Praise for *Aga.... ... .*

"Cabot's tale will appeal to Tracie Petersen fans and readers who enjoy tales of forgiveness and inspirational western historical romances."

Booklist

"A beautifully written, emotionally charged story. Highly recommend."

Interviews and Reviews

"Cabot takes two misunderstood characters and sweetly gives them hope, purpose, and of course romance while entertaining readers with their story."

Reading Is My Superpower

Praise for *After the Shadows*

"Cabot is becoming a must-buy. Her sensitivity and realistic portrayal of characters often on the margins of history really shine in this new historical series."

Library Journal starred review

"Cabot skillfully links diverse plotlines in a tightly woven narrative, putting forth an uplifting message about the value of all human life that's moving without detracting from the plot's suspense."

Publishers Weekly

"A captivating historical romance. There is plenty of drama and excitement, but ultimately the hopeful message displays the courage it takes to overcome grief and love again."

The Historical Novel Society

Books by Amanda Cabot

HISTORICAL ROMANCE

SECRETS OF SWEETWATER CROSSING

After the Shadows

Against the Wind

Into the Starlight

MESQUITE SPRINGS

Out of the Embers

Dreams Rekindled

The Spark of Love

CIMARRON CREEK TRILOGY

A Stolen Heart

A Borrowed Dream

A Tender Hope

TEXAS DREAMS

Paper Roses

Scattered Petals

Tomorrow's Garden

WESTWARD WINDS

Summer of Promise

Waiting for Spring

With Autumn's Return

Christmas Roses

One Little Word: A Sincerely Yours Novella

CONTEMPORARY ROMANCE

TEXAS CROSSROADS SERIES

At Bluebonnet Lake

In Firefly Valley

On Lone Star Trail

INTO *the* STARLIGHT

AMANDA CABOT

Revell

a division of Baker Publishing Group
Grand Rapids, Michigan

© 2024 by Amanda Cabot

Published by Revell
a division of Baker Publishing Group
Grand Rapids, Michigan
www.RevellBooks.com

Printed in the United States of America

Library of Congress Cataloging-in-Publication Data
Names: Cabot, Amanda, 1948– author.
Title: Into the starlight / Amanda Cabot.
Description: Grand Rapids, Michigan : Revell, a division of Baker Publishing
  Group, 2024. | Series: Secrets of Sweetwater Crossing ; #3
Identifiers: LCCN 2023039716 | ISBN 9780800740665 (paperback) | ISBN
  9780800745820 (casebound) | ISBN 9781493445493 (ebook)
Subjects: LCGFT: Christian fiction. | Novels.
Classification: LCC PS3603.A35 I58 2024 | DDC 813/.6—dc23/eng/20231002
LC record available at https://lccn.loc.gov/2023039716

Scripture quotations are from the King James Version of the Bible.

Cover design by Laura Klynstra
Photography by Ildiko Near, Arcangel
Author photograph © Val Rothwell Photography

This book is a work of fiction. Names, characters, places, and incidents are the product of the author's imagination or are used fictitiously. Any resemblance to actual events, locales, or persons, living or dead, is coincidental.

Baker Publishing Group publications use paper produced from sustainable forestry practices and postconsumer waste whenever possible.

24 25 26 27 28 29 30   7 6 5 4 3 2 1

For Lorie McDonald,
a woman of many talents
and a true friend.

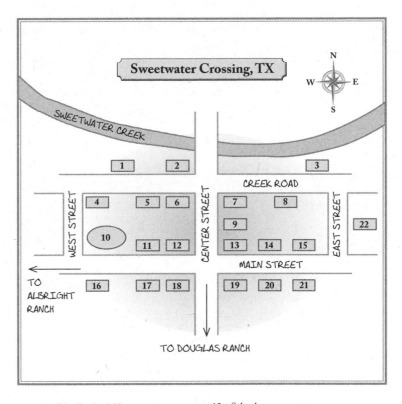

1 – Mrs. Sanders's Home
2 – Cemetery
3 – Finley House
4 – Saloon
5 – Tearoom
6 – Teashop
7 – Parsonage Annex
8 – The Albrights' Home
9 – Parsonage
10 – Park
11 – Library

12 – School
13 – Church
14 – Mayor's Home and Office
15 – Mercantile
16 – Livery
17 – Sheriff's Home and Office
18 – Ma's Kitchen
19 – Doctor's Office
20 – Post Office
21 – Dressmaker
22 – Miss Heppel's Home

One

Dreams weren't supposed to die, but Joanna Richter's had, all except one.

The concerts at Munich's glorious Odeon and Vienna's incomparable Musikverein had nurtured the dream she'd cherished for almost as long as she could remember, but it had crumbled, destroyed by something the doctors told her was invisible to the human eye. The majesty of the Swiss Alps had sown the seeds of another dream, one that had withered before it could fully flower. Now there was only one left.

Joanna smiled as she entered Sweetwater Crossing. It might lack the museums and monuments that Grandmother Kenner had called the essentials of a civilized city, but this small town in the Texas Hill Country had something far more valuable: her home. It wouldn't be the same with both Mama and Father gone, but the house itself wouldn't have changed. It would shelter her and maybe, just maybe she'd be able to find a new purpose for her life here, a chance to finally be the best at something.

She slowed the buggy, wanting to savor the first few minutes of her homecoming. Other than the new parsonage that had been built after the last one burned, the town looked the same, and oh, how comforting that was. She'd once sought change. Now she valued stability. Being here would provide that.

Warmth flooded through Joanna's veins as she turned onto Creek Road and approached her destination. It was there, just as she remembered it. Her smile broadened as she gazed at the building where she'd spent most of her life. The stone that Clive Finley had chosen for the three-story house was strong and durable, unlikely to crumble or burn, giving her a feeling of safety and security. The columns that supported the veranda stood tall, as though proud that their role was more than decorative, or so Joanna had claimed when she was a child. The double staircase served as a reminder that there was more than one way to reach a destination, and the three dormer windows seemed to herald the presence of the three Vaughn girls, even though she and her sisters never slept in those rooms.

Her sisters had laughed when she'd described the house that way, saying she was being fanciful. Perhaps she was, but this was Joanna's home, her beloved home. It hadn't changed, though she had, as one by one her dreams had vanished.

She frowned at the memory of why she'd been so eager to leave Sweetwater Crossing. The disappointment that had verged on despair. The overwhelming sense of failure. The realization that there would be no happily-ever-after with a handsome rancher for her. That dream had been the first to die. Fortunately, she had told no one—not even her sisters—what she'd dreamt. And now there was no need.

As she had so often in the past, Joanna guided the buggy between the stone pillars marking the entrance to Finley House and along the curved drive that led to the house itself. When she'd reined in the horse, she inhaled deeply in an attempt to calm her nerves, regretting the action a second later. It was only when the pain in her lungs subsided that Joanna could climb out of the buggy, and even then her hands had begun to shake. It was one thing to know that her parents were not there, quite another to enter the house that held so many memories and not see them. Reminding herself to take shallow breaths, she mounted the front steps and knocked on the door. After a year and a half, Joanna Vaughn Richter was home.

It seemed forever but was no more than thirty seconds before the door opened and the petite blond with deep blue eyes who looked so much like Mama that Joanna could hardly breathe stared at her.

"Joanna?" The woman's voice trembled more than Joanna's hands had, and her eyes widened in what appeared to be shock. "Is it really you?"

Joanna nodded. "It's me, Emily."

The last time she'd seen her older sister had been only hours after Emily's wedding, when she and her handsome groom had left Sweetwater Crossing to return to George's ranch. Emily had been beautiful then—everyone in town acknowledged her as the prettiest of the Vaughn girls—but that beauty paled compared to the Emily who now smiled at Joanna. There was a new softness to her sister's face, a gleam in her eyes that hadn't been there before, transforming her into the picture of a happy woman.

"I can't believe it." Emily took a step forward and wrapped her arms around Joanna's waist as she'd done so many times when they'd been children. It had become more awkward once Joanna grew to her full height—half a foot taller than Emily— but Emily had always persisted in her efforts to soothe Joanna when she'd been distressed. Today it was Emily who appeared distressed. "Louisa and I've been so worried about you."

"I'm sorry." Though the words were inadequate, they were the only ones Joanna had. "I should have written, but I couldn't." For so many reasons.

Emily broke the hug, then reached out to take one of Joanna's hands and lead her indoors. "It doesn't matter. Nothing matters except that you're back and safe."

Despite the warmth of the September day, the house was cool. That shouldn't have been a problem, but something triggered a coughing spasm, the first Joanna had had since she'd arrived in Texas. The doctors had warned her against becoming overly excited. Perhaps that was the cause, because there was no doubt that she was excited to be home. Excited and at the same time a bit apprehensive, knowing that even though the house itself had not changed, many other things had.

She bent over, trying to stop the coughing. When she could again breathe freely, she looked at her sister. "I'm sorry," she said, wondering how many more times she would have to apologize.

Emily's blue eyes, so different from Joanna's brown ones, reflected concern. "You're ill. What can I do? Should I call Louisa?" As if she'd only just registered the unrelieved black Joanna wore, Emily asked, "Why are you in mourning? Was it your grandmother?" She shook her head. "Oh, listen to me. I should be helping you, but instead I'm bombarding you with questions."

"It's all right, Emily." When they were growing up, Emily had felt that her role as the oldest meant she had to care for Joanna and Louisa, and that caring had included what had sometimes felt like an inquisition. "I should probably sit down and drink a bit of water." The air here was heavier than it had been in the Alps, and the doctors said that could make breathing more difficult.

"Of course." Emily wrapped her arm around Joanna's waist again. "Let's go to the kitchen. I've got pudding on the stove, and if I leave it too long, it'll be a scorched mess."

Once Joanna was seated at the kitchen table with a glass of water in front of her, Emily began to stir something that smelled like chocolate. "We have a few minutes to talk before Mrs. Carmichael and Noah come back from their walk." She paused and turned to look at Joanna. "Noah's my son—my adopted son—and you remember Mrs. Carmichael. She takes care of Noah while Craig is at school." A chuckle accompanied Emily's explanation. "There I go again. If you got my letters, you know all that. Craig tells me I'm prone to chatter when I'm excited."

There was no missing the smile that crossed Emily's face when she spoke of her husband. Her second husband.

Joanna brushed aside thoughts of George. Nothing good would come from thinking of him, just as nothing good would come from remembering how often she'd wished she'd been a petite blond like Emily instead of a tall brunette, especially when George had had eyes only for Emily. "The last letter I received said you were going to marry the schoolteacher and that Louisa brought a man with a broken leg to recuperate here."

"Oh my." Emily made no effort to hide her dismay. "That was months ago. So much has happened since then. Louisa did more than set Josh's leg. She married him."

Little sister Louisa was married. Joanna knew she shouldn't have been surprised, and yet she was. Before she could speak, Emily continued. "I don't understand why you didn't receive my letters. I thought it took only a few weeks for mail to reach Munich."

"I haven't been in Munich since early February." Though she tried to suppress it, Joanna coughed again. "I caught scarlet fever." And had almost died, although she wouldn't worry Emily with that information. "It turned into pneumonia. That's when Grandmother took me to Switzerland, because the air was supposed to be better there. She arranged for mail to be forwarded, but it appears most of it wasn't."

Abandoning the pudding for a moment, Emily gave Joanna

a quick hug. "My letters don't matter, but I hate that you were sick and so far away. I wish I'd known."

It might have been comforting to have had Emily or Louisa with her during the long recovery, but they would have tried to convince her to return home, and at that point, Joanna had still entertained dreams of an illustrious career and hadn't wanted anyone to try to dissuade her.

"There was nothing you could have done. The sanatorium was one of the best in Europe, and the treatments helped." As much as they could. Joanna paused, debating whether to tell her sister the final prognosis, then decided she might as well be honest. "The doctors warned me that my lungs will always be weak"—too weak to allow her to continue her training and eventually embark on a concert tour of her own—"but if I'm careful, I can live normally."

Emily fixed one of her appraising looks on Joanna. "I'll make sure you're careful, and so will Louisa."

Joanna smiled, knowing they would. Emily would cook meals she was certain would strengthen her, and Louisa would study medical books to determine whether anything more could be done.

"I'm so glad you're home again." Emily returned to stirring the pudding. "The important thing is for you to rest, and there's no better place than right here."

Though her sister's gesture encompassed more than the kitchen, Joanna studied the room where she'd spent so many hours watching Mama cook and then helping her wash the dishes. The curtains at the window were new, but that was the only change she could see, other than Mama's absence. The wooden table where Joanna had eaten cookies after school still had the small gouge from a broken glass, and the cupboards still had mismatched knobs after Louisa had unscrewed one and lost it in the yard. It was a simple room compared to some of the châteaux she'd visited, but that simplicity was a balm to Joanna's spirits.

"I feel better just being here."

Emily tasted the pudding, then added another spoonful of sugar. "I hope you're not angry that I turned our home into a boardinghouse." For the first time since Joanna had entered the house, her sister's voice held a note of uncertainty.

"How could I be angry? You did what you had to to save our home." Though the news that both of her parents had died had been devastating, Joanna understood the actions her older sister had taken to ensure that Finley House would remain the family home. "Now that I'm here, I can help you, if you still have a room for me, that is."

"No helping until you're fully recovered, but of course there's room for you. Beulah's in your bedroom. I could move her, but I'd rather not, now that she's become accustomed to it. Would you mind moving into my old room or Louisa's? She and Josh have taken over the third floor."

More changes. The thought of returning to the room she'd had for as long as she could remember had buoyed Joanna during the long journey from Europe. Now it appeared that that dream had also died. What other changes were awaiting her?

"Beulah?" Rather than upset Emily by admitting her disappointment that her room hadn't been kept for her, Joanna seized on the familiar name. "Beulah Douglas lives here?"

Emily nodded. "I thought I'd written about that. She stays here during the week so she can attend school, then goes home on Friday afternoon. It's been a good arrangement for everyone, especially Noah. He misses her on the weekends."

A shadow crossed Emily's lovely face. "There I go again, talking about other things. You haven't told me why you're in mourning, but I assume it's for your grandmother. When did she die?"

"A few hours after my husband."

"Stop! I can't do it."

Burke Finley stared at the woman seated next to him, not bothering to hide his shock. That was the last thing he'd expected Della Samuels to say. Not once during the ten days they'd been traveling had she complained, not even when the accommodations were at best mediocre and the food barely edible. Now that they'd reached Texas's Hill Country and were within an hour of the town she claimed was the one place on Earth she wanted to visit before she died, it seemed that something had changed her mind.

"What's the matter, Aunt Della?" The petite woman whose brown hair bore silver wings, confirming that she'd lived for more than forty years, wasn't his aunt, though she would have been his aunt by marriage if his uncle had lived. Still, for as long as Burke could recall, he'd addressed her as Aunt.

"I can't do it." Della's eyes, the same light blue as the dress she wore today, filled with tears. "I thought I wanted to go to Sweetwater Crossing, but now I'm afraid to. It probably sounds silly to you after I begged you to take me there, but I'm afraid that I'll be disappointed. What will I do if it's not as special as Clive told me it was?"

Burke gave her a professional assessment. Her color was a bit high, but she was showing no signs of heat distress, and her respiration was steady. Perhaps her concern wasn't the town itself but her fiancé's grave. "There's no need to visit the cemetery." Though others made weekly pilgrimages to their loved ones' final resting places, he rarely spent time at his mother's grave, preferring to remember her alive. There was no question of visiting his father's grave, for he was buried on a battlefield hundreds of miles from home.

"We don't have to go to the cemetery, but I thought you wanted to see the house he built for you and talk to the man who's living there."

According to the stories Burke had heard, the house Clive

Finley had designed for his bride-to-be was larger and more beautiful than the one on the plantation she'd called home. Legend had it that Della's daddy was so opposed to his daughter's moving to Texas that he wouldn't agree to the marriage unless Clive could give her the same luxury she'd grown up with. And so Burke's uncle had built a house that rivaled those the plantation owners used to flaunt their wealth.

There should have been a happy ending to the story, but there wasn't. Though Clive's house had been finished, he'd died before he could return to Alabama to claim his bride and had left the house in the care of his closest friend.

"I thought I wanted to see it," Della admitted. "Now the whole idea seems overwhelming." Her breathing grew ragged, making Burke doubt his previous assessment of her health.

"Let's get out and rest a bit," he said, gesturing toward a large live oak tree. "The shade looks welcoming." One way or another, he had to convince Della to continue, for while she might be ready to return home, he was not. There was nothing waiting for him in Samuels, Alabama. Nothing good, that is.

She shook her head. "Just turn around."

She'd regret it. Burke was certain of that, and so he said, "I never thought you were a coward." He was the coward, not wanting to return to the town where he'd spent that horrible morning. Though Felix had insisted that no one other than he would know the truth and that everyone made mistakes, Burke knew that Edna was right: some things were unforgivable.

Trying to block the memories that would haunt him for the rest of his life, Burke fixed his gaze on Della. "You don't really want to go back, do you?"

Della stared at the live oak, then slowly shook her head. "You're right. I'm not a coward and I don't want to go back, but I'm afraid. I've had the image in my mind for over twenty years. What if it's wrong? What if I'm disappointed?"

Though he wished it were otherwise, Burke couldn't make

any promises. All he could do was encourage her. "There's only one way to know."

This time Della smiled. "You're right. You know, Burke, if you weren't such a fine doctor, you could be a minister. You're good at comforting people."

"It's a nice thought, but any skills I have are for healing bodies." And even those were in question. He'd always found being a physician rewarding, but even before the morning when everything had changed, Burke had begun to wonder whether serving the residents of a small town was what he was meant to do. He was no longer needed in Samuels. Felix could handle the practice, especially since he planned to let Edna assist him.

Had Della realized that? Was that why she'd suddenly decided to come to Texas and insisted Burke accompany her? He wouldn't ask. All he knew was that he needed a new direction for his life. Perhaps two weeks in the Hill Country would help him find it.

"How much farther is it?"

Burke was heartened by the anticipation he heard in Della's voice. "Less than five miles."

Her smile broadened. "Let's go. I owe it to Clive and to me." Her apprehension apparently gone, Della leaned forward and studied the countryside, giving Burke a running commentary as they approached their final destination.

"Clive was right," she said softly. "I like the Hill Country."

So did Burke. The rolling hills with their limestone outcroppings, the meadows ringed by live oak trees, the fields bright with wildflowers were all appealing. And when they reached Sweetwater Crossing, the appeal only increased.

The town Clive Finley had chosen was more attractive than Burke had expected, its main street lined with well-cared-for buildings. The mercantile, mayor's office, and church occupied one side of a block, with the dressmaker, post office, and a doctor's office on the other. Burke gave the doctor's office a longer look than the other buildings, noting that the front door had been freshly painted and that the windows gleamed. Whoever the town's physician was, he cared about appearances.

"Do you want me to ask for directions?" They were approaching what appeared to be the center of town, a corner that housed the church, the school, and a restaurant as well as the doctor's office.

Della shook her head. "I'm sure we can find it on our own. Clive said it was next to the creek."

As he guided the buggy into the intersection, Burke looked both directions, grinning when he spotted a bridge a block and a half to the right. "That must be the creek." He turned toward it, silently praying that Della would not be disappointed. Though she'd begun speaking of it a scant two months ago, she'd admitted that she'd dreamed of coming here for many years. It was only after her father's death that she'd decided to make her dream come true.

"Which way do you want to go?" Burke asked when they reached the corner of Center and Creek streets. If the house was next to the creek, it would be on the north side.

Della shuddered when she saw the cemetery on the northwest corner. "Not that way."

Burke turned east, remaining silent as they passed a small house, then a larger one on the south side of the street. Though he would have expected similar homes on the northern side, there were none, simply a large expanse of grass and trees. Then he saw it.

"That's it!"

Della's excitement matched his own. The house his uncle had built was magnificent, far larger and more elaborate than anything Burke had seen in Sweetwater Crossing. While the other buildings were situated close to the street, this one was farther back, with a curved drive leading from the wall that marked the front of the property to a three-story house. A double staircase led the way to the front door, while four columns supported a second-floor veranda. Della's home in Alabama was beautiful, but this one surpassed it in both beauty and grandeur.

"Oh, Burke. It's just the way Clive described it." She leaned over the side of the buggy, pointing to the pillars that marked the ends of the wall. "Look. They say Finley House." Tears glistened in her eyes as she turned to Burke. "Thank you for insisting that we come. I'll remember this for the rest of my life." She paused, then asked, "Do you think Pastor Vaughn will let us go inside?"

Burke smiled and repeated what he'd said less than an hour ago. "There's only one way to know."

⟡

"Your husband?" Emily's eyes widened with shock. "You're a widow?"

The tremor in her voice reminded Joanna that Emily had been a widow when she'd returned to Sweetwater Crossing a year ago and was probably remembering the grief of the first few months without her beloved husband.

"Kurt and I were married in July, two months ago today." It had been a wonderful day, one of the happiest of Joanna's life, but the happiness had been almost as short-lived as her first dream of marriage and happily-ever-after.

"He and Grandmother died a month later. According to the doctor, it was spoiled chicken." If Louisa were here, she'd want more details, but that should be enough for Emily. "My stomach was queasy that day, so I didn't eat any, and Marta didn't like the spices, so she had only a little. The doctor said that's why she survived."

As she continued to stir the pudding, Emily raised an eyebrow. "Who's Marta?"

"Kurt's sister. She was at the sanatorium too." If it hadn't been for Marta, Joanna would not have met Kurt, and if she hadn't met Kurt, she wouldn't have known the wonder of love and marriage.

Before she could say more, the back door flew open, and a young boy raced in, then flung his arms around Emily's legs. "Me saw new horse, Mama!"

The brown-haired boy, whom Joanna guessed to be three or four years old, must be Noah, the schoolmaster's son.

"I'm sorry, Emily. You know how he gets around horses." Joanna recognized the gray-haired woman who'd followed Noah into the kitchen as Mrs. Carmichael, the widow who'd lived in the parsonage once the Vaughns moved into Finley House. A few inches shorter than Joanna, her back still straight despite her seventy years, Mrs. Carmichael was one of the kindest women Joanna had ever met. It was no wonder Emily had welcomed her as a member of her newly forged family.

The widow glanced at the table, then stopped, her surprise evident. "Do my eyes deceive me, or is it really Joanna Vaughn?" She bent down to give Joanna a hug.

"Your eyes are as sharp as ever, Mrs. Carmichael, but I'm Joanna Richter now."

"Come see horse, Mama." Ignoring the other adults, Noah tugged on Emily's skirt.

Emily shook her head. "Later. Remember your manners, Noah. This is my sister, Miss Joanna. What do you say to her?"

"Is it your horse?"

She probably shouldn't have laughed at the boy's single-mindedness, but Joanna did. "Yes, it is." She was about to tell Noah that she'd introduce them later when she heard a knock on the front door.

"I'll answer that," Joanna said. Emily had pudding to cook, and Mrs. Carmichael appeared tired from her walk. Even though she had been gone for more than a year, this was still Joanna's home. Greeting visitors was partially her responsibility.

She rose and walked through the hallway that bisected the first floor, wondering whether she'd recognize whoever had come to call. Perhaps the Albrights, who lived across the street, had seen her arrive and wanted to welcome her back. But the couple who stood on the front porch were strangers.

The man appeared to be close to her age with auburn hair, green eyes, and a square chin that kept him from being conventionally handsome. Though the woman at his side was old enough to be his mother, Joanna saw no resemblance between them. What she saw was apprehension on the woman's face and in the way she clung to the man's arm.

"Can I help you?" Joanna asked, unsure whether she should invite them inside. Perhaps they were simply lost and needed directions.

"We're looking for Joseph Vaughn. I understand he lives here."

Joanna's first thought was that the man's voice was deep and melodic, making her wonder whether he sang in a choir, but it was overshadowed by the pain the name evoked. Joseph Vaughn was—or, rather, had been—her father.

Before she could explain that he'd died more than a year ago, Noah raced into the hallway, his rapid footsteps followed by Mrs. Carmichael's more deliberate ones.

"Me see! Me see!" Apparently Noah wanted to greet the visitors.

When Joanna reached out to keep him from catapulting himself onto the porch, Mrs. Carmichael stopped and put her hand on her heart. Blood drained from her face as she stared at the doorway.

"Clive! Clive Finley! You're back!"

Two

Burke shook his head. He shouldn't have been surprised, because folks back home told him he resembled his uncle, but he hadn't expected anyone in Sweetwater Crossing to have such vivid memories of Clive that they would mistake him for his long-dead relative.

"I'm sorry, ma'am, but I'm not Clive," he told the gray-haired woman. Though she was too old to be the minister's wife, she acted as if she lived here. "I'm his nephew Burke, and this is Miss Della Samuels, the lady my uncle planned to marry. We came from Alabama hoping Pastor Vaughn could tell us more about my uncle's final days. And, of course, Della wanted to see this house."

The woman who'd opened the door stared at them, her expression reflecting sorrow rather than the shock and curiosity the older woman had displayed. Perhaps the sorrow had nothing to do with Burke and Della but was the result of a recent bereavement, because there was no mistaking her mourning garments. Taller than the woman he'd once planned to marry by four or five inches, she was a brown-eyed brunette rather than a blue-eyed blond like Edna, and unlike many women whose complexions appeared sallow when they were in mourning, she wore the unrelieved black well.

"Come in, come in," she said, ushering them into a wide hallway with twin staircases that mirrored the ones leading to the front porch. While Della gasped at the magnificence of what should have been her home, the younger woman turned toward the child. "Noah, please ask your mama to join us in the parlor."

When the four of them were seated in a room whose elegance rivaled any he'd seen in Alabama, with elaborate crown molding, delicately patterned wallpaper, an intricately carved mantel, and a rosewood piano, the brunette's expression changed to chagrin. "Pardon me. I seem to have forgotten my manners. I'm Joanna Vaughn—that is, Joanna Richter—and this is Mrs. Carmichael."

Her correction of her surname caused Burke to glance at her left hand. As he'd surmised, she wore a gold band that appeared new, confirming his assumption that her marriage was recent.

Della remained silent, as if overwhelmed by the house, but the gray-haired woman did not. "You gave me quite a shock, young man. I thought you were Clive come back from the grave." Mrs. Carmichael's smile was rueful. "Silly me. I should have realized that he would have aged. You can't be much older than Clive was when he lived here."

Before Burke could respond, a petite blond entered the room, trailed by the boy Mrs. Richter had called Noah. Had she not been introduced as Mrs. Richter's sister Emily Ferguson, he would not have believed them to be related, for there was no physical resemblance between the two women.

"I'm so happy to meet you both." Mrs. Ferguson turned to address Della when the introductions were complete. "My father considered Clive his closest friend and often said he wished he could have met the woman who inspired this house."

24

Apparently not noticing the past tense the woman used, Della raised a questioning eyebrow. "I want to thank you for allowing Burke and me to come inside. Finley House is even more beautiful than Clive said in his letters." She paused for a second. "Where might I find Pastor Vaughn? There are so many things I want to ask him."

The sisters exchanged a glance, Mrs. Richter's frown confirming Burke's supposition that the man was deceased. "I'm afraid you won't be able to do that. Our father died last year."

Della made no effort to hide her distress. Tears filled her eyes, and she clasped her hands. "I'm so sorry for your loss."

She was more than sorry. She was devastated. Burke knew that Della had been counting on Clive's friend to provide the answers she sought. While one of her goals had been to see the house, that paled compared to her desire to learn more about her fiancé's life in this small town.

Almost as if she understood, Mrs. Richter gave Della a sympathetic look. "I'm sorry you've made such a long trip for naught."

Without waiting for a response, she turned to her sister. Burke's assumption that they were engaged in silent communication was confirmed when Mrs. Ferguson said, "If you don't have any other plans, I hope you'll stay here until you're ready to return to Alabama."

"Stay. Nice horse stay." The boy who'd been staring out the front window appeared to have paid more attention to the adults' conversation than Burke would have expected from one so young. Noah couldn't be more than three or four.

A faint smile crossed Della's face. "Thank you, but we couldn't impose." The look she gave Burke said she wanted nothing more than to spend a few days in what would have been her home if Clive had lived, but years of putting others' interests ahead of her own kept her from admitting it.

Once again, Mrs. Richter seemed to have read Della's

thoughts. "It's no imposition," she assured Della. "There's no hotel in Sweetwater Crossing, so my family is used to having guests."

No hotel. When she'd asked Burke to accompany her, Della had indicated that they'd take rooms in a hotel. Now she shrugged, her somewhat sheepish expression confirming that she hadn't realized the town lacked one.

Mrs. Ferguson nodded her agreement with her sister. "After our parents died, I turned Finley House into a boardinghouse. Right now it's mostly family, but there's plenty of room for both of you."

The sheepish expression vanished, and Della's eyes lit with pleasure. "We had planned to be here for two weeks. If that's too long for you . . ."

"Nonsense. You're welcome to stay here for as long as you wish." Mrs. Ferguson's tone was firm.

When Mrs. Richter tried but failed to suppress a cough, Burke gave her a professional appraisal. She was thinner than most women, and the flush that colored her cheeks was not a blush, nor was the cough a casual clearing of the throat. Try though she might to hide it, Mrs. Richter was recovering from a serious illness, probably lung-related. Now, however, was not the time to discuss that.

Burke turned to her sister. "We will, of course, pay for our room and board." It was the least they could do.

"Nonsense." Mrs. Ferguson's reply was immediate. "My family wouldn't have had a home like this if it weren't for you."

Mrs. Richter seemed to agree. "The least we can do is give you a place to stay."

"Thank you. You're both kind and generous." Della appeared almost overwhelmed by the prospect of spending two weeks in this house.

"I'd best get back to the kitchen, because the others will be here soon," Mrs. Ferguson said as she looked at the clock on the mantel. "Joanna, would you show our guests to their rooms? Miss Samuels can have our parents' room and Mr. Finley the blue one. The linens are all fresh."

"Perhaps we could have a tour later," Burke said when Mrs. Ferguson left the room. "I know Aunt Della has been looking forward to seeing all of Finley House."

Della nodded. "I wondered whether it was as beautiful as Clive claimed, but what I've seen so far is even grander than I expected." She smiled as she looked at the crown molding and the stained woodwork that framed the four generously sized windows.

"Father said this house was Clive's wedding gift to you. I'll show you the rest later, but before we go upstairs, there's something down here that I want you to see." Mrs. Richter rose and walked to the pocket doors at the south end of the parlor. Though it was only a short distance, Burke noticed that she stopped midway across the room to catch her breath before she said, "According to my father, this room was meant to be a surprise."

When Mrs. Richter slid the doors open, Della gasped. "A library!" Her eyes filled with tears that might have been from happiness or regret that she would not share her delight with the man she'd lost. "Clive knew how much I love reading, but I had no idea he'd done this." Della entered the room and walked to the floor-to-ceiling shelves on the opposite side, gazing at the books, caressing some of the spines. "I told him once that I was a librarian at heart."

Burke hadn't known that. "And so he gave you your own library."

A magnificent library. What Burke guessed to be several hundred books filled the shelves, beckoning an avid reader to choose one. Though he would have furnished the room with at least two comfortable chairs, someone—probably Pastor Vaughn—had turned it into an office with a desk, desk chair, and two plain wooden chairs for visitors. This, Burke guessed, was where the minister had written sermons and met with parishioners.

Her breathing once more normal, Mrs. Richter moved to Della's side. "I hope you don't mind, but until a couple years ago, this was Sweetwater Crossing's unofficial library. My father lent books to anyone who wanted to read."

Far from being annoyed or angry, Della beamed with pleasure. "Books are meant to be shared."

Burke agreed, but one part of Mrs. Richter's explanation puzzled him. "What changed?" he asked. "You said 'until a couple years ago.'"

"It's simple. The town opened a separate library. It's not as extensive as this, but what she was paid as the librarian helped a young widow support herself and her daughter."

"Perhaps we can visit it. As you can tell," Della said with a smile as she pulled a volume from a shelf and opened it to the first page, "I love being surrounded by books."

"Me like books too." Noah, who'd been playing quietly in the parlor, skidded to a stop next to Della. "Read to me."

"You know better than that, Noah." Mrs. Carmichael put a restraining hand on the boy's shoulder. "What do you say?"

He looked perplexed for a second before saying, "*Please* read to me."

Della nodded. "Perhaps later. We could choose a book from the other library."

Mrs. Carmichael shook her head. "I'm afraid it's closed now. Alice was the librarian, but she married our interim pastor, and they moved back to his home in Louisiana."

Mrs. Richter appeared startled by the explanation, raising new questions in Burke's mind. Della, however, was focused on the library itself.

"That's a shame. Every town needs a library."

"But we didn't have one in Samuels," Burke reminded his honorary aunt. "I'm surprised you didn't establish one."

"I wanted to, especially after Clive died, but my father wouldn't allow it."

Burke tried to control his anger at the man who'd attempted to control every aspect of his daughter's life. Anger solved nothing, and the man could no longer be held accountable.

Obviously shocked by the revelation, Mrs. Richter gestured toward the shelves. "Consider this yours for as long as you're here. I know that's what both Clive and my father would have said. Now, let me show you your rooms. I imagine you want to rest after your journey."

What Burke wanted to know was why she had trouble breathing. Was it pneumonia or something else? What treatments had she received? And if it was pneumonia, how had she contracted the disease that killed so many?

You're not her physician, he reminded himself. *You're a guest in her home, nothing more.* But the questions refused to be dismissed.

✍

"Emily, what's going on?"

Joanna's heart began to pound at the realization that for the first time in far too long, the three Vaughn sisters were together. This was the moment she'd dreamed of so often on the journey across the ocean, the true homecoming she'd longed for.

Her younger sister rushed into the kitchen, the possessive grip she had on a black medical bag telling Joanna how precious it was to Louisa. "I saw two unfamiliar buggies in front of the house."

In the second before Louisa registered her presence, Joanna noted that Louisa's blue eyes, so like Emily's, sparkled more than she'd remembered and that her face had a new softness, perhaps because she, like Emily, was happily married. *Oh, Kurt, I wish you were here to meet my family.*

Brushing aside the sorrow that threatened to overwhelm her

every time she thought of how his life had been cut short, Joanna rose from the chair Emily had insisted she take when she'd returned from escorting their guests to their rooms. "I'm responsible for the first."

"Joanna!" Her eyes widening in surprise, Louisa dropped the bag and covered the distance between them in two quick strides. "I wish I'd known you were here." She shot an accusatory look at Emily, who was peeling potatoes, her expression reminding Joanna of their childhood when Louisa had been quick to find fault with their older sister. "You should have told me the instant she arrived." Turning to Joanna, she grinned, then gave her a quick hug before stepping back. "It's wonderful to see you, but you're too thin."

Emily had always been the slender one, but now Joanna claimed that distinction, albeit not by choice.

"That's the result of scarlet fever and pneumonia." Though she tried not to, Joanna coughed and leaned against the table. How she hated feeling like an invalid. "I'm better now, but the doctors warned me that I'll always be weak."

Louisa gave her the same appraising look that Mr. Finley had when she'd coughed. "I'm not going to accept that, because they could be wrong, but we'll talk about that later. Right now all that matters is that the three of us are together again. It's almost like old times." She glanced at the shiny gold ring on her left hand. "Of course there've been some changes. Emily and I are married ladies now with the best husbands in the world."

"I'm looking forward to meeting your husbands." Even though her heart ached for Kurt, Joanna did not begrudge her sisters their happiness. She extended her left hand. "I was married too, but he and Grandmother died. That's why I'm in mourning." She was surprised Louisa hadn't commented on her black dress.

"Oh, Joanna, how awful!" Louisa gave her another hug, then practically pushed her back into the chair. "You should sit down and take a sip of water. That'll help your cough. Then I want to hear all about your time in Europe and your marriage. You can start by telling me why you brought two carriages."

This was vintage Louisa, expecting everyone to answer her questions merely because she was the youngest. Joanna smiled at how quickly they'd resumed their childhood roles.

Before she could reply, Emily spoke. "Joanna didn't bring two. A woman named Miss Della Samuels and a very handsome young man who Mrs. Carmichael claims looks exactly like Clive Finley came in the other one."

Louisa's eyes widened. "Our Clive Finley?"

"One and the same. Miss Samuels was Clive's fiancée." Joanna continued the explanation. "She came here to see if Finley House was as beautiful as he claimed."

"Is it?"

"According to her, even better." That acknowledgment and the woman's pleasure at the library had warmed Joanna's heart, almost mitigating the pang she'd felt when strangers had arrived the very day she'd returned. Though she'd known that Emily had turned Finley House into a boardinghouse, Joanna's heart hadn't been ready for the reality of sharing her home with others or that someone would be staying in the room her parents had once occupied. Emily and Louisa had had more than a year to adjust to their parents' absence, but seeing Finley House without them revived the sorrow that had diminished over the months.

"Miss Samuels and Mr. Finley are staying here for two weeks." Once again, Emily offered an explanation. "I think she wants to learn everything she can about the town that might have been her home. It would be easier if Mama and especially Father were here. They could tell her so much."

Louisa nodded but kept her gaze fixed on Joanna. "Our guests sound interesting, but I'm more interested in you. Tell me everything that happened in Europe."

"We only have half an hour before supper," Joanna protested, knowing that Louisa would ask a hundred questions, each of which would demand a lengthy answer.

"Then you'll have to talk fast."

～

The room looked the same. The wainscoting was as highly polished as she remembered, the pale brocade wallpaper that stretched from the wainscoting to the crown molding as pretty as her memory. The table and chairs hadn't changed. What had changed was that there were nine people seated here tonight rather than five and that Emily and Craig occupied the places that had been Mama and Father's.

It was right that they had assumed those seats. After all, this was their house now. And that, Joanna realized, was the biggest change of all. Her memories were of being a child here, part of a small family. Now the anchors of that family, her parents, were gone, and that changed everything.

She took a sip of water, trying to calm her thoughts, and forced herself to listen to the conversation going on around her.

"What do you do for a living, Burke?" Louisa's husband Josh asked as he passed a bowl of mashed potatoes to their guest.

When the group had assembled in the dining room and Emily had begun the introductions, Miss Samuels—Della, that is— had suggested they dispense with formality and address each other by their given names. "You're treating us like family, and that's what family does." Everyone had agreed.

Even before they'd begun to eat, Joanna realized that the decision helped them relax, making them seem like if not family at least old friends rather than people who'd just met.

She smiled as she thought of the two men who *were* family: her new brothers-in-law. Craig was a taller and more mature version of his son, with hair and eyes as dark brown as hers, while Josh was blond and blue-eyed, both his hair and eyes a deeper hue than Kurt's. Though she'd spent only a few minutes with her sisters' husbands, that had been enough to show Joanna how deeply both of them loved their wives, and she'd said a prayer of thanksgiving that her sisters were so happy in their marriages.

Burke took a spoonful of the potatoes Josh had passed to him and responded to his question about his profession. "I'm a physician."

A doctor! Joanna tried not to frown. No wonder he'd given her those appraising looks when she coughed or stopped to catch her breath. She'd been too ill to retain many memories of the doctor who'd treated her in Munich, but the ones in Switzerland had studied her as if she were a specimen, not a woman whose dreams they'd shattered. She had no need for more of that.

Oblivious to Joanna's dismay, Josh smiled at their guest. "So is my wife."

Louisa was quick to contradict him. "That's a bit of an exaggeration. I've had training as a doctor and a midwife, but I'm not a full-fledged physician."

Della paused from buttering a roll. "If I know Burke, and I do, he'll be happy to answer any questions you might have. If he doesn't know the answer, he'll find it."

The man whose auburn hair would make him stand out in a crowd nodded. "I'll certainly try. My partner and I used to take turns challenging each other with questions about obscure ailments. It was a friendly competition, and we both learned from it."

Was it only Joanna's imagination that Burke's expression had seemed strained when he'd mentioned his partner?

Craig didn't appear to have noticed anything unusual, because he nodded in approval. "That's an interesting technique. It might be a way to motivate some of my pupils. I don't know whether Emily mentioned it, but I'm Sweetwater Crossing's schoolmaster."

"Pa teaches," Noah announced. "Uncle Josh sells things."

Louisa gave Noah a fond glance. "That's one way to describe it. Josh opened a tearoom and specialty shop a few months ago, and he now owns the mercantile."

"A tearoom?" Della appeared intrigued. "I wouldn't have expected one here."

"It's been remarkably successful." Louisa's pride in her husband's venture was apparent. "We'll have to have tea at Porter's next week."

This time it was Burke whose interest seemed piqued. "Porter's? Any relation to Porter and Sons in New York?"

It was Josh's turn to nod. "I used to be part of P&S. Now I'm just a small-town proprietor." He paused for a second before adding, "That was the best move I've ever made."

"How did you manage to come to Sweetwater Crossing?" Burke asked.

With a quick smile for his wife, Josh answered, "It's a long story. I'll save it for another night, because I think Craig wants to know more about the way you and your partner challenged each other."

"There's not much more to tell you. We called it Stump the Doctor—not a particularly imaginative name, but it made us both better physicians."

"I think you're right, Craig. It could benefit your pupils. Instead of asking all the questions yourself, you could have the students challenge each other about whatever they're studying. You might even turn it into a game with prizes for the winners," Joanna suggested. Miss Albright, the woman who'd taught her and her sisters, had been effective in imparting knowledge, but she had done nothing as innovative as making learning a game.

Feigning indignation, Craig turned to Emily. "Why didn't you tell me your sister had such good ideas? All I heard was that she was an accomplished pianist."

"And she is," Louisa assured her brother-in-law. "That's why she was in Europe studying with some maestros."

Joanna wished her sister hadn't said that. It wasn't that she planned to keep her time abroad a secret, but today had been so eventful and exhausting that she wanted nothing more than to retire to her room.

"Europe." Della's eyes lit with interest. "That sounds fascinating. I want to hear about it."

Before Joanna could offer an excuse, Emily spoke. "Another night, perhaps. Joanna had an even longer journey than you and Burke did." For once, Joanna was grateful that Emily was being a protective older sister.

"Of course. We all need to rest," Burke was quick to agree.

"Now that that's all settled, let's have some dessert." Emily rose to begin clearing dishes.

While they were enjoying their chocolate pudding, Louisa turned to Burke. "If you're willing, I'd like to learn everything you know about lung diseases."

"Certainly." He looked at Joanna, but this time his gaze seemed less clinical, instead reminding her of the way Kurt had looked the day they'd met. Perhaps Burke didn't regard her as a specimen after all.

Chapter

Three

He wasn't sleepy, but Burke hadn't wanted to intrude on the two couples' evening, and so when both Della and Joanna retired to their rooms, he'd climbed the stairs to his and was now seated on the veranda that spanned the back of the house. Perhaps the view of the slowly moving creek would help him sort out his impressions of the day that had been filled with surprises.

The first had been the house Clive had built for Della. Though Finley House reminded Burke of Della's childhood home, there was one noticeable difference: this house felt like a home, a place filled with warmth and welcome, while the plantation house her grandfather had built had always struck Burke as cold.

The difference was the family that lived here. The three Vaughn sisters bore little physical resemblance, although Emily and Louisa had the same vivid blue eyes, but they all treated him and Della almost as if they were part of their family, as did Josh and Craig. Even little Noah and Mrs. Carmichael had been more welcoming than he would have expected.

That had been the second surprise. And then there was Joanna. The ring on her left hand and her second surname told him she was married, while the combination of her husband's absence and her mourning clothing made him believe she was a widow. It was one thing to be recovering from a serious physical ailment as she was, but when deep emotional loss was added, the prognosis became complicated.

What could a physician do? That was a question Burke had posed to Felix as part of their Stump the Doctor challenge. It was also one of the few times neither of them had an answer.

"Do you mind if I join you?" Mrs. Carmichael interrupted Burke's reverie as she emerged from her room onto the shared veranda. "It's been such an exciting day that I know I won't be able to sleep for hours."

Nor would Burke. Rising, he gestured toward the chair next to his. "I'd welcome your company." Perhaps talking to her, even if it was about inconsequential things, would help him relax enough to sleep.

When she was seated, Mrs. Carmichael shifted slightly so she was facing him. "I still can't believe Clive's fiancée came here. Of course it's been decades, but I still recall how eager we were to meet the woman he loved so dearly. At first folks thought she must be a pampered girl who'd demanded a huge house, but Clive soon set them straight. Once they heard about her daddy, opinions changed mighty fast, but the curiosity never died."

Feeling the need to defend his uncle's choice of a bride, Burke said, "Della is the least selfish person I've ever met. She's devoted her whole life to making others happy."

The widow nodded. "I can see that. She's kind and generous, and you're a good man to have brought her all this way, especially since it meant leaving your patients."

"My partner is handling them." There was no need to tell Mrs. Carmichael or anyone that he welcomed the opportunity to leave Alabama. "Besides, I was almost as curious as Aunt Della. Neither of us knew what we'd find."

"I doubt you expected it to be a boardinghouse."

"True, but I also didn't expect such a welcoming family."

Though the sun had set, the waxing moon revealed Mrs. Carmichael's smile. "Joseph Vaughn set a fine example for his daughters. He loved them all equally."

Her statement was almost as unexpected as the family itself. Though Burke had no memory of his father, his mother had lavished the same love on him as she did on Antonia and Hester.

"Pardon me for asking, but why wouldn't he?"

"It's a complicated family." The widow's smile was undiminished. "Joseph was the pastor in a town about fifty miles away. When his wife died giving birth to Joanna, he wanted to leave the memories behind, so when he heard about the opening for a minister in Sweetwater Crossing, he came here."

Though the story differed from his own, Burke felt a connection to Joanna's father. They'd both come to Sweetwater Crossing to escape memories when death changed their lives irrevocably. Joseph Vaughn had remained and forged a new life. While Burke wouldn't be here permanently, if he was fortunate, he might accomplish what the town's former minister did and find a new direction for his life.

After pausing to take a breath, Mrs. Carmichael continued. "Prudence Abbott was a young widow with a child of her own. That's Emily. Practically from the day they met, sparks flew between Prudence and Joseph, and they married a month later. Louisa's their child. She's the only one who grew up with both parents."

No wonder the three sisters bore so little physical resemblance. Burke nodded. "You're right. The family is complicated. My mother was a romantic at heart and would have been pleased by the evidence of second chances at happiness." He, on the other hand, had yet to have his first.

Her nod said that Mrs. Carmichael agreed with Ma. "Emily found her second chance. She was a widow when she returned to Sweetwater Crossing last year." For the first time, the older woman's smile faltered. "I hope Joanna will be as fortunate. It's sad that her husband died after they'd been married only a month."

Burke's supposition that she was a widow had been accurate. "Was he an American?"

"No. I don't know much about him other than that he was German and they met in Switzerland. You'll have to ask her if you want to know more, but you might want to wait a day or two. The poor dear only arrived today."

Burke tried to mask his surprise. He recalled Emily saying something about Joanna's longer journey, but he'd assumed that she had been back for several days and was still recovering.

"Don't you dare tell the others," Mrs. Carmichael continued, "but Joanna has always been my favorite of the Vaughn girls. I sometimes thought she felt a bit lost being the middle child, so even though I hated to see her leave, I knew the time in Europe would be good for her."

Mrs. Carmichael shook her head. "Look how that turned out. She caught some horrible disease and lost her husband. It doesn't seem fair, but I won't give up hope that things will turn around." She wrinkled her nose as she looked at Burke. "You probably think I'm an old busybody. I'm not. I'm also not a matchmaker, but if I were, I couldn't have found better mates for Emily and Louisa. I want Joanna to be as happy as they are."

So did Burke. Though he couldn't explain the reason, something about Joanna had touched a chord deep inside him, making him want to protect this woman. She wasn't a patient. He hadn't known her long enough to call her a friend. Still, the urge—more than that, the need—to ease her suffering and restore her health so that she could seek a second chance at happiness could not be denied.

Mrs. Carmichael raised her hand to her mouth, stifling a

yawn. "It seems the day is finally catching up with me. Good night, Burke."

"Good night."

As he settled back in the chair, Burke closed his eyes for a moment, reflecting on what he'd been told. Though he cautioned himself not to place too much weight on initial impressions, there was no question that Joanna was the most intriguing of the three sisters. He sensed that she possessed an adventurous streak, since she'd left her family to go to Europe. And then there was her strength. Not physical strength, because her breathing was definitely strained, but internal strength.

Burke's instincts told him she was a woman who could stand on her own, one who didn't need a man to take care of her, even under devastating circumstances, and yet, despite knowing that, he wanted to help her heal both her body and her spirit.

❧

"Come in," Joanna said when she heard the soft knock.

"I thought you'd be asleep." Emily closed the door behind her, frowning slightly at the sight of the lighted lamp and the book in Joanna's hand.

"So did I, but my mind is whirling in a dozen directions all at once." Part of that was the strangeness of being in Emily's former room rather than her own. Though both bedchambers were on corners of the second floor, Emily's faced the back and had access to the rear veranda, whereas Joanna's had only a front-facing window. Even though she'd once coveted this room, today Joanna would have preferred the familiarity of the one where she'd slept for so many years.

Rather than admit that to Emily, she said, "I hoped Miss Austen's story would help me relax, but there are so many things to think about."

"If you're like me, that starts with our new visitors." Emily perched on the side of the bed next to Joanna.

While that wasn't foremost in Joanna's mind, she had indeed thought of Burke and Della and hoped they were finding it easier to relax than she was.

"I never imagined I'd meet Clive's fiancée." Della might be more than a decade older, but even in the brief time they'd spent together, Joanna felt an affinity with her, perhaps because they'd both lost loved ones, perhaps because Della's passion for books matched her own for music.

"What amazes me the most is meeting a man who looks so much like Clive. I always wondered about his appearance, because I can't remember Father describing Clive."

Joanna nodded. She'd never envisioned Clive Finley being a redhead with green eyes, but there was no denying that Burke was an attractive man. What intrigued her was more than his physical appearance. Burke was clearly devoted to Della, but though he seemed happy to be here, Joanna sensed an underlying sorrow. It wasn't the kind of sorrow Kurt had when they'd first met, caused by his wife's tragic death. Rather, Joanna had the impression that Burke was haunted by something in his life.

There was no reason to tell Emily that she was concerned about one of their visitors, especially not tonight when Joanna's emotions were so tumultuous. Instead, she pretended that her thoughts had not taken a detour.

"All I recall is Father talking about their friendship and how he wished Clive had survived the war. I know he wondered which battle was his last."

"We could ask Della. She should know."

Once again, Joanna nodded. "I'll do that in the morning, even though I don't like reminding her of her loss." Joanna hated talking about Kurt's death, even to her sisters. Recounting his final hours brought the sorrow she'd tried so hard to suppress back to the surface and reopened the wounds his absence had inflicted. Joanna could only hope the passage of time had made it easier for Della to speak of her beloved's death.

"Perhaps you should wait," Emily suggested. "After all, she and Burke will be here for two weeks. Why not give them a chance to form some happy memories of Sweetwater Crossing before you ask about Clive?"

"That's good advice, O wise older sister." Joanna pretended to doff her hat and bow, wanting to lighten the atmosphere.

Emily's lips curved into a smile. "I'm glad you recognized my wisdom. You and Louisa were often rebellious subjects."

"That's only because whenever we played, you insisted on being the queen. You claimed it was your prerogative as the eldest." Joanna gave her sister a quick hug. "I don't think I said it often enough when we were growing up, but I love you."

"Not as much as I love you."

Joanna chuckled. "There you go again, trying to be the best."

Holding her hands up in surrender, Emily joined in the laughter. When their laughs turned into giggles and finally stopped, she spoke. "One of the reasons I knocked when I saw your light is I wanted to give you something happy to think about." She paused. "Are you ready?"

"For happy things, always." There'd been far too few of those recently.

Emily rose and smoothed her skirt over her abdomen, revealing a small but unmistakable bump.

"Is that what I think it is?"

Her sister's eyes sparkled with joy. "It is. You're going to be an aunt."

"Oh, Emily, that's wonderful!" Joanna drew her sister into a long hug, relishing the news and the way it dispelled the malaise that had clung to her all afternoon and evening. "When is the baby due?"

"Early February." Emily's voice cracked with emotion. "Craig and I are thrilled, especially because Louisa is back and can deliver your niece or nephew. She'll probably never tell you—you know how modest our sister can be—but she saved a baby's life a few months ago. The parents named him after her."

"A boy named Louisa?" The thought made Joanna giggle again.

"Oh, Joanna, your sense of humor hasn't failed, has it? His name is Louis Gleason."

"An admirable name, but let's not talk about someone else's baby. How are you feeling?"

Emily wrinkled her nose. "Better now that the morning sickness is over. I've started to feel the baby move. They're just little flutters, but it feels like a miracle."

"And it is. I remember Mama saying that each new life is a miracle."

Emily nodded. "And a gift from God." She clasped one of Joanna's hands. "I'm sorry about all that you've gone through, but I'm grateful that you're back home. I want my baby to be close to his or her aunts."

"Aunt Joanna. I like the sound of that. Have you and Craig thought about your baby's name?" Though she and Kurt had been married only a few weeks, they'd agreed that their first son would be named Kurt, and their daughter would bear Joanna's mother's name, Anna.

Emily shrugged. "We've talked, but there's still plenty of time to decide. All we know is that it won't be a combination of our names. Can you imagine a child named Cremily?"

Shaking her head in mock dismay, Joanna said, "The poor child. At least Joanna is a normal name." Everyone in the family knew that her mother had wanted to name her Josephine Vaughn, honoring her father Joseph, but when Mother died in childbirth, Father had changed their daughter's name to Joanna. "That way you'll never forget that your mother's name was Anna," he'd told Joanna.

"We're in no hurry to choose a name," Emily continued. "At this point, we're focused on rejoicing."

"As you should be. You'll be a wonderful mother." One thing Joanna had known for as long as she could recall was that Emily had deep maternal instincts. "I'm surprised you and George didn't have a child. You were married long enough."

Inexplicably, Emily appeared uncomfortable with the idea. "It didn't happen," she said, "but God has given me another chance to be a mother."

"And me a chance to be an aunt." It would be another change, but this was a happy one.

⟨⟩

"You broke your promise!"

"Everyone makes mistakes."

"I'll never forgive you."

"Her anger will fade. In the meantime, it's best if you keep your distance."

Though Burke was hundreds of miles away, their voices echoed through his mind, first Edna's, then Felix's, reminders of that horrible morning when he'd returned to the infirmary and discovered Edna hysterical with grief as she cradled her mother's body. Burke's patient, the woman who might have been his mother-in-law, had died sooner than he'd expected. Hours later after Edna had left, Burke had discovered the cause of death: four grains of morphine were missing.

"I only gave her two," he'd told Felix. They both knew that was all that Mrs. Arnold should have even though her pain was extreme. Four would have been a lethal dose.

"You were more than tired. You were exhausted. If you weren't, you'd have written the amount you dispensed on her record." Though Felix had tried to excuse him, reminding him that Mrs. Arnold's cancer was so advanced that she wouldn't have lived much longer anyway, Burke knew there were no excuses for what had happened. He'd taken an oath to do no harm, but he had. Irreparable harm.

Wrenching himself back to the present, he stared out the French doors. The light of the almost full moon shone on the creek. A few stars twinkled in the ebony sky. If he opened the door, he'd probably hear an owl hoot or a nocturnal creature scurry through the grass. Had it not been for the memories that tormented him, Burke would have called it a peaceful night, but there was no peace in his heart, simply remorse that he'd cut a life short.

If only there were a way to make amends. But nothing could erase his guilt. That was something he'd have to bear until he took his last breath.

⁓

"Have you thought about what you'd like to do today?" Emily asked as she passed the plate of toast to Della.

As had been customary when their parents were alive, Saturday breakfast consisted of nothing more than scrambled eggs and toast. Father had claimed that a meatless meal helped him think more clearly and resulted in better sermons. There were no sermons to be written today, but no one seemed to mind the simple fare. Josh and Craig piled eggs on their plates, and Noah grinned when his toast crunched.

Both Burke and Della appeared more rested than they had yesterday, but the pain Joanna had seen in Burke's eyes had not lessened. Though he smiled as he accepted the bowl of peach jam, the smile did not reach his eyes, making her wonder whether he'd slept as restlessly as she had.

Della nodded as she spread jam on a piece of toast. "I want to visit Clive's grave."

"His grave?" Joanna blinked in surprise. "I don't understand. He's not buried here." When Burke looked as startled by her response as she'd been by Della's request, Joanna continued. "My father believed Clive was killed in the war. He'd told his friends that he was going back to Alabama to fight with the men he'd grown up with, so no one was surprised by anything other than the suddenness of his departure, but Father had expected to hear from him. When no letters came, he wanted to write to you to ask what had happened, but he couldn't recall the name of the town where you two lived. Father spent the rest of his life regretting that he didn't know when or where Clive died."

Emily and Louisa's nods confirmed Joanna's statement. Josh and Craig, who were relative newcomers, remained silent, but Mrs. Carmichael said, "That's what we all believed."

The blood that had drained from Della's face rushed back, and she shook her head vehemently. "That's not possible, Joanna. Your father sent me a letter, telling me what happened." Obviously distressed, she pushed back her chair and rose. "Please excuse my poor manners, but I can't swallow another bite until this is settled. I need you to see the letter."

She left the room, her footsteps echoing as she climbed the stairs.

"Lady sad." Noah crumbled a corner of his toast.

She was indeed.

A few minutes later Della returned and handed a well-worn envelope to Joanna. "It's all here."

Her own appetite forgotten, Joanna slid the single sheet of paper from the envelope and began to read aloud. "'Dear Miss Samuels, I regret to inform you that Clive Finley died of dysentery last evening. The doctor did everything he could but was unable to save him. I extend my condolences to you.' Signed Joseph Vaughn."

Della nodded slowly. "You see."

Joanna fixed her gaze on Della. "What I see is that my father did not write this letter. It's not his penmanship." She extended the sheet to Emily and Louisa for confirmation. When they'd both agreed that this was not Father's handwriting, Joanna continued. "Furthermore, he always included a Scripture reference in his letters. There's none here."

"But if he didn't write it," Burke asked, "who did?"

That was a question Joanna could not answer. "I don't know. I don't recognize the writing. Do you, Mrs. Carmichael?"

She studied it longer than Emily and Louisa had, then shook her head as she handed it back to Della. "I'm afraid I don't."

"There's one more thing." Louisa joined the conversation. "I remember Doc Sheridan saying Sweetwater Crossing was unusual because it had never had a case of dysentery."

"So the letter is all lies." Burke made no effort to hide his anger, though Joanna knew it wasn't directed at any of them. Undoubtedly, he was concerned about the effect this revelation was having on Della.

"It appears that way," Joanna agreed.

Della's dismay was obvious. "I don't understand." She picked up the letter and stared at it as if seeing it for the first time. "Who could have sent this and why would they have lied to me?"

Joanna wished she had an answer. As it was, her head was reeling with the realization that what she'd believed about the man who'd built this house was false. "I have no idea. All I know is what my father told us. There were four men who became close friends: my father, Clive, Doc Sheridan, and Mr. Albright. They used to get together every Saturday evening to talk about whatever it is men talk about when there are no ladies present. According to my father, those times were highlights of the men's lives, and they never missed one."

Della nodded as if she'd heard the same story.

"No one knew why Clive didn't join them that Saturday in early 1861. It was supposed to be their last evening together, because Clive was planning to leave the following Monday." Joanna continued the story. "Afterwards, they speculated that he'd gotten a message to return to Alabama immediately, but the postmaster said there'd been none. All anyone knew was that they never saw Clive again."

When Della remained silent, as if trying to absorb what she'd heard, Burke's green eyes narrowed as he addressed Joanna. "We need to learn the truth. I know your father is deceased, but maybe the other two men can help. Even though it's been a long time, they might recall something."

Emily shook her head. "Doc Sheridan died earlier this year. That only leaves Mr. Albright. Unfortunately, he and his wife are visiting friends who moved to Austin, and I'm not certain when they're expected back."

Della, who looked as if she'd aged a decade in the last ten minutes, attempted to brush away the tears that streamed down her face. "I can't believe it. It's almost like losing Clive a second time."

Four

It wouldn't be like losing Father a second time, but though it would undoubtedly be difficult, Joanna needed to see where he'd died. She'd refused Emily and Louisa's offers to accompany her, knowing this was one thing she had to do alone, and so with legs that were remarkably steady, she made her way to the barn.

To her relief, she found a peaceful scene. For the first time in her memory all three stalls were filled. Her father's horse greeted her with a whinny, while Emily's and Josh's regarded her more cautiously. Grandmother's horse—Joanna's now—and the one Burke had driven were at the livery. It was an ordinary morning in an ordinary barn with no reminders of the tragedy that had occurred here.

After saying a silent prayer for both her father and the man who'd killed him, Joanna left the barn, blinking as her eyes adjusted to the bright sunshine.

"Do you tell your secrets to the horses?"

She turned, startled by both Burke's presence so close to the barn and the question. She thought he'd be trying to comfort

Della after the revelation that what she'd believed about Clive were lies.

"I used to," he continued. "When I was upset, I'd confide in them."

Joanna had no trouble picturing the boy Burke once was hiding his emotions from his family, instead pouring out his heart to a horse. Boys, Miss Albright had taught her pupils, weren't supposed to cry, for tears were a sign of weakness. Even now, Joanna suspected Burke rarely expressed his feelings, particularly the darker ones like sorrow and regret.

She'd shed her share of tears when Kurt and Grandmother died, but she hadn't wanted to put her grief into words, even with Marta. Kurt's sister had railed at the doctors, then spent hours lamenting the loss of her only sibling. Joanna had simply listened.

Her eyes now accustomed to the sunlight, Joanna fixed her gaze on Burke, wondering why he'd come out here.

"I think Louisa may have talked to the horses, but I never did," she told him. "The piano was my refuge." Though this was an unusual conversation to be having with someone she had just met, Joanna found she didn't mind sharing her inner thoughts with Burke, because her instincts told her she could trust him. While his question may have sounded casual, she sensed that it was the result of genuine caring, not idle curiosity.

"My family soon learned that if I was playing Chopin's Funeral March, they should leave me alone."

Burke extended his arm, waiting for Joanna to place her hand on it before he took a step toward the house. "I'm no musician, but even I know that's an intense piece. What did you play when you were happy?"

She smiled, remembering. "Many things. I found Beethoven's Moonlight Sonata soothing. One of Chopin's preludes was good when I felt a mixture of emotions. It starts and ends quietly, but there's a thunderstorm in the middle."

"I can't say that I recognize those, but Aunt Della might. Perhaps you'll play them for us while we're here."

"Perhaps." The thought was appealing. Music had always soothed Joanna, and prior to her illness, it had been the primary focus of her life. Still, there could be hurdles to overcome. "Since I haven't played in months, I'm afraid my fingers might not do what I tell them to." Herr Ridel had insisted on hours of practice each day, warning that muscles needed regular exercise.

Burke gave her hand a long look, as if trying to identify possible weakness. That was, Joanna supposed, the result of his medical training. Though she'd expected him to offer an opinion of her hands' readiness, he said, "If you weren't talking to the horses, why were you in the barn? That doesn't seem like the best place to spend such a beautiful morning."

It wasn't. Joanna hesitated for a moment, then realized that since Burke would be here for two weeks, he might hear what had happened to Father. It was best that he learn the truth from her.

"I needed to see where my father died. I was already in Europe, but last year Emily found him in the barn with a noose around his neck." Though Joanna tried to keep her tone even, it wavered as she recounted what had happened that Saturday in August.

Burke stopped abruptly, his green eyes wide with shock. "That must have been horrible for your sister."

"It was a horrible time for both Emily and Louisa. Louisa left Sweetwater Crossing soon after that, but Emily wouldn't believe that Father had taken his own life and spent months trying to discover what really happened."

"Did she succeed?"

"Fortunately, yes." Joanna couldn't imagine what it would have been like to go through the rest of their lives with the cloud of Father's death hanging over them. "He was murdered, but the killer tried to make it look like suicide. Emily doesn't like unsolved mysteries, and neither do I."

Though there had always been questions about Clive Finley's disappearance, as far as Joanna knew, no one had believed there was anything sinister about it. But now, faced with the falsehoods in the letter Della had received, the situation took on a different color.

"I want to learn what happened to Clive. I know it's been more than twenty years, but the answer has to be here in Sweetwater Crossing."

Joanna wasn't certain who was more surprised by her statement: Burke or herself. The words came out seemingly of their own volition, but as she uttered them, she was filled with a sense of rightness. Della deserved to know the truth, and Joanna needed to know who'd sent the letter pretending to be her father.

Burke nodded as if he understood her reasoning. "Would you like a partner or even an assistant as you search for the answers? I don't know anyone here, but I'd like to help. I hate to see Aunt Della so upset."

"So do I." The woman's distress had made Joanna's heart ache. Though she hadn't been able to help Emily expose their father's killer, she was here now and had nothing else to occupy her days. Her homecoming hadn't been what she'd expected, but maybe this was why she'd arrived at the same time as Della and Burke. Maybe this was what she was meant to do.

"There has to be a way to uncover the truth," she told Burke.

"Then let's work together."

"I'd like that."

⸎

The surprises continued. As if the revelation that the letter Della had cherished for so long was a lie wasn't enough, there had been the equally shocking news that Joanna's father had been murdered. And now, though Burke had thought she might have retreated to her room to recover from what she'd learned, Della was waiting for him and Joanna as they returned from the barn. Her tears had dried, but sorrow still shone from her eyes.

When they were close enough to hear, she looked at Joanna. "Where is the cemetery?"

Apparently Della had forgotten that they'd caught sight of it when they arrived yesterday.

"Directly west from here." Joanna tipped her head to indicate the direction. "It's on the northwest corner of Creek and Center. You can't miss it."

Della gave a quick nod, acknowledging the directions. "I know it's futile, but I want to see it."

"Would you like me to accompany you?"

This time Della shook her head. "Thank you, Joanna, but no. Just Burke."

And so they headed for the place where Clive Finley was not buried. Della's steps were firm as they approached the cemetery, but after half an hour of reading the inscriptions on all the headstones, her energy seemed to flag. "Joanna was right," she said slowly. "Clive's not here. I simply didn't want to believe it."

Wishing there were something he could do to lessen her disappointment, Burke looked around. Spotting the steeple gave him an idea. "There's one more place to try. The church will have burial records." While unlikely, Clive might have been buried outside the cemetery. Burke knew that some families had small cemeteries on their ranches, wanting to keep their loved ones' remains close.

A spark of enthusiasm lit Della's eyes. "You're right. It's possible that the minister can help us."

Suspecting they'd find the minister in the parsonage, Burke knocked on the door of the stone building next to the church. The man who opened it appeared to be close to fifty, old enough to have remembered Clive if he'd lived here then. Burke doubted that was the case, since Joseph Vaughn had been the town's minister for many years, but he needed to ask. Few would comment on the current pastor's medium height, graying brown hair, or brown eyes. Instead, his most distinguishing characteristic was his thinness. It wasn't, Burke thought, the result of an illness but rather a trait he'd inherited.

"Good morning." His smile was warm and welcoming. "I'm Harold Lindstrom. How can I help you?"

After Burke introduced himself and Della, he said, "We wondered whether we could see burial records for early 1861."

If Pastor Lindstrom was surprised by the request, he gave no sign. "I didn't live here at the time, but the records are next door in the church. May I ask whose you're seeking?"

"Clive Finley."

A small gasp confirmed that Della had managed to surprise him. "The man who built Finley House?" There was a note of incredulity in the reverend's question.

"Yes. Della is the woman he planned to marry."

The minister gave Della a sympathetic look. "As I said, I wasn't here then, but I heard that he died in the war."

When Della did not respond, Burke continued the explanation. "My aunt was told otherwise. We're trying to explore every possibility."

"Certainly." Harold Lindstrom led the way to the church, then ushered them into a room off the narthex. With space for only the minister's desk and chair, two other chairs for visitors, and open shelves filled with books behind the desk, the office was smaller than Burke would have expected.

Once they were seated, the minister pulled one of the volumes from a shelf and laid it on the desk. "Here we are, the war years. Sadly, too many of Sweetwater Crossing's men are buried elsewhere. My predecessor listed their names and as much information as he had, even though they aren't in our cemetery."

When Burke started to open the book, Della shook her head. "Let me." She leafed through it for a few seconds, then studied one page carefully. "There's nothing. Clive is not buried here." Her voice was steadier than Burke had thought possible, but the way she clasped her hands together to hide their trembling told him she was as devastated by the absence of any reference to Clive as she'd been by the revelation that the letter she'd received so many years ago was filled with falsehoods.

"Thank you, Pastor Lindstrom," Burke said as he helped Della to her feet. There was no reason to linger, and unless he was mistaken, Della was on the verge of tears but didn't want a man she'd met only a few minutes earlier to see them.

The somber expression in the minister's brown eyes made Burke suspect he'd reached the same conclusion about Della's state. "I wish you'd found what you sought."

"It's not your fault," Della said softly. "You can't show me records that don't exist."

Her head held high, she walked out of the church. That was Della, doing her best to project strength, regardless of her true feelings.

"This trip hasn't been what you hoped for, has it?" Burke asked as they made their way slowly toward Finley House. While there'd been no reason to linger in the minister's office, there was also no reason to rush to their temporary home. "Would you like to start back to Alabama on Monday?"

"No." Once again, Della's voice was firm. "It may seem foolish to you, but I feel closer to Clive than I have in years. He may not be buried here, but this is where he lived. I want to stay for the full two weeks."

"All right." It was more than all right, for Burke had no desire to leave early. Though he had yet to resolve the questions about his future, there were reasons to remain in Sweetwater Crossing, including his desire to help Joanna solve the mystery of his uncle's death.

~~

Perhaps it was because she and Burke had discussed music. All Joanna knew was that she felt drawn to the parlor. The piano was in the same spot it had always been. The music she'd left in the bench was undisturbed. Some things hadn't changed, but she had.

She seated herself in front of the piano, opened the fallboard, then winced when she pressed a few keys. Her beloved piano was woefully out of tune.

"Oh, Joanna, I'm so sorry." Emily, apparently drawn by the sound, entered the parlor. "If I'd known you were coming home, I would have tried to have it tuned. To be honest, though, I don't know who could have done it now that Mrs. Sheridan is gone."

Though the doctor's wife was only a mediocre musician, she'd taught herself to tune pianos when she'd insisted that her daughter learn to play and had always tuned the Finley House piano.

"I suppose we could ask Miss Heppel," Emily continued. "She stopped giving lessons earlier this year, but she's still the church pianist."

Joanna smiled, thinking of the woman who'd nurtured her love of music. It had been Miss Heppel who'd written to Grandmother Kenner, telling her Joanna had the makings of a concert pianist and urging her to take her to Europe on her next trip.

Joanna's maternal grandmother had been so angry when her father had moved to Sweetwater Crossing shortly after Joanna's birth that she'd never visited her only grandchild. She had, however, sent occasional letters and gifts from her extensive travels.

When the invitation to accompany her to Europe and be tutored by masters had arrived, Joanna had been shocked but had agreed immediately. Not only was it the opportunity of a lifetime, but it would also take her away from Sweetwater

Crossing and the dream that had died almost as soon as it had been birthed.

Looking up at her sister, who stood at the end of the bench, Joanna said, "I'm surprised Miss Heppel is no longer teaching. Who took her place?"

"No one."

Another change. Though Joanna had been home less than twenty-four hours, those hours had revealed one change after another. Perhaps that was why she felt as if she were adrift, floating through a landscape that looked only slightly familiar.

"I imagine Miss Heppel would help us."

"We don't need her," Joanna told her sister. "The first thing Herr Ridel did was teach me to tune. He said every pianist should know how, because we couldn't be assured that instruments would be ready as promised. 'Emergencies happen, and so does sloppiness,' he said."

Joanna rose and studied the strings. "I suspect it'll take less time to make this sound good than to convince my fingers to perform. Don't be surprised if you hear some horrible sounds."

But that didn't happen. Once the piano was tuned, Joanna began five-finger exercises, then graduated to her favorite Chopin prelude, and as she did, she felt herself relax, remembering how music had always soothed her. It didn't change what had happened—Kurt and Grandmother were still dead—but the pain that clenched Joanna's heart lessened while she was playing. That, her mother had told her, was a gift from God.

⁓

Leaving Della on the front porch where she claimed she wanted to rest and reflect for a few minutes, Burke entered the house, then stopped abruptly, almost mesmerized by the music coming from the parlor. Though he'd listened to music in church and at various social functions, he'd never heard any that touched his emotions so deeply. He sank onto the staircase and gave himself over to listening.

At first the notes were soft, like gentle rain. Then they grew louder, conjuring the image of thunder and a heavy downpour. Finally, they became soft again. The storm was over. As the final chord died, he rose and entered the parlor, clapping as he did.

"That was magnificent. Is that the Chopin prelude you mentioned earlier?"

Joanna turned and nodded. Though she was still clad as she'd been when they'd walked from the barn, her demeanor had changed. Her shoulders were straighter, the angle of her head more confident, her expression more peaceful.

"It's Opus 28, Number 15." She gestured toward the sheet music in front of her. "I thought I'd forgotten it, but once I started playing, the notes came back to me."

Burke was impressed that she'd memorized what seemed to be a complex piece. Perhaps that was what came from repetition. He took a step closer, then when she gestured an invitation, sat on the edge of the piano bench.

"Your family didn't exaggerate when they said you're an accomplished musician. I don't claim to be an expert. All I can tell you is that I've never heard music so filled with emotion. It was glorious, and that's a word I've never used before."

Joanna's pleasure was evident in the soft blush that colored her cheeks. "Thank you. My grandmother took me to Europe to determine whether I had any genuine talent."

"What did you learn?"

"That I might have become a concert pianist if only . . ." She paused so long that Burke feared she would not complete the sentence. At last she said, "Everything changed when I caught scarlet fever and then pneumonia. The doctors said my lungs were permanently damaged and I'd never have enough stamina for a concert tour."

Pneumonia. No wonder Louisa had asked him to teach her

everything he knew about ailments of the lungs. Her sister hadn't died, but her life had been irreparably changed by the dread disease. Doctors kept searching for better ways to treat it, but so far no one knew how to prevent it.

Burke's heart began to race. Was this the answer to his question about the future? Was he meant to do more than treat disease? No one had been able to prevent pneumonia, but that didn't mean it was impossible. A century ago, people despaired of preventing smallpox until Edward Jenner developed a vaccine. Surely it was possible to eradicate pneumonia with a vaccine just as Jenner had done with smallpox. The question was, was Burke the right man to do it?

After taking a deep breath to slow his heartbeat and bring him back to the present, Burke studied Joanna, searching for signs of weakness. "I hadn't realized playing was so strenuous."

Those brown eyes that reminded him of hot chocolate had lost the sparkle they'd had when she accepted his compliment. "It's not the performing itself. It's the schedule. There are so many stops and so many rehearsals that there's very little time to rest. The doctors warned me I could do further damage if I overexerted."

The discouragement in her voice touched Burke's heart and made him resolve to help her. "And so you abandoned your dream."

"Yes." Discouragement was replaced by resignation. "Being a concert pianist wasn't always my dream. I had others that died before I went to Europe, but when I saw how powerful music can be and the way it touches so many people, I knew that was what I wanted from my life." She gazed at him for a moment before adding, "It's more than that I *wanted* to be a musician: I felt as if that was what I was meant to do."

Burke understood the feeling. From the first time he'd assisted the town's older doctor, he'd believed that healing people was his mission in life. It had given him a sense of fulfillment.

But even before the fatal overdose of morphine, that fulfillment had begun to fade. Della had joked that Burke had outgrown Samuels, and perhaps she was right. He knew that old life was gone. It was time to find a new one.

"It might still be possible for you to be a concert pianist," he told Joanna, wracking his brain for ways to increase her pulmonary stamina. "Your doctors might have been wrong."

She shook her head. "They weren't."

Her voice was devoid of hope, and that disturbed him more greatly than the diagnosis itself. Somehow, someway he'd prove those other doctors wrong.

Chapter
Five

"My mother would probably chide me for saying this, but you appear a bit nervous." Burke's expression was almost sheepish, as if he expected Joanna to reprimand him. How could she, when he'd spoken the truth?

It was a beautiful Sunday morning, cooler than many at this time of the year, with a light breeze. The rest of the family preceded them on their way to church, Emily and Louisa walking beside their husbands and little Noah, and Della engrossed in a discussion with Mrs. Carmichael. The first half block had been uneventful, with Burke commenting on how different the weather was from Alabama. And then he'd said that.

As Joanna's steps faltered, she turned toward him, shocked that he'd read her emotions so easily. No one—not even her family—had done that. She paused for a second, not sure how to respond, then realized there was no reason to dissemble.

"It's probably silly of me to be nervous, but this will be the first time I've seen someone other than my father standing in the pulpit." That thought had disturbed her sleep and wakened her far too early this morning. And then there'd been breakfast.

It had seemed somehow wrong to eat what had been their traditional Sunday meal when her parents weren't here to enjoy it. Emily and Louisa may have become accustomed to the changes in their lives, but this was Joanna's first Sunday in Sweetwater Crossing without her parents.

Though breakfast had been difficult, the worst was yet to come. Soon she'd be entering the building that had played such a vital role in her life. It would look the same. Joanna knew that. But the service wouldn't be the same.

"Pastor Lindstrom seems like a good man." Burke's words and his gentle smile were designed to reassure her. "When Aunt Della and I met him yesterday, he struck me as sympathetic."

"I'm sure he is." But he wasn't Father, and that was the problem. Trying to distract herself, Joanna continued. "Emily said Reverend Lindstrom is the third minister since Father. Apparently the first one wasn't right for Sweetwater Crossing, and the second minister was temporary from the beginning. He married Emily's friend Alice, the one who used to be the librarian, and moved back to Louisiana."

Though she wasn't babbling, Joanna felt as if she were on the verge of it. "Emily assured me I'd like the new minister and would have a chance to get to know him better when he joins us for lunch today. I should be happy. It's just . . ."

"A change." Burke completed the sentence. "And you've already had too many of them."

Joanna nodded, once again surprised by his understanding. Coming home had been so different from her expectations. "You're right. I feel overwhelmed by the way everything in my life has changed, but how did you know?"

Burke's green eyes deepened with what might have been sorrow. "I've had some changes in my life that left me feeling that way."

"Changes like leaving your practice, if only for a month or so, to come here?"

He shook his head. "That was actually a good change. Others weren't as benign."

Though Joanna wanted to delve into what those other changes had been, she knew better than to pry. Besides, they'd reached the church and, as was the family's custom, did not linger to speak to anyone despite curious glances directed at her and Burke. Instead, she followed the rest of the family into the sanctuary to the second pew.

That was yet another change, another reminder of Father's death. Previously she'd sat in the first pew, the one reserved for the minister's family. Now that pew remained empty, because the current minister had no family.

Afterward Joanna could not have told anyone what subject Pastor Lindstrom had chosen for the sermon or which hymns they'd sung. She was dimly aware of Miss Heppel playing the piano in the loft and had the fleeting thought that her former teacher wasn't as skilled as she recalled, but that seemed unimportant when a thin man no taller than she took his place behind the pulpit. Though Father had been gone for more than a year, the reality of his death came crashing over Joanna as she watched someone else lead the congregation in the familiar liturgy.

Burke was right; change was difficult. And yet as the service ended and Pastor Lindstrom pronounced the benediction from the sixth chapter of Numbers, Joanna felt her spirits lift. The Lord had indeed given her peace.

⁓

Burke smiled and gave thanks for the way Joanna relaxed after the benediction, as if a burden had been lifted from her shoulders. One of his prayers had been answered.

She rose to exit the pew, her lips curved in a wry smile. "I need to warn you that you may feel as if you're running a gauntlet when we step outside. Folks will want to meet you and Della."

"And talk to you." Under most circumstances, people would have been welcoming her home, but Burke had seen the speculative looks that had been directed their way and heard the whispered, "It's about time the middle Vaughn girl returned. Imagine, staying in Europe after her parents died. She should have been here with her sisters."

Joanna shrugged. "There'll be some of that, but you and Della are the main attraction, particularly for those who remember your uncle. Are you ready?"

"As ready as I can be." He touched Della's shoulder to get her attention. "How about you, Aunt Della?"

"I'm looking forward to meeting the townspeople. I know I shouldn't have been staring, but some of them look old enough to have known Clive." Her smile broadened. "Pastor Lindstrom's sermon couldn't have been more appropriate. 'Ask and it shall be given you; seek and ye shall find.' Matthew 7:7 was the encouragement I needed."

"That's a message we should all remember." And one whose truth was evident, for another of Burke's prayers had been answered. Despite the string of disappointments Della had encountered since they'd arrived in Sweetwater Crossing, her normal optimism had returned.

He left the church, Joanna on one side, Della on the other, while the rest of their party followed. As they emerged into the sunlight, two middle-aged men approached them, their expressions curious. Though both were brunets of the same height, one man's hair was light brown and his eyes blue, while the other had darker hair, brown eyes, and a paunch.

"Welcome to Sweetwater Crossing," the lighter-haired man said, extending his hand to Burke. "I'm Malcolm Alcott, the town's mayor." The gesture and words were courteous, but the mayor's blue eyes radiated barely veiled hostility.

Apparently unaware of his companion's reaction, the other man extended his hand. "And I'm Sheriff Andrew Granger.

Welcome to the finest town in the Hill Country." His welcome rang with sincerity.

If Sweetwater Crossing was like many other towns, these men were among the most powerful and were exercising that power by being the first to greet a newcomer. Though common courtesy dictated that they include Della in their welcome, neither man appeared eager to acknowledge her presence, leaving Burke to suspect they were like Della's father and held women in low regard.

The mayor's eyes narrowed. "You remind me of someone I used to know."

"Good morning, Mr. Mayor and Sheriff Granger." Though the men were ignoring her as well as Della, Joanna wasn't allowing that to continue. "Please let me introduce you to Miss Della Samuels and Burke Finley. They've come from Alabama and are staying with us at Finley House."

The men gave Della the briefest of nods before turning their attention back to Burke. "Your name's Finley?" The sheriff studied him. "Are you Clive's son?"

"No, sir. I'm his nephew. Miss Samuels is the woman he'd intended to marry."

The mayor nodded, his gaze never veering from Burke. "That explains it. The resemblance is remarkable."

"So I've been told."

Della took a step forward, her eagerness to speak to someone who might have known her fiancé evident. "I came to learn what I could about Clive's time here."

When there was no response, Burke spoke. "If you two knew him, perhaps we could talk to you when you're not busy." A casual conversation in the churchyard wouldn't be enough for him, particularly given the mayor's hostility that had yet to fade and the way both men were ignoring Della. Burke wanted to sit with them, not leaving until he was satisfied he and Della had learned everything they knew.

The men exchanged an uncomfortable glance. "It's been a long time," the mayor said.

"Yes, it has," Joanna agreed. Unlike Della, who seemed to have accepted the men's behavior, she refused to be nothing more than a bystander. "But even after all these years, you might recall something. I'm certain you want to help Miss Samuels in any way you can."

The mayor's nod seemed perfunctory. "I'll think on it, and so will the sheriff. Right, Andrew?" When the other man inclined his head in agreement, they took their leave, their spots quickly claimed by others who wanted to meet the newcomers and speak to Joanna. To Burke's relief, none of the women who'd been so critical of her was among them.

A woman with almost black hair and gray eyes was one of the last to leave the church. While others walked in pairs or small groups, she remained alone as she approached the Vaughn family, her eyes fixed on Joanna.

"Joanna, my dear, I could hardly believe my eyes when I saw you walk into the sanctuary. Welcome home!" She touched Joanna's hand. "I can see that you're busy now." Though she gave Della an appraising look, to Burke's surprise, she merely glanced at him, then averted her head. "Please say you'll visit me tomorrow. I want to hear all about your studies. Shall we say 10:00?" Without waiting to be introduced to Della and him, she hurried away.

"My apologies," Joanna said when the dark-haired woman was out of earshot. "Miss Heppel isn't usually so abrupt. I think my return caught her off guard. She's our church pianist and the woman who taught me to play."

"She seems very fond of you. Were you her protégé?"

Joanna smiled at Della's question. "I hadn't thought of myself in that way, but perhaps."

Half an hour later, when Burke was convinced he'd met everyone in Sweetwater Crossing, though he could recall only a few names, Joanna said, "We can leave now." The crowd had dispersed, the few who remained conversing with her sisters and their husbands.

Moments later, a new couple approached them. Joanna's expression changed from pleasure to concern, perhaps because the woman, who was almost as short as Emily, appeared on the verge of fainting. She gripped her husband's arm for support, then seemed to regain her composure.

Taking a step toward them, Joanna greeted the woman whose blue eyes were fixed on Burke. Her light brown hair and features were unremarkable, but her gaze was piercing, reminding him of his first schoolteacher, who'd always seemed to know when mischief was afoot and frequently stopped the perpetrators before they could play their pranks.

"Miss Albright—oh, excuse me, Mrs. Neville—I'm so glad to see you. And, Mr. Neville, please accept my congratulations on your marriage. You couldn't find a better woman." It appeared that Joanna was going to ignore Mrs. Neville's previous discomfort.

Turning to Burke and Della, Joanna continued. "When she was still Miss Albright, this lady was our schoolmarm. She taught my sisters and me the three Rs and so much more."

He'd been right in thinking this woman had taught school. Had marriage been the reason she'd retired, or did she suffer from an ailment that left her so pale and dependent on her husband? Not wanting to make her uncomfortable with his assessment, Burke turned his attention to Mr. Neville. Like his wife, he had no distinguishing features. His brown hair and eyes were ordinary, but the way he regarded his wife was not. Mr. Neville was clearly infatuated with the woman who wore his ring.

"First of all, Joanna, you've reached the age where you can address Thomas and me by our first names. More importantly, it appears you've forgotten some of the manners I taught you."

Burke wasn't certain whether the former schoolmarm's disapproval was real or feigned, but he was relieved to see color return to her cheeks and that she was no longer in danger of fainting.

"Aren't you going to introduce your friends?" she asked, her voice tart.

"My apologies, Gertrude." Another woman might have been chagrined by the criticism, but Joanna's demeanor remained calm as she performed the introductions.

Gertrude Neville nodded at Della before returning her gaze to Burke. "He looks just like Clive, doesn't he, Thomas?"

"He certainly does." Thomas fixed a warm smile on Della. "I can see why Clive built that house for you. It's a beautiful home for a beautiful woman." Turning back to his wife, he said, "Don't you agree, Gertrude?"

"Indeed."

❧

"Where in Louisiana do you live?" Harold Lindstrom asked as he passed the mashed potatoes to Della. "Several of the parishioners told me that's where you're from."

Joanna watched, amused by the way the gregarious pastor who'd insisted they address him by his first name kept his attention focused on Della. There were eight other people at the table, but though he'd addressed each of them at the beginning of the meal, now the majority of his questions were directed at the woman for whom Finley House had been built. Though it might be because they were of a similar age, Joanna suspected a different cause. The way Harold watched Della reminded her of the way she'd regarded George, the man who'd become Emily's first husband.

George Leland had been the most handsome man Joanna had ever seen, a blond, blue-eyed prince, or so she'd thought at the time. And, though she was now embarrassed to admit it, she'd believed her heart was broken the day he asked Emily to be his bride. It was only after she'd met and married Kurt, another handsome blond, blue-eyed man, that Joanna had realized what she'd felt for George had been nothing more than infatuation.

"We live in Samuels, Alabama, not Louisiana." Burke's explanation brought Joanna back to the present. "And, yes, before you ask, the town was named for Aunt Della's family. Her great-grandfather was one of the first residents."

"Is your family still there?" Once again, Harold's question was for Della.

She shook her head and placed a spoonful of potatoes on her plate. "Only family of the heart—Burke's two sisters. But let's not talk about me. What brought you to Sweetwater Crossing?" The sparkle in Della's eyes left no doubt that this was more than a casual inquiry.

When Emily had mentioned the new minister, she hadn't said much other than that the church elders were impressed with his credentials. If she knew why he'd left his last church, she hadn't told Joanna.

Harold wrinkled his nose, as if the answer were unpleasant, and reached for the gravy boat. "My last congregation decided they wanted a younger minister, one with a wife and children. They said a married man would be better able to counsel the town's increasing number of young families."

Laying down her fork, Della sniffed in indignation. "Jesus wasn't married, nor are Catholic priests."

A rough laugh was Harold's response. "I'm neither Jesus nor a priest. I will admit that I was unhappy with their decision at first. I'd been there more than fifteen years and thought I was part of the community. But when the invitation to come here happened almost immediately, I suspected this was part of God's plan for me." He started to pour gravy onto his potatoes. "Now that I'm here, I know it was the right move."

"Based on today's service, I would agree." Della's expression was earnest, underscoring her words. "You preached a fine sermon. It doesn't often happen, but I felt as if you were addressing my personal needs. Was that because we met yesterday and you knew why I'd come to Sweetwater Crossing?"

Though obviously pleased by her praise, Harold shook his head. "The inspiration for the sermon came before I met you. Friday afternoon, to be exact."

Once again, the conversation seemed limited to Della and Harold, with Joanna feeling like an onlooker. It didn't matter, though, because she found the subject interesting and the couple's fascination with each other intriguing.

Rather than being disappointed, Della seemed encouraged by the timing of Harold's decision to base his sermon on the seventh chapter of Matthew. "That's when Burke and I arrived. Some might say it was a coincidence, but I don't believe that."

For the first time since he'd tipped the gravy boat, Harold looked at his potatoes, seemingly surprised that he'd flooded them with gravy. "Nor do I."

$\backsim\hspace{-0.3em}\circ$

"We need to talk," Joanna told her sisters, gesturing to the kitchen table after they finished washing the dishes. Harold, Della, Burke, and Mrs. Carmichael were seated on the back veranda with Craig and Josh while Noah napped. Though Emily and Louisa had started to follow the others outside, Joanna had stopped them, knowing this was a conversation the three of them needed to have.

"It was an interesting lunch, wasn't it?" Emily said. "I had the hardest time not laughing when Harold poured half the gravy on his potatoes."

Louisa chuckled. "I have to give him credit. He ate it as if it was his normal serving, when we all know it wasn't." Her chuckle deepened. "I could almost see the attraction between him and Della. It was like iron filings near a magnet."

That was part of what Joanna wanted to discuss. "At first

I thought it was one-sided, but it didn't take long for me to realize Della was just as entranced as Harold."

"Smitten." Emily smiled as she twisted her wedding band. "It reminded me of the way Alice and David looked when they first met."

Louisa nodded. "It sounds like the stories about Mama and Father. Do you suppose there's something about being Sweetwater Crossing's pastor that brings love to people who weren't expecting it?" She tipped her head to the side as she asked, "Do you suppose she'll stay?"

Joanna had had the same thought. "Maybe. I know Della and Burke plan to visit for only a couple weeks, but you heard her. She has no blood relations in Alabama. For the right reason, Della might be convinced to stay here."

Her smile once more restored, Louisa nodded. "For the right man."

It was time to broach the subject that might change all their lives. "I've been thinking about something," Joanna told her sisters. "What happened at lunch only confirmed my thoughts. That's why I wanted to talk to you two."

"Why do I have the feeling we won't like what you're going to say?" Emily asked.

"Because you might not." She gave them a second for her warning to register. "I realized this is Della's house. Clive built it for her. Yes, he asked Father to take care of it while he was gone, but the truth is, even though we've lived here and paid the taxes, we aren't the rightful owners. Della is."

Emily and Louisa remained silent for a long moment, absorbing the implications. At last, Emily spoke. "I recall Father saying Clive gave him a document that stated he wanted our family to have Finley House if he didn't return."

"And he didn't return." Louisa seized the only claim the Vaughn family had to the house.

"That's true," Joanna agreed, "but we know it was supposed

to be Della's home. None of us thought we'd ever meet Clive's fiancée, but now that she's here, I believe we owe her the house."

Louisa and Emily exchanged a look before Emily nodded. "You're right, Joanna. We need to offer it to her."

❧

Something had happened while the three sisters had stayed in the kitchen after lunch. Their tension was unmistakable, their smiles more than a little forced as they asked him and Della as well as their husbands to join them in the parlor, leaving Mrs. Carmichael to wait for Noah to waken from his nap.

"Is something wrong?" Burke asked when they were all seated. "You look very serious." Though the question could have been directed to any of the sisters, he looked at Joanna as he spoke.

"We are serious." She turned to Della, her expression more somber than Burke had ever seen it. "My sisters and I have discussed it, and we agree that this is your house, not ours. Clive built it for you."

Della's shock mirrored Burke's. Blood drained from her face, then rushed back as the magnitude of the sisters' offer registered. She was silent for a moment, perhaps trying to marshal her thoughts. Finally, she leaned forward, tears glistening in her eyes.

"Oh, my dears, do you mean you'd give me your home?"

"It's not truly our home. My family have simply been caretakers. Finley House was meant for you." Emily, perhaps in her role as the eldest, provided the explanation, although Burke suspected the idea had been Joanna's.

Della ignored the single tear that made its way down her cheek. "It's very generous of you to even offer me the house, but I cannot accept it. First of all, I have no need for another house. Now that my father's gone, I have the one in Alabama. But more importantly, Clive built the house for us to share."

She looked around the parlor, clearly admiring the furnishings and the crown molding. "When I came here, all I wanted was to see the building. You've given me far more than I expected."

Tears continued to well in her eyes, evidence of the deep emotions that the sisters' generosity had aroused. "You didn't have to, but you welcomed me into your home and treated me like part of your family."

Burke understood Della's feelings, for he too felt as if he'd become an honorary member of the Vaughn family. He and Della had been here a mere two days, but those days had brought him a sense of belonging that surprised him with its intensity.

Della's gaze moved from Emily to Louisa, resting on Joanna. "I could never, ever take your home from you, but thank you for offering it. That's the kindest thing anyone has done for me in many years."

Joanna nodded slowly. "If you change your mind, the offer stands. My sisters and I believe this is your house in ways it was never ours. From everything we've heard, Clive designed each of the rooms with you in mind, imagining you entertaining people here, setting the dining room table for your family, spending hours deciding which book to read next. Finley House was made for you, Della. As Emily said, my family have been caretakers."

Della shook her head. "That's where you're wrong. Your family turned this house into a home. I have no desire to take that from you. Simply spending a few days here has been a dream come true." She paused, her expression becoming wistful. "If only I knew what happened to Clive, my life would be complete."

Chapter

Six

She should not have eaten that ham sandwich. Joanna laid a hand on her stomach as she descended the stairs for breakfast, giving thanks that the queasiness had diminished. Ham had never agreed with her, but she hadn't wanted to cause Emily more work by asking for something different, and so she'd accepted half a sandwich at suppertime and satisfied the rest of her unusually robust appetite with potato salad and a piece of apple pie. She'd paid the price this morning.

"Good morning," she said with a bright smile as she entered the kitchen, determined that no one would know she wasn't feeling her best. "Did you make apple pancakes?" Joanna hoped she'd be able to eat at least one. Her smile brightened at the sight of the pot of tea that Emily had placed next to the coffee. Though Joanna normally savored a cup of coffee with breakfast, tea seemed like a safer choice today.

"I remembered that you like pancakes, and I had a couple apples left over from the pie." Emily flipped one of the cakes, revealing a properly browned side. "Beulah will be sorry she missed them, so please don't mention breakfast to her."

"I won't." The sip of tea accomplished what Joanna had hoped and settled her stomach.

"Who's Beulah?"

Joanna turned to greet Burke, who was looking particularly handsome this morning with his sometimes-unruly hair tamed and his face freshly shaved, but it was Emily who responded. "She's one of Craig's pupils. Beulah spends Monday through Thursday nights with us because she lives too far out of town for her mother to bring her in each day."

Though it was an unusual arrangement, Burke asked no questions. Joanna continued the explanation. "I don't want you to be surprised when you meet her. Beulah is what some would call simple."

"I happen to hate that term, and it's one we never use here," Emily said firmly. "Beulah's one of the sweetest children you'll ever meet, but she doesn't look like everyone else, and she's slower to learn than the rest of the class."

Burke took the chair next to Joanna and accepted the cup of coffee Emily offered. "Beulah sounds like a boy back in Samuels. I'm surprised she attends school. He was kept at home."

"And so was Beulah." A nod confirmed Emily's words. "When Craig and I saw how much she wanted to go to school, we devised this plan. It's worked out well for all of us." And was another example of Emily and Craig's kindness.

Burke placed his cup back on the table and nodded. "I'm looking forward to meeting her."

The sincerity in his voice raised him another notch in Joanna's esteem. If Father were here, he would have approved of Burke. Joanna certainly did.

⁓

"I imagine your office was larger than this," Louisa said as she unlocked the front door to the doctor's office Burke had noticed the day he and Della arrived and ushered him inside.

A hallway bisected the building, with two doors on its right, a door and an open stairway on the left. Louisa led the way into the room on the left. "This is where I spend most of my time. Please let me know if you have any suggestions for improvements," she said as she opened the shutters and let sunlight stream into the room. "Doc Sheridan was a good doctor, but he was also a bit old-fashioned."

Burke gave the room a quick appraisal. "It appears you have everything you need." A desk, an examining table, cabinets filled with medicines, a small bookcase with manuals. His office had those functions divided into two separate rooms, one where he and Felix met patients and kept records, the other for examinations and basic treatment. Though Louisa's single room was smaller than either of the ones Burke had had, it was well-equipped and probably adequate for a town the size of Sweetwater Crossing.

He pulled a book from the shelf, opened it, and glanced at the first page. "A newer version is available."

Louisa shrugged, as if not surprised. "Does it have more information about lung disorders?"

"I believe it does." Burke flipped to the pulmonary section and nodded. "It definitely does. Some of the treatments listed here are no longer used."

"I'll order the new edition. I'm sure you know that my interest is more than academic. I want to do everything I can to help my sister."

Burke nodded. "Joanna told me she had pneumonia. It's a terrible disease and one I think should be eradicated."

Louisa's eyes shone with approval. "I agree. Let me show you the rest of the office, and then we can discuss ways to treat pneumonia." She opened the door to the room on the opposite side of the hallway. "As you can see, this is the infirmary."

Spotlessly clean, it held two beds and a small stove, presumably for heating water and food for the doctor and patients.

"You're right that my office in Samuels was larger. We had five beds in our infirmary, but that's because we served more people. Even after the slaves were freed, many remained to work on the plantations and needed medical care all too often."

When Louisa opened the final door, Burke chuckled. "Now, that's something I didn't expect. I'm not surprised that you have a room for storage, but a piano?"

"Mrs. Sheridan was insistent that their daughter learn to play, but it was too difficult to get the instrument upstairs, so Doc left it here." Louisa flashed a wry smile. "Phoebe's one of my dearest friends, but even I wouldn't call her a talented musician. Her playing was so bad that the only times she could practice were when Doc was on house calls."

"Is there a full apartment upstairs?" When Burke had first seen the two-story building, he'd assumed the doctor used the second floor as his residence.

Louisa nodded. "Josh and I talked about living there, but we have more space at Finley House, and neither of us wants to rent it out." She gestured toward the open staircase. "There wouldn't be enough privacy if we had patients staying in the infirmary, and even though we could put locks on the door, we'd worry about all the medicine. There's no reason to think it would happen again, but someone contaminated the contents of one of my jars a few months ago."

"A wise decision." Burke had not had that problem in Samuels, but no one other than Felix and Edna had entered his office when he wasn't there.

As the front doorbell tinkled, Louisa smiled. "There's our first patient."

Burke shook his head. "Yours, Louisa. I'm here as an observer."

"And, I hope, as an adviser." She raised her voice to greet the woman who'd entered the hallway. "Good morning, Mrs. Oberle. How can I help you today?"

The brown-haired lady whose mustard-colored dress would have made Burke's sisters shudder began coughing. When she'd managed to control the spasms, she looked at Louisa, her dark eyes filled with hope. That was the kind of trust every physician strove to earn.

"I need more of that cough medicine." If Mrs. Oberle noticed Burke, she gave no sign.

"Let me listen to your lungs." When Louisa led the way into the examining room and helped her patient onto the table, Burke followed, remaining in the doorway to avoid alarming Mrs. Oberle. After Louisa carefully adjusted her stethoscope and performed a complete auscultation, she nodded her approval. "Your lungs are clearer than last week. That means they're healing."

The woman did not appear to share Louisa's optimism. "Not as fast as I want."

Though she didn't say it, her tone left little doubt that she believed Louisa should be doing more, and her hopeful expression faded. Rather than let Louisa lose a patient's confidence in her skill, Burke decided to intervene. "Healing takes longer than any of us would want."

Mrs. Oberle turned to stare at him, as if registering his presence for the first time. "Who are you?"

"This is Dr. Burke Finley. He and his aunt are visiting us." Louisa performed the introduction.

"Finley? Like Finley House?"

"Yes." Once again, Louisa answered. "He's Clive Finley's nephew. His aunt was Clive's fiancée."

The woman's brown eyes radiated curiosity. "Well, now, that's interesting. And you say you're a doctor?"

"Yes, ma'am."

Curiosity turned to approval. "I hope you'll stay a while. If you do, maybe I can convince my husband to see you. His gout's been paining him something fierce." She gave Louisa a look filled with chagrin. "I'm sorry, Louisa, but you know how men are. They don't think women should be doctors." Her gaze moved back to Burke. "I'm glad you're here, Dr. Finley."

So was he. Even though it was only temporary, the prospect of helping Louisa with her practice was appealing.

⁂

"I'm so glad you came." Miss Heppel clasped both of Joanna's hands and drew her inside. "You don't know how much I missed you while you were gone. None of my other pupils cared about learning to play. The only reason they took lessons was because their mothers insisted." She shook her head in a self-deprecating move. "But you don't need to hear me complain. Let's sit for a while, and then I hope you'll play for me. I want to hear how much you've improved."

Joanna took the seat her former teacher indicated and looked around the parlor. The grand piano that many would have said was too large for the room still dominated it, leaving space for little more than the settee, low table, and two upholstered chairs. Miss Heppel still had not replaced the wallpaper, though it had faded more than Joanna recalled, and the curtains bore additional rents from sun rot.

By any standard, it was a shabby room, and yet Joanna's heart leapt with pleasure at the sight of the place where she'd spent so many hours, repeating a single measure more times than she could count until she'd satisfied Miss Heppel, basking in her teacher's praise when she'd mastered a particularly difficult piece.

After placing her reticule on the floor next to her, Joanna began to peel off her gloves. When she'd laid them carefully on top of the reticule, she smiled at her hostess. "Do you know that this is the first time I've sat anywhere other than on the piano bench?"

Miss Heppel started to reply, then reached out to grab Joanna's left hand, staring at her ring. "You're married!"

"I was," Joanna explained, "but he died. That's why I'm in mourning."

"Oh." Miss Heppel was speechless for an instant. "I assumed it was for your grandmother."

"She died too."

"Oh, my dear, I'm so sorry. I had no idea you'd suffered a double loss." She took a deep breath. "Shall we speak of happier subjects? Or maybe you could play something for me and give me a chance to compose myself."

As Joanna walked the few steps to the piano, she debated which piece to play. It wouldn't be Chopin. Miss Heppel did not share Joanna's enthusiasm for the composer, even though she taught her pupils to play his music. Deciding on Liszt's Piano Concerto No. 2 in A Major, Joanna opened the fallboard and began to play. When she reached the final chord, Miss Heppel began to applaud.

"I was right. You're remarkably talented. Europe was good for you."

"It was, and yet . . ." Joanna paused, not sure how much to reveal.

"It wasn't your home. Sweetwater Crossing is." Miss Heppel's gray eyes rested on Joanna, as if daring her to disagree.

She couldn't. No matter how many changes she'd found, no matter how uncomfortable she sometimes felt, this was still Joanna's home.

⁓

"I doubt we'll see any more patients today." Louisa seemed resigned to having a small practice. "I'll stay for another hour, but there's no need for you to sit here and be bored. I can read the journal you lent me."

"Are you sure?"

"I am."

Grateful for the reprieve from what had indeed proved to

be a boring afternoon, Burke rose and gathered his hat and bag. Though he hadn't told Louisa everything he'd learned about pneumonia, when he'd seen her eyes begin to lose their focus, he'd realized he'd given her too much information too quickly. She needed time to absorb today's discussion before they proceeded.

"I thought I'd stop in the mercantile," he told her.

"Good choice." Louisa chuckled. "Josh's other businesses—the tearoom and teashop—cater mostly to women. That's why he hired women to manage them and spends most of his time at the mercantile. You'll be more comfortable there."

Burke crossed the street and headed east, passing the mayor's office on his way to the mercantile. Though he was tempted to enter and ask Mayor Alcott whether he remembered anything about his uncle, Burke decided it would be best to give him and the sheriff a few days. If the men approached him or Della of their own volition, they'd be more likely to share whatever they recalled, and maybe by then the mayor would have recovered from whatever had caused his unexpected reaction to Burke.

He paused for a second before opening the door to what Louisa claimed was Josh's preferred place to spend the day. The exterior of the store was unremarkable, but the displays in the large plate glass window were artfully arranged and contained items designed to appeal to men, women, and even children.

"See anything you like?" Josh asked when Burke entered the store.

"Those peppermint sticks look appealing." So did the store itself. The aisles between counters were wider than those in the Samuels mercantile, giving it an air of luxury even though most of the merchandise was ordinary.

"I didn't see prices on anything in the window. Do you let customers bargain?"

"No. I sell the candy at cost or sometimes even a little less, depending on the customer's situation, but everything else has fixed prices. The candy pricing is deliberate. My grandfather told my cousin and me that mothers find it difficult to refuse a begging child and that once they're inside the store, they'll discover other things they either need or want."

It was an interesting concept. "Has the strategy proven as effective here as in New York?"

"Yes." Josh gestured toward the counters filled with merchandise. "I've added items the previous owner never stocked and have been able to get rid of almost all of his mistakes."

Burke looked around, trying to spot what Josh considered a mistake. The only items that appeared out of place were two fishing poles propped against the wall in the back corner.

When he saw the direction of Burke's glance, Josh chuckled. "You found them. I've been told they're excellent fishing poles, but no one in Sweetwater Crossing seems interested. I suppose I could simply throw them out, but I can't bring myself to do that." He raised an eyebrow. "You wouldn't be interested, would you?"

Burke shook his head. "I won't be here long enough to go fishing."

When two ladies entered the store, a petite woman emerged from a room in the back to assist them, leaving Josh with Burke.

"Sweetwater Crossing is a long way from New York. I'm curious about how you ended up here."

Shrugging, Josh said, "It wasn't my plan, that's for certain. I broke a leg when my horse threw me. Fortunately, Louisa found me and brought me here to set it. By the time it healed, I'd realized that Sweetwater Crossing was a special place."

It was unique. That was undeniable. "Don't you miss the excitement of a big city?" The farther he'd traveled from Samuels, the less desire Burke had to return. His next home, he'd decided, would be in a city. Not only would no one there know about the horrible mistake he'd made, but the sheer size would provide the opportunity to explore new ways to use his training.

He might even be able to begin work on developing a vaccine for pneumonia.

Josh clasped his hand on Burke's shoulder. "You're mistaken if you believe Sweetwater Crossing lacks excitement. It may be a small town, but it has its share of secrets and intrigue. Now, let me get you one of those peppermint sticks you wanted."

∽

"Are you certain this is a good idea?" Joanna asked when Burke suggested that walking would benefit her lungs. They'd finished supper, and rather than sit on the front porch as they had the previous evening, he'd recommended a walk. "The doctors in Switzerland told me I needed to avoid overexerting myself. They said that could cause more damage."

His green eyes darkened, making her wonder whether her questioning him had hurt him. That hadn't been her intention. Joanna trusted Burke, but she couldn't forget the sanatorium physicians' advice. They were, after all, reputed to be the best in the world at treating lung diseases.

"What they told you is true for the first weeks after pneumonia, but your lungs have healed enough now that exercise which makes you breathe a bit harder is good for them. It's like stretching a muscle in your arm or leg, a way to strengthen the muscles in your lungs."

Remembering how Louisa had touted the benefits of stretching when Emily had had a cramp in her leg, Joanna nodded. "All right. I defer to your knowledge." She pulled her shawl from the hook near the door and draped it over her shoulders.

"I wish all my patients were as agreeable," he said as they descended the front steps.

Joanna blinked in surprise and turned to glare at him. "I'm not your patient." The words came out with more force than she'd expected, but the thought of Burke viewing her as someone under his professional care was unexpectedly distasteful.

It must be because she'd been an invalid for far too long. She'd chafed at the poking and prodding that had characterized her days in Switzerland and had made a silent vow to never again be admitted to a hospital.

This time there was no sign of pain in Burke's expression. Instead, he appeared almost amused by her caustic reply and bent his arm so she could place her hand on his elbow as they made their way toward the street.

"Few people enjoy being under a doctor's care, particularly for an extended period, but I hope you're my friend and that you'll consider my advice that of a friend who wants only the best for you."

A friend. That was decidedly more appealing than being a patient. If Burke was her friend—and Joanna hoped he was—he would be the first man to carry that distinction. George had been . . . She didn't know how to complete the sentence, and so she wouldn't. George was gone. Herr Ridel had been her teacher; Kurt became her suitor almost as soon as he arrived at the sanatorium. Her suitor, her fiancé, and then her husband. As memories rushed through her, Joanna sighed.

Burke slowed their pace, his demeanor once again solemn. "You look sad. Is the thought of being my friend so unpleasant?"

Once again, she'd caused pain when that hadn't been her intention. "No, not at all. I was remembering my husband."

"Would it help to talk about him? One of the things I learned in medical school was to be a good listener."

Shaking her head, Joanna said, "It's too beautiful a night for sad thoughts." And, despite the happiness of the few weeks they'd spent as man and wife, most of Joanna's memories of Kurt were sad ones.

She took a deep breath, held it, then exhaled slowly as Burke had advised before she spoke again. "I love this time of the day when daylight fades and the first stars come out. When

I was a child, I used to think there was something magical about starlight. It's so different from the light of the sun and the moon. The way stars twinkle makes them seem special. I used to tell myself that I was special when I walked into the starlight."

Her sisters had laughed when she'd told them that, not understanding how much she wanted to feel special, but Burke did not. "I never thought of stars that way. I was fascinated by the moon and how it changes from day to day. I particularly like crescent moons."

"But the moon hides its face every month. The stars don't. They're more dependable." And dependability was something Joanna prized. "Oh, listen to me, arguing the merits of stars versus the moon. You must think I'm a bit crazy." Emily and Louisa certainly had.

"Not at all. Everything you said confirms what I already knew: you're an artist. You deal with more ethereal things than most people, including me. Everything I do is grounded in facts. I don't let my imagination fly very often."

He acted as if that was a failing, but Joanna knew it wasn't. As Burke had said, it was simply a difference between them.

She quickened her pace, then said, "There's nothing more important or more valuable than saving lives." Even though she hadn't enjoyed the treatments she'd received, she knew she wouldn't be alive if she hadn't endured them.

Burke's lips thinned for an instant, telling Joanna whatever he was going to say disturbed him. "Unfortunately, I wasn't able to save all of them."

"But you did your best." Joanna was certain of that. "That's all anyone can do. The rest is in God's hands."

Though his arm relaxed ever so slightly, perhaps because of her reassurance, Burke shook his head. "It shouldn't have happened."

Joanna heard the anguish in his voice and wished she could

do something to lessen it. "Do you want to tell me about it? I may not have gone to medical school, but I've learned to listen."

She'd listened to Grandmother when she'd claimed that a year or so in Europe was what Joanna needed. She'd listened to Marta complain about her illness, brag about her brother, then blame the doctors for his death. She'd listened to Kurt recount the story of his ill-fated first marriage. She'd listened and listened and listened, but none of that seemed as important as listening to Burke now.

He shook his head again. "This is one story you don't want to hear."

Chapter

Seven

"What a charming building." Della smiled at Joanna and her sisters as they approached their destination.

The four of them had walked west on Creek, crossing Center to reach the place where they would spend the next hour savoring food that Joanna hoped her stomach would accept. It had rebelled this morning, even though she'd eaten no ham yesterday. The only explanation she could find was that she was suffering from what the doctors in Switzerland called overactive nerves, the result of her conversation with Burke. She'd hated— yes, hated—the pain she'd heard in his voice, but though she believed that talking about what had happened would help him, a bit like lancing a boil to let the poison drain, she'd been unable to convince him to confide in her.

That failure had led to endless speculation, which had led to a restless night filled with dreams whose details she was unable to recall other than they'd been filled with danger. And that had led to this morning's queasy stomach. Overwrought nerves could cause stomach ailments, or so Louisa had once told her.

Fortunately, by the time noon arrived, Joanna's normal good health was restored.

"It's clever the way it looks like two houses that were connected." Della stopped at the end of the walk to admire the buildings Louisa used to refer to as dollhouses.

For once Emily said nothing, leaving it to Louisa to explain the origin of the tearoom and teashop she and Josh had created. "That's because that's what happened."

Like Della, Joanna was impressed. "It's hard to believe these were Mrs. Locke's and Mrs. French's homes a year ago." A fresh coat of paint on the trim, the extended porch that connected the two small houses, and the simple but elegant sign proclaiming this as Porter's had transformed ordinary dwellings into a thriving business.

Della's eyes widened in surprise. "People lived in such small houses?"

Each of the original buildings was constructed of stone with two windows on one side of the door, a porch on the front, and an outside staircase. Where they differed was that the house on the west had its windows and stairs on the west side while the one on the east had them on the east, giving them a symmetry that Louisa said had appealed to Josh.

"They're called Sunday Houses," Joanna explained, "because farmers who lived a distance away would stay there when they came into town to shop on Saturday and attend services on Sunday. They weren't designed as full-time homes, but two of Mrs. Carmichael's friends moved into their Sunday Houses permanently when they were widowed. They said the three rooms were all they needed—a small kitchen, gathering room, and bedroom."

Though she said nothing, Della's expression showed she was still astonished by the thought of such a small living space. That was understandable since she'd grown up in a plantation home as large as Finley House. Joanna knew she would have trouble moving from Finley House to one of the Sunday Houses. While she didn't need a lot of space, she needed more than they afforded.

"After the widows died," Louisa said, continuing the story as she led the way toward the entrance, "their houses were vacant until Josh saw them. We joke that he fell in love with them before he did with me and that they're the reason he stayed in Sweetwater Crossing."

Della shook her head. "That's absolute nonsense. That husband of yours is clearly smitten with you."

Joanna agreed. There was something truly endearing about the way both of her sisters' husbands doted on them. Kurt hadn't been as demonstrative in public, but she'd never doubted his love. As he'd said the day he'd asked her to marry him, they filled empty spots inside each other, giving them both a new chance at happiness.

Joanna paused at the steps leading to the expanded porch and turned toward Louisa. "I'm impressed with how connecting the two porches makes the teashop and tearoom look like they were meant to be a single building." It was a simple change and yet a brilliant one.

Her younger sister's smile revealed her pleasure at the compliment. "We're happy with the way everything turned out." She directed her next words to Della. "I hope you and Joanna enjoy the tea. It's become a favorite with many of the ladies in town."

"Including me," Emily said.

When Louisa opened the door on the right and ushered the others inside, Joanna grinned. "Someone likes blue." And that someone, she was certain, was Louisa. Joanna had noticed the blue background on the sign outside and wondered if it was a harbinger of the interior. It was. Not only did the wallpaper boast a blue pattern, but each of the six tables had blue-rimmed china arranged on pale blue tablecloths.

"Did you choose the linens and china?" she asked her sister.

"Josh and I did that together."

"But it was your idea."

"Well . . . yes."

Della, who'd been watching the exchange, nodded. "I knew it. The room has a woman's touch."

"Welcome to Porter's, ladies." The dark-haired woman whom Joanna recognized as Louisa's friend Caroline gave them a welcoming smile. "I'm glad to see you're back in town, Joanna, and I'm pleased to meet you, Miss Samuels."

She led the way to what appeared to be the tearoom's premier table, one next to the window. "I hope you'll enjoy your tea."

Joanna almost laughed at the fact that Caroline, who'd been one of the star pupils when Gertrude had taught etiquette, had failed to introduce herself.

"I was going to introduce you as Caroline Brownley, but the ring on your hand tells me you have a new name."

"Yes, I do." Caroline's eyes, a lighter green than Burke's, sparkled with delight. "I'm Caroline Knapp now. My husband is the man responsible for the renovations on these buildings."

"Raymond's a very talented man." Louisa never hesitated to give credit where it was due. "He built the parsonage, and he's going to build a house for Josh and me."

This was the first Joanna had heard that Louisa and Josh were planning to move out of Finley House. Before she could ask for more information, Louisa squeezed her friend's hand. "I'm glad to see you so happy, Caroline. You're the ideal wife for Raymond."

"And he's the ideal man for me. Now, ladies, what kind of tea would you like? We have individual pots, so each of you can choose your favorite." She pulled a card listing the varieties of tea from the pocket in her apron and placed it on the table. "If you have difficulty reading it, let me know. Gertrude insisted we needed calligraphy, and you know how hard she is to resist once she's made up her mind."

All three sisters nodded, remembering the way their former teacher had drilled concepts into their heads.

Within minutes, Caroline had brought a platter of small sandwiches and scones along with the beverages the quartet had chosen. As Joanna had expected, everything was exquisitely prepared and presented, the savory flavors of the sandwiches complementing the sweet jams and honey they spread on the scones.

Della let out a sigh of contentment as she smoothed marmalade onto a piece of scone. "This is marvelous." She looked around the room, appearing to be studying every aspect. "I know Clive never saw this, but it's another appealing part of your town. He was right when he told me Sweetwater Crossing would be the right home for us."

"Why did you and he want to leave Alabama?" That was part of the story Joanna had never heard.

"It was Clive's idea. He'd heard so much about Texas that he was determined to discover whether the stories were true. Once he saw Sweetwater Crossing, he fell in love with it the way Josh did with the Sunday Houses."

Della's smile became wistful. "I would have gone anywhere with Clive, but my father tried his best to keep me in Alabama. That's why he insisted Clive build such a big house. He was sure Clive would fail and that I'd have to stay in Samuels." This time she frowned. "As it turned out, I did have to stay with Father, but now I feel as if I've come home." She wrinkled her nose. "That probably sounds silly since I've been here only a few days, but that's the way I feel."

Joanna tried not to frown at the realization that Della, a newcomer, felt more at home here than she, who'd spent most of her life in Sweetwater Crossing, did at Finley House. Perhaps the feeling that everything had tilted off its axis was nothing more than a residual effect of her illness. Though the doctors had warned her that full recovery could take a long time, she doubted that was the primary reason it seemed as if she, like Mrs. Carmichael, was a boarder in what had been her home.

Oblivious to the direction Joanna's thoughts had taken, Emily placed her cup back on its saucer and leaned toward Della. "I hope you know that you're welcome to stay at Finley House as long as you'd like. I know I speak for the rest of the family when I say we enjoy having you with us."

Joanna agreed. "If my parents were alive, they would say it was fitting that the woman who inspired Finley House lived there."

"You could even stay permanently," Emily continued. Her slightly mischievous smile told Joanna she had donned her matchmaker hat and was thinking of Harold Lindstrom. Though the Sweetwater Creek elders weren't as adamant as the ones at Harold's previous church, Joanna knew they preferred a married man as minister.

"That's right." Louisa climbed onto the matchmaking bandwagon. "Once Josh and I move out, you could have the whole third floor. We have our own sitting room, and Josh has a small office up there."

She had planned to wait until they returned to Finley House to ask Louisa why they were building a separate home, but Joanna wouldn't let this golden opportunity pass.

"Where will your house be?" *And why do you need it?* Though the second question was more important, she did not ask it.

"You know how Father used to say Finley House had enough land for at least three homes?" When Joanna nodded, Louisa continued. "We decided on the west end of the property. We'll be right on the corner of Center Street."

"So you'll have a good view of Porter's." Della smiled as if she considered that an admirable reason for Louisa to leave her childhood home.

"There's also a view of the cemetery," Louisa pointed out. "Neither was the reason we chose that location. The primary attraction was the big live oak. Our plan is to situate the house so the tree's in our front yard. I want to hang a swing from one of the branches, and Josh—practical Josh—likes the idea that the tree will block some of the summer sun and keep the house cooler."

"Plus, they'll have more privacy in their own home." Emily's smile was rueful. "Craig and I do our best, and so does Mrs. Carmichael, but Noah's at the inquisitive age. No matter how many times we tell him not to, he manages to elude even the most watchful eye and climb those stairs to the third floor."

Della's chuckle said she found Noah's antics amusing. "He's a boy. Burke was just as adventurous when he was that age."

Joanna caught her breath as the image of a boy with red hair, green eyes, and a mischievous grin flitted through her brain. Had Burke been as adorable as Noah? Yes, her instincts told her. Even more so.

"Have we convinced you to stay?" Emily steered the conversation back to the point she'd been trying to make.

"I'm not sure about permanently, but the thought of extending my visit is enticing," Della admitted, her voice thickening with unshed tears. "You're all kind to make me feel so welcome. I wish there were something I could do to repay you. I know you don't need anything at Finley House, but I want to contribute to the town."

"There is something you could do."

Joanna suspected Della was as surprised as she was by Emily's quick response. Was whatever she was about to suggest part of her sister's attempt at matchmaking?

"I believe I told you that my friend Alice was the librarian and that the library's been closed since she moved away. Would you consider serving as our librarian for however long you're here? The town would benefit from that, even if it's only temporary."

Della's radiant smile left no doubt of her response. "I can't think of anything I'd enjoy more."

⁓

He still wasn't accustomed to the doorbell. He and Felix hadn't had one on their office, but according to Louisa, her predecessor had believed it an essential part of a medical establishment. When he heard the tinkle, Burke rose and walked toward the hallway, wondering who had come in Louisa's absence.

"I wondered if you'd stay here while my sisters and I take Della to tea at Porter's," she had said the previous afternoon when she explained her plan. "We'd invite you, but the tables are for four."

"And afternoon tea is not something most men enjoy." Burke completed the sentence.

"Also true. I doubt anyone will come, but I'll feel better if you're here."

She'd feel even better now that a potential patient had entered the office. Burke studied the man who was lumbering through the hallway, clearly having difficulty putting weight on his right foot. Taller and larger than most, he walked at a quarter the normal speed of a man his age, the winces that he tried to suppress confirming Burke's initial diagnosis.

"Good afternoon, sir." Burke extended his hand to the dark-haired patient whose eyes, almost the same shade of brown as Joanna's, radiated pain. "I'm Dr. Finley."

"Herb Oberle." The man's grip was firm, a good sign. "The wife tole me you was here. Ken you help me? Doc Sheridan tried, but it din't do no good." Mr. Oberle pointed to his feet. "It's the gout."

Exactly what Burke had assumed from Mr. Oberle's gait, although he needed an examination for confirmation. "Let's take a look at your foot." He ushered him into the office.

When Mr. Oberle removed his boot and sock and extended his foot, Burke nodded. As he'd expected, the man's large toe was swollen.

"It hurts somethin' fierce," Burke's patient said. "Wakes me up purty near every night. I tell you, Doc, it's the worst pain I ever knowed. The wife tells me it ain't true, but I could swear the sheet weighs a ton. Ken you help me?"

"I hope I can. What did Dr. Sheridan prescribe?"

Mr. Oberle shrugged. "Some big pills. I cain't 'member what he called 'em."

"But they didn't help."

"No, sirree. Turned my innards inside out, but din't help the pain."

Keeping his expression neutral, though he suspected Dr. Sheridan had given the man one of the purgatives that had little effect on gout, Burke asked, "What do you eat for supper most nights?"

His patient blinked in surprise. "Same things most folks do— meat, some potatoes, big piece of pie."

"Does the meat include liver and kidneys?"

Mr. Oberle grinned. "Sure does. The wife don't like 'em, but I sure do."

"Do you drink milk with your meal?"

A look of pure horror crossed the man's face. "'Course not. Beer's the only thing I drink. What would folks think if the fella who brews the best beer in the county drank milk?" He narrowed his eyes as he regarded Burke with suspicion. "How come you're askin' what I eat and drink?"

Knowing it was critical to establish his credibility, Burke adopted his most conciliatory tone. "Some doctors believe there's a connection between what we eat and drink and gout.

If they're correct—and there's some evidence that they are—beer and rich meats like liver and kidneys cause gout."

Horror changed to curiosity. "How come Doc Sheridan never said that?"

"He may not have read the same journals that I do." When Felix had joined the practice, he'd continued his subscriptions to Eastern medical journals, admitting that he rarely read them but that he thought Burke might find them useful.

Mr. Oberle was silent for a moment, then shook his head. "I cain't stop drinking beer."

Burke wasn't surprised by the response, particularly from a man whose livelihood was based on the fermented beverage. "The choice is yours. I can't force you to do anything you don't want, but given the intensity of your pain, I would strongly advise you to consider eliminating beer."

After a silence that seemed to last a week, Mr. Oberle's expression turned from hostile to cautious. "You won't tell no one?"

"Of course not."

"All right." The man grimaced as he tugged his sock over his swollen foot. "I'll try it."

After his patient left and Burke had entered the details of the appointment in Louisa's record book, he grinned, remembering how he'd debated which journals to bring with him, finally settling on two from Boston. They were typically less interesting than the ones from Philadelphia, but he'd been drawn to one in particular. It was no coincidence that that one had included the article about diet and gout. That was clearly the hand of God at work.

$\backsim$

"Take a deep breath, hold it for four seconds, then exhale slowly."

Joanna was grateful that Burke had waited until they reached the end of the driveway before he issued the command. If they'd been inside the house or on the front porch and Louisa had overheard him, she would have interrupted, wanting to know why he was advising that. And, much as she loved her sister, Joanna did not want to share her time with Burke. He'd been in Sweetwater Crossing only a few days, but in those few days, he'd become more than a visitor, more than a boarder in Finley House. He'd become a friend and a confidant, and Joanna cherished the time they spent together.

She wouldn't tell him that, of course, for it wasn't seemly. Instead, she responded to his instruction. "Herr Ridel taught me to take deep breaths before I played. He claimed it would calm my nerves."

Joanna saw surprise on Burke's face. "I can't imagine you being nervous. You always seem composed."

That was so far from the truth that she chuckled. "Believe me, I was a bundle of nerves when I had to play before strangers."

"Did deep breaths help?"

"Yes."

He nodded, as if he'd expected her response. "They'll also help your lungs heal."

"Are you going to tell me deep breaths are a form of stretching?"

It was Burke's turn to chuckle. "How'd you guess?"

She took a deep breath, held it as he'd advised, then exhaled slowly. "When I do that, I feel as if they're expanding."

"They are. Three more breaths, and then we can continue walking."

When they began strolling along Creek, Joanna spoke again. "I heard you had your first patient while Louisa was gone."

"Based on the timing, I suspect he waited until he saw your sister leave. His wife was in the office yesterday and warned Louisa that he didn't trust what he called lady doctors." Burke paused for a second. "I'm not sure he trusted me at first, but he finally agreed to do what I suggested . . . at least for a few days."

Joanna knew better than to ask what the man's ailment had been or what Burke had recommended. Instead, she said, "I'm glad you were willing to keep the office open so Louisa could join us for tea. She wouldn't have come otherwise, but it was a special afternoon with the three of us and Della. In only a few days, your aunt's become part of the family."

Burke quickened the pace ever so slightly, an action Joanna suspected was meant to make her breathe more quickly. "I've never seen her so happy." His breathing hadn't changed, but Joanna's was more labored. "I know Della said it was only temporary, but once she starts working in the library, I'll be surprised if she wants to leave."

"My sisters and I hope that's true. Being at the library may help her learn more about Clive. She talked to Mrs. Sanders—she's the manager of the teashop—today, but her only memories of Clive were that all the single girls fancied themselves in love with him."

Burke raised an eyebrow. "What did Della say about that?"

"She laughed and told Mrs. Sanders she couldn't blame them. After all, she fell in love with him too."

"And unlike many, she never fell out of love."

Burke's quiet observation startled Joanna. It was an unexpected direction to take their conversation. "I don't think it's possible to fall out of love, not if it's true love."

She paused for a second, wondering why Burke had raised the specter of love dying. It almost sounded as if he'd had firsthand experience, yet even if he had, that didn't explain why he'd said "many." Surely Della's experience demonstrated the durability of love. Even now, decades later, she still loved Clive.

Sensing that Burke was waiting for her to continue, Joanna said, "Kurt and I were married only a short time, but he'll always have a special place in my heart." Because, unlike what she'd once believed to be her first love, her feelings for Kurt had been more than a passing fancy. Perhaps what Burke had experienced or witnessed had been infatuation masquerading as love.

"Do you think you'll marry again?"

The question was as unexpected as Burke's comment about falling out of love. Joanna was silent for a moment, unsure of her response. Widows often remarried, particularly if they were young. Yet others did not, claiming they'd lost the one man they could love. Would she be like Emily, blissfully happy in her second marriage, or Mrs. Carmichael, content as a widow?

"I don't know."

Chapter
Eight

"I feel like I'm royalty the way everyone is being so kind to me." Della arranged her skirts as she settled into the carriage for their ride to what Joanna still called the Albright ranch, even though its owners were now named Neville.

"First that wonderful tea yesterday, and now an invitation to lunch. You're all spoiling me."

Though the smile that lit Della's face confirmed her pleasure, Joanna felt compelled to offer a caveat. "I should probably warn you that I have no idea how good the food will be. Gertrude was an excellent schoolmarm, but I'm not certain she ever learned to cook. I recall her mother telling mine that she despaired of teaching Gertrude to make even the simplest of meals." That was one reason Joanna had suggested she and Della visit in the afternoon rather than come midmorning and stay for lunch. Gertrude, however, had overridden Joanna's protests that it was too much work for her and had insisted that Della and Joanna join her for a meal.

"According to Mrs. Albright," Joanna continued as they made their way out of Sweetwater Crossing, "Gertrude spent the time she should have been in the kitchen honing her culinary skills either reading or trying to convince her mother to plant flowers."

"She sounds like a woman after my heart." Della nodded her approval of their hostess's priorities. "Few things can compare to a good book or a beautiful flower. You know how much I love books. Clive was almost as passionate about flowers."

But when they reached the ranch, though the grounds were well-maintained, there were no flowers in sight, making Joanna suspect that while Gertrude had been successful in bending pupils to her demands, she had failed to persuade her mother that flowers were essential. What she didn't understand was why Gertrude hadn't planted flowers now that this was her home and not her mother's.

While Joanna was still looping the reins over the hitching post, Gertrude emerged from the house. Standing on the front porch, she beckoned them inside, her eyes sparkling with more warmth than she used to display in the classroom, her light blue dress more flattering than any she'd worn to school. Unlike the woman who'd seemed almost fragile on Sunday, this Gertrude appeared happy and confident.

"I'm so glad you could come today." Though she nodded at Joanna, her attention was focused on Della, her eyes cataloging every detail from the hat perched on top of Della's head to her high-buttoned shoes. "I've been looking forward to getting to know you better. Clive told me you love books as much as I do."

Gertrude hooked her arm around Della's and led the way into the house. "Tell me, what do you think of the Brontë sisters? Do you prefer *Wuthering Heights* to *Jane Eyre*?" Before Della could respond, she continued. "Clive laughed when I compared him to Mr. Rochester and informed me in no uncertain terms that he did not have a mad wife locked away in the attic."

If Della found this an unusual welcome, she gave no sign but simply followed their hostess into the parlor. When she and Joanna had divested themselves of their hats and gloves and were seated on the horsehair settee across from Gertrude, Della said, "I'm surprised Clive recognized the reference to *Jane Eyre*. He and I shared many interests, but books were not one of them."

That was a story Joanna hadn't heard, an unexpected insight into the man who'd built her home.

"I hadn't realized that, but it makes the library at Finley House all the more remarkable. My father called it a treasure not only because of the number of books but also the variety. He said almost every subject he could imagine was included."

Gertrude looked as if she wanted to disagree with Joanna. Pursing her lips, she said, "The library wasn't the only thing that was remarkable. So was Clive." A faint smile softened her face, and for a second Gertrude appeared younger than the thirty-eight Joanna knew her to be.

"Did you know Clive well?" Della's eyes glowed with the possibility of learning more about her fiancé's life in Sweetwater Crossing. Though Joanna hoped she would, the smile and the way Gertrude's demeanor had changed so dramatically made her wonder whether she had been one of the young women who'd been attracted to Clive. According to both Mrs. Carmichael and Mrs. Sanders, most of the single girls had been fascinated by or perhaps infatuated with Della's intended.

Gertrude shook her head, her expression once more solemn. "He didn't pay much attention to me or to anyone who wasn't involved in building his house. I got to see him more often than many people, because my parents and I had supper with him each Saturday, but all I remember him talking about was the house he was building." She paused, then turned to Joanna. "Did you know that Clive lived in what we called our Sunday House, even though it's almost as large as Finley House?"

"No, I didn't." Neither Father nor Mama had mentioned either Clive's staying across the street or that the Albrights called their large in-town home a Sunday House, but by the time Joanna and her sisters had been old enough to care about the man who'd built their house, years had passed, and that might have seemed unimportant.

"It would have been an ideal location," Joanna added. The Albrights' house had been the first built on Creek and, until Finley House was constructed, had been the largest. While it wasn't directly across from Finley House, it was close enough that Clive would have had only a short walk to oversee the construction.

As she shifted slightly in her chair, Gertrude nodded. "That's why Papa offered it to him. The house was empty except for Saturday night, because we were all out here."

Though the location of Clive's temporary residence seemed insignificant to Joanna, Della appeared intrigued by this newly revealed detail of her intended's life. The smile she gave Gertrude was filled with gratitude for the tidbit of information. "Your Sunday House is much larger than the others."

Gertrude chuckled, as if she'd been privy to Della's reaction to the other Sunday Houses. "That's because my parents always planned to live there permanently when my father retired from ranching. Papa liked the idea of being closer to Joanna's father and Doc Sheridan and seeing them more than once a week."

But both men were dead, as was Clive.

"So now the ranch is yours." Joanna wondered how Gertrude was adjusting to the changes in her life. "I still have trouble realizing that you're no longer teaching."

"You and most of Sweetwater Crossing." Gertrude's chuckle turned into a full-fledged laugh. "They all thought I was a confirmed spinster like Minerva Heppel."

"But Thomas changed your mind." Joanna wished she'd been here to see the courtship. Louisa had said it was brief and had surprised many, although the more cynical had declared it a wise move on Thomas's part to merge his ranch with the larger Albright one.

"He did, but that's enough about me. Let's eat lunch, and then I want to show you my favorite part of the ranch." Gertrude rose and led the way into the dining room.

The meal was surprisingly good. When Della complimented Gertrude on the chicken fricassee, she laughed and said she'd discovered that cooking was like everything else. If you found the right book of instructions, you could learn anything. Though the biscuits had been tender, the tough crust on the pecan pie was evidence that Gertrude's culinary education was still incomplete.

"We'll leave the dishes here," she said when the meal was over. "I'm afraid we may have rain this afternoon, but I don't want you to miss my special spot. Come, ladies, let's enjoy the sunshine while it lasts."

Once they were outside, Gertrude stood between Joanna and Della, linking arms with both of them. "Tell me, Della, which of Jane Austen's books do you consider her best?"

While the two women discussed the merits of *Persuasion* versus *Pride and Prejudice*, Joanna studied the area they were crossing, trying to imagine what Gertrude considered special about it. The meadow ringed by live oaks and mesquite was pretty, but so were dozens of other meadows. She saw nothing exceptional here.

"We're almost there," Gertrude said as they climbed a small rise. "What do you think?"

There, close to a spreading live oak but far enough away that the branches did not shade it, was a flower bed. It was small—perhaps three feet wide and seven feet long—but every inch was covered with plants, most of which were still blooming. If this were a desert, Joanna would have called it an oasis. Here, in the middle of a green meadow, the tiny garden provided a refreshing splash of color.

"Oh, Gertrude, it's beautiful." Della's voice was filled with awe at the variety of flowers.

Joanna didn't know which flowers grew in Alabama, but Della's reaction made her surmise that many of these were new to her.

"I can see why this is your favorite place," Della continued, "but why is it so far from the house? I would have thought you'd want to be able to see it from inside."

There was one reason Joanna could imagine. "Perhaps it was designed as a refuge. As dearly as I love my sisters, there were times when I craved solitude. I turned one of the unused rooms on the third floor into my sanctuary."

When Gertrude laughed again, Joanna realized this was a far different Gertrude from the woman who'd been her schoolmarm. That Gertrude would smile with approval when a pupil gave the correct answer, but Joanna had no memories of laughter or even chuckles.

"The reason is far more prosaic," her former teacher told them. "My mother believes flowers are a waste of fertile soil, because you can't eat them or feed them to cattle. I disagreed, so I dug and planted the bed myself. I only told her and Papa about it when the first flowers were in bloom. And now, even though I could plant flowers everywhere, I've decided to keep this as the only place they grow. That makes it special."

This was another side to Gertrude that Joanna would never have guessed. "When did you plant the bed?"

"Years ago. Before the war."

Della knelt and fingered the red petals of a flower Joanna could not identify. "Regardless of the reason you created it, this is a beautiful spot. I haven't seen your whole ranch, but it's definitely my favorite place too." Rising, Della smiled at their hostess. "I can't explain why I feel this way, but there's something extra special about this flower bed. I wish Clive could have seen it. He loved flowers almost as much as I love books."

Gertrude appeared surprised. "Did he? In that case, let's call this Clive's flower bed."

❧

"Your former teacher intrigues me," Della said when they'd taken their leave and headed back to town.

"In what way? I never thought of her as intriguing." Although today had revealed new and unexpected facets of Gertrude's personality.

"I suspect she's not as happy as she pretends." When Joanna raised a brow, Della shrugged. "I could be wrong, of course. Since my father died, I've spent a lot of time thinking about happiness and trying to decide whether those closest to me are happy. You, for example, are an inherently happy person, even though the last year has been so difficult."

The assessment surprised Joanna. "I never thought of myself that way, so I'm not certain you're correct."

"It's only my impression." Della was silent for a moment before she said, "I wish I could say that Burke is happy. If anyone deserves happiness, he does, but he's always been too serious. I suspect that's because he didn't have a father or any adult males close to him while he was growing up."

"I didn't realize that. He doesn't talk much about his past."

"That's Burke. It's no secret that his father left for the war when Burke was four. Like so many other men, he never returned. Burke's mother had her hands full raising him and his two older sisters." Della stared into the distance, perhaps trying to compose her thoughts. "I did what I could, but like his mother, I had no experience with young boys. What she and I learned is that they're very different from girls."

It was an interesting observation. "That's another thing I never thought about. As you know, my situation was very different. There were only girls in my family, and we were fortunate that our father survived the war. He was badly wounded at Gettysburg and lived with constant pain, but we had both parents with us until last year."

106

"Sadly, true happiness seems to elude Burke. First no father, then Edna—" Della stopped abruptly, her face flushing as if she'd said too much.

Joanna knew better than to pry, but she couldn't stop herself. "Who's Edna?"

"The woman Burke planned to marry."

Joanna seemed different tonight, Burke reflected as he settled her shawl over her shoulders. She had the same glow his sisters had when they were pregnant, making him wonder if she too was expecting a child, but that was a subject no gentleman, not even a doctor, would raise. It was up to the woman to introduce it, and many waited until their increasing girth made their condition obvious.

He wished he understood what had changed, why she seemed more pensive, why he'd caught her giving him speculative looks. According to Della, they'd had an enjoyable lunch with Gertrude Neville, so Burke doubted that was the cause. He hoped Joanna would explain her unusual mood while they were walking, but until they reached the bridge which had become their nightly destination, they chatted about inconsequential things. Then as they both leaned on the railing and peered at the slowly moving water, she surprised him.

"Do you believe dreams come true?"

Startled by the unexpected question, Burke replied with one of his own. "Do you mean dreams like the ones in the Bible that God used to send messages?"

Joanna shook her head. "Maybe dreams wasn't the right word. That's how I've always thought of them, but aspirations might be better."

It was a question worth pondering. "I suppose they do for some people. You sound as if you don't believe that."

Gripping the railing, she said, "I used to. My head used to

be filled with dreams, but one by one, they either died or were destroyed. I thought I was going to be the first of us girls to marry, but the man I fancied didn't want me." She turned and fixed her gaze on him, her expression earnest. "Look at what happened to my dream of being a concert pianist." The cough that punctuated her statement underscored the problem. "Now I'm almost afraid to entertain new ones."

Was this the cause of her pensive mood? Rather than ask and possibly embarrass her, Burke chose a different tack. "Do you believe happiness is tied to having dreams come true?"

She dropped her gaze and stared at the creek for a few seconds before responding. "It always seemed that way to me, but Della has a different perspective. She told me some people are intrinsically happy, and she thinks I'm one of them."

That was a partial explanation for Joanna's mood. When Della was in one of her introspective moods, she often posed questions or made statements that caused others to reconsider what might previously have seemed like tenets of their beliefs.

"Do you disagree with her?" Burke wasn't certain he'd classify Joanna as intrinsically happy, but he hoped Della was correct. This woman who'd suffered so many losses in such a short time deserved to be happy.

"I'm not sure. As I told her, it's not something I've given a lot of thought. Growing up, I remember feeling desperately unhappy when I realized that Mama wasn't my real mother. She never treated me any differently than she did Emily and Louisa, but when they were annoyed with me over something, they'd remind me that she wasn't my mother. I hated that."

As Burke recalled the conversation he'd had with Mrs. Carmichael the day he'd arrived in Sweetwater Crossing, he realized that she'd been right in believing that life hadn't always been easy for Joanna as the middle child. "You three seem to be close now."

"We are. Those were childish spats, and I've long since recovered from them. What about you?"

"Are you asking if I'm a fundamentally happy person?" Burke wasn't. He was neither an optimist nor a pessimist. He was a realist.

"Maybe, but I'm more curious about your dreams. If one of them was to become a physician, it's come true."

"That was my first dream," he admitted. "When I saw soldiers who survived the war returning home with missing limbs, some blind, most in pain, I wanted to help them. I was too young to do anything other than give them a cup of water or a piece of bread, but I vowed that when I grew up, I'd learn how to ease suffering."

"And you did. Now that that dream came true, have you replaced it with another?"

This was one of the most unusual conversations Burke had had. Edna would never have asked him about his dreams, and even though Della would sometimes probe his thoughts, aspirations was one subject she had never addressed. Though he was reluctant to reveal another aspect of himself, he didn't want to disappoint Joanna by refusing to answer.

"Yes," he said slowly, "but this one is unlikely to come true."

"I know I shouldn't pry, but I hope you'll trust me enough to tell me what it is."

When she phrased it that way, how could he refuse?

Burke took a deep breath, exhaling slowly before he spoke. "I can never atone for what I did, but I need to find a new direction for my life. Meeting you has made me think I've found it. Instead of simply treating patients the way your doctors in Switzerland did, I want to find a way to prevent pneumonia."

❦

Joanna stared at her reflection in the mirror, wondering if she'd made a mistake in donning the green poplin. While it was the darkest shade of green the modiste had had, it was not black. Some might be scandalized that she hadn't observed the full mourning period for Kurt and her grandmother, but when she'd spotted the dress in the back of the armoire where she'd hung it the day she arrived, she'd felt compelled to put it on, even though she did not normally change clothes before supper.

What she wore would make no difference to Burke. She knew that, just as she knew that no matter how fervently she wished she could do something to assuage the pain that had been evident when he'd spoken of dreams that would never come true, she could not. If there was one lesson Joanna had learned in Europe, it was that no one could assume another's pain. Recovery was something each person had to do individually.

Once again, Burke had alluded to a tragic episode in his past, one related to a patient's death. Once again, he'd given no details, though it was evident he blamed himself. Once again, Joanna had wished she could reassure him, but she couldn't, not when he made it so clear that he did not want to discuss what had happened.

Instead, she'd asked him more about how he hoped to prevent pneumonia, and they'd talked about how different her life might have been if there'd been a vaccine for it as there was for smallpox.

Not once had Burke mentioned Edna, the woman who'd broken their engagement one day before her mother died, then shocked the town by marrying Burke's partner a week later. Though Della had recounted only the basic details, Burke's silence on the subject confirmed Joanna's belief that Edna's actions were part of the sadness he could not hide and were likely the reason for his comment about falling out of love.

Joanna couldn't lessen Burke's guilt over his patient's death or his regret over his broken engagement, but she hoped that searching for information about Clive would give him a sense of purpose and lessen the pain. They'd start after supper tonight.

"What a lovely dress," Louisa said when Joanna entered the kitchen. Though Emily consistently refused their help, both sisters were just as consistent in offering and tried to arrive in the kitchen well before a meal was ready to serve in case Emily would allow them to assist her.

Louisa studied the gown with its deceptively simple lines. "Did you buy it in Paris?"

"Grandmother and I never got there. This came from Munich, but the designer claimed he'd studied in Paris." When she'd buttoned the bodice, Joanna had noticed that it fit more snugly than it had before and realized that she was regaining the weight she'd lost while ill.

"It's good to see you out of mourning." Emily looked up from the sauce she was stirring and gave the dress an appreciative smile. "Mama and Father would have approved. I'm sure you remember that they used to say what mattered was what's in our hearts, not the outward trappings."

They had, and that was part of what had helped Joanna make the decision. "Grandmother Kenner would have been scandalized, but I just couldn't bear another day in black. Those dismal clothes were a constant reminder of the past and what I lost. I want to focus on the future." And maybe, if she was fortunate, that future would be a happy one.

"That's a wise approach." Though Emily could sometimes be critical, she was also quick to voice her approval. "Now, would you taste this sauce and let me know whether it's sweet enough?" She dipped a spoon into the sauce and offered it to Joanna.

"Did you make bread pudding?" Joanna asked when she'd tasted the butterscotch sauce and pronounced it exceptionally good.

Emily nodded. "I thought it might be a way to celebrate Della's first day at the library. She mentioned she's never eaten it before."

Louisa pulled a clean spoon from the drawer and dipped it into the sauce. "She's in for a treat."

An hour later, Della was the first to speak after Craig offered the blessing for supper. "This has been the most exciting week I can recall. So many wonderful things have happened: tea at Porter's, lunch with Gertrude, and being at the library."

Mrs. Carmichael nodded as if she understood the reason Della smiled when she mentioned the library. "Did you have many patrons?"

Craig didn't wait for Della's response. "Judging from the line I saw outside the door during recess, I'd say she did."

Della's smile grew. "Oh yes. So many people came. Most said hello, borrowed a book, and left right away, but a few stayed to talk."

The blush that stole onto the older woman's face made Joanna suspect she knew the identity of at least one of those who lingered, but she wanted confirmation. "Who stayed the longest?"

"Harold."

Nine

"Will I like what's coming next?" Burke asked as he closed the front door behind him and Joanna. As they'd gone into the dining room for supper, she'd said there was something they should do before they took their evening walk but wouldn't elaborate.

"There's no way of knowing." A shrug accompanied her words. "I didn't mean to sound so mysterious, but I was concerned that Della might overhear me and didn't want to do anything to spoil her day."

"She seemed excited about working at the library, didn't she?" Excited was almost an understatement. Della had been as giddy as a schoolgirl when she'd recounted how she'd spent the day.

"I think she was even more excited about Harold's visit."

Burke nodded. "I noticed that too." Della reminded him of his sister Antonia when Ned, the man she'd ultimately married, first moved to Samuels. There'd been the same almost secretive smiles, the same blushes. Antonia and Ned had a happy ending, but creating one for Della and Harold would be more difficult unless Della decided to remain in Sweetwater Crossing.

It had been less than a week since they'd arrived, surely not long enough to make such an important decision, but with her position as the town's librarian and the open-ended invitation to live at Finley House, it was possible Della had already considered that. And if she did decide not to return to Samuels, it would be easier for Burke to embark on the next phase of his life: moving to a big city.

Della's decision was at least a week away. What was important now was whatever Joanna had in mind for the evening.

"Where are we going?" They'd descended the steps and were making their way along the drive.

Joanna nodded toward the house diagonally across the street. "Emily told me the Albrights returned today. We agreed not to say anything to Della until you and I talked to them."

Burke tried to understand the sisters' logic. Everyone knew how eager Della was to meet the remaining member of what had been a foursome. "Was it because Mr. Albright was one of Clive's friends and you thought he might have distressing information about him?"

"Not necessarily. When we visited Gertrude, she mentioned that Clive lived in the Albrights' house while Finley House was being built."

"So besides Mr. Albright being one of the four men who met each Saturday evening, Mrs. Albright would also have had more than a passing acquaintance with my uncle. It seems probable that they know more about him than anyone in Sweetwater Crossing." Which was why Della should have accompanied them tonight.

"I've thought that from the beginning." Joanna stopped when they reached the pillars that marked the entrance to Finley House. "It's important that Della talk to them, but I think they should meet you first—"

Suddenly Joanna's decision to delay Della's meeting with the Albrights made sense. "Because you want them to see how much I resemble my uncle." Burke completed the sentence.

"Exactly. I wanted them to get past the surprise and give them some time to search their memories for details about Clive before Della visits them."

That might make the initial meeting easier for everyone. "You're very thoughtful."

Joanna appeared uneasy with the praise. "My parents taught us to try to imagine how the other person would feel before we spoke or did something."

Had Edna ever thought about how Burke would feel when she announced her plans to marry Felix? He shook himself mentally. It was time to stop thinking about Edna. She was part of his past, not his present or future.

"They gave you a valuable lesson."

When they reached the Albrights' home, Joanna knocked on the door. A few seconds later, it was opened by an older version of Gertrude Neville. Though Mrs. Albright's hair was gray, her eyes were the same shade of blue as her daughter's, and other than the slight sagging around her jaw, her facial features were almost identical to Gertrude's.

"Joanna!" The woman's smile was warm and welcoming. "What a nice surprise! I hadn't heard you'd come home." As her gaze moved beyond Joanna and rested on Burke, blood drained from her face, then rushed back. "Clive! Clive Finley!"

Burke wondered if she always spoke in exclamations or if it was only tonight. In either case, he understood why Joanna had wanted them to pave the way for the Albrights' introduction to Della.

A second later, Mrs. Albright turned. "Wilbur, come here this instant! You won't believe your eyes!"

Heavy footsteps announced her husband's approach. Wilbur Albright was a few inches taller and perhaps five years older than his wife with a posture that proclaimed that he was a man used to commanding respect and carefully tailored clothing and gold cuff links leaving no doubt of his wealth.

"Who are you?" he demanded. "You can't be Clive. You're too young."

Mrs. Albright laid her hand on her husband's arm as she said, "But he looks just like Clive."

"If you'll invite us inside, we'll explain everything." Joanna was the voice of reason in the unfolding drama.

"Yes, yes, of course." Mrs. Albright appeared abashed. "What am I doing, forgetting my manners?" She ushered them into the parlor. While their home was smaller than Finley House and lacked the impressive double staircase, this room's crown molding and the marble mantel underscored the Albrights' position as the town's richest family.

When they were seated on chairs that appeared to have been chosen for style rather than comfort, Joanna spoke again. "Mr. and Mrs. Albright, I'd like you to meet Burke Finley. The reason he looks so much like Clive is that Clive was his uncle."

Mr. Albright nodded slowly. "I would have said his son, but that's not possible. You're a bit too old for that. I know Clive had no children when he lived here, although he talked about how he and his fiancée—I can't recall her name—hoped to fill all the bedrooms in their house with children."

Della, being gently reared and conscious of propriety, had never discussed the children she and Burke's uncle had pictured running through Finley House, perhaps sliding down the banisters of the twin staircase.

"We hoped you could tell us what else you remember about him," Joanna explained. "You see, Burke didn't come to Sweetwater Crossing alone. He brought Della Samuels."

"That's the name you couldn't recall, Wilbur. Della Samuels was the woman Clive planned to marry." A faint smile crossed

Mrs. Albright's face, perhaps because she'd remembered something her husband hadn't.

"She wanted to see the house he built and learn what happened to him," Burke explained.

Shaking his head, Mr. Albright looked from Burke to Joanna and back to him. "I can tell you what he did when he was here, but to this day, I can't explain why he left without a farewell. That's not something the man I believed I knew would have done, but it proved that I didn't know him as well as I thought. Even if he'd been summoned back to Alabama, he should have said goodbye to Doc and Joseph and me." Though it had been more than twenty years, it was obvious that that memory still rankled.

"Your father tried to discover when and where Clive was killed," Mrs. Albright told Joanna. "There were so many battles in that horrible war!" Another exclamation. "He wanted to contact Miss Samuels, but he couldn't recall the town where they lived."

"It was Samuels, named for Della's family, but Clive never returned. Della received a letter saying he died here of dysentery."

Mr. Albright shook his head at Burke's explanation. "That story's as false as old Mrs. Douglas's teeth. Clive wasn't sick a single day."

Joanna's quick intake of breath made Burke wonder whether she was recalling her own illnesses. "Maybe so," she said, "but someone pretending to be my father sent a letter to Della."

The Albrights exchanged confused looks before Mr. Albright spoke. "I don't understand. Who would have done that?"

"That's what we're trying to learn. Joanna and I hoped you could help us."

"We'll try. I'd like to meet Clive's sweetheart." This time Mrs. Albright spoke softly.

"I know she'd like to meet you."

Though Mr. Albright did not disagree with his wife, he had

a different concern. "Make sure she brings the letter. I want to see it."

⁓

"I don't think they'll be able to help her." Joanna hated how her voice quavered. She'd kept it steady while they were with the Albrights, but now that she and Burke were outside, she could not hide her distress. "I don't know why I'm so upset. I knew it was unlikely they'd know anything more than Mrs. Carmichael and the others did."

Burke bent his arm so she could place her hand on it, then laid his hand on top of hers as he said, "It's natural to hold on to hope. It's also possible that the Albrights will recognize the handwriting on the letter."

"Possible but not likely. The only person in town besides its author who would have seen the letter was the postmaster, and he's no longer alive."

"As much as I wish it were otherwise, I have to agree with you that it's unlikely the Albrights will be able to identify the person who wrote the letter. Like you, I want to hold on to hope, but it's not always easy."

Though the words were matter of fact, they brought unexpected tears to Joanna's eyes. As she blinked rapidly to keep them from falling, she struggled to understand why she'd become so emotional. That wasn't normal for her, but then again, few things had been normal since she'd returned to Sweetwater Crossing.

"Where are the happy endings?" she demanded, surprising herself with the fervor in her voice. "Every time I believe I've found one, it disappears. Look what happened to my husband."

"Do you want to tell me about him?" Joanna hadn't told her sisters everything about Kurt, but though Mama might have warned her about the dangers of confiding too much in someone she'd just met, it felt right to share the story with Burke.

Perhaps the difference was that Emily and Louisa were both happily married, while Burke, who was clearly no stranger to sorrow, was more likely to understand how deeply what Kurt had endured had affected Joanna.

She nodded slowly. "Kurt didn't believe happy endings were handed to us; he claimed we had to create them."

When Burke said nothing, Joanna continued. "When he and I met, we'd both suffered losses. You already know mine: the doctors' assessment that I'd never be strong enough to tour. Kurt's was worse: his wife had died less than a month earlier, and he blamed himself."

The instant the words were spoken, Joanna regretted them, fearing they would remind Burke of the death for which he blamed himself. The circumstances were different, and yet self-inflicted guilt was a heavy burden to bear, regardless of the cause.

Burke's hand tightened on hers, making Joanna fear she had indeed resurrected unpleasant memories, but his next words reassured her. "If you intended to shock me, you did. Why did Kurt feel responsible?"

Doing her best to keep her voice calm, Joanna began the explanation. "He said Irmgard was moody. Some days she'd be the happiest person he knew—the word he used to describe her was ebullient—other days she'd sink into depression and refuse to leave her bed. He never knew which Irmgard would be waiting for him when he came home." Joanna had tried but failed to imagine how difficult that must have been for him.

"I wonder if she suffered from *la folie circulaire*."

"What's that? I know enough French to know that it means circular insanity, but is it a real disease like pneumonia?"

Burke nodded. "According to what I've read, a Frenchman named Jean-Pierre Falret gave it that name thirty or so years ago, but physicians have seen the symptoms for centuries." This time Burke shook his head. "I'm sorry that I interrupted you. Blame it on my medical curiosity, which sometimes gets the best of me. Please continue with the story."

Joanna took a deep breath, then exhaled, grateful that he had slowed their pace to lessen her exertion. They might not walk all the way to the bridge tonight, but that was unimportant. What mattered was finishing this conversation.

"Kurt and Irmgard had an argument one night, and the next morning he woke to discover she was gone. He searched everywhere, but she'd left no trace. It was weeks later when he learned that she had fled to a cousin's home. By the time Kurt arrived, it was too late. Somehow, Irmgard had been trapped inside the barn when it burned. All that was left was her badly charred body." Joanna shuddered, remembering Kurt's face when he'd recounted that part of the story. "He was convinced that if he hadn't allowed their argument to escalate, Irmgard would still be alive."

Loosening his grip on her hand, Burke began to stroke it, perhaps sensing how much power the sad story still had over her. "That's not simply shocking. It's tragic."

"It was. He told me the only thing he wanted to do was blot the horrible scene from his memory. When he couldn't do that, he decided distance might help and came to the sanatorium to visit his sister. I was with Marta when he arrived."

Joanna closed her eyes for a second, remembering how distraught Kurt had appeared but how a few minutes with Marta had lessened the strain lines around his eyes. Within an hour, the three of them were laughing at Marta's exaggerated stories of one nurse's eccentricities.

"Later Kurt claimed God had brought us together and that I was his chance to rebuild his life and create a happier one."

Burke slowed their pace further. "But then Kurt died, leaving you alone, so whatever happiness you had was brief."

Joanna heard the tension in Burke's voice and wondered whether he was thinking of Edna and the wedding that had not taken place. "That's true, but our time together was long enough for both of us to realize that we shouldn't expect someone else to heal us. We supported each other and we found happiness together, but the actual healing was something we had to do individually." She paused and looked at Burke. "Does that make sense?"

"It does. More than that, it's a lesson I need to learn." He paused so long that Joanna wondered if he wanted to change the subject. Then he said, "I didn't lose a spouse the way you and Kurt did, but I did lose someone I loved and who I thought loved me. The girl I thought I was going to marry fell in love with my best friend."

"Edna?"

"Did Della tell you about her?" Burke sounded surprised.

"Don't be angry with her. I don't think she meant to say anything, but once Edna's name slipped out, she told me a little bit."

"I can't be angry with Della for very long. Edna and I were sweethearts from the time we were old enough to know what that meant. It didn't matter what the occasion was. We were a couple." Burke sighed as if the memory was bittersweet. "Folks expected us to marry before I went East for medical college, but I knew I wouldn't have much time to spend with her. That didn't seem like the right way to start a marriage."

"You were probably right." Joanna had heard that doctors' training was intense and left them with little time to sleep, much less have a normal life.

"When I finished school and returned to Alabama, Edna's father was ill. We both agreed that wasn't a good time for us to marry. Then when he died, her mother became ill and Edna said it wasn't a good time to talk about a wedding."

Though Joanna wouldn't voice her thoughts, she was beginning to suspect that Edna wasn't as eager for marriage as Burke had been.

"Soon after, the man who'd become my closest friend at medical school wrote to see if I'd be interested in having him as a partner. Felix was tired of living in New England and wanted to see whether Alabama was as beautiful as I'd claimed. I knew that if he came, I'd be able to spend more time with my bride, so I agreed."

"And he and Edna fell in love."

"As I said at the beginning, it's a common story, but it still came as a shock to me. I should have realized what was happening, because Edna was a different person when Felix was around—happy, almost carefree, even though her mother's condition continued to worsen—but I was shocked when she told me she loved him and even more shocked when she married Felix a week after her mother's death."

Joanna sensed there was more to the story than Burke had said, but she wouldn't pressure him to reveal more than he was comfortable doing.

"I'm sorry she hurt you, but you deserve a woman who loves you with her whole heart."

"Do I?"

Chapter

Ten

Joanna smiled as she laid her hand on her stomach. There was no change on the outside. It was too soon for that, but she could no longer ignore the nausea that plagued her every morning, leaving her feeling both weak and hopeful. If what she thought was true, one of her dreams would come true.

She descended the stairs carefully, not wanting to stumble if her legs refused to support her, then entered the kitchen. As she'd hoped, both of her sisters were there, Emily stirring what appeared to be pancake batter while Louisa sipped a cup of coffee.

"Is something wrong? You look terribly pale." Louisa gave her a professional appraisal.

Sinking onto a chair, Joanna shook her head. "I think something might be very right. I think I may be pregnant. How do I know for sure?"

Louisa took the chair next to her, reached for her hand, checked her pulse, then began asking questions, including whether Joanna had found herself on the verge of tears more often than normal. When she finished, her eyes sparkled with satisfaction. "I usually suggest an examination to be certain, but from what you've said, I have no doubts. You're going to be a mother early next May."

Emily, who'd been listening carefully, nodding at many of Joanna's answers, abandoned her cooking to give Joanna a big hug. "What wonderful news! I'm so happy for you. Just think, our children will grow up together."

Even though she'd been fairly confident of the reason for her nausea, having it confirmed made Joanna's mind whirl, and she was suddenly beset with worries. Was she ready to be a mother? Would she be a good one? What would it be like raising a child in a house where she felt like a boarder? Was that fair to her baby? And then there was the biggest question, the one she hesitated to voice, even to herself.

"I didn't think it was possible," Joanna told her sisters. "Kurt and I were married such a short time that when I started feeling ill, I thought it was something I'd eaten or some kind of virus. I even worried that I might be like Kurt's first wife who sometimes imagined she was ill."

"What you're feeling is not imaginary," Louisa assured her.

Emily nodded in agreement before turning back to her cooking. "Some people conceive on their wedding night. Oh, Joanna, this is wonderful news."

Joanna smiled at her sister's apparent need to repeat herself. "It is wonderful and I'm excited, but it would be better if Kurt were here to share the excitement." The excitement and more, much more.

Biting her lip as the worries roiled through her, Joanna decided it was time to share her greatest fear. "I'm afraid of what it will be like for my child not having a father." Though Burke had never referred to the loss of his father, Joanna knew how much the absence of a father had weighed on many of her classmates, particularly the boys. The horrible war that had divided the nation had created far too many widows and fatherless children.

"I won't suggest you marry again to give your child a father." Emily flicked a drop of water onto the skillet to test its heat. "Craig told me how much he hated it when well-meaning people claimed he owed it to Noah to find a new wife."

"But he did," Joanna reminded her. "Although seeing you two together tells me you married for love, not duty."

Emily smiled. "We did, but coming back to you, even though Kurt is gone, Craig and Josh will be part of your baby's life."

"He or she will never lack for love." This time it was Louisa who added confirmation.

It wouldn't be the same, and yet having uncles close by would have to be enough, because like Craig, Joanna had no intention of marrying simply to give her child a father.

"The baby is a gift," she told her sisters. "It's a part of Kurt that I never dreamed I'd have, and it'll have the two best aunts any child could ever want." She paused, then corrected herself. "Three aunts. Wait until Marta hears." She'd write her sister-in-law a letter after breakfast. "My baby's going to have aunts on two continents."

"You'll be a great mother."

Though Joanna hoped Louisa was right, she couldn't dismiss her concerns so easily. Raising a child alone would be far more difficult than it would have been if Kurt had lived. Still, the thought of the life growing inside her filled her with joy.

"If I'm half as good as our mother, the baby will be blessed." Joanna already was. Instead of the happy ending she'd sought, she'd been given a happy beginning.

⁓

"Is there something I should know about your sister?" Burke asked Louisa after they'd entered the office. "All the while we were eating those delicious pancakes, you and Emily looked like you were having trouble keeping a secret. I doubt it had anything to do with the new combination of spices Emily tried."

The way Louisa kept her attention focused on the shutters she'd just opened told Burke he was correct in his assumption, but she said only, "Nothing I can tell you right now."

"I see." Unless he was mistaken, his suspicion that Joanna was pregnant was correct. Burke's stomach clenched at the realization that, like him, this child would grow up without a father, then relaxed a bit as he thought of Craig and Josh. In the few days he'd been in Sweetwater Crossing, he'd seen how Josh had treated Noah and knew that he'd be a good uncle to Joanna's child. And Craig would undoubtedly lavish love on her baby just as he did on his son and would on the child Emily was carrying. Though she lacked a husband, Joanna would not be raising her child alone.

When Louisa turned and walked toward her desk, Burke settled into the chair on the opposite side that he'd claimed as his own. "If you won't answer questions, maybe I can. Is there anything I can tell you?"

Louisa shrugged, her smile wry. "I already know what you're going to say, but I'll ask again. How do I convince men that I'm competent enough to treat them?"

If she'd asked about a specific ailment, he could have given her a definitive response. As it was, all Burke could say was, "I wish I could encourage you, but you and I both know that some people will never change their minds, no matter what the evidence says." People like the residents of Samuels who hadn't valued his opinion because they'd known him since he was in diapers. Though they hadn't been numerous, they had been vocal. Burke had thought he'd accepted their lack of trust, but it had rankled when they'd sought Felix's help instead of his.

"Then my best hope is that the town will hire a male doctor who'll let me work alongside him. I know I still have more to learn. If he's like Austin—he's the doctor in Cimarron Creek who taught me so much—he could be my mentor."

Though Burke hated to discourage her, he felt compelled to say, "Not everyone is capable or willing to be a mentor." The majority of the men he'd met in medical college would have refused to work with a woman, declaring that women had no business trying to be doctors.

"But you've proven you're both willing and capable." Louisa raised an eyebrow. "Is there any chance I could convince you to be that doctor?"

"I'm afraid not. Even if Della decides to stay, I'll be leaving when our two weeks are over." Being a small-town doctor was not the right life for him. The past six months in Samuels had proven that. It was time to move on, to find a city that felt like home, and learn whether he was the man who could discover a way to prevent pneumonia.

Once again, Louisa flashed a wry smile. "I was afraid you'd say that. As punishment for not agreeing, you'll have to listen to me play the piano."

"I never realized you were vindictive," Burke said with a short laugh as Louisa rose and headed for the storage room where the piano was housed, "but I can't believe it will be so bad. If you have even a fraction of Joanna's talent, it'll be a pleasant experience."

It was not. The piano was in desperate need of tuning, and Louisa hit more wrong than right notes. Still, Burke said nothing. Living with two sisters had taught him the folly of appearing to take a woman's bait.

A minute later, although it felt like much longer, the noise—he wouldn't dignify it by calling it music—stopped, and Louisa returned to the office.

"Either you're partially deaf or you were plugging your ears. Still, I give you credit for not demanding I stop massacring the music."

"It's your office."

"But those were your ears that were being assailed. I won't

subject you to that again. The piano was worse than I expected. It needs Joanna's help."

Louisa settled behind the desk and began sorting through the mail she'd picked up at the post office this morning. "There's a package for you." She held out a thick envelope.

Burke nodded when he recognized the handwriting and smiled when he opened the package. "It's two more medical journals. I didn't expect Felix to send them since I'm only going to be here a short time, but I'm glad he did. I almost always find something of value in them, and even though you did torture me, I'm happy to share these with you."

He opened the first and scanned the table of contents, his attention caught by an article titled "Physician Searches for Means of Preventing Pneumonia." His heart pounding with anticipation, Burke began to read, anticipation turning to excitement. This was more than he'd hoped for. He read the article a second time, taking note of everything it said and what was not said.

Burke wanted to move to a large city, one far from Samuels. Dr. Fielding, the subject of the article, lived in San Francisco. Burke wanted to create a vaccine to prevent pneumonia. So did Dr. Fielding. The California physician was working alone. Though Burke had expected to do the same, he knew that two minds were better than one, particularly for research and experimentation. There was no mention of Dr. Fielding wanting or needing an assistant, but the doctor had only begun to explore possibilities. An assistant could help with that work and perhaps contribute new ideas.

Would the man even consider someone with no credentials other than a degree and a burning desire to find a way to prevent a dreaded disease? There was only one way to know. As Burke reached for a piece of paper and his pen, he tried to picture himself in San Francisco. He'd heard the city had many hills. Would Joanna like them? They wouldn't be like the mountains she'd seen in Switzerland, but they might remind her of the Hill Country.

He shook his head at his foolishness. Why was he imagining himself and Joanna together in San Francisco? Even though she'd traveled to Europe, she had no reason to leave Sweetwater Crossing. This was her home. This was where her family lived. This was where she would raise her child. Only a deluded man would think otherwise.

⁓

"I'm so glad you could all join us," Mrs. Albright said after she'd greeted Joanna, Della, and Burke. "Wilbur and I've been looking forward to this evening."

Like Joanna and Della, Mrs. Albright had dressed for the occasion, choosing a gown of almost the same shade of silver gray as her hair. Della had donned a blue plaid taffeta dress trimmed with navy blue velvet ribbon, while Joanna wore the black silk gown she and Grandmother had chosen for her performances. Though black, it wasn't a mourning gown and evoked only pleasant memories.

"I'm happy to be here," Joanna told Mrs. Albright. And she was, for she wanted to learn as much as she could about Clive Finley's time in Sweetwater Crossing. Perhaps one of the Albrights' recollections would help her discover who'd sent that letter of lies. "Is there anything I can do to help you?"

"Thank you, but no. Gertrude's assisting me. Wilbur and Thomas are in the parlor." Mrs. Albright tipped her head toward the doorway on the right. "Wilbur's most anxious to meet you, Miss Samuels."

Though Joanna hadn't realized the Albrights would invite their daughter and son-in-law, it was a thoughtful gesture, since Gertrude had known Clive and might have more memories to share with Della than she had that day at the ranch.

As Della, Burke, and Joanna entered the parlor, Mr. Albright and Thomas rose. "Welcome to Sweetwater Crossing, Miss Samuels." The older man smiled as he extended his hand to Della. "Clive spoke of you so often that I almost feel as if I know you."

When the greetings were completed, Della took the seat their host indicated, smoothing her skirts as she said, "I wish he'd been a better correspondent. When Clive did write, those letters included apologies for their brevity and infrequency. Most of what he told me was about the house and the delays when some of the building materials were stolen."

Mr. Albright frowned for a second, then nodded. "It's been so long that I'd forgotten that. Clive was perplexed by the thefts because of what was taken. As I recall, there was some crown molding, some wainscoting, even a piece or two of furniture. He said he could understand the missing furniture, because that could be easily resold, but there wasn't enough molding or wainscoting for even a small room, so he had no idea why anyone had taken it."

Thomas appeared surprised by the revelation. "I never heard anything about thefts."

"That's because Clive didn't want it to be common knowledge." Thomas's father-in-law nodded slowly. "He feared that might encourage the thief to continue. After that, Clive spent more time there, overseeing even the smallest of details."

Joanna nodded at the new insights into the man who'd built her home. While she didn't understand his desire for secrecy about the missing items, she did understand his desire for perfection. First Miss Heppel, then Herr Ridel and the European maestros had pointed out that a single wrong note ruined a whole piece of music.

"That's why everything about Finley House turned out so well," she said. "My parents never stopped marveling at its beauty."

Burke, who'd been sitting silently, spoke. "You said my uncle spent a lot of time at the house, but he must have done other things. What were they?"

Before Mr. Albright could respond, his wife stood in the doorway. "Supper is ready. You can continue your discussion in the dining room. Now come. Let's eat."

As Joanna had expected, the meal was delicious. Roast chicken was accompanied by scalloped potatoes, green beans, yeast rolls, and peach jam.

"Thank you for serving chicken, Mother Albright," Thomas said as he helped himself to a particularly large serving. "Not keeping the chickens is the only disagreement Gertrude and I have had."

Joanna's former teacher wrinkled her nose. "I spent too many years getting pecked when I collected eggs to want to ever do it again, and even though I despised those chickens, I didn't like wringing their necks."

"This is hardly appropriate dinner conversation," Mrs. Albright chided her daughter. "Wilbur and I were happy to bring the chickens when we moved here permanently."

"I don't miss them," Gertrude said firmly, "but Enoch does, doesn't he, dear?" She turned toward her husband.

"I suspect the attraction is the other horses." Thomas looked around the table, as if gauging everyone's reaction to the discussion. "Enoch's my horse, a gift from Gertrude's parents. He's an excellent mount, but horses are herd animals, and his herd are the two horses that used to share the stable with him." A chuckle accompanied Thomas's words. "When we get close to this house, he picks up his pace, clearly anxious to be with his former stablemates."

Mrs. Albright's expression left no doubt that she considered horses almost as unacceptable a topic of conversation as chickens. In an attempt to appease her hostess, Joanna said, "This is the best jam I've ever tasted."

"Thank you, Joanna. It's my mother's recipe."

Gertrude passed the plate of jam to Burke. "Clive, I told my mother we needed to serve it tonight, because I remembered how much you enjoyed it."

Joanna saw Burke's momentary confusion before he realized that Gertrude had mistaken him for his dead uncle, but it was Della who spoke. "Burke," she said, emphasizing his name, "isn't one for preserves. I, on the other hand, believe good jam makes even the best of rolls even better."

Burke shrugged. "We didn't have fruit trees, and even if we had, my mother wouldn't have had time to make preserves. She did make the finest butter in the county, so I grew up buttering my rolls."

"Then you'll want this, Burke." Gertrude passed him the butter dish. "I apologize for calling you Clive. It's simply that you look so much like him, and you're sitting where he did all those years ago."

"My daughter's right," Mrs. Albright said. "I had the same reaction when I first saw you. I thought you were your uncle. And now seeing you here takes me back in time."

Mr. Albright nodded in agreement with his wife. "It was a privilege to know Clive. I often thought of him as the son I never had—a man of high morals."

"You're right." Mrs. Albright stopped spreading jam on her roll and looked directly at Burke. "He was unfailingly polite but never let his head be turned by all the attention the girls paid him."

"No, indeed. The only company he kept was with Joanna's father, Doc Sheridan, and me." A look of pure nostalgia crossed Mr. Albright's face. "Saturday evenings were the highlight of the week for us."

"Did you have supper together?"

Mr. Albright shook his head at Burke's question. "Doc and the preacher ate with their families. Clive stayed here with us. The four of us met afterwards to smoke a cigar or pipe and talk about the week we'd had and what was in store for the next week." He looked at his son-in-law. "It probably sounds boring to you young folks, but we enjoyed it."

"Not boring, sir. Gertrude and I have similar conversations each evening, don't we, honey?"

She nodded, then began asking Burke for his impressions of Sweetwater Crossing. It was only when they'd finished dessert that her father spoke again.

"Have I waited long enough?" he asked his wife.

"Yes, Wilbur." She gave him a fond smile before addressing Della. "I told him I didn't want anything to interfere with our meal."

"But I can't stop thinking about that letter you received." Mr. Albright continued the explanation. "I hope you brought it with you."

"I did. It's in my reticule."

And that was hanging on the coat-tree in the hallway along with her cloak.

"Then let's adjourn to the parlor." Mrs. Albright rose. "We can see it better there."

When they were all seated, Della opened her reticule and withdrew the worn envelope, handing it to Mr. Albright. He studied it, then gave it to his wife, who scrutinized it as carefully as he had. When she shook her head slightly, he spoke.

"Nothing in that letter is true. I don't understand who would have sent it or why."

He was saying nothing Della didn't already know. Joanna watched as the older woman did her best to hide her disappointment. "Does the penmanship look familiar?" she asked.

"Not to me," Mr. Albright was quick to respond.

"Nor to me." His wife handed the letter to Thomas. "I doubt you can help Miss Samuels, but would you look at it?"

He gave it a cursory glance, then shook his head. "I never saw anyone write quite like that. What about you, Gertrude? You've taught penmanship. Does anything look familiar to you?"

Though her study was more thorough than her husband's, the answer was the same. "I certainly never taught anyone to write like that. And, Thomas, you know our schoolmaster would have sent us to the dunce stool if we'd crossed our T's that way." She turned to Della. "I'm sorry, Della. I know you'd hoped for a different answer."

Her disappointment now clearly visible, Della turned to Burke, leaving him to be the one who said, "It appears we've reached another dead end."

⁓

"I know I've said it before, but I want to say it again. I'm so happy that we're both expecting babies next year." Emily smiled at Joanna as the two of them washed breakfast dishes.

They'd spent an uneventful Sunday. Della had been quieter than usual, perhaps still troubled by the lack of new information about Clive. To Joanna's relief, she'd seemed to have regained her normal enthusiasm this morning and was humming softly when she left to open the library. With everyone else gone, Joanna and Emily had the house to themselves, something that had rarely happened when they were growing up.

In typical oldest sister fashion, Emily directed the conversation. After she'd asked about Joanna's morning sickness, she'd reiterated her excitement over their pregnancies.

It was exciting that they could share their experiences, and yet . . . Joanna asked the question that had plagued her for days. "Do you suppose Louisa feels left out?"

Emily's smile faded ever so slightly. "I hope not. She and Josh have only been married a few months, and not everyone conceives as quickly as you and I did."

But that hadn't happened during Emily's first marriage. Joanna wouldn't pry, but she couldn't stop herself from saying, "I'm surprised you and George didn't have any children. Remember how he used to ask me to play Brahms's Lullaby?"

He'd sat on the bench next to Joanna, his smile so warm that she—foolish, foolish girl—had believed he was as attracted to her as she was to him, but like Clive Finley, George had had eyes for only one.

"When I asked him why he wanted to hear that song so often, George said it was one he hoped to sing to his babies. That made me think he was eager for children."

Emily turned to stare at the back door, her lips tightening with what appeared to be discomfort. "He was," she admitted, "but it didn't happen. Let's talk about happier things. Have you thought about names for your baby?"

Eleven

"Are you feeling all right?"

As worry lines formed between Louisa's eyes when she saw Joanna in the hallway of her office, Joanna realized she should have anticipated her sister's concern. This was the first time Joanna had come here, and given her medical history as well as what some would call her current delicate condition, it was no wonder Louisa feared she was ill.

Joanna offered a reassuring smile. "Today's better than most mornings, and I haven't been coughing very much. I'm sorry if I alarmed you, but I wanted to talk to Burke." And, though she'd expected him to be with Louisa, he was not.

Ushering her into the main room of her office, Louisa said, "It's his day to go to the post office. He should have been back by now, but you know how Jake Winslow likes to talk."

"Especially to men." The postmaster was famous for being long-winded. "Poor Burke. He's a captive audience."

"Did I hear my name?" Burke entered the office so quietly that Joanna, even though she'd been anticipating his arrival, did not hear him. She'd been studying the room where Doc Sheridan had once stitched a cut on her arm, looking for changes Louisa had made but finding none.

"You certainly did." Louisa gave Burke a wry smile before she continued. "My sister came to talk to you. I didn't ask what couldn't wait until supper, but I know her well enough to say that she's determined to do something today."

When Burke settled in the chair next to her, Joanna turned toward him and wrinkled her nose. "As you can see, my little sister believes she knows everything." She emphasized the adjective, as she'd done so many times when they were growing up. "Unfortunately for me, this time Louisa's correct. There is something I was planning for this afternoon, but I wanted to make sure you were in agreement before I did it."

Louisa lifted an eyebrow. "And just what are you proposing to do?"

"Besides asking you to leave us alone?"

When Louisa let out an exaggerated huff before heading to the storage room and pounding on the piano, Joanna turned to Burke. "Were your sisters like us, deliberately trying to annoy each other even though they knew that by the end of the day they'd be best friends again?" Louisa's pretended anger was done in fun and reminded Joanna of the happy times she'd shared with both Emily and Louisa.

Burke shrugged. "I don't know. I did my best to stay away when I heard squabbling."

"You're a wise man." Settling back in the chair, Joanna said, "I didn't mean to be mysterious, but I also didn't want Louisa's opinion. I keep thinking about Della and how disappointed she was on Saturday. I was too. I thought the Albrights would be able to help resolve the questions about Clive, but they didn't appear to know anything we hadn't already heard."

Joanna shook her head slowly. "I probably shouldn't have had such high hopes. After all, my father was Clive's closest friend, and he went to his grave believing Clive had left sooner than expected to join an Alabama regiment and that he died in the war. There was no reason to believe Mr. Albright would have thought any differently."

"Whoever wrote that letter knows the truth."

"Exactly. There has to be a way to discover who did that." Joanna kept her gaze fixed on Burke, trying to gauge his reaction to what she was about to propose. "The Albrights may have known Clive better than most of the town, but they weren't the only ones who spent at least some time with him. I want to talk to everyone who might have a clue to what happened to him."

Burke nodded his approval. "I assume you've decided where to start."

"That's what I wanted to discuss with you. Several people have mentioned how many girls were attracted to your uncle. Even if it was only infatuation, they probably sought opportunities to be near him. I know it's been a long time, but women tend to remember unrequited love." Joanna suspected she'd remember her foolish attraction to George for the rest of her life. "They may recall something—even a small detail—that will help us put the puzzle together. That's why I thought I'd talk to them."

"And you don't want me to accompany you."

"How did you guess?"

Burke shrugged as if the answer should be apparent. "You said you wanted my agreement. You already know I want to do everything I can to solve the mystery of my uncle's death, so something must be different about talking to those women. The only thing I could imagine is that you don't believe I should be involved."

Though Burke didn't seem annoyed, Joanna wanted him to understand her reasoning. "I'm not trying to exclude you. It's just that I thought the women might be more comfortable talking to me alone. There are some things we women will share with another woman but wouldn't dream of saying in front of a man."

Once again Burke nodded. "You're undoubtedly correct about that, but there's an even better reason I shouldn't go with you. Your ladies might be uncomfortable with me because of my resemblance to my uncle. Who's on your agenda?"

Joanna almost sighed with relief that Burke was so agreeable. More than agreeable. Understanding.

"I want to start with Beulah's mother. If I'd thought about it sooner, I could have spoken to her when she brought Beulah into town this morning, but it might be better to talk to her at her home. Her mother-in-law lives with her and may remember more than Miriam does. Afterwards, I'll see what Miss Heppel has to say."

Burke picked up the round paperweight Louisa had inherited from Doc Sheridan and tossed it from hand to hand. "Unless Louisa needs me here tomorrow, we can talk to some of the older men . . . together."

The smile that accompanied Burke's final word sent a surprising warmth surging through Joanna. A warmth that was as unusual as it was unexpected. Both Louisa and Emily had told her that tears could be common at this stage of her pregnancy, but neither had mentioned what felt almost like attraction. How odd.

Joanna was still mulling over her reaction to Burke's smile when she guided the buggy onto the Douglas ranch. Though modest compared to the one Gertrude and her husband now shared, it was well cared for, with a few flowers still blooming next to the porch.

Alerted by the sound of the approaching vehicle, the woman who'd been cutting dead blossoms swiveled her head, then stood. Beulah's mother was close to Joanna's height, but her hair was many shades lighter and threaded with gray, her eyes blue rather than brown.

"I wasn't expecting you. Did something happen to Beulah?" Miriam Douglas's voice reflected both surprise and concern.

"No. I'm sorry to have alarmed you." Miriam's first thought was for her daughter, something Joanna should have anticipated. "Beulah's fine. I came because I wondered if I could talk to you and Mrs. Douglas for a few minutes."

As the tension in her shoulders dissipated, Miriam nodded. "Of course." She gestured toward the house. "Let's go inside. Mother Douglas will be happy to see you again. All Beulah can talk about is you and the newcomers who are staying at Finley House."

Once again Joanna chided herself for her thoughtlessness. Even though Miriam delivered Beulah to the schoolhouse and picked her up there rather than coming to Finley House, Joanna could have made the effort to spend a few minutes with her.

"Come inside." Miriam led Joanna into the small but immaculately clean kitchen that was redolent of freshly baked cake. "Look who came to see us."

A second later, the gray-haired woman who Mama had claimed refused to let age stop her from doing things that those a decade younger wouldn't have attempted emerged from the adjoining room. After giving Joanna a welcoming smile and hug, she studied her for a moment, then nodded, her eyes radiating satisfaction.

"Miriam, you din't tell me we was gonna have visitors. I reckon it's good that I just took that pan of gingerbread out of the oven. Joanna here will surely wanna have a piece." Mrs. Douglas's smile broadened as her gaze returned to Joanna's midsection. "Ginger's good for settlin' stomachs when you're in the family way. Now sit down. Sit down."

As she took the chair Mrs. Douglas had indicated, Joanna stared at the older woman in astonishment. "How did you know? I haven't told anyone other than my sisters."

Beulah's grandmother chuckled. "You're glowin'. Miriam looked the same way when she was carryin' Beulah. I cain't count the number of pots of ginger tea I made for her. Right, Miriam?"

"Yes, Mother Douglas. And they helped."

But it was milk that the older woman insisted Joanna drink with her gingerbread, saying it was good for both her and her baby.

When Miriam had joined Joanna and her mother-in-law at the kitchen table and had accepted Joanna's compliments on the gingerbread, she turned to her mother-in-law. "Joanna said she has some questions for us."

"And I got some for her, like how long that handsome young fella's gonna stay. When I saw him in church, I nearly dropped my teeth. He sure do remind me of Clive Finley."

Thankful that she'd been given a way to introduce her questions, Joanna nodded. "That's who I wanted to talk about. You know that Miss Samuels was Clive's fiancée. I'm trying to help her learn more about Clive's life here and wondered what you recall about that time."

Miriam swallowed her cake, then said, "He caused quite a stir among my friends. They all wished he'd forget his sweetheart and marry them." She gave her mother-in-law a quick smile. "If I hadn't been promised to Hiram, I might have felt the same way, but no one could compare to Hiram."

"You two were meant for each other. I knowed that the first time I seen you together. Hiram had a lovin' look in his eye. Gladys—you remember her, don't you, Miriam?—said Hiram looked the same way Malcolm did when he saw Minerva. 'Course her son weren't as lucky in love as you and Hiram were."

It took Joanna a second to realize that Mrs. Douglas was referring to Mayor Alcott and Miss Heppel. Perhaps because her parents had discouraged gossip, but more likely because it had happened so far in the past, this was the first she'd heard of any romantic interest between them. The mayor had been married for as long as Joanna could remember, and Miss Heppel was what the town called a confirmed spinster.

"It sure were amusin' watchin' them gals tryin' to outdo the others," Mrs. Douglas continued. "I heard tell they brung Clive cakes and pies."

Miriam's eyes widened for a second. "You're right, Mother Douglas. I'd forgotten that. What I remember is the way all the girls hoped he'd dance with them at the church social."

"Did he?"

"Nope." Mrs. Douglas answered before Miriam could speak. "Not a one. He sure were a mighty fine dancer."

Joanna made no effort to hide her puzzlement. "I thought you said he didn't dance with the girls."

"He din't. He wouldn't favor any of them single gals, but he sure as shootin' danced with everyone what was married."

This was a new facet of Clive's personality and one Joanna suspected would amuse Della, but though the conversation continued, she learned nothing that lent clues to what might have happened to the man who built Finley House. She could only hope her next visit would be more fruitful.

⁓

"I'm so glad you came," Miss Heppel said, repeating the greeting she'd given Joanna last week. The speed with which she opened the door made Joanna suspect she'd been watching for her. "Your visits are making Monday my favorite day of the week, after Sunday, that is. The peace I feel when I'm playing hymns reminds me that our Lord is a God of love and forgiveness."

Miss Heppel pursed her lips the way she had when Joanna had hit a wrong note, only this time her displeasure appeared directed at herself. "I didn't invite you here to listen to me. I want to hear more about your time in Europe."

When she was seated on the chair across from her former

teacher, Joanna said, "I did come to listen to you. I was hoping you might be able to help me."

A faint flush colored Miss Heppel's cheeks, making Joanna wonder how often people asked for her assistance. "Of course I'll help you if I can. What can I do for you?"

"It's really for Della Samuels. There are questions about how Clive Finley died, so Burke and I are trying to learn everything we can about his life here. I'm sure you remember him."

Miss Heppel nodded vigorously. "How could anyone forget the man who built that huge house? I don't mean to offend you, Joanna, because I know you love your home, but you must realize how unsuitable it is for Sweetwater Crossing. The best I can say about it is that those stairways are attractive, even if a bit ostentatious, but it's a building that doesn't belong here."

Miss Heppel's vehemence, so different from her normal calm demeanor, puzzled Joanna. "The house has served us well," she said, choosing to ignore the unflattering description of Finley House. "I think it must have been interesting to see it being built."

Miss Heppel shrugged. "Like most of the town, I occasionally snuck inside when the workers were gone. Curiosity is powerful, even when you know you shouldn't give in to it." She folded her hands as if preparing to pray. "Haven't you ever done something you regretted?"

"Yes, of course I have." Most recently, being jealous of Emily when George had asked her to marry him and causing her family unnecessary worry by being such a poor correspondent while she was in Europe.

"Then you know how I feel. Unfortunately, I can't undo the past."

"I can't imagine that anyone would begrudge you a look at the house." That seemed an odd thing to be dwelling on decades later. "Is there anything else you can tell me about Clive?"

A shake of the head was Miss Heppel's first response. "It

was a difficult period in my life. My father had just died very suddenly—Doc Sheridan said it was a heart attack—and my mother had to sell the livery. That's when I started giving piano lessons. We needed the money, you see. I didn't have time to think about anything else."

She frowned before giving her head another shake. "I'm sorry that I can't be more helpful, but it was a long time ago, and memories fade. Let's talk about something more pleasant. Tell me about your husband. It must have been love at first sight. Isn't it glorious when that happens?"

Joanna's confusion must have shown, because Miss Heppel said, "Oh, yes, I was in love once upon a time. Unfortunately, my story doesn't end with 'and they lived happily ever after.'"

Joanna's hadn't either.

Chapter

Twelve

Burke picked up the package he'd put in the back of the buggy, hoping his hostess would be as pleased by it as his patient had predicted. While yesterday had been uneventful, this morning had been busier than he'd expected, because Louisa had asked him to accompany her when she called on a pregnant woman, explaining that the woman's six-year-old had a sore throat.

"I don't believe it's scarlet fever," she said, "but after Joanna's experience, I don't want to take any chances. That's why I want your opinion."

Burke had agreed readily, looking forward to the challenge of doing more than removing infected splinters and treating rashes. And, like Louisa, he hoped the child did not have scarlet fever but was prepared to order the household to quarantine if needed. Fortunately, the boy had not contracted the dreaded disease. There was no strawberry tongue or scarlet skin, though the child's condition was still serious.

"He's burning up with fever, he cries when he tries to swallow, and he says his ears hurt something fierce. Can you help him?" The mother led Burke and Louisa into her son's bedroom, refusing to leave him, even though Burke had suggested she would be more comfortable not watching the examination.

As he'd suspected from the symptoms she outlined, the boy had severely swollen tonsils, what some called tonsillitis, others preferring the term quinsy.

"Has this happened before?" he asked.

The mother nodded. "But not this bad. I'm scared." She touched her son's forehead, biting her lip as he winced from even the slight pressure. "Can't you give him morphine? Doc Sheridan said that was the best way to treat pain."

Trying not to shudder at the thought, Burke shook his head. While it was never easy to watch a child in pain, morphine was not the answer. It might lessen the pain, but it would not resolve the infection. If left untreated, the boy's quinsy would only worsen, leaving him unable to open his mouth fully and possibly deaf for the week or two until the abscess ruptured.

"Your son's tonsils are badly infected," Burke told the mother after he'd shown Louisa how he'd made the diagnosis. "I can give you something for him to gargle, and that may help, but the best thing is to open and drain the abscess. Are you willing for me to do that?"

"Will it make the pain go away?"

"It will."

"Then go ahead."

Once he'd convinced the mother to sit on the opposite side of the room so that he and Louisa could work without interruption, Burke opened his medical bag and began to prepare for the procedure, explaining each step to Louisa. Though she said nothing while he swabbed the boy's tonsils and carefully inserted the lancet, he heard her quick intake of breath when the abscess began to drain. Only minutes later, the boy was able to speak.

"It doesn't hurt." The child's amazement was mirrored in Louisa's expression.

"Thank you," she said softly. "I learned so much today."

The mother insisted on a tangible payment. With tears of relief streaming down her face, she handed Burke a plucked chicken. "Emily will know what to do with it."

Burke hoped that was the case. "I have something for you," he told his landlady as he entered the kitchen bearing the chicken.

Emily took one look at the contents of the sack and laughed. "Let me guess. You tried to refuse, but your patient wouldn't listen."

"She said you'd know what to do with it."

"I do indeed. This one will make a fine roast. Now, shoo. I know you and Joanna had plans for the afternoon. She's waiting in the parlor."

The sound of music told Burke that Joanna was doing more than waiting. She was playing something soothing, although whether that was for herself, Emily, or even him, he did not know.

"Don't stop," he said when her fingers stilled and she started to rise from the bench. "That was beautiful. What is it called?"

"It's a piece by Johannes Brahms, the first of his piano trio. I was simply passing the time until you came."

Though there was no condemnation in her voice, Burke felt the need to apologize. "It's later than I expected, but if you're still agreeable, I'm ready to visit whichever man is first on your list."

She rose, straightening her skirt and heading toward the front door. "I thought we should start with the mayor." As she pinned on her hat, she said, "I'm surprised he hasn't talked to you after you asked him and the sheriff to share their memories. It seems odd, since some call him a windbag. While I wouldn't use that term, Mayor Alcott can be pompous, and he never hesitates to voice his opinion."

"He probably believes his position as mayor makes him an expert on most things."

Like Joanna, Burke had been surprised by the mayor's silence but attributed it to the hostility he'd seen the day they'd met. Perhaps today would be different.

"Finley, I've been meaning to talk to you," the mayor said when Burke and Joanna entered his office, "but there hasn't been time. Being mayor of this fine town demands almost every hour of the day."

To Joanna's credit, her only reaction to the blatant exaggeration was a faint tightening of her lips, as if she was trying to suppress a laugh. He was grateful that the man appeared less adversarial today, perhaps because he'd had over a week to become accustomed to Burke's resemblance to his uncle.

"I realize you weren't mayor back then," Burke said, attempting to appeal to the man's vanity, "but you strike me as someone with an excellent memory." When Alcott preened, Burke continued. "What do you recall about the time my uncle lived here?"

The proud smile turned into a scowl. "Not much. That was the year I decided to run for mayor. Some folks thought I was too young, but I managed to convince them to support me. Campaigning and wooing my wife were more important than thinking about the man who was trying to outdo the rest of us by building that monstrosity of a house."

When Joanna flinched at the description of her home, Burke said as mildly as he could, "Everyone's entitled to an opinion. I, for one, find the house beautiful. And," he added, "I suspect the taxes Joanna's family pays on it help the town's coffers."

Alcott inclined his head. "That much is true."

An hour later, though Burke had learned nothing of value about his uncle, he and Joanna had been subjected to a lengthy discussion of the changes the mayor had made in Sweetwater Crossing and how he'd won reelection by a landslide.

When they managed to escape—that was the only word Burke thought appropriate—and were out of earshot, he turned to Joanna. "Who was his opponent?"

"There wasn't one. No one else wants the job."

Burke suspected that wasn't the whole truth and that the mayor had intimidated anyone who considered opposing him.

"What about you?" he asked her. "It's a shame women can't vote or run for office, because you'd be a good mayor."

Joanna stared at him for a second, then burst into laughter, a sound that made the beautiful music she'd played earlier today pale in comparison. It was a full-bodied laugh, clear as a bell, and more infectious than most germs, leaving others no choice but to join in.

When her laughter subsided, she pretended to glare at him. "If I didn't know better, I'd say you've spent too much time in Mr. Miller's saloon and that what I heard was whiskey talking."

Burke feigned innocence. "I made you laugh, didn't I? That was my intention." Laughter turned Joanna from pretty to stunning, bringing welcome color to her cheeks and a sparkle to her eyes. "You should do it more often."

He might not have learned anything from the mayor, but the afternoon was far from a failure, for Burke now had a new mission. He would do whatever he could to make Joanna laugh at least once a day.

"Will you share the joke with the rest of us?" Craig asked as he passed the bowl of peas to Joanna. "You've been wearing a Cheshire cat grin since we sat down for dinner."

Joanna felt heat rise to her cheeks. Though she was still amused by the idea of running for mayor, she hadn't realized it was obvious. "It's not really a joke," she told Craig. "Burke made the most ridiculous suggestion this afternoon, and I can't help smiling whenever I think about it." She'd done more than smile. She'd chuckled, and when she'd been alone in her bedroom, she'd laughed aloud.

Della laid her fork on her plate and looked from Burke to Joanna, her expression inscrutable. "That doesn't sound like the Burke I know. His suggestions are usually very well thought out and sensible."

"This one wasn't."

Burke's lips twitched with amusement. "How do you know it wasn't?"

"Because the whole idea is preposterous."

Beulah, who'd been listening intently, turned to Joanna. "What did Mr. Burke say?"

"He said that if laws were different I should run for mayor."

Emily exchanged a quick look with her husband before she fixed her gaze on Joanna. "And you told him you wouldn't consider it."

"Of course I did." The talents God had given her did not include serving in public office. "I doubt a woman would ever be elected mayor, even if women could vote."

"Why not?" Beulah seemed perplexed, addressing her question to Craig, perhaps because he was her teacher.

"It's never been done," he told her, "but that doesn't mean it won't happen someday."

Mrs. Carmichael nodded. "Folks here have mighty strong opinions about their elected officials. I remember the opposition when Malcolm Alcott first ran for mayor."

"He told us people thought he was too young." Though Joanna wasn't certain how old he was now, she suspected he'd been about her age when he'd decided he should be mayor.

"Not just that. He was young and single. In folks' minds, that meant he hadn't settled down enough to run the town." Mrs. Carmichael broke her roll in two and began to butter it. "There were rumors that he was sweet on Minerva Heppel, but the grapevine must have been mistaken, because Malcolm started courting Mary Watson, and the next thing we knew, they were married."

This was the second time Joanna had heard the mayor's name coupled with Miss Heppel's. Was he the man who'd broken her heart?

Joanna's musings were cut short when Craig said, "You might not want to ever be mayor, Joanna, but I wondered whether you'd consider teaching some of my pupils to play the piano. A few of the mothers said they'd approached Miss Heppel, but she refused. I sense that there's a real need."

Once again, Beulah was the first to react. "Would you teach me?"

Seeing the enthusiasm on the girl's face made Joanna wish Craig had waited until Beulah left the table before posing his question. While it wasn't as outlandish as Burke's, Joanna's answer was the same.

"I can't do that, Craig. One thing I learned in Europe is that teaching requires talents I don't possess. From everything I've heard, you're an excellent teacher. I wouldn't be even passably good. It wouldn't be fair to your pupils to have me try to teach them."

"Oh." Beulah blinked to keep the tears that filled her eyes from falling. "I want to play like you."

What could she say to comfort the child? As she searched for an answer, though she couldn't explain why she did it, Joanna looked at Burke. He said nothing, and yet the sympathy she saw reflected from his eyes heartened her and gave her an idea.

"Can you keep a secret, Beulah?" she asked.

When the girl nodded, Joanna continued. "If you promise not to tell anyone, I'll teach you to play scales. We can practice after school every day."

Beulah's radiant smile banished the last of Joanna's doubts.

"I'm gonna learn to play the piano! Wait till my mama

hears." The smile faded a second later. "I'm sorry, Miss Joanna. I know it's a secret. I won't tell her."

"It's all right to tell your parents and your grandmother," Joanna assured the girl. "It's only a secret from the other pupils."

Nodding as solemnly as if they'd negotiated a peace treaty, Beulah said, "Okay. Just my family." She picked up her glass of milk, then set it down again and smiled at Joanna. "I'm so happy."

"So am I." Louisa, who'd been uncharacteristically silent during the discussion, spoke. "Today that's thanks to Burke. Not only did he make my sister laugh again, but he's teaching me so much. I learned how to diagnose and treat quinsy." She gave him a smile, then turned it on Della. "I hope you'll both stay for more than two weeks."

So did Joanna.

Thirteen

"I'm still trying to decide whether the view from the front veranda is better than the back."

Burke turned to look at Della, who was seated next to him on the parlor settee. Though she normally remained silent while Joanna entertained them with a few musical numbers after supper, tonight she continued to whisper. "What do you think?"

"I haven't been on the second-floor front veranda, so I can't weigh in." He kept his voice as low as Della's, not wanting to disturb the others but realizing that this was a ploy and that Della wanted to talk to him privately. She could have waited until Joanna ended the piece, but perhaps she hadn't wanted to delay the nightly walk he and Joanna took.

"There's no time like the present to remedy that," Della said as she rose, expecting Burke to follow her.

He did, and when they reached her room, he dutifully admired the view before saying, "What's bothering you?"

She settled onto one of the chairs that flanked the doors to the veranda, motioning Burke to the other. "I can't fool you,

can I? Bother is the wrong word, but there's something I want
to discuss with you."

Burke suspected the discussion had been precipitated by
Louisa's comment at supper, but he said simply, "Go ahead."

"I know I told you two weeks here would be enough, but
Sweetwater Crossing has turned out to be very different from
my expectations. I never thought I'd be living in Clive's house
or that the people would be so welcoming. I never thought I'd
find myself working here, much less as a librarian."

A faint blush stole its way up her cheeks, telling Burke that
while she wouldn't admit it, Della could also have said, "I never
thought I'd meet someone like Harold."

"You're not ready to return to Alabama, are you?"

It was what he and Joanna had suspected. While it was too
soon to know whether Della would remain here permanently,
Burke wouldn't be surprised if that happened. And if she and
Harold discovered that what they felt for each other was true
love, it could be the best thing that had happened to Della in
decades.

"No, I'm not ready to leave," she admitted. "I like it here,
but your situation is different." Della fixed her gaze on him, her
light blue eyes filling with tears. "Felix is expecting you back in
a couple weeks. I don't want to interfere in your life any more
than I already have."

When Burke started to protest, to tell her that far from interfering, bringing her to Texas had given him a chance to re-
evaluate his life, Della held up a hand to stop him. "I'd like to
stay here a while longer. I thought I could take a stagecoach or
train when I'm ready to leave."

That was something he'd never permit. "You know I don't
want you to travel alone."

Della nodded, then brushed away the tear that had slid down
her cheek. "I suspected you'd say that. All right, Burke. We'll
return when we planned."

He reached across the small distance and laid his hand on hers. "You didn't let me finish. When you leave—*if* you leave, because I'm not convinced you want to do that—we'll go together, but it doesn't have to be immediately. You heard Louisa. If the other sisters agree that we can remain for a while, I'll let Felix know that my plans have changed."

Burke wouldn't tell Della that Felix and Edna would probably be relieved or that Felix had advised Burke to reassess his future, even going so far as to say that he was no longer needed in Samuels.

"Are you certain?" Della blinked away the last of the tears. "I know you're training Louisa and treating some patients, but it's not like it was in Alabama."

"No, it's not, but I'm happy to help Louisa."

Witnessing Louisa's enthusiasm as she learned something new was more rewarding than he'd expected, but there was more to do, much more. The cases Burke had handled had confirmed that Sweetwater Crossing needed a fully trained doctor. While Louisa had developed the basic skills when she'd worked with the doctor in Cimarron Creek, there were still gaps in her knowledge. Even a few more weeks under Burke's tutelage would help.

He was in no hurry to leave. Besides, if Fielding agreed, he would return to Alabama only if he needed to accompany Della back home. Then he'd head to San Francisco.

Burke wasn't ready to tell Della about the hope that had lodged in his heart that Fielding would welcome an assistant, but he wanted to share it with someone. Not just anyone, he realized, but Joanna. Only Joanna.

"Are you sure you're not saying that to placate me?"

He countered with a question of his own. "Have you ever known me to lie?"

"No," Della admitted, "but there's always a first time."

"This isn't it."

She studied him for a moment, then, apparently satisfied by what she saw, nodded. "Let's talk to the sisters."

∽◌

"There was no question that we want you to stay," Joanna told Burke as they descended the front steps. As they did each night, they spent five minutes on the veranda while Joanna took and held deep breaths. Fresh air, Burke had said, was better for her lungs than the air inside the house. It was only when she'd completed what he called the breathing exercises that they began their walk.

"Louisa's thrilled at the idea of learning more from you, and Emily loves having you and Della as boarders."

"What about you?"

Joanna smiled, thinking of the way her life had changed since he and Della had arrived. "I'm grateful for all that you and Della are doing. You're making Sweetwater Crossing a better place to live. Thanks to Della, we have a library again, and you're providing medical care to men who'd never consult Louisa."

Though the crescent moon provided little illumination, the lights that spilled from Finley House's windows allowed Joanna to see that Burke wasn't convinced. Could it be because she hadn't revealed her personal feelings?

"You're making a difference in the town," she continued. "I appreciate that, but even more, I'm grateful for what you've done for me. I feel healthier than I have in almost a year. My lungs are stronger, and I have more energy. That's because of the exercises you've prescribed. They've been better than all the medicines the doctors in Europe gave me."

Burke's shoulders relaxed, telling Joanna she'd been right in thinking he needed to hear that.

"I thought you looked better." He paused, then let out a mirthless laugh. "That's the wrong word. It sounds like I was commenting on your appearance and implying that you aren't always attractive. You are. What I should have said was that you look healthier."

Joanna couldn't help chuckling. "There's no need for an apology. I knew what you meant. I'm happy that you're staying at least for a while longer, because it's good for us." Most of all herself. "But what about you? You said your new dream was to find a way to prevent pneumonia. As much as I love Sweetwater Crossing, I don't see how you can do much research here. Very few of our residents have caught pneumonia. Have you abandoned your dream?"

They'd been walking more briskly than usual and were approaching Center Street. Though it was too dark to see them, Joanna knew there were stakes in the ground, marking the outline of what would be Louisa and Josh's home. The town was changing in more ways than she'd envisioned on the seemingly endless journey home from Europe. Her dreams had changed. Had Burke's?

"Abandon my dream?" The way Burke shook his head emphasized his denial. "To the contrary. I'm pursuing it. One of the journals Felix sent me had an article about a physician in San Francisco who's trying to discover how to prevent pneumonia. He wants to develop a vaccine like the one that's been successful in practically eradicating smallpox."

Burke paused for a moment, appearing to be debating whether to say anything more. "I haven't told anyone—not even Della—but I wrote to this man asking if I could participate in his research." He took a deep breath and exhaled slowly before he continued.

"My mother used to tell me that I was impulsive and should think about important things before I acted. Maybe I should have waited, but when I saw the article, it appeared to confirm everything I'd been considering. When I met you and realized how much pneumonia was affecting your life months after you contracted it, I started thinking that doctors ought to do more than treat pneumonia. There ought to be a way to prevent it. I already knew that I didn't want to return to Alabama, so this seemed like a good solution."

The lump that lodged in her throat surprised Joanna. It was silly to be so dismayed by the thought of Burke going to San Francisco. After all, it wasn't as if she'd thought he would remain here indefinitely, and yet there was no denying that the idea disturbed her.

"Have you received an answer?" By some small miracle, her voice sounded normal.

"Not yet. It's been less than a week since I mailed my letter." Burke stared into the distance, then gave a short laugh. "I don't know what I was thinking. Maybe I wasn't thinking at all, but I asked Dr. Fielding to reply to me here. It was almost as if I knew Della and I would be staying for more than two weeks."

Joanna wasn't sure what to say, and so she remained silent.

When they reached the bridge, Burke touched her arm. "You won't tell Della or anyone, will you? Della has enough things on her mind right now. I don't want to add to them."

"Of course I won't tell her. We're all entitled to secrets." Joanna leaned on the railing, looking down at the slowly moving water, wondering whether Burke's uncle had ever stood here, talking about secrets with one of his friends.

"We are indeed," Burke said. "And those secrets should only be shared with people we trust."

The lump in Joanna's throat disappeared as warmth flowed through her at the realization that Burke had put her in that special category.

She turned to face him, wanting him to see how deeply he'd touched her. "I'm honored that you trust me."

His smile warmed her even more than his words had. "I've learned to be careful about who I trust." Burke's brief silence made Joanna wonder whether he was thinking of his partner or his former fiancée, but when he spoke, his reference was closer to home.

"As much as I admire your sister for her persistence, I wouldn't tell Louisa anything I didn't want repeated."

Joanna shared Burke's caution but wondered how he'd come to that conclusion. "Louisa wouldn't deliberately betray a trust. It's simply that sometimes things slip out." She took a breath before she added, "I'm surprised she hasn't told you my secret. Not that it'll be secret much longer. You may have already guessed it. Did you know—"

Before she could complete the sentence, Burke laid a cautioning finger on her lips. "Just because I told you my secret doesn't mean I expect you to do the same."

The wonderful warmth that had dissipated Joanna's worries increased as she reveled in the touch of his finger. "I know that. You're not a man who gives a gift—and entrusting your secret to me was a gift—because he expects something in return. I want to tell you."

And that surprised her. Never before had she felt so comfortable with a man, so willing to tell him her deepest thoughts and fears. Not even Kurt had engendered this desire to confide in him. Joanna couldn't explain it. All she knew was that what she felt for Burke was unique.

As he nodded slowly, she sensed that he understood what she'd said, perhaps even what she'd been thinking.

She tipped her head up and smiled at him. "I'm expecting a baby."

Chapter

Fourteen

October first. The beginning of a new month. If all went as he hoped and Fielding agreed to hire him, it could be a month filled with exciting new possibilities. In the meantime . . . Burke slid his arms into his jacket and tried not to frown at the memory of things that hadn't gone the way he'd hoped.

It had been five days since Joanna had confirmed his suspicions that she was pregnant. He must have said appropriate things, because she'd continued by telling him how happy she was that a part of her husband would live on after him, but all the while she'd been speaking, Burke had felt as if someone had punched him in the solar plexus.

It was ridiculous to be jealous of a dead man, and yet Burke could not deny that for one fleeting moment he'd wished the baby was his. And if that wasn't ridiculous, Burke didn't know what was. He had no intention of remaining here, so why had he pictured himself standing beside Joanna, holding a child— their child—in his arms?

Fortunately, Joanna had not mentioned her pregnancy again, and the following few days had been uneventful. Burke had written to Felix, telling him their return would be delayed, perhaps indefinitely. He and Joanna had spoken with Mrs. Tabor, the proprietor of the town's restaurant, and Sheriff Granger. Though both had been friendlier than the mayor, they'd had nothing new to tell them, nor had the half dozen women Joanna had visited on her own. The quest to discover what had happened to Uncle Clive was at a standstill.

Forcing his lips into a smile, Burke opened his door and entered the hallway. Judging from the delicious aromas wafting upstairs, breakfast was almost ready.

"It's all right, Burke." Della, who'd emerged from her room at the same time, gave him a smile that might have been reassuring if he knew what she meant by her unusual greeting.

"What's all right?"

She smiled again and patted her hair as if to assure herself that every strand was in place. "I know you and Joanna have been talking to everyone who might know something about Clive. You obviously didn't learn anything important or you would have told me. That's all right." Della took a step forward, clearly more comfortable with the situation than either Burke or Joanna. They'd both admitted their discouragement when the conversations had proven fruitless.

"I've reconciled myself to not knowing how Clive died or where he's buried," Della continued. "Even if I did know that, it wouldn't bring him back."

"That's true, but I hate unsolved mysteries." Burke's mother had told him that life was filled with ambiguities, that it wasn't always possible to answer every question, but he'd never been comfortable with uncertainty.

Della's expression radiated sympathy. "I know you do. It's your nature to want to solve problems, but this appears to be one without a solution." Though Della laid her hand on the banister, she did not begin to descend the stairs. "I've accepted that, and you should too. Meanwhile, if I'm not mistaken, Emily has a sausage casserole waiting for us."

Breakfast did indeed feature a mouth-watering sausage dish. For some reason Beulah did not like it, so Emily reserved it for days when the girl was not here.

When Craig had blessed the food, Josh took a healthy serving of the casserole, smiling at Emily when he'd swallowed the first bite. "Excellent as usual. Do you think you could teach Louisa to make it? Your cooking is one of the things I'll miss once we move into our new home. My wife is a good cook, but she'd be the first to admit that she can't match your culinary skills."

"And I would never try to match her healing." Emily smiled. "Since Louisa won't charge me for her services as a midwife, I offered to deliver meals to your new home at least once a week."

"When is it scheduled to be completed?" When Joanna had pointed out the stakes outlining what would become the foundation for Josh and Louisa's house, Burke had realized that the newlyweds wouldn't be far away from Emily and Joanna. Now that all three sisters were back in town, it seemed they wanted to remain close to each other.

Louisa looked up from the piece of toast she'd been busy buttering. "Raymond says it'll take three or four months. We'd hoped to be able to move in before Christmas, but that probably won't happen."

She turned to her husband. "Don't worry, Josh. You won't starve there. Even though I refused my sister's generous offer, Emily and I agreed that you'll eat here whenever I'm away from home with a patient."

"That's a good plan." Mrs. Carmichael added her approval. "Josh may own a tearoom, but I suspect he'd be hard-pressed to do more than boil water for tea and open a can of escargots. Most men can't cook."

"You're right about me, Mrs. Carmichael," Josh agreed, "but Craig's an exception."

Emily's husband shrugged. "I had no choice. Noah and I had to eat." And before he'd come to Sweetwater Crossing, Craig had been a widower.

Apparently mollified by the culinary arrangements, Josh turned to Joanna. "I know you said you don't want to teach anyone other than Beulah, but I have another suggestion. If I buy a piano, would you play in the tearoom? It wouldn't have to be all day or even every day, but I know the customers would enjoy it."

Burke had to admire Josh's strategy. He'd obviously been trained as a salesman, because his suggestion was carefully phrased, making it difficult for Joanna to refuse.

But she did. "Thank you for offering, Josh, but your tearoom is complete as it is. You don't need music there. The food and decor are enough." She turned to Louisa. "Don't you agree?"

Louisa held up both hands in the universal signal of surrender. "Don't ask me. No matter what I say, one of you will be annoyed. How am I supposed to choose between my sister and my husband?" She turned to Burke. "You're impartial. What do you think?"

"I'm the wrong person to ask, because I've never eaten there, but since you asked me, I think you should accept Joanna's decision."

She favored him with a grateful smile. "Thank you."

"He's a good man."

Joanna closed the piece of sheet music and looked across the room at her sister as the final note faded. Today, though she normally had other chores to perform, Emily had asked Joanna to play for her for a few minutes after they'd finished the breakfast dishes. The gleam in her eye when she'd made the request had told Joanna that Emily had motives other than listening to music. Her sister's comment confirmed it.

"Who?" Joanna feigned innocence.

"Burke, of course. I like the way he defended you, and unless I'm mistaken, he's attracted to you."

That was classic Emily, wanting everyone to be as happy as she was. In this case, she was mistaken.

"We're friends; that's all."

Her sister's lips twitched with amusement. "Maybe. Maybe not." She leaned forward to lessen the distance between them. "Mama would say I shouldn't pry, but I have to ask: have you thought about marrying again, especially now that you're expecting?"

When Joanna did not respond immediately, Emily continued. "Kurt wouldn't have wanted you to live the rest of your life alone, would he?"

"That's something we never discussed. He was the healthy one." Joanna was silent for a second, trying to recall the day they'd spoken of the future. Why wouldn't Kurt's face come into focus? She could picture blond hair and blue eyes, but the features were blurred.

"What's wrong?" Emily rose from the settee and wrapped her arms around Joanna's shoulders. "You look as if you've seen a ghost."

Joanna shook her head. "Only if ghosts have blank faces." She shook her head again, trying to make sense of what had happened. "What's wrong with me, Emily? It's only been a few months, but I can't remember what Kurt looked like. I wish I had a daguerreotype of him. What will I tell my child when he asks about his father?" Though Louisa had reminded Joanna that babies came in two varieties, she was certain this child would be a boy.

Emily tightened her grip on Joanna's shoulders, trying to comfort her the way she had when they'd been children. "Perhaps Kurt's sister has one she can send you."

"That's a good idea. I'll ask Marta, but it still doesn't explain why I've forgotten so much. You remember what George looked like, don't you?"

To Joanna's surprise, Emily shuddered. "Unfortunately, yes."

"What do you mean, unfortunately?" Joanna shifted so that she was face-to-face with her sister. "George was the most handsome man I've ever seen. I think I fell in love with him—at least a little bit—the day I first saw him. All I could think about was how wonderful he was and how I hoped he'd ask me to marry him."

Oh, dear. Why had she said that? She'd never intended to let Emily know how foolish she'd been, how she'd been so infatuated that she'd done everything she could to gain George's attention, to prove that she was the Vaughn sister best suited to be his bride.

Emily's lips flattened in a gesture Joanna remembered from their childhood, one that meant she was trying to control her anger. Was she about to remind Joanna that the commandments said "thou shalt not covet"?

"I know it was wrong," Joanna said, trying to make amends, "but I was terribly jealous of you. You were leaving home to live a fairy tale, but my dream of happily-ever-after was shattered."

When Emily met Joanna's gaze, her eyes bore more pain than Joanna had ever seen. She took a deep breath, as if trying to calm herself, then said, her voice low and filled with anguish, "You may not believe it, but you were the fortunate one. There was no happily-ever-after."

"I never understood what George was doing in the saloon that night." Emily had revealed that he'd died in a saloon fight when they'd been married a little over a year. "I didn't know he was a drinker or a fighter."

"George's death was a blessing."

Speechless, Joanna simply blinked in astonishment. When she recovered the ability to speak, her voice sounded like a croak. "What do you mean?"

Emily sighed. "My life with George was far from happy. If it was a fairy tale, it was one of the gruesome ones."

Whatever Joanna had expected her sister to say, it wasn't that. She couldn't question the truth behind Emily's words because she hadn't been there, but Joanna didn't understand how everything could have changed so drastically. "You both looked so happy at your wedding."

"We were happy then," Emily admitted. "It took several months before I realized that George didn't love me. He loved the idea of blond, blue-eyed children. That's why he chose me, because I had blond hair. If you'd been the blond, you'd have been his bride."

The story was so preposterous that Joanna shook her head. "That can't be true."

"It was. All George wanted was a blond boy to carry on the family name."

"But you had no children."

Once again, Emily shuddered. "According to George, that was my fault. He claimed I was a bad wife and had to be punished." She wrapped her arms around her ribs and winced, as if remembering pain.

"Did he . . ." Joanna could not complete the sentence. The thought was too horrible to put into words.

Her sister had no such compunctions. "Hit me? Yes. Each month was worse than the one before." Emily's lips curled in a mirthless smile. "When the sheriff told me George had been killed, all I could think was that now the pain would stop."

"Oh, Emily." Joanna hugged her sister, wishing there were something she could do to erase the past. "I had no idea what you went through." She'd been heartbroken when Kurt died, grieving for the future they would never share, and had believed that Emily had felt the same bone-deep sorrow she had.

Her sister laid her head on Joanna's shoulder as she'd done when they were young women and Joanna's height had surpassed Emily's. "I didn't want anyone to know. Craig knows, of course, and I told Louisa." The pain that had shone from Emily's eyes had lessened. "You had your own loss to deal with, so I didn't want to burden you with my story, but I couldn't let you continue to think that George was a good husband. He wasn't."

Joanna tightened her hold on Emily. "I'm so sorry." Though the words felt inadequate, they were all Joanna could offer.

"It's over. Believe me, Joanna, every day I thank God that that part of my life has ended and that he brought Craig into my life. I tell him he's God's gift after the shadows, the man who showed me the meaning of true love."

"And soon you'll have a baby." For the first time since their conversation had begun, Joanna smiled. "George was wrong."

Emily's smile matched hers. "Yes, he was."

Chapter

Fifteen

"I'll probably be gone for a couple hours," Louisa told Burke as she picked up her black doctor's bag. "I need to check on two women. One of them likes to talk"—she paused and then added—"a lot. I suspect she's lonely."

"And you're a good conversationalist." Louisa was more gregarious than Joanna, who was reserved around people she didn't know well, preferring to express herself through her music as she was now.

"If you want, you can close the office when Joanna's finished. I doubt we'll have any patients. For some reason, Wednesdays are the least busy days of the week. That's why I schedule my midwife visits then."

"I'm in no hurry to leave." Now that Joanna had tuned the piano, ending the less than melodious hour while she tightened and loosened strings, pressing the same key so many times that Burke wanted to shout "enough," she was playing melodies. And, as often happened when she was at the keyboard, he found himself relaxing, becoming caught up in the music, feeling as he had as a child when his mother had read him stories that transported him to another world.

Louisa shrugged as she headed for the front door. "All right, then. It's your decision."

Burke settled back in the chair and closed his eyes, enjoying the music that was flowing through the office. Afterward, he couldn't have said how long he'd sat there. All he knew was that the doorbell's tinkle and the sound of heavy footsteps accompanied by moans startled him.

As the music stopped abruptly, Burke rushed into the hallway, his practiced eye assessing the visitor. Herb Oberle, the man whose gout he'd treated, clutched his right arm close to his body, the blood-soaked sleeve leaving no doubt what caused the moans.

"Right this way, Mr. Oberle." Burke ushered him into the examining room and helped him onto the table. "Let's see what's wrong."

"That dang fool mule done kicked me."

As he carefully removed the man's shirt, Burke kept his face impassive, though the sight of a bone protruding through Oberle's skin and the badly mangled flesh told him this would be no simple operation. "It looks like your mule did more than kick you."

Oberle winced as Burke swabbed blood from the area around the break, needing to confirm the extent of the injury. "That ornery critter sure did. He stomped on me." As he looked at the damage the mule had inflicted, which was more apparent now that Burke had wiped some of the blood away, he shuddered. "That hurts worse than the gout."

"It's a serious injury." Though he would never alarm a patient unnecessarily, Burke made it a practice not to minimize a condition.

The man whose livelihood revolved around brewing beer

gave Burke a look verging on despair. "You can save my arm, cain't you? I cain't work without it."

"I'll do my best." That was all Burke could promise. Any time a bone was broken, there was the possibility of complications, and compound fractures increased the probability of infection because of the punctured skin. Skin, one of Burke's professors had declared, was the body's first line of defense. When it was compromised by a cut or abrasion, infection was likely to result, and when skin was as badly damaged as Oberle's, the danger was multiplied.

"It will take a while to set your bone and stitch up the skin." Burke wouldn't tell his patient that the underlying tissue had been torn and would require many sutures if it was to heal. "I won't lie to you. This will be painful. That's why I'm going to give you some chloroform. It'll put you to sleep and make the procedure easier for both of us."

Oberle shook his head vehemently. "I don't want that."

"Mr. Oberle, you need it. Setting your arm will be painful. So will repairing your skin."

"Nope." Another shake accompanied the refusal. "Don't want none of that. Doc Sheridan done give me some when I broke my leg. Made me sicker than a dog."

Burke nodded slowly, acknowledging his patient's fears. "He may have given you too much. The right amount should not make you ill."

"Don't want none. Do you hear me?" Oberle's voice had risen to a shout.

"Yes, sir, I do." Though Burke disagreed, he would not gainsay his patient. The man had a right to refuse sedation, even though it would make Burke's job more difficult.

"I won't give you any chloroform, but you need to do your best not to move when I'm pulling your bones back together." Burke raised his own voice to ensure that Oberle understood the gravity of the situation. "Close your eyes and try to relax."

"Promise you'll save my arm."

"Promise me, Burke. Promise you won't leave her." Edna's voice echoed through Burke's brain, reminding him how the worst twenty-four hours of his life had begun. He'd given her his promise, only to have it thrown back at him the next morning. *"You promised,"* Edna had shrieked. *"It's your fault. All your fault."*

Wrenching himself back to the present, Burke looked at his patient. The man's fear was palpable, making him wish he could provide a guarantee. But he could not. "I'll do my best," he repeated. That was all he could promise.

As his patient closed his eyes, soft music began to fill the office. While he cleansed the arm and prepared to realign the pieces of bone, Burke kept an eye on Oberle's condition, wishing he'd been able to sedate him. Though Oberle was accustomed to pain from his gout, this would not be a pleasant experience.

To Burke's relief, the man began to relax, and while it was evident that he felt pain when Burke positioned the bone and even more when he sutured the skin, Oberle's reaction was less violent than it had been during Burke's initial examination, and by the time the cast had hardened, his patient was laughing as he regaled Burke with a story of how his mule—the same one that had broken his arm today—had overturned and then drunk a jug of beer.

"I reckon he was gettin' his revenge on me," Oberle said as he climbed off the table and prepared to leave. "Thanks, Doc. This weren't as bad as I was expectin'."

It could be coincidence, but Burke didn't believe that for a minute. Watching Oberle's remarkable calm reminded him of the story in the Bible when David played his harp to soothe Saul's spirit. Never before had Burke seen evidence of music's therapeutic power, but he knew that was what he'd witnessed today. Joanna's talent was a gift from God, a gift she'd shared with Herb Oberle.

"I'm happy to see you again," the proprietor of Ma's Kitchen said as Joanna and Burke entered the restaurant, "but I'm sorry to say that I haven't remembered anything more about your uncle."

Burke smiled at the heavyset woman whose snub nose gave her a slightly mischievous look, even when she was at her most serious. "Thank you for trying, but that's not why we're here. Joanna and I wanted to celebrate something, and dinner at Ma's seemed like the best way to do it."

If Mrs. Tabor had been an insect, her antennae would have been vibrating. As it was, an inquisitive expression crossed her face, telling Joanna she wouldn't rest until she'd discovered the cause for celebration.

"Certainly." Mrs. Tabor nodded as she led them to a table near the front window. "Louisa prefers this spot, so I thought you might like it too." She waited until they were seated, then leaned forward, as if they were conspirators. "I suppose I shouldn't, but I'm going to be a nosy old woman and ask what you're celebrating."

Joanna did her best to hide her smile, letting Burke respond. "Joanna helped me with a patient this afternoon."

"You did?" Mrs. Tabor studied Joanna as if seeking evidence that she'd developed new skills. "I thought Louisa was the one who did the doctoring."

"She is. All I did was play the piano." Joanna still had trouble believing Burke's contention that it had made a difference, but he was convinced it had, just as he was convinced that God's prompting was the reason she'd decided to tune the piano today.

"I didn't do much, but I'd never turn down an opportunity to eat here." The number of times the Vaughn family had dined at Ma's while Joanna was growing up could be counted on one hand, making this a treat.

Apparently satisfied with the story, Mrs. Tabor straightened her spine. "I'm serving meatloaf and baked fish tonight. There's spice cake for dessert."

"Which do you recommend?" Burke asked her.

Before the restaurateur could respond, the sound of two men arguing caused everyone to stare at them.

"Excuse me for a moment." Mrs. Tabor strode across the room. Though her words were not audible, her posture left no doubt that she would not tolerate such behavior, and within seconds, one man stormed out, leaving the other to finish his meal.

"I'm sorry you had to hear that," Mrs. Tabor said when she returned to Joanna and Burke's table. "I assure you that that's an unusual occurrence." She paused for a second, then shrugged. "Maybe there was a reason that happened, because it jogged my memory. The only time I can recall an outburst like that was when your uncle lived here. He normally ate at the Albrights', but he came here one night. The next thing I knew, he and Malcolm Alcott were shouting at each other. Everyone knew Malcolm had a temper, but Clive was so mild-mannered that it was the talk of the town for the next few days."

Burke's expression said he was as intrigued by this new revelation about his uncle as Joanna was. "I don't suppose anyone knew what the fight was about."

Mrs. Tabor shook her head. "You're right about that, Burke. Both men claimed it was nothing more than a friendly dispute. Friendly." She scoffed. "If you'd been here, you'd have known it was anything but friendly. Now, have you decided whether you want meatloaf or fish?"

Joanna had no difficulty choosing. "I'll have the fish. That's one thing Emily doesn't like to cook." She considered removing the bones too much work.

When Burke ordered the same, Mrs. Tabor returned to the kitchen.

"I wish we knew more about that argument." Though Joanna knew that everyone could be roused to anger if given enough provocation, the image of a public altercation did not jibe with the picture she'd formed of Burke's uncle.

"So do I, but since it was so long ago, it's unlikely the mayor recalls it."

"And even if he did, he'd probably revise the story to make himself appear to have been the victim."

Burke chuckled. "I suspect you're right. Let's put that behind us and enjoy the evening. I'm glad we're here."

"So am I," Joanna told Burke. "Your invitation was kind, but it wasn't necessary. Playing the piano is a joy for me, not a chore."

"Did you ever consider that I might simply have wanted an excuse to have supper with you?"

The question took her aback. When Joanna shook her head, Burke said, "I did. I thought we might both benefit from a change in our routine. As much as I enjoy your sister's cooking, meals at Finley House can be a bit . . ."

He paused, perhaps searching for the correct adjective.

"Loud?" Joanna volunteered. Though she'd never admit it to Emily, there were times when the noise overwhelmed her. Perhaps it was because her companions for over a year had been adults. Noah and at times Beulah were a far cry from her sedate grandmother and the dignified men who'd taught her. Still, she had no right to complain or even comment, because Finley House was Emily's now. Joanna lived there, but even though it was the same building that had been her home for most of her life, it no longer felt like her home. It was Emily and Craig's.

"Loud?" Burke shrugged. "I was going to say exuberant, although meals can't be exuberant. It's the people eating those meals."

Joanna waited until Mrs. Tabor had set their meals before them before she responded. "Emily tells me Beulah has become more talkative in the past few weeks. She's not sure why, but Craig says she's no longer the last one to volunteer an answer at school. As for Noah, from what Mrs. Carmichael has said, he's always been determined to make his opinions known."

Burke took a bite of the fish and declared it delicious. "Yours is a lively household, no doubt about it. That probably won't change much when Louisa and Josh move out."

"And then we'll have Emily's baby and not too long afterward mine." It should have felt awkward discussing pregnancies with a man who wasn't her husband, but it didn't. Though she couldn't explain why, nothing about Burke conformed to Joanna's idea of normal interactions with a member of the opposite sex. She was more relaxed with him than she'd been with any man, including Kurt.

"When is your baby due?"

"Louisa says early May. Why?"

Burke's smile warmed her more than the bite of piping hot fish she'd just swallowed. "I had another reason for inviting you to dine."

"An ulterior motive?" The almost flirtatious tone of her voice surprised Joanna. She wasn't a flirt, never had been, and yet tonight she sounded a bit like one. Oh, how she hoped Burke hadn't noticed.

Fortunately, when he answered, there was no sign that he'd misconstrued her question. "You could call it that, although I prefer to say it's my second motive. You weren't in the room, so you couldn't see what was happening, but there's no question that Mr. Oberle's surgery was easier because you were playing the piano. Music soothed him almost as much as chloroform would have."

"Why didn't you give him chloroform?"

"He was adamant in his refusal. Even when I disagree, I won't go against a patient's wishes. The fact is, Joanna, you helped me immensely. My patient was calmer, and so was I."

Burke's expression was solemn. "Here's my second reason for inviting you to have supper with me: I wondered whether you'd be willing to do it again. You know Louisa and I don't treat serious injuries every day, but I believe your music would also be beneficial during less critical procedures. I could use your help, and when she sees how effective your music is, I'm confident Louisa will want you to continue after I leave."

Burke wasn't finished. "I know you refused Craig and Josh's suggestions, but I hope you'll consider mine. You don't have to answer immediately. All I ask is that you consider it."

Joanna took a deep breath, trying to settle her roiling thoughts. Though the reminder that Burke would be leaving had turned the previously delicious fish to dust in her mouth, her heart had soared at his suggestion. Playing for patients was something she'd never considered, a far cry from performing on a concert stage, and yet . . .

As she took another breath, the memory of her father reminding his congregation that God had given each of them a talent but allowed them to choose how they used that talent flashed through her brain. Father's sermon had included the story from Matthew of the three servants who'd been given talents and how two of them had invested wisely. Joanna did not want to be the one who'd done nothing with her talent, incurring the master's wrath.

She thought of her time at the sanatorium. Would her suffering have been reduced if there'd been music? Perhaps. Perhaps that was why the prospect of being able to lessen someone's pain filled her heart with hope and a sense of rightness.

"I don't need more time to think about it," she told Burke. "My answer is yes. You're a wonderful doctor. If you believe my music can help you, I'll play for you and your patients whenever you need me."

Burke's smile left no doubt that he was happy. So was she.

Chapter

Sixteen

"I'm glad you could come," Gertrude said as she ushered Joanna into her parlor two days later. "I wanted us to have some time alone. You've been home for weeks now, and I haven't heard about what happened in Europe and how you met your husband."

She gestured toward the plate of spiced cookies and the two glasses of buttermilk on the table. "Help yourself. Even my mother says my cookies are good."

They were. Joanna nibbled one and complimented her hostess before she said, "The first months in Europe were wonderful. I learned so much from Herr Ridel and the masters he persuaded to teach me."

"I'm not surprised. I knew that if you had the right teacher, you could become an excellent musician. Minerva Heppel tried, but she's not a gifted teacher."

While it was true that Miss Heppel could not compare to the musicians Joanna had met in Europe, she had given Joanna a good foundation, a fact that she pointed out to Gertrude.

"Your loyalty is admirable, Joanna, even if a bit misplaced."

When Joanna refused the offer of another cookie, Gertrude pushed the plate aside. "Now, tell me about your husband. I heard you met him at the sanatorium. Was he a patient?"

Joanna shook her head. "His sister was. Kurt was there to visit her."

"And you fell in love at first sight." Gertrude put down her glass to meet Joanna's gaze. "It feels like a miracle when that happens, doesn't it?"

Though Gertrude spoke as if from personal experience, she'd known Thomas for years before she married him, and rumor had it that he'd proposed more than once. If it had been love at first sight, why hadn't they married sooner?

Joanna doubted her former teacher would appreciate being questioned about the apparent discrepancy, and so she did not. Instead, she said, "I didn't think of it as a miracle, but Kurt's love felt like a gift." And now the memory of the time they'd spent together seemed like a dream or a story she'd read, not something that had happened to her. If it weren't for the child she was carrying, she might have doubted she'd ever been married.

Gertrude nodded vigorously. "His love was a gift, no question about that. First love is special." She paused to take a sip of buttermilk. "I heard you and Burke had supper at Ma's the other night."

"We did." It was clear that Gertrude's curiosity had been piqued, so Joanna obliged her. "He wanted to thank me for playing the piano while he set a patient's arm."

"Herb Oberle."

There were no secrets in Sweetwater Crossing. "Yes. He also asked if I'd consider playing while he and Louisa treat other patients."

To Joanna's surprise, Gertrude frowned. "Music won't sway him. Minerva tried that and failed."

What on earth was Gertrude talking about? Miss Heppel

had barely spoken to Burke, and he'd never heard her play anything other than Sunday hymns. How could that possibly sway him, and—more importantly—why would Miss Heppel want to sway him?

Joanna's confusion must have shown, because Gertrude gave her head a self-deprecating shake. "Please excuse me. Sometimes my mind wanders. What I meant to say was that Burke could turn a girl's head. I hope you won't let that happen, because you'd be making a mistake if you married him. Second loves can never compare to the first, and second marriages are always disappointing."

Gertrude was speaking the way she had in the schoolroom when she'd declared that two times two equals four. That was an incontrovertible fact. Her view of second loves and second marriages was not. Gertrude was wrong.

"I think you're mistaken." There was no question that Emily's second marriage was vastly better than her first, and Kurt had told Joanna their marriage was happier than his to Irmgard. Gertrude had no need to know that. Instead, Joanna said, "My parents were very happy together, and it was a second marriage for both of them."

"Are you certain they were happy? I heard the only reason they married was because each of them had a child. Your mother had Emily, your father you. They didn't want to raise them alone, so they married." Gertrude took a short breath, then continued. "I can't condemn them. Giving children two parents is an admirable reason to enter into matrimony a second time, but your situation is different. You have no children, and so you'd be making a mistake if you married again."

Knowing that her secret would not remain secret for much longer, Joanna shook her head. "My situation's not so different, Gertrude. I'm expecting a baby next spring."

"You are?" Gertrude stared at her for a long moment, as if assuring herself that Joanna was telling the truth. "I shouldn't admit it, but I envy you. All I wanted was his baby, but it wasn't meant to be."

Remembering that Louisa had mentioned Gertrude losing a baby last spring, Joanna started to express her sympathy, but her former teacher forestalled her.

"Be careful, Joanna. That's a precious gift you're carrying. A baby is even more precious than a man's love."

⌒

"You're a wonderful doctor." Try though he might to dismiss them, Joanna's words lingered in Burke's memory along with the warmth in her expression when she'd uttered them. She might believe it was true, but she wouldn't have said that if she knew what he'd done.

It had been almost two full days since their supper at Ma's, two days of debating what he should do. Should he tell Joanna, knowing she'd never regard him in the same light, or should he let her continue to believe he was a better man than he was? Honesty won.

"Do you realize that I've been in Sweetwater Crossing for three weeks and I've never been to the park?" Burke waited until Joanna finished the piece she was playing before he spoke.

Louisa had closed the office early, saying any patients who needed them knew where to find them, and while she'd gone across the street to spend some time with Josh at the mercantile, Burke had returned to Finley House, determined that today would be the day he'd tell Joanna. He could have waited for their usual evening walk, but he wanted to see her face when she heard the story of the worst day of his life.

"You haven't been to the park?" Joanna appeared surprised. After a quick glance at the clock on the mantel, she rose. "Shall we go there now?"

While they strolled into the center of town and headed west on Main to reach the park, they spoke of ordinary things. Joanna mentioned her visit with Gertrude and her confusing reference to Miss Heppel, then listened while Burke recounted his discussion with Louisa regarding the best way to treat chicken pox.

It was only when they were seated on a bench far enough from the street that they'd have privacy that he said, "I brought you here for a reason."

"Do you have another ulterior motive?" Joanna's grin told him she was expecting something lighthearted.

Burke shook his head. "No ulterior motive, but I couldn't let you continue to harbor false impressions of me. You deserve to know what happened in Alabama."

The sparkle fled from Joanna's brown eyes. "Is this about the patient you couldn't save? I know that's been weighing heavily on you, even though I'm certain you did everything you could to save him."

If only that were true. "It's not that simple, Joanna. I wish it were true that I tried my best to save her, but I made a horrible mistake, and as a result a woman died."

Joanna's eyes widened and her breath caught as she struggled with his revelation. "You said it was a mistake."

"One that should not have happened."

She was silent for a moment before she said, "Why don't you tell me everything? You don't need to tell me her name if you don't want to."

That was Joanna, worrying about his divulging something he shouldn't. "It doesn't matter now. Her name was Mrs. Arnold, and she was Edna's mother."

"The woman you expected to be your mother-in-law."

Burke nodded. "We all knew that she was dying of cancer, but once Edna realized how much her mother wanted to see her married, she and I were determined that she'd live long enough to attend our wedding."

He paused, remembering how the feisty woman's health had declined much more rapidly than either he or Felix had expected and how she'd become a shadow of herself. "She was in such extreme pain that she needed morphine several times a day."

"My father relied on morphine when his war wounds grew too painful," Joanna said softly, "but he didn't need daily injections."

"He was fortunate. Edna's mother would rally occasionally, but the day Edna broke our engagement, she took a turn for the worse. We brought her into the infirmary so I could give her morphine during the night."

Burke took a deep breath, not wanting to continue but knowing he had to. "The last thing Edna said to me that night was, 'Don't leave my mother alone.' I promised her I wouldn't."

A bird settled on the branch of a nearby tree, its song so beautiful that it seemed to be saying, "God's in his heaven— All's right with the world." Both Robert Browning and the bird were wrong. All was not right, at least not in Burke's world. He wasn't certain it would ever be.

"I stayed awake all night, not wanting to leave Mrs. Arnold's side, but after I gave her another injection just before dawn, once I saw she was sleeping peacefully, I went outside to clear my head. When I returned, Edna was there screaming because her mother was dead."

The tears that shone in Joanna's eyes told Burke how deeply the story was affecting her. "I don't understand. Why do you believe you were responsible for her death?"

"Because I gave her twice as much morphine as I should have. I was so tired that I didn't write the amount I'd dispensed on the chart we kept by her bed, but when Felix and I checked our supply later that day, there was no question that double the normal amount was gone. I must have been more tired than I realized, because I would never have done that knowingly, but there was no undoing it. Mrs. Arnold was dead, and it was my fault."

"It was an accident, a tragic mistake." Joanna's voice trembled with emotion, becoming stronger as she said, "You can't let that overshadow all the good you've done. You're kind and caring, and I stand by what I said at Ma's. You're a wonderful doctor."

Joanna was the one who was kind and caring, but while it would be easy to accept her praise, Burke could not. "I'm not a wonderful doctor, Joanna. Because of me, a woman died."

She shook her head. "How can you be so certain that that wasn't part of God's plan? You said Mrs. Arnold was in extreme pain. Perhaps he used what you consider a mistake to end her suffering."

It was Burke's turn to be astonished. "Do you really believe that?"

"If my father were still alive, he'd tell you that God's ways are not ours. He might also quote Romans 8:28."

Burke wracked his brain, trying to recall the verse she'd cited. "Is that the one about all things working for good?" When Joanna nodded, he shook his head. "I wish I could believe that, but—"

Joanna wouldn't let him complete his sentence. "Believe it, Burke. Believe it."

He stared at her for a long moment, wanting to accept the comfort she was offering, wishing he deserved it.

"Believe it, Burke." Joanna reached for his hand and laid hers on top of it, as if her touch would convince him even if her words did not.

The bird whose song had seemed to mock him continued to trill, but this time Burke heard only the beauty. A week ago, even a day ago, he wouldn't have thought it possible, but the warmth of Joanna's expression as well as the earnestness of her voice cracked the shell he'd erected around his heart, and for the first time since that awful morning, Burke caught a glimpse of hope.

Chapter

Seventeen

Midnight. Joanna frowned as she looked at her watch. She should have been asleep hours ago, but the memory of Burke's anguish when he'd told her what had happened to Edna's mother and the blame he'd accepted kept her tossing and turning. When she'd finally admitted that she wouldn't sleep, she'd lit her lamp and attempted to read, but the novel that she'd found fascinating yesterday held no appeal tonight.

Poor Burke! Joanna's heart ached at the thought of what he'd endured. Burke would never deliberately harm a patient. It wasn't simply that he would have been violating his Hippocratic oath. He would also have been betraying his own innate integrity.

She could understand Edna's grief, but where was Burke's partner in all this? The fact that Burke did not want to return to Alabama made Joanna believe that their friendship had been irrevocably damaged, and that was almost as tragic as Mrs. Arnold's death.

She closed her eyes and said a silent prayer that Burke would find some peace in what she'd told him. It was important—no, it was essential—that he forgive himself.

She wouldn't refer to the conversation again, because that might revive memories Joanna hoped he would put aside, but if Burke did, she would do her best to reassure him. Even if they never spoke of it again, she would do everything she could to show Burke that she trusted him. More than that, she wanted him to know that she cared for him. Deeply.

༉

"Did something happen over the weekend?"

Della's question made Burke blink in surprise. His honorary aunt had waylaid him—that was the only word to describe what had happened—when he'd left his room and invited him into hers. Now they were seated on her veranda when he would have preferred to be downstairs waiting for Emily to serve breakfast.

"Why do you think something happened?" Answering a question with another one sometimes distracted Della enough that she'd go on a tangent.

"Because you've looked more relaxed the last couple days. I haven't seen you this much at peace since before Felix came to Samuels." She pursed her lips. "I never did think it was a good idea to have two doctors."

This was the first time Della had expressed any concerns. "Why didn't you tell me that before I agreed that he should be my partner?"

Della's smile was wry. "Would you have listened to me?"

"Probably not. Felix was my friend as well as a good doctor. It made sense to have him as my partner."

"Even though he stole your girl?"

A month ago, Burke might have flinched at the memory. Today he only shrugged. "Felix may have done me a favor. If Edna was so easily stolen, she wasn't the right woman for me."

"On that we're agreed." Della laid her hand on Burke's and gave it a small squeeze. "I know you well enough to say that you won't confirm this, but I suspect that the reason you're finally at peace is because you've found the right woman . . . right here in Sweetwater Crossing."

It was a quiet Monday morning, one month and a day since she'd returned and since Burke and Della had arrived in Sweetwater Crossing, a month that had brought changes Joanna had not anticipated, including the new life nestled beneath her heart. She smiled as she walked south on Center Street, thinking of the changes that were yet to come.

Her morning sickness had ended, and her body had begun to change shape. Soon she'd need to let out seams or buy new clothes. Gertrude had offered her some of her larger shirtwaists, but the skirts she'd worn when she was expecting her baby were inches too short for Joanna. It was time to visit the town's dressmaker. If Thelma Scott had nothing ready-made, she'd sew what Joanna needed, but there was one stop on Joanna's list before she went there.

"Good morning." Della rose from behind her desk when Joanna entered the library. "Of course you're welcome to browse, but I'm surprised to see you. I thought you'd be with Louisa and Burke."

"They're out calling on patients." Which gave Joanna time for this much overdue visit, since Miss Heppel wasn't expecting her until this afternoon. "I feel remiss that I haven't been here before. I have no excuse."

"And no particular reason to come. After all, you have more books at home than we do here, and if you simply wanted to talk, there are plenty of opportunities at Finley House."

Joanna smiled at Della's attempt to make her feel comfortable. It was no wonder that the library was far busier than it had been when Emily's friend Alice had been in charge. Della's warm welcome and genuine desire to help others would encourage almost everyone to return.

"But I wanted to come, if only to see what changes you've made. Mrs. Carmichael said I wouldn't recognize the library."

Della chuckled. "As you can see, that's an exaggeration. All I did was rearrange a few things."

The shelves that had been placed perpendicular to the back wall now lined it, making it easier to read the titles and providing space for the biggest change, a small seating area designed to invite patrons to linger.

"These chairs and table are new." The few nicks and scratches on the low table did not detract from its appeal but confirmed that it was meant to be used. So did the slightly worn arms on the upholstered chairs. The overall effect was as welcoming as Della herself.

"I found them in what had been Alice's living quarters and believed they'd be better served here," Della explained. "I thought patrons might want to read a few pages before borrowing a book. And when we're not busy, some stay for a bit of conversation. I never thought a library had to be a silent place."

"I agree. Do many people come just to talk to you?"

"Some." When a blush stole onto Della's face, Joanna suspected that Harold was one of them. The rumor mill had reported that he was a frequent visitor to the library, provoking speculation that he was interested in more than books.

Harold was not the reason Joanna had come. She walked to the shelves, fingered a few titles, trying to decide where to start.

"You're not looking for a book, are you?"

Joanna turned. "No. I wanted to talk to you away from Finley House."

"Then come sit down, and we'll talk." When they were both

seated in the comfortable chairs, Della said, "Let me guess. You're going to apologize because you haven't discovered what happened to Clive."

Was the woman clairvoyant? "How did you know?"

"Burke and I had a similar discussion a few weeks ago. I'll tell you what I told him—being here has accomplished more than I expected. Living in Finley House has given me the opportunity to say goodbye to Clive."

Della fiddled with the watch she kept pinned to her bodice, something Joanna had noticed she did when she wanted a moment to think. "I realized I'd never done that. Oh, I knew he wasn't coming back, but seeing the town he loved and meeting some of the people he knew has been good for me. Now I can truly accept that Clive was part of my past and that it's time to decide what I want my future to be." Her eyes reflected uncertainty. "Does that make sense?"

"It does. Listening to you makes me realize that I should do the same thing. Nothing will bring Kurt back. I need to plan for the future."

Della's relief that she'd been understood was obvious. She reached out and touched Joanna's hand briefly. "It seems to me you've already begun to do that. Helping Louisa and Burke's patients is a wonderful use of your talent. And, of course, you have your baby to look forward to. Babies are such a joy." Della's eyes grew misty. "I would love to hold him or her."

"I hope you'll be here to help me spoil him." Joanna smiled, picturing Della and Mrs. Carmichael serving as substitute grandmothers. "I saw you raise your eyebrows when I said 'him.' Emily and Louisa keep reminding me that the baby could be a girl, but I'm convinced I'm having a boy."

This time it was Joanna who extended her hand to touch Della. "I may be speaking out of turn, but I don't believe I'm the only one who wants you to become a permanent resident of Sweetwater Crossing." She paused, wondering whether she should continue, then decided she might as well. "I've heard that our minister is a frequent visitor here and that he stays longer than most."

Another blush colored Della's cheeks. "I was afraid people would talk, but Harold said we shouldn't worry about gossip. He and I discuss books, flowers, favorite foods, even local politics. The subject doesn't matter. Simply being with him is invigorating." Della bit her bottom lip in a gesture that confirmed her uneasiness. "Oh, Joanna, I sound like an infatuated schoolgirl, don't I?"

Joanna shook her head. "I'd say you sound like a woman who's attracted to a very good man."

Once again, Della appeared relieved by Joanna's words. "It's hard to explain, but the way I feel reminds me of when Clive and I were courting. It's similar and yet different, perhaps because I'm old now."

"Not old. Older, more mature, and probably wiser." It seemed strange to be giving romantic advice to an older woman, yet another example of how different everything was since Joanna had returned to Sweetwater Crossing.

Della stared at the door, perhaps wondering whether Harold would soon open it. "There are times when I believe what I feel is love, but I'm too old for that, aren't I?"

"Definitely not." Joanna infused her words with conviction, wanting to reassure this woman who'd lost her first love. No matter what Gertrude said, second loves could be wonderful. "We're never too old to fall in love." She paused for a second, giving Della time to absorb her declaration. "You didn't ask, but I'll volunteer my opinion anyway. I think Harold feels the same way about you. I saw the attraction between you two the day he had Sunday dinner at Finley House and flooded his plate with gravy because he was looking at you and not the potatoes. From what I can tell, that attraction has only grown."

190

Looking both unconvinced and hopeful, Della stared at Joanna as if trying to assess her sincerity. "Do you really think so?"

"I do."

⁓

"I'm glad you were with me today," Louisa said when she and Burke returned to the office. "This was the first time I've encountered a rash like Mrs. Miller's."

Louisa removed her hat and took her seat behind the desk, relaxing for the first time since they'd left the saloon owner's home. Though she'd done her best to maintain a neutral expression while Burke assessed their patient, he'd seen the tension in Louisa's shoulders when she'd realized that the training she'd received hadn't prepared her for today.

"I wouldn't tell her, but that was the most severe case of lichen I've seen. Usually there's only a slight fever, and the pimples are not so inflamed." Burke settled into the chair across from Louisa and crossed his legs at the ankles. Like Louisa, he was glad to be back here. While it was satisfying to alleviate someone's pain, Burke appreciated a respite between patients.

"The zinc ointment should reduce the itching, and an alkaline bath each night will allow her to sleep more easily," he told Louisa. Mrs. Miller had summoned her because of the rash, which was accompanied by intense itching and stinging.

"Your treatments are better than the whiskey her husband prescribed." Now that they were away from the Miller residence, Louisa didn't attempt to hide her amusement at the thought that three shots of whiskey could cure a severe rash.

"I'll have you know that whiskey has its uses." Burke adopted a professorial tone. "Why, I've cleansed countless wounds with it."

"Yes, of course, but that's not what Mr. Miller suggested."

Louisa feigned lifting a glass to her mouth, then burst into laughter.

Burke shared her mirth. "What did you expect from a saloon owner? He believes whiskey should be imbibed."

"Just as Mr. Oberle believes beer is the only acceptable beverage. I'm surprised he didn't offer us any."

When they'd called on him and Mrs. Oberle before returning to town to see Mrs. Miller, Burke had been surprised by the pervasive smell of beer, though he'd seen no sign of any inside the house.

"I suspect Mr. Oberle realized that morning was too early for a glass of beer." Burke wouldn't tell Louisa that Herb Oberle had admitted that his gout had subsided after he stopped drinking beer and eating so many rich meats. He'd confided that to Burke while Louisa was examining his wife and had repeated his insistence that no one in Sweetwater Crossing know that he was doing nothing more than sampling each batch of beer to ensure that it met his standards.

"Maybe." Louisa sounded skeptical. "I'm glad I didn't have to refuse and insult him." She folded her hands and leaned forward on the desk, seemingly wanting to close the distance between them. "Thanks to you, I'm learning so much. Until today, I thought lichen was something that grows on a rock."

"That's one definition. Mrs. Miller's rash is another."

Louisa settled back in the chair. "Are you as pleased with Mr. Oberle's healing as you told him?"

"I am. Even though I did everything I could to disinfect the area, there's always a risk of infection with compound fractures and as much tissue damage as he sustained. Fortunately, there was no sign of infection today, and he was able to wiggle his fingers."

Louisa wiggled hers, mimicking Burke's patient. "Mr. Oberle seemed amused when you told him he might be able to predict storms once his radius healed. That's something I hadn't heard."

"That may not happen to everyone, but it does to me. The site of my break aches when the weather is changing." Burke rubbed his right forearm, which he'd dubbed his human barometer. It had been close to two decades since he'd fractured it, but though the healing had been complete, he still had periodic reminders of the injury.

Louisa's expression turned serious as she watched Burke. "How did you break your arm? I doubt a mule crushed it."

"Fortunately, my family had no mules. I can't imagine what my mother would have done with one as ornery as the Oberles'." After Burke had completed his examination, Herb Oberle had insisted on introducing him and Louisa to the animal that had caused such damage.

"My explanation is less colorful. I fell out of a tree. I was hiding from my sisters because they wanted me to attend a tea party with them and their dolls and lost my balance. They both laughed, because they thought a broken arm was an appropriate punishment for trying to avoid them."

"But you weren't laughing."

"No, I wasn't. I wouldn't let them see me cry even though the pain was pretty bad, but I came close to it. Once the cast was on, the worst part was being unable to fish for six weeks."

"You know how to fish?" Louisa appeared impressed by what Burke considered an ordinary skill.

"Doesn't everyone?"

"Not my family. The fish in our creek are too small to eat, so no one bothered to teach us." She gave Burke an appraising look. "I know there are larger fish in the river around five miles from here. If you really want to fish, you might want to take Joanna with you. She needs to do something more than play the piano."

Burke nodded. A little exercise and fresh air would benefit Joanna. Time with her would benefit him. "I may do that." And he knew where to start.

"I had an enlightening conversation with Della this morning," Joanna told Emily, who was buttering the top of the loaf of bread prior to putting it into the oven. She wouldn't mention the one she'd had with Miss Heppel, who appeared to have just heard about Joanna's playing while Burke treated Mr. Oberle.

"You can tell a lot about a man by how he feels about music," Miss Heppel had said. "Almost everyone finds the right melodies soothing, but there are exceptions. I knew Malcom wasn't the man for me when he told me all music sounded the same to him. How could I have even considered marrying a man like that?" Then, as if she'd said too much, she'd moved to the piano bench and invited Joanna to play a duet with her.

The comment had lasted only a few seconds, but it lingered in Joanna's memory. Was this what Gertrude had meant when she'd alluded to Miss Heppel's trying to sway a man with music?

Emily's chuckle brought Joanna back to the present. "I'm guessing what you and Della discussed had nothing to do with books."

"You're right. It didn't. I learned that what we thought was true: there's a definite attraction between her and our minister. I suspect all they need is a little nudge and we'll be hearing wedding bells."

"I'm good at nudging." After Emily slid the loaf into the oven, she turned back to Joanna. "I think I'll start by inviting Harold to have supper with us every Friday. That's an evening when not many parishioners would ask him, and we have an extra spot at the table those nights because Beulah's back on the farm. What do you think?"

"I think you're becoming a matchmaker."

"I've been called worse." Emily reached for the carrots she planned to add to tonight's stew and started to peel them. "We'll see whether I have a talent for it. Once we get them on the road to matrimony, there's another couple I want to nudge."

"Who's that?" Joanna wracked her brain, trying to think who would be Emily's next target. Thelma Scott? Emily had mentioned that the dressmaker was lonely. One of the widows?

Her sister smirked. "You and Burke."

Eighteen

"Are you sure you don't need to help Louisa today?" Joanna asked as Burke helped her into his carriage. While they'd been eating supper yesterday, he'd told her he had a surprise for her this morning and to wear her oldest dress. Both of her sisters pleaded innocence after Emily confirmed that as a widow Joanna did not need a chaperone, but Josh had winked at Burke when he'd issued the invitation, making her suspect he'd been involved in whatever Burke planned.

Curious and admittedly eager to see what Burke had in store for her, Joanna had donned a dark brown dress with a twice-turned hem, one she would not have worn in public had it not been for his recommendation. When she'd tried it on last night, she'd discovered that it was tight around her waist, and so she'd let out the seams, exposing darker fabric. Mama would not have approved, but Joanna's shawl covered the evidence of her alteration.

Burke settled onto the seat next to her and reached for the reins. "Louisa will be fine on her own. One of the things I've learned since I came here is that I don't need to work every minute of every day. Others are capable too."

The slightly acerbic tone told Joanna he was thinking of someone other than Louisa. "Including your partner."

"Former partner." When Joanna raised an eyebrow, Burke continued. "I received a letter from Felix yesterday saying he was having no difficulty handling all the patients now that Edna's helping him." As he guided the carriage past the town limits, Burke loosened his grip on the reins, apparently confident that the horse could be trusted not to run. "Reading that erased my last doubt. Whether or not Dr. Fielding accepts me as his assistant, I will not return to Alabama permanently. Even if Edna could forgive me, the town no longer needs me."

"You still haven't heard from Dr. Fielding?" Joanna knew how frustrating it could be to wait for a response. She hadn't received a letter from Marta since she'd been home, despite her sister-in-law's promise to write regularly, and while transatlantic mail took longer than posts from San Francisco, the delay made her worry about Marta's health.

"It's possible I'll never hear from him. Not everyone responds to each letter."

The discouragement she heard in Burke's voice made Joanna want to lighten his mood. "Have you been talking to my sisters? I was a horrible correspondent when I was gone."

He shook his head, but whether in response to her question or her statement wasn't clear. "Surely they understood when they learned how ill you'd been."

How Joanna wished that had been the only reason she hadn't written to her family. "It started before then. I was so caught up in my new life that nothing else seemed important. I don't think I sent my parents more than three letters before I caught scarlet fever." She bit her bottom lip, thinking of how her silence must have hurt them. "I never imagined that I wouldn't see either of them again."

This stretch of the road was straight, allowing Burke to take his eyes off it. "We can't change the past," he said, his green eyes solemn. "We can only go forward."

But had he? Though he'd seemed more relaxed since the day they'd spoken of Mrs. Arnold's death, Joanna suspected it was still weighing heavily on Burke.

"Going forward is what Della told me she'd resolved to do when we talked the other day." Joanna paused, unsure whether she should pose the next question. "Has she spoken to you about Harold?"

Burke seemed confused. "Not much. Why?"

"My sisters and I believe there's a romance brewing between them. How would you feel if she stayed here permanently?"

His response was immediate. "Happy for her. Other than the house she inherited, there's nothing tying Della to Samuels. She deserves a second chance at love, and Harold is a fine man."

"That's what we think too." Joanna studied the area they were passing, trying to imagine where Burke was taking them. "Are you sure you know where we're going? There's nothing out this way for miles and miles."

"That's not what Louisa said."

The mention of her sister's name surprised Joanna. "Louisa was part of this?"

"She gave me the idea. Josh helped with the matériel."

"Matériel? That sounds like we're going on a military excursion."

"No armies will be involved." As they rounded a bend and the sparkling surface of a slowly moving river was revealed, Burke guided the carriage off the road, stopping a few yards from the water.

Still puzzled, Joanna turned toward him. "There's nothing here but the Guadalupe."

"And fish, or so I've been told."

"We're going fishing?" His recommendation of old clothes

made sense if that was true, but there was a problem. A big one. "I don't know how to fish."

"So I've been told." Burke's lips quirked into a smile. "There's a first time for everything."

"So I've been told."

As she'd hoped, Burke laughed when she repeated his words. "I know there's such a thing as beginner's luck, but I hope you don't expect me to catch anything." He might not be disappointed, but Joanna hated the idea of any kind of failure. Even though she knew it was because of things outside her control, she felt as if she'd failed as a pianist and a wife.

Seemingly unaware of the depressing turn her thoughts had taken, Burke gave her a reassuring smile. "From what you've told me, the bigger problem would be if you catch something, since Emily doesn't like to cook fish."

"That's true, but what's the point of fishing if it isn't to catch something?"

"Fun," Burke said as he helped Joanna descend from the carriage. "Whether or not we catch anything, you'll have the fun of fishing. That was one of my favorite pastimes as a boy." A nostalgic smile lit his face. "Even though I was the youngest, I caught more fish than my sisters, because they never learned the first rule of fishing: you have to be quiet, or you'll scare the fish away."

"Wasn't it difficult not to talk to your sisters?" Joanna couldn't imagine Noah remaining quiet for any length of time, but Burke would have been older, so silence might not have been a problem.

He chuckled. "Sometimes I would make faces at them, but that only made them chatter more, so most of the time I just ignored them. As strange as it may sound, I find fishing both relaxing and exciting."

Burke reached into the back of the carriage and pulled out two rods and a covered pail that she assumed contained bait.

"What do you think of these? Josh told me they're the finest bamboo rods he's ever stocked."

Joanna eyed them and smiled. No wonder Josh had been so pleased by the prospect of today's outing. "Did he also tell you they're the only ones he'll ever stock? When he took over the mercantile, Louisa said he grumbled about some of the merchandise the Bentleys had bought, and these rods were among them. Josh claimed it would have been easier to sell an albatross than fancy fishing rods."

"These aren't albatrosses. Look at how flexible they are." Burke demonstrated that characteristic. "With the right bait, the fish will practically hook themselves." He grabbed both rods in one hand, the pail in the other, and began to walk toward the river, keeping his pace slow enough that Joanna had no problem staying at his side.

"That sounds like an exaggeration."

Burke's smile was wry. "Fishermen are infamous for that. Now, let's get you started." He handed one rod to Joanna, then stood on the bank and lifted his. "The first thing is to learn how to cast."

"Don't we need bait?"

"Not yet. Watch me." To Joanna's surprise, instead of flinging the rod forward, he tipped it up and backward, then flicked it forward, stopping when the hook rested on the water's surface.

"You make it look easy." But it wasn't. Joanna was certain of that.

"It isn't difficult. It simply takes some practice." Burke laid down his rod and moved to stand behind Joanna. "Let me show you how." He positioned her hands on the rod and line, then lifted her arms to demonstrate the correct motion.

There was nothing inappropriate about it. She'd been closer to men when she'd danced. And yet nothing—not even the waltzes that some still considered scandalous—had felt like this. With Burke's arms touching hers, his body so close that she could feel the heat radiating from it, she felt protected and, odd as it seemed, cherished.

Joanna took a deep breath, trying to settle her thoughts. This was nothing more than a fishing lesson, and yet all of her senses were heightened, making her wish the lesson would never end.

Two hours later, the man whose touch had scrambled Joanna's thoughts untangled the line that she'd caught in a tree for what felt like the hundredth time. "So, what do you think of fishing?" he asked.

"You were right. It was fun, but I wish I'd caught something."

"You did."

Joanna shook her head and tried to hide the smile at her catch. "An old shoe doesn't count. I'm convinced the fish don't like me."

"But I do. Doesn't that count?"

"It does."

❧

Joanna was more tired than she'd expected by the end of the day and wondered if Burke would object if she canceled their nightly walk. To her surprise, no one had mentioned the fishing excursion at supper, perhaps because Beulah might have thought she should have been included. But Beulah was no longer in the dining room. When Mrs. Carmichael and Della had taken Noah to the parlor, Beulah had joined them, claiming she wanted to read her new book to him. Now there were only six adults left.

Josh's gaze moved from Joanna to Burke. "I thought one of you would say something, but since you didn't, I have to ask. How did you like my bamboo rods?"

Burke kept his expression as solemn as if he were weighing in on a subject of great importance. "Mine was the best rod I've ever used." Joanna knew he wouldn't brag, but he'd caught

half a dozen fish, releasing each of them, since her attempts
had been unsuccessful.

"What about you, Joanna? Did you like the rod?"

"I have to agree with Burke. It was the best one I've ever
used." She paused for a second. "Of course, it was also the
only one I've ever used, but I had fun."

"Then the day was a success."

"I'd say so." Burke winked at Joanna. "Wouldn't you?"

"Yes." Unlike the fish that Burke had tossed back into the
river, the shoe she'd caught was drying in the barn, a souvenir
of her first fishing excursion.

When Josh and Louisa exchanged pleased looks, Craig
grinned. "I'm sure my wife is happy that you didn't bring her
any fish to clean and cook."

"He's right," Emily said. "I consider that a successful end to
my sister's introduction to fishing. But now that we're alone, I
have something for the six of us." She reached into her pocket
and withdrew four envelopes. "Joanna and Burke get individual
ones. Louisa, you and Josh have to share, as do Craig and I."
She handed Burke, Louisa, and Joanna theirs.

As she'd expected, Joanna's name had been inscribed on
the heavy cream-colored envelope. What she hadn't expected
was that rather than script, it had been written in calligraphy.

"I assume these are from Gertrude," Emily said, "since her
mother brought them over this afternoon."

Louisa fingered the envelope with her name and Josh's on
it. "I'd forgotten Gertrude knew calligraphy."

"She tried to teach us," Joanna reminded her sisters, "but
none of us could master it. It's true art like those Chinese characters she showed us."

Emily frowned. "I'd forgotten about them."

"So had I."

When both of her sisters appeared disappointed by their
memory lapses, Joanna attempted to reassure them. "The only

reason I remember is that I tried to find a similarity between the Chinese brushstrokes and musical notes."

"Did you?" Though she wouldn't have thought he'd be interested, Burke appeared to care about her response.

"No." Joanna opened the envelope and slid out a carefully written card. "Gertrude's invited us to supper Saturday evening." She bit her lip, debating whether to share her concern. "I know it would be rude to refuse, but even Gertrude admits that she doesn't excel at cooking."

Emily shrugged. "Even if she isn't the best cook, I'd appreciate an evening when I don't have to prepare the meal. And with all of you there, it should be fun."

"But not as much fun as fishing," Louisa quipped.

As she'd undoubtedly intended, everyone laughed.

When they reached what the sisters still referred to as the Albright ranch, although it was now Gertrude and Thomas Neville's home, Burke studied the building. Unlike Finley House with its three stories, this house had been constructed with only one floor. It was probably almost as large as Finley House, but instead of being designed to impress by standing tall, it sprawled across expansive grounds. This was a true Texas house, well-built but unpretentious.

Burke revised his opinion when Thomas ushered them indoors. Though the interior was more casual than Finley House and the Albrights' two-story home in town, the dining room displayed the same elegance that Burke had seen in Della's father's home: fine china, delicate crystal, heavy silver flatware, all arranged on a lace tablecloth that allowed the beauty of polished mahogany to shine through its intricate pattern. It was a room designed to impress guests.

Perhaps that was the reason the sisters had worn what Burke suspected were their finest gowns. Years of listening to his sisters discuss fashion told him that while not made of silk or satin, the lower necklines and lace trim proclaimed that these were not ordinary dresses. Emily kept a shawl wrapped around her, presumably to hide her expanding midsection, but Joanna's gown merely hinted at the new life she carried.

Their hostess, dressed in a gold gown with more ruffles than Burke had seen on a single garment, greeted them with a broad smile. "It's so nice to have you all back in town," Gertrude told the sisters as she hung their cloaks on a coat-tree. "Sweetwater Crossing wasn't the same without all three Vaughn girls here."

Joanna was the first to respond. "We each left for different reasons, but speaking for myself, I'm happy to have returned. My sisters have given me the support I needed." That was, Burke suspected, a reminder that while she had eschewed traditional mourning clothing, Joanna was still a recent widow.

Gertrude gave a short nod, then extended her hand to Burke. "Clive, I hope Miss Samuels doesn't mind that she wasn't invited tonight. I wanted the party to be for the younger generation."

Burke decided to ignore both her mistake with his name and the fact that Gertrude was part of the same generation as Della. "I'm sure she wasn't insulted. She and Mrs. Carmichael were planning to cook a simple supper with Noah."

Craig, who'd rested his hand on the back of Emily's waist, grinned. "They're brave women. My son is fascinated with the kitchen, but at three, he's hardly old enough to cook."

"What I heard was that he was supposed to tear the bread for bread pudding." Emily tipped her head up to smile at her husband. "He can't make too much of a mess doing that."

"Don't be so sure."

Having observed the state of Noah's plate when he finished supper, Burke suspected Craig's skepticism was well-founded.

After letting out what sounded suspiciously like a scoff, Gertrude led the way into the dining room, "We'll keep you here long enough for the older women to have the kitchen cleaned and ready for tomorrow's breakfast."

Once again, Burke was surprised by her reference to age. Mrs. Carmichael was indeed an older woman, but Della was almost the same age as Gertrude. Why was she placing so much emphasis on age?

As Emily had predicted, the evening was pleasant. Despite Joanna's concerns, the food was good, although it could not compare to Emily's cooking or the meals at Ma's Kitchen. The conversation was lively, ranging from Thomas's experiences as a rancher to the hope that the new minister would not change too many of the town's Christmas traditions. It was only when he saw Joanna stifle a yawn that Burke realized how much time had passed. He caught Emily's eye, then tipped his head toward Joanna, relaxing when she nodded and turned to Gertrude.

"This has been a delightful evening," she told their hostess, "but morning will come all too soon. Thank you for inviting us."

As everyone rose to make their farewells, Thomas cleared his throat. "Thank you for coming. This has been a special time for Gertrude and me. I can't remember when I've seen my wife so happy."

She touched her husband's hand, then let her gaze travel to each of her guests. Surely it was Burke's imagination that it lingered on him. "It has been special," she agreed. "I feel like I'm fifteen again."

Chapter

Nineteen

She shouldn't still be thinking about it, Joanna told herself as she turned onto Center Street the following Friday morning, heading for the post office. It had been almost a week since Gertrude's party. She, her sisters, and the three men had spent more than four hours at the Albright ranch, four enjoyable hours. Why then was she remembering the brief awkwardness when Gertrude had called Burke Clive?

After their initial shock at the resemblance between Burke and his uncle, no one else had made that mistake, but this wasn't the first time Gertrude had misspoken. Why? While it might have been a slip of the tongue for someone else, Gertrude had always been a stickler for accuracy. That was what bothered Joanna most. She wouldn't embarrass her former teacher by asking, but she was puzzled. Surely Gertrude was too young to be having the memory problems that sometimes plagued older people.

Fixing a smile on her face, she entered the post office, grateful to see that Mr. Winslow was engrossed in a conversation with another customer. If today was like other days, he'd attend to her, then return to his discussion, sparing Joanna a long conversation about topics no more interesting than how many eggs Mrs. Winslow's chickens had laid.

"Good morning, Mr. Winslow." Joanna approached the counter. "Do you have anything for me or my family?"

The postmaster grinned. "Sure do. There's three letters for Mr. Porter and one that came all the way from Europe for you."

Her earlier discomfort faded, and Joanna's heart soared at the prospect of a letter from Marta. "Nothing for Dr. Finley?" She knew he'd been waiting anxiously for a response from Dr. Fielding, and she'd hoped that it had arrived.

"Nope. Not today."

Biting back her disappointment, Joanna accepted the mail and headed for home. Rather than return the way she'd come, she turned east on Main and then north on East, completing what she thought of as the circuit.

She was walking briskly, trying to imagine what would be in Marta's letter, when she passed Miss Heppel's home. To Joanna's surprise, the piano teacher stood on her front porch.

"Joanna." Miss Heppel's voice carried clearly. "I was just thinking about you, and here you are. I know it's not Monday and you're probably busy, but won't you come in for a few minutes?"

Though she was eager to read Marta's letter, it could wait, and something in Miss Heppel's tone told Joanna this was more than a casual request. "Certainly."

When they entered the small house where Joanna had spent so many hours trying to perfect her playing, Miss Heppel led her directly into the parlor. "I should offer you a cup of tea or coffee, but I was hoping you'd play a duet with me. I woke this morning with a need—that's the only way I can describe it—to play Schubert's Fantasia with you. Will you indulge me?"

"Of course. You know how much I like that piece." And

perhaps the pleasure of playing a duet with her former teacher would banish the last of Joanna's malaise.

When they reached the final chord, Joanna's spirits had risen along with the music, and so when Miss Heppel suggested they play it again, Joanna agreed.

"Thank you, Joanna." Miss Heppel closed the sheet music, signaling there would not be another encore. "I appreciate this more than you'll ever know. My thoughts were turbulent this morning. Now they're settled."

So were Joanna's. Music had healed or at least soothed both of them. If Burke were here, he might have declared this an example of the power of music to do what medicine could not.

Joanna looked at Miss Heppel, trying to gauge her mood. "Is there anything I can do for you?"

Her former teacher shook her head. "My dear, you've done more than anyone could expect. You've shared your time and talent with me. That's a gift I'll cherish as long as I live."

A wistful expression crossed her face, turning her eyes as dark as storm clouds. Though Joanna had seen Miss Heppel in pensive moods before, this was different, more intense, evidence that something had disturbed her this morning.

"I always enjoy playing with you." Joanna felt the need to reassure the older woman. "I wish we'd done it when I was taking lessons."

Instead, Miss Heppel had insisted Joanna learn both parts of a duet, telling her that would prepare her to play it one day when she found the right partner. It was only since she'd returned and she and Miss Heppel had played together that she'd experienced the full beauty of the pieces.

"You weren't ready then. My playing would have overwhelmed yours." Once again, a fleeting look that might have been regret marred Miss Heppel's normally beautiful face. "You needed time to deepen your understanding of human

208

emotions. As tragic as some of your experiences were, they molded you into a mature, caring woman." She shook her head. "I don't know what's gotten into me this morning. I never used to be so maudlin. I apologize, Joanna. You have other things to do, and so do I." She rose. "Thank you again for indulging me."

It was a clear and almost abrupt dismissal, something Joanna had not experienced before. "It was my pleasure," she said as she walked toward the door. "Goodbye."

When she entered Finley House a few minutes later, Joanna was still reflecting on her time with Miss Heppel. Mama used to say that changes in the weather affected people's emotions. Perhaps that's why both Joanna and her teacher had been in uncharacteristic moods today, for there was no question that their visit had been unlike any other. What she needed now was a cup of coffee, a chance to read Marta's letter, and some ordinary conversation with her sister.

She entered the kitchen, reassured by the sight of Emily kneading bread dough. Mrs. Carmichael must have taken Noah for a walk to give Emily a few minutes without interruptions.

Emily quirked an eyebrow as she looked up. "Mr. Winslow must have been especially talkative today. I thought you'd be back half an hour ago."

On an ordinary day, she would have. "He wasn't the cause of the delay. Miss Heppel saw me walking by and asked me to play a duet with her."

"And you couldn't refuse."

"No, even though I wanted to open Marta's letter the minute I saw it."

Emily poured a cup of coffee and handed it to Joanna. "I won't interfere, because I know you've been anxious to hear from her."

"Thank you. I have." After she'd taken a sip of coffee, Joanna slit the envelope and withdrew a single sheet of paper, quickly scanning it. Since Marta's English was far better than Joanna's German, she'd written in Joanna's native language.

"Good news?" Emily asked when Joanna slid the letter back into the envelope.

"Yes. The doctors have declared her cured, so Marta's going back to Germany. She promised to write again once she's at home."

"You look as if something's bothering you." Emily formed the dough into a loaf and placed it in the buttered pan for its final rise.

"She said nothing about the baby, so our letters must have crossed in the mail." Joanna frowned. "I hope she received mine before she left Switzerland. I really wish I could have seen her face when she read it, because if there's one thing I know, it's that when Marta learns she's going to be an aunt, she'll be almost as excited as I am." They'd both mourned the loss of Kurt, but the life that was growing inside Joanna was his legacy, the beginning of a new generation of Richters. "Just in case my letter wasn't forwarded, I'll write again tonight."

"How are you feeling?" Emily laid a hand on her midsection and smiled. "I'm finding this a wonderful experience."

So was Joanna, now that the morning sickness had ended. "I'm healthy, but . . ." She searched for the right word. "Unsettled."

"In what way?"

"I know I should be planning for the future, but it seems murky. You and Louisa know what yours will bring. You'll continue to run the boarding house and care for your children. Louisa will continue being the town's midwife and doctor and will move into the house she and Josh are building. I'm unsure what I should do. Helping Louisa by playing the piano doesn't seem like enough."

Emily's blue eyes were filled with both understanding and sympathy. "I'm going to tell you what our father would have. You need to be patient. God will provide answers in his time."

"I know you're right. I only wish patience wasn't such a difficult lesson to learn."

∽

"Is something wrong?" Burke waited until Joanna finished her breathing exercises and they started down the driveway before he posed the question that had plagued him since supper. "You seemed quieter than usual."

"How could anyone talk when Noah decided to entertain us with stories of making piecrusts?"

Burke had to admit that the tale had been entertaining, though he'd eyed the apple pie Emily had served with more than a bit of caution after hearing Noah's story.

"He didn't really do that, did he?"

"No." Joanna's smile said she sensed his need for reassurance. "He and Emily are good at pretending. She said he used to be content with just using the rolling pin on the floor, but now that he realized she's flattening something, Noah wants to do the same thing."

"So she lets him roll pastry on the floor?" There was more to child-rearing than Burke had imagined.

"No flour and lard. Emily gives him a wrinkled handkerchief. According to her, Noah can spend an amazing amount of time trying to get the wrinkles out."

Burke had to laugh at the picture Joanna was painting of a child using a rolling pin the way an adult would use a flatiron. "It sounds as if Emily's mastered the art of mothering. I doubt my mother would have thought of that."

"You probably didn't spend a lot of time in the kitchen."

"I can't say that I did. The barn was my favorite spot. That and the creek."

"Is that because your sisters didn't like either place?"

Burke nodded. "Good guess." Or was it only a guess? Joanna seemed to understand him better than anyone he'd met.

When they reached the end of the drive and headed west on Creek, Burke increased their pace. Though it meant shortening their time together unless they lingered on the porch when they returned to Finley House, he wanted to assess Joanna's strength. To his relief, her breathing remained normal. There was no question that her health had improved in the last month.

As a light breeze caused her to draw her shawl closer around her shoulders, Burke wondered how Joanna would react if he wrapped his arms around her. That would warm her, but it would break all the rules of propriety. Keeping his hands firmly at his sides and willing himself to think of something—anything—other than how good it would feel to hold her in his arms, Burke said, "Don't think I haven't noticed that you avoided answering my question."

"I can't get anything past you, can I?" Joanna paused, and for a second he doubted she'd tell him anything. Then she shrugged. "I wouldn't say anything's wrong, but I feel unsettled. I wish the path to my future was clear. Emily and I talked about it today. It's easy for her to advise patience, because she's living the life she always dreamt of, but I don't like looking into the future and seeing nothing but a blank page."

A blank page. A letter that hadn't come. No matter how you described it, it was a feeling Burke understood all too well. "I know what you mean. Some days—and today was one of them—I'm convinced that either I won't hear from Dr. Fielding or he'll reject me. That makes me wonder what I'll do with the rest of my life."

An owl's hoot caused Joanna to startle and lose her balance. Instinctively, Burke reached out to steady her, putting an arm around her shoulders and drawing her close to him. For the second that she stood there regaining her equilibrium, he savored the sweet smell of her perfume and the softness of her curves pressed against him.

As if she was suddenly aware that others might observe and misconstrue their closeness, Joanna took a step away.

"There must be other doctors you could work with." If she'd been affected by their proximity, her voice gave no indication.

Burke willed his own voice to be as calm. "Possibly, but I don't know of any. The delay makes me question whether I'm pursuing the wrong dream. Maybe research isn't what I should be doing." The subject might not be pleasant, but it had brought his heart rate back to normal.

"What would you do if not that?"

"I don't know." That was the problem. "When I left Alabama, I was convinced that being a small-town doctor wasn't for me, but the time I've spent in Sweetwater Crossing has been more fulfilling than I expected."

Helping reduce Herb Oberle's pain from gout had given Burke almost as much satisfaction as treating the man's broken and mangled arm. Herb was only one person, not the thousands whose lives he could change if he could prevent pneumonia, but if Burke hadn't been here, Herb might have lost his arm.

"You've done a lot for us, and it's only been a short time." Once again, Joanna seemed determined to reassure him, although this time the stakes were far higher than piecrusts. "Louisa says she learns something from you every day, and you've definitely helped me. I can breathe more easily, and I'm stronger, all thanks to you."

Though Burke wanted to take credit, he knew there were other factors at work. "Don't discount the tincture of time."

"The what?"

Burke smiled, recalling his fellow students' amazement the day they'd been introduced to the term. "One of my professors reminded us that many conditions will heal without medicines or treatment if given enough time. He knew patients might not believe that, so he called it the tincture of time and gave them a bottle of harmless colored water to drink each day."

"In other words, he advocated patience. Just like Emily. I wish I had more of it. I hate being in limbo, not knowing what I should do. I want to feel useful."

And that was the crux of it, wasn't it? It was normal to want to believe that one's life made a difference.

"You are being useful, Joanna. Never doubt that. Your music helps my patients and me."

"You?" She seemed surprised even though Burke knew he'd told her that her music had benefited him.

"Yes, me." The best days were the ones when she was in the office. "My patients aren't the only ones who need soothing. I think more clearly when you're playing, and problems don't seem as serious." Burke paused for a second, wondering whether he should tell her everything that was in his heart, finally admitting the truth. "I don't know what I'd do without you."

And, like his uncertain future, that was a problem. He couldn't say when it had begun. All he knew was that his feelings for Joanna had deepened. They had begun as friendship and admiration. Now they were harder to define. Thoughts of her popped into his brain at unexpected times, and whenever he was pondering a question, he asked himself what Joanna would say.

Burke couldn't explain it, because he'd never felt this way about Edna or any other woman. No one else had dominated his thoughts the way Joanna did. It made no sense, but thoughts of Joanna disturbed and yet comforted him at the same time.

What was happening to him?

❧

"Did your arm predict this, Burke?" Louisa gestured toward the window where rain was sheeting down the panes. Though the Sunday breakfast Emily had served was as delicious as ever, Joanna's younger sister was clearly displeased with the weather. Perhaps that explained her nonsensical question.

Burke did not appear to find anything unusual. "It did," he admitted. "Do you want me to warn you next time?"

Joanna stopped spreading peach jam on a piece of toast to stare at him. "What are you two talking about?"

"Ever since I broke my arm as a child, I get twinges or sometimes actual pain when the weather is changing. I thought something was wrong with me until one of my professors said it's a known effect of a broken bone."

Before Joanna could ask whether this was the same professor who'd introduced Burke to the concept of a tincture of time, Josh spoke. "It's too bad Louisa wasn't there to treat you. My leg was badly broken, but weather has never bothered it." Josh's pride in his wife's skills was evident.

Though Louisa flushed with pleasure, a look of worry crossed Della's face. "I hope the weather doesn't keep people away from church today. Harold is planning a service of thanksgiving."

"Isn't that normally in November?" Craig, who'd been instructing Noah on the fine art of eating bacon with a fork rather than his fingers, joined the conversation.

"That may be the official date," Della said, "but Harold wanted to remind us all that we should give thanks every day."

It was an excellent suggestion, one Joanna decided she would do her best to follow.

Mrs. Carmichael chuckled. "I'm thankful for large umbrellas."

"Puddles. I like puddles."

Though everyone else smiled at Noah's declaration, Emily kept a sober mien. "I don't want to see any splashing in puddles on the way to or from church. If you get mud on your Sunday clothes, there will be no chocolate cake for you."

Noah was silent for a moment, weighing the consequences of a few minutes' pleasure splashing. "Okay," he said at last.

There was no splashing, although Joanna's hem was damp by the time they arrived at the church. As she'd expected, the sanctuary was full. Inclement weather was no reason for the congregation not to worship. If anything, the parishioners seemed in better moods than usual, joking about how good it felt to be warm and dry. The good humor continued throughout the service, with Harold's sermon provoking some titters and a few outright laughs when he suggested giving thanks for the rain, because it washed the windows.

"And now," he said as he concluded the homily, "please rise and join me in singing 'Come, Ye Thankful People, Come.'"

As Miss Heppel played the opening chords, the congregation rose and began to sing. A second later, a loud crash and the sound of dozens of keys being pressed at the same time caused everyone to turn to see what had happened.

Burke did more than turn. He rushed out of the pew, heading for the stairs to the loft with Joanna close behind him, offering silent prayers for the woman who'd become a friend as well as her teacher.

Please, Lord, let her be all right. But even as she prayed, Joanna knew that only the direst of emergencies would have caused Miss Heppel to stop playing and create such a racket. Whatever it was, Joanna needed to be there to help the woman who'd started her on the road to being a pianist.

Her heart pounding with alarm as well as the exertion of rushing up the stairs, she could do nothing but stare when she reached the top. *No, dear God, no.*

Joanna had been in the loft perhaps a dozen times, but never before had she seen anything like the scene that greeted her and Burke. Miss Heppel's head had hit the keyboard; her hands hung limply at her sides. The music had faded, leaving no sound save Joanna and Burke's breathing.

216

There should have been more. There should have been moans or groans. There should have been a third person breathing. But the piano and the pianist were silent.

While Joanna remained frozen with shock, Burke moved toward the piano, his expression grim. Gently, as if unwilling to disturb her, he turned Miss Heppel's head, frowning at the sightless eyes staring straight ahead.

His voice was low and filled with sorrow as he confirmed Joanna's fears. "She's gone."

Twenty

Joanna wiped the tears from her eyes. This was the third funeral she'd attended in as many months, the third time seemingly healthy people had died with little or no warning, Kurt and Grandmother within hours of eating the spoiled meat, Miss Heppel doing what she enjoyed most, playing the church's piano.

Even though it was a Thursday, most of the town had put aside their daily responsibilities to honor her memory and see her laid to rest. Harold had spoken of Miss Heppel's devotion to the church and, though tears had welled in her eyes, Joanna had taken her former teacher's place at the piano, playing "Come, Ye Thankful People, Come," a hymn that she would always associate with Miss Heppel. A new month had begun, but for many, including Joanna, it felt like the end of an era.

Miss Heppel was gone. Burke said she appeared to have had a bad heart, but if that was true—and Joanna had no reason to doubt his diagnosis—no one in Sweetwater Crossing had been aware of it. Louisa had found no entries in Doc Sheridan's journals for Miss Heppel, and Mayor Alcott had declared that she had been in good health when she'd consulted him the previous Friday.

"If it's any consolation," Burke said as he escorted Joanna from the cemetery to the parsonage annex where the congregation would share a cold collation, "a major heart attack happens so quickly that there's almost no pain."

"I hope that's true." Both Kurt and Grandmother had suffered greatly in their final hours, Grandmother even begging to die so she would be freed from pain. Joanna was grateful that Miss Heppel had been spared that agony.

"I wonder whether she had a premonition that she was close to dying. She wasn't like herself when I saw her on Friday, and before I left, she told me she'd remember the duet we played for the rest of her life. I'd never heard her say anything like that."

They'd reached the annex, but while others were streaming inside, Joanna found herself reluctant to enter. The meal and the conversation that accompanied it were the final steps in honoring Miss Heppel, steps Joanna wanted to delay as long as she could.

Though Burke nodded as if he understood, the respite was brief.

"I'm sorry to interrupt, but I couldn't help overhearing what you said." Mayor Alcott laid his hand on Joanna's shoulder. While it was probably meant to be a gesture of comfort, she found it as condescending as his tone. If he had always been like this, it was no wonder Miss Heppel had not wanted to marry him.

"I think you're correct," the mayor continued, speaking to Joanna as if Burke were not present. "Minerva may have had some idea that her time was coming. You see, she wrote her will Friday afternoon and asked me to ensure it was legal."

If his words were supposed to console Joanna, they failed, just as his touching her shoulder had, although they did rouse her curiosity. It wasn't unusual for someone in Sweetwater

Crossing to consult the mayor on legal issues, since he was the closest to an attorney that the town had, but it was unusual for Miss Heppel to have done that. As far as Joanna knew, they'd exchanged no more than basic pleasantries for decades, perhaps because Miss Heppel had refused his offer of marriage.

She couldn't imagine why the mayor was telling her about Miss Heppel's will, but Joanna felt the need to say something in response. "My father claimed people often waited too long to make their final wishes known because they didn't want to consider their own mortality."

"Minerva appeared healthy." The mayor seemed determined to continue the discussion. "When she told me what she intended, I suggested she think about it for a few days, but she insisted she needed to get everything done right then."

Joanna nodded. "She always knew what she wanted."

"Dillydallying or dithering," she had told Joanna, *"is what lazy people do. Once you've made up your mind, don't delay. There's no better time than the present."*

Remembering her teacher's advice, Joanna said, "I'm not surprised she didn't want to wait."

The mayor gave Joanna another of those looks that were designed to assert his superiority. "You may be surprised by what I have to tell you. Minerva wanted you to have her house. She told me that you're the only person in Sweetwater Crossing who would appreciate her piano."

For a moment, the words refused to register, and Joanna looked to Burke for confirmation that she'd heard correctly. "It's a very fine piano," she said, addressing the part of the mayor's explanation that made the most sense. "As good as the ones I used in Europe. If I had a place for it, I'd be honored to accept it."

Burke touched her hand, his fingers warm against skin that had chilled when the mayor had approached Joanna. "From what Mayor Alcott said, you do have a place. Miss Heppel gave you her house."

"That's right. The house and all its contents. Everything she owned belongs to you." The mayor reached into his pocket and withdrew a key. "This is yours now."

A house. A home of her own. A place where she and her baby could create a future together, one where they weren't dependent on anyone else. They'd be close to Emily and Louisa and their families, but they'd be free to do whatever they wanted without feeling beholden to anyone.

How had Miss Heppel known that was what Joanna needed? She had never told Miss Heppel that she felt like a boarder in what had once been her home or how she sometimes worried that Emily would expect her to raise her child the same way she and Craig were raising Noah.

Joanna hadn't dared to dream of moving out of Finley House, fearing Emily would view it as a rejection of her love. It was one thing for Louisa to leave the family home. Even Emily had admitted that a newly married couple might need more privacy than Finley House afforded. Joanna had had no reason. Until today. Miss Heppel's gift had given her a choice. She could sell the house or she could do what Miss Heppel had intended and live there. There was no question which choice Joanna would make.

"I don't know what to say." She wasn't ready to share her thoughts with anyone, not even Burke.

"You don't have to say anything," Burke told her as he squeezed her fingers. Turning to the mayor, he continued. "Thank you, Mayor Alcott. As you can see, Joanna's overwhelmed by the gift." He placed his hand on the small of her back and guided her toward the street, somehow realizing that she was unable to enter the annex and engage in conversation with the other mourners. "Do you want to go home?"

"Not right away. I want to go to Miss Heppel's house." Joanna wasn't certain she'd be able to go inside today, but she needed to stand in front of it, to look at the building that had been an important part of her past, the building that would be the site of her future.

"Your house," he corrected softly.

"My house." Joanna took a deep breath, trying to settle her emotions. When they were far enough away that no one would overhear them, she spoke. "I can't believe it. My prayers have been answered in a way I never imagined. It's much smaller than Finley House, but it would be mine, a place for me and my baby." And even though she hadn't admitted it to herself, that was what she had sought. She wanted—no, she needed—her own home. "The baby and I will be close to my sisters, but we won't be sharing someone else's home."

When they reached the piano teacher's house, Joanna stopped. Taking a deep breath and exhaling slowly, she reveled in the peace that settled over her as she gazed at what would become her new home. The feeling of being a visitor in Emily's home was gone, replaced by the prospect of having a house of her own, one filled with music and memories of the duets she and Miss Heppel had played, one where her baby could crawl, then walk, and maybe one day play a duet with her.

"It's exactly what I needed, Burke. Exactly."

⁓

"Good morning, Burke."

Though the bell had alerted him to a patient's arrival, Burke was surprised by the identity of the man in the hallway. This was the first time the minister had come to the office. "Good morning, Harold. What can I do for you?" A cursory inspection revealed no obvious problems, but not all ailments were evident at first glance.

The man who'd caught Della's eye seemed nervous, a state Burke had never associated with him. "It's not an illness or injury that brings me here. I want to talk to you."

"And whatever it is can't wait until supper." As far as Burke knew, Harold would join them again tonight. As had become her custom, each Friday Della took special pains with her appearance, knowing that she'd see Harold at supper. Today Joanna had commented on the new collar and cuffs Della was wearing. Last week, it had been a different way of styling her hair, a change so subtle that Burke couldn't identify it but one that had met with the sisters' approval.

"I wanted to talk to you privately." Harold emphasized the final word.

Realizing that he'd failed to invite the man who was not a patient into his office, Burke gestured toward the doorway. "Come in. Have a seat. Louisa won't be back for a while."

"That's what I hoped when I saw her leaving in her buggy."

This talk—this *private* talk—had been carefully planned. That much was obvious. The subject was not.

When they were both seated, Harold fixed his gaze on Burke. "I never imagined myself in this position, asking permission from a man so much younger, and yet here I am." The man who displayed such confidence in the pulpit was clearly uneasy. He ran his hand through his hair, then stared at his fingers, as if surprised by what he'd done.

"I'm forty-eight years old, and though I've counseled many, this is the first time I've done this." He cleared his throat, swallowed deeply, then paused before the words came tumbling out. "I love Della and want her to be my wife, but tradition says I need to receive her father's permission before I propose."

Burke remained silent. By any measure, this was an extraordinary conversation but one that filled his heart with happiness. Della, it seemed, would have the happily-ever-after that had eluded her for so long.

Harold started to muss his hair again, then wrenched his hand back to the chair arm. "I know you're not a blood relative, but you're the closest thing to a family Della has. Do I have your permission to marry her? I promise you that I'll do everything in my power to make her happy."

"I know you will." Burke gave a short shrug. "Like you, I never pictured myself in this situation, but of course you have my blessing. When do you plan to ask Della?"

His relief evident, Harold smiled. "Tonight after supper. I thought I'd take a page out of your book and invite her to walk with me. The bridge over the creek struck me as a romantic site."

Burke had never viewed it in that light, but that was of no import. "Unless I'm mistaken, Della will find any place romantic as long as you're with her. You're a lucky man, Harold. She's a wonderful woman."

"I know." His mission accomplished, the minister left the office, his step lighter than it had been ten minutes ago.

Burke settled back in his chair, thoughts tumbling through his brain. Della would accept the proposal; he was certain of that. She'd stay in Sweetwater Crossing and create a future with Harold, the future she wanted and deserved. Joanna's future was taking shape as well. Though she hadn't yet agreed, she was the logical person to become the church pianist and, now that she had a home of her own, she could even offer lessons to children if she chose to.

The two people for whom Burke harbored the deepest feelings were ready to begin the next stage of their lives. He was the only one who was still uncertain of what the future would hold.

If only Dr. Fielding would answer his letter.

⁓

"Are you certain you don't want me to go with you?" Emily asked when Joanna entered the kitchen, wearing her cloak and ready to don her hat. "The roast is in the oven, so I have nothing else to do for at least an hour."

Joanna shook her head. "Thank you, but this is something I need to do alone."

It had felt wrong to enter Miss Heppel's house yesterday after the funeral, so all she had done was stand in front of it for a few minutes, trying to accept the magnitude of the gift. Though she'd considered going there this morning, something had held her back. Perhaps it was the sense that crossing the threshold would signal the end of Miss Heppel's life even more than the funeral had. But she was ready now, ready and almost eager.

She walked slowly along East Street, studying the house as she approached it. The trim was freshly painted, the shrubs meticulously cared for, the front walk free of leaves. Everything was in order, just as Miss Heppel's life had been. It was time to see what awaited her inside.

Joanna pulled the key from her pocket, unlocked the door, and stepped into the parlor. As she'd expected, the house felt empty and lifeless, the light coating of dust on the piano evidence of Miss Heppel's absence. The familiar room seemed different today without its mistress, and yet as Joanna looked around the room where she'd spent so many hours, she could envision herself sitting in the wing chair, warming her feet by the stove when her fingers tired of making music.

Glancing into the kitchen, she nodded. While not as familiar as the parlor, it still evoked memories of the days she'd helped brew a pot of tea and cut shortbread for them to enjoy as they discussed the merits of a Beethoven sonata versus a Chopin prelude. Those days were over, but the memories would remain.

Though she'd been inside the house countless times, Joanna had never ventured beyond the kitchen and parlor. There'd been no need to enter either of the bedrooms, one on each side of the short hallway leading from the parlor. As she opened the door on the right, Joanna smiled. Small and simply furnished with a narrow bed, a chest of drawers, and a trunk along one wall, this would become the nursery. Her smile broadened as she pictured her baby sleeping here.

She closed the door and turned, her hand hesitating to turn the other doorknob. Entering Miss Heppel's bedroom seemed like an invasion of her privacy, and yet Joanna knew she had no choice. Once she moved, this would be hers, the place where she rested, the place where she dreamed.

Resolutely, she opened the door, stepped inside, and gasped. It wasn't possible, and yet she knew her eyes had not betrayed her. Though three walls were ordinary, the fourth was identical to the Finley House dining room. The same wainscoting that covered the bottom half of the dining room walls and the same crown molding that accented the ceiling embellished Miss Heppel's bedchamber.

Joanna had never seen a room like this with one wall so different from the others. It almost felt like a shrine, yet surely that was ridiculous.

She took another step into the room, her eyes narrowing when she recognized the bedside table as identical to those in the room Clive Finley had furnished for himself and his bride. Half a dozen books with familiar bindings were stacked on the table. Joanna picked up the volume on top and opened it. There was no question: its twin was part of the Finley House library.

Trying to slow her heart, which had begun to pound at the enormity of what she'd discovered, Joanna was unable to dismiss the implication that the woman who'd given her this house was a thief. These were the items Clive had told Della had disappeared when Finley House was being built. It couldn't be a coincidence.

Why had Miss Heppel taken materials destined for another building? And just as importantly, why had she felt the need to recreate so much of Joanna's childhood home? It made no sense.

Twenty-One

Joanna was thankful she and Burke were taking their nightly walk, because she didn't want anyone to overhear what she was about to tell him. She couldn't explain it, but when she'd left Miss Heppel's house, her first thought had been that she wanted his advice about what she'd seen. In the past, she would have confided in one or both of her sisters, but she doubted they'd understand how deeply the scene had affected her. Burke would. She knew that instinctively.

When they reached the end of the drive, she started to turn right as they did most evenings, but Burke shook his head. "Let's go the opposite way."

Where they walked didn't matter, but Joanna couldn't stop herself from asking why he was changing their routine.

"Harold's planning to ask Della to walk with him tonight. They'll probably go that way."

Thoughts began to whirl through Joanna's brain. As far as she knew, the older couple had never strolled after supper. "Do you know why he wants to go walking?"

A small shrug was Burke's initial response. "I do," he admitted, "but I can't betray a confidence. I imagine you'll hear about it later tonight."

The smile she heard in his voice answered her question. "If the reason is what I think it is, it'll be wonderful news."

"It just might be. Now, tell me what's bothering you."

"I didn't realize it was so obvious." Joanna had done her best to appear unconcerned during supper.

"Your sisters didn't seem to notice."

"But you did." That was part of the reason she wanted to confide in Burke. He understood her better than her own family did. "You're right. I saw something today that disturbed me, and I wanted your reaction."

"Something about your new house?"

"Yes." When Burke's footsteps slowed, Joanna shook her head. The story would be easier to tell if she was walking, the rhythm of moving first one foot then the other helping her keep her thoughts in order. "I was surprised—shocked would be a better word—by what I found." And she still was. When she'd finished her explanation, Joanna asked, "What do you make of it?"

They'd turned onto East Street and had reached Miss Heppel's house. Burke stopped, gazed at it for a second, then resumed his normal pace. "I'm not sure. It could be coincidence, but like you, I doubt it. It could be that the wainscoting and crown molding were left over from the construction and Clive gave them to Miss Heppel's parents. He may have ordered extra pieces after some were stolen."

"But that doesn't explain the books and the night table. Those couldn't have been extras." As much as Joanna wished there were an innocent explanation, she could not find one. "I believe these are the things Clive told Della were missing and the reason the house took longer to finish than he'd hoped."

"I suspect you're right. I didn't know either Miss Heppel or her parents, but I'm as puzzled as you about why they would have stolen anything. And if they did steal, why wouldn't they have taken enough for a whole room, not just one wall?"

Joanna tried to recall everything Miss Heppel had told her. "Her father died around the time Clive came to Sweetwater Crossing, and her mother had to sell the livery. It's possible they needed money, but since it appears they kept everything rather than try to sell it, that doesn't make sense." Joanna paused. "I wonder whether I should say anything to Della."

"You could tell her what you found, but I wouldn't recommend it." Burke's voice was soft but firm. "She told me she's finally put the past behind her."

Joanna nodded. "Della said the same thing to me."

"I can't imagine what would be gained by showing her the room or even telling her about it."

"Then you'd recommend saying nothing to anyone." As far as Joanna knew, no one had been in Miss Heppel's bedroom, because she'd been buried in the dress she was wearing Sunday morning and visitors to the house would have had no reason to enter her private chamber.

Though the evening was not cold, Joanna shivered and drew her shawl closer as she looked up at Burke, waiting for his response.

"It has to be your decision," he told her, "but that's my advice."

It was good advice. There was, however, another problem. "I'm not sure I can sleep in that room. It feels strange and almost eerie to me."

The bed was positioned so that the last thing she saw each night and the first thing to catch her eye each morning would be the wall with the wainscoting and crown molding. Unfortunately, the size of the room made rearranging the furniture impossible.

Burke slowed his pace, perhaps sensing the turbulence of her thoughts. "I can understand that, but you'll need a bedroom if you're going to live there. Even if you used the other room and turned that one into the nursery, you'd still have to go in there. It wouldn't take too much effort to remove the wainscoting and crown molding and paint that wall a new color. You could even cover all of them with wallpaper. That would give the whole room a new appearance."

Once again, Burke had good ideas. Joanna had been so distressed by the sight of items from Finley House that she hadn't thought of ways to change the room. "I could donate the books to the library or put them in the Finley House library. The night table can go into the attic." Perhaps at some point in the future, she'd give it to someone who would appreciate a piece of fine furniture.

"Would that make you comfortable living there?"

"I believe it would. The rest of the house suits me well, and if I make those changes, I'll be able to enjoy all of it." Joanna tightened her grip on Burke's arm, wanting to show her appreciation. "Thank you. I knew you'd be able to help me."

"I'm glad I could and that your future is becoming more settled. Did Harold ask you to serve as church pianist?"

Feeling more comfortable than she had since they'd begun walking, Joanna resumed their original pace. It was a beautiful evening, one she wanted to enjoy.

"Yes, and I agreed."

"I thought you would." Burke's response was immediate. "What I don't know is how you feel about the position. Playing hymns in a small church is not the same as playing secular music in a concert hall."

Rather than remind Burke that that dream had died, Joanna said, "You're right. I won't be performing, but I might be doing something even better. When I climbed the loft stairs this afternoon and sat in front of the piano, I felt closer to my father than I have since I left Sweetwater Crossing."

She'd gone there directly from Miss Heppel's house, hoping she'd find a measure of peace, and she had. "I could picture Father smiling and saying he was proud that I'd chosen to serve God that way. It's true that hymns are not as challenging as the music I played in Europe, but that doesn't mean that they don't touch people. They do."

Burke laid his hand on top of hers and gave it a small squeeze. "I agree. My mother once told me that if people made a difference—a positive difference—in one person's life, their own lives were a success. By serving as the pianist, you have the opportunity to influence many more than one."

The wistful tone of Burke's voice told Joanna he was thinking of Dr. Fielding and wondering why he hadn't received a response. "So do you, Burke. More importantly, you've already done what your mother said. You've made a difference in more than one life. Just ask Louisa or Herb Oberle. You're a success."

Burke shook his head. "I don't feel like one. It's not only what happened to Mrs. Arnold. I keep thinking that God intends me to do more than treat individual illnesses."

"There's time."

"Maybe." The way Burke pronounced the word made Joanna suspect he meant to say "no." "I don't want to sound morbid, but we never know how much time we have. What I do know is it's time to see if Harold and Della have returned."

⚭

"Harold told me he asked for your permission to marry me." More than a hint of amusement colored Della's voice.

"He did, and of course I said yes." Burke paused for a second, savoring the happiness he saw on Della's face. After everyone had congratulated him and Della, Harold had remained for another half hour, then took his leave when Emily's yawn made it clear that she needed to sleep. Though Burke had expected Della to accompany the others upstairs, she'd remained in the parlor, her expression telling him she wanted some time with him.

"I imagine my response was as quick as yours," he told her. The flush that stole its way onto Della's cheeks confirmed Burke's suppositions.

"Harold and I are both old enough to know our minds. There was no reason to make him wait for my answer." She wrinkled her nose. "The hardest part will be waiting almost two months for our wedding. I would have married him tomorrow, but Harold wanted me to have enough time to settle everything back home." A chuckle accompanied Della's words. "I don't know why I called Samuels home. It no longer feels like that to me. Home is where Harold is, and that's here."

"But he's right. You do have things to settle, like your house."

Leaning forward ever so slightly, Della said, "That's what I wanted to discuss with you. I'd always thought I'd give you the house, but I can't picture you returning there, not with everything that's happened."

Burke's honorary aunt was even more perceptive than he'd realized. "You're right. I can't imagine doing that either. I sent Felix a letter yesterday, telling him the practice is his." Even if Dr. Fielding did not accept Burke as his assistant, he knew that Samuels would never again be his home.

Della studied him for a moment. "Are you certain?" When Burke nodded, she said, "Then you won't mind if I sell my house to Felix and Edna, will you? I won't make it an outright gift as I would have for you, but I'll set the price so low that they won't refuse."

"Why? I thought you didn't approve of Felix."

Della shook her head. "I didn't approve of him as your partner. But, as you said, he's a good doctor. Samuels needs him, so I might as well give him and Edna a reason to stay."

"You think of everything, don't you?"

Another shake of the head was Della's first response. "I still haven't found the way to get you to admit that you're in love."

⁓

As Burke placed his hymnal back in the rack, he reflected that today's service had been different from the previous ones in several important ways. First, and most noticeably, Joanna was no longer seated next to him but was in the loft with the piano. And because she was, the hymns were more beautiful than before. Miss Heppel had been a competent pianist, but Joanna's playing was far superior. She made the keys sing, or so it seemed to Burke.

That wasn't the only difference. Ever since she and Harold had returned from their walk Friday evening and announced their engagement, Burke hadn't seen Della without a smile. Her happiness must have been contagious, because everyone at Finley House was in better spirits than Burke had ever seen them.

And then there was Harold. Though he'd tried to maintain a solemn mien during the service, his gaze continued to return to Della, and each time, the corners of his mouth would curve upward. The man was besotted. No doubt about it.

Harold cleared his throat. "Before I conclude today's service, I have two announcements. The first is that Mrs. Joanna Richter, whom many of you knew when she was Joanna Vaughn, has agreed to be our pianist. I hope you'll join me in thanking her."

Though it was normally frowned upon, almost everyone turned to smile in the direction of the loft.

"My second announcement is more personal." This time Harold made no effort to hide his happiness. "I am honored to tell you that Miss Della Samuels has agreed to be my wife. We hope you'll all be with us as we are joined in marriage on December 26."

The spontaneous applause left no question that the town was pleased. And if anyone found it inappropriate for Della to stand next to the minister to accept congratulations as the congregation filed out of the sanctuary, no one said a word. Today's was a service few would forget.

While the rest of the Finley House residents left the church, Burke remained at the back of the sanctuary, waiting for Joanna to come down from the loft. She'd explained that, although it had not been done in the past, she intended to play a hymn—she referred to it as a recessional—while the parishioners walked outside. Only when the last one had departed would she leave the piano.

Though he'd expected to be alone, a man clapped him on the shoulder. "Finley."

Mayor Alcott made Burke's name sound like an epithet. He had no idea what he'd done to alienate the man, but their every encounter had included barely concealed hostility.

"I don't like to conduct business on a Sunday, but folks have been pressuring me. They want a permanent doctor. Louisa does what she can, but she's not a real doctor, and even if she were, few men would consult her. The town needs a man."

When Burke did not respond to the mayor's assertion, he continued. "Folks urged me to advertise for a new doctor before you arrived, but now they're calling on me to convince you to be that doctor. Will you?"

Alcott's expression reminded Burke of a small boy who'd bitten into a sour lemon. While others might want Burke to remain, the mayor did not. Still, the request was a logical one, especially now that Della would become a permanent resident. Most people would assume that Burke would want to remain with her. Under some circumstances, he would have, but he wouldn't hold out any false hopes to the mayor.

"I appreciate everyone's faith in me," he said, keeping his eyes fixed on Alcott as he stressed the word *everyone*, "but I can't make that commitment."

"Why not?" The question verged on pugnacious, telling

Burke the pressure on the mayor was intense. Unwilling to discuss his hopes with this man, Burke said, "I applied for another position and am waiting to see whether I was accepted."

Alcott's eyes narrowed, and Burke saw a hint of relief in them. The townspeople couldn't blame the mayor if Burke received another offer.

"I'll give you until December to make up your mind."

It should have been a conciliatory statement, but it sounded more like a threat.

Joanna's heart was overflowing as she descended the loft steps. Her first Sunday as church pianist had been even more rewarding than she'd anticipated. Every note she'd played had felt as if it was coming directly from her heart, and the sound of voices singing in harmony had brought tears to her eyes. Burke had been wrong when he'd said she wouldn't be performing in a concert hall. This was God's concert hall, with every note dedicated to his glory.

"You look happy," Burke said when she reached him.

"I am. This last hour was one of the happiest of my life." The accolades she'd received in Europe faded in comparison with the satisfaction she'd felt playing simple hymns. And then there was the reflected glow of others' joy.

"I'm so happy for Della and Harold," she told Burke as he escorted her out of the church. "Seeing them together makes me wish I'd been here when my sisters were falling in love. My heart sings when I see the way Della and Harold look at each other."

Burke's smile widened. "Besotted. That's the way I describe it. My sisters had the same look when they were being courted. I imagine you and your husband did too."

Had they? Joanna's steps faltered when she realized she could not recall Kurt looking at her the way Harold gazed at Della. Had he? Had she had stars in her eyes? Again, Joanna could not remember. What she did recall was her excitement over the prospect of leaving the sanatorium and starting a life with Kurt. They'd planned to visit his parents in Germany, then come to Sweetwater Crossing. Only after they'd spent time in both places would they decide where to make their permanent home.

The one thing Joanna knew for certain was that neither she nor Kurt had been besotted. They'd cared deeply for each other, but their marriage had been based on the desire to help each other heal, not on what some might call a grand passion.

Rather than tell Burke all that, Joanna said simply, "Even though it's been only a few months, my memories have faded, and that makes me feel guilty. I don't even have a picture of him." She still hoped that Marta would send her a daguerreotype, but there had been no word from her sister-in-law after that one letter.

"What will I tell Kurt's son when he asks about his father?"

"That you loved him. That's what my mother told me when I asked. It wasn't much, but it was enough to satisfy me."

And if it satisfied Burke, perhaps it would satisfy Joanna's child. "I don't know how you do it, Burke, but you always know the right thing to say."

His lips twisted in a wry smile. "I'm not certain the mayor would agree. It obviously pained him to ask me to become the town's permanent doctor, and his displeasure increased when I wouldn't give him a definitive answer."

"Mayor Alcott has always been prickly."

Burke raised an eyebrow. "Is that how you describe him? I might not have been so charitable. But rest assured that whether or not I stay will have nothing to do with his persuasive ability."

That sounded as if Burke hadn't completely dismissed the idea of remaining in Sweetwater Crossing. Though she tried to keep her expression neutral, Joanna's heart leapt at the possibility. "Are you considering it if Dr. Fielding is so misguided as to refuse to hire you?"

"I like the way you phrased that—misguided. I'll have to remember that if he doesn't accept me. To answer your question, I don't know what I'll do if that happens."

"You won't have to make that decision. I'm confident he'll want your help." And when Burke left, there would be a hole—a huge hole—in Joanna's life.

Twenty-Two

Bang! The sound of the front door crashing against the wall interrupted the dinner conversation that, for once, wasn't dominated by Noah's stories of his adventures. To Burke's amazement, the boy apparently enjoyed eating fried chicken with his fingers so much that he felt no need to talk, but now the pleasant adult conversation had come to an abrupt end.

Before Emily or Craig could rise to greet whoever had entered the house, Gertrude burst into the dining room, her face contorted with distress.

"Help! Burke, you've got to help him!"

"Lady sad." Like the adults' discussion, Noah's silence had ended, leaving him looking confused.

While Emily attempted to reassure her son, Burke rose and strode to the distraught woman's side. Keeping his voice low and calm, he asked, "What happened and to whom?"

"It's Thomas. I never saw him in so much pain." Gertrude clutched Burke's arm and stared at him, tears streaming down her face. "You've got to help."

"Is he at your parents' house?" That was the most likely

explanation for Gertrude's coming without a cloak or gloves, but he needed to be certain.

"We were having dinner with them like we do most Saturdays. I don't know what's wrong, but it's serious."

Removing her hand from his arm, Burke gave Gertrude a reassuring nod. "I'll be with him in a few minutes, once I collect my bag." He turned to Joanna, knowing he could depend on her to help calm her former teacher. Even without music, Joanna was a soothing person. "Would you accompany Gertrude back to her parents' house?" The woman's wailing was upsetting Noah unnecessarily.

When the two women had left with Joanna's arm wrapped around Gertrude's waist to steady her, Burke looked at Louisa. "I hope you'll assist me."

The expression in her blue eyes was dubious. "Gertrude didn't ask for me."

"But I did." Not only would Burke benefit from having an assistant, but the ailment might be one Louisa hadn't encountered previously. They'd both benefit.

When they'd gathered their medical bags, Burke and Louisa hurried across the street and entered the Albright house without knocking. It took only seconds to see that everyone was gathered in the dining room. Gertrude and her parents stood staring at Thomas, who lay on the floor, writhing in pain. Only Joanna seemed to grasp what a patient needed, for she knelt next to him, held his hand, and murmured soothing words.

That was Joanna—kind and caring, knowing instinctively what should be done. Perhaps it was because she'd been a patient so recently, but Burke suspected what he was seeing was an intrinsic part of her.

He crouched next to his patient, trying to determine the cause of his pain. From the way Thomas was moving, Burke believed it was below his waist but not related to his hips or legs.

Keeping his face from betraying his concern over the difficulty of treating internal ailments, he asked, "Where does it hurt?"

Thomas continued to moan as he used his free hand to point to his lower right abdomen. This was what Burke had feared. Unbuttoning the man's coat, he noted that the area was bloated.

"Did the pain start there?" This time Thomas shook his head and pointed to his navel, increasing the likelihood that Burke's initial diagnosis was correct.

"Is he going to be all right?" Gertrude demanded. Her tears had stopped, perhaps because her mother had wrapped one arm around Gertrude's waist and was stroking her hair with the other.

"We'll do the best we can." The plural pronoun was deliberate. Though no one had commented on Louisa's presence, Burke wanted it clear that she would assist him. "Thomas, we need to get you to our office to treat you." He looked up at Mr. Albright. "How quickly can you get your buggy ready?"

The man appeared dazed and shook his head as if he were confused.

"I'll get mine." Joanna sprang to her feet and started for the door. "It'll be faster."

With Joanna in the driver's seat, Burke and Louisa managed to lift Thomas into the buggy. She drove quickly but carefully, doing her best to keep from jolting the patient, then helped Burke and Louisa transfer Thomas onto the examining table in the office, leaving Gertrude and her parents to follow on foot. To Burke's relief, his patient seemed calmer once he left the Albright house, and the examination proceeded smoothly. But when Gertrude and her parents arrived, Thomas's pulse accelerated.

"Wife worries too much," he muttered.

That was all Joanna needed to hear. She'd been standing near the door, waiting to see whether Burke needed any more help. Without consulting him, she walked into the hallway and urged

Gertrude and her parents to take seats. "No one's allowed in the treatment room," she said firmly as she closed the door to keep them from peering inside.

Burke and Louisa exchanged grateful looks. "Your sister's amazing," he said when he was certain he would not be overheard. Not only had Joanna been the one who'd attempted to comfort their patient, but she'd understood what he and Louisa needed.

"What's wrong with me?" Thomas asked when Burke concluded his examination.

"It's what I thought based on the location of your pain." The examination had confirmed his initial diagnosis. While some physicians might disagree, Burke believed patients needed to understand the situation and refused to minimize the dangers.

"You have acute appendicitis. That means there's an inflammation of a small part of your body called the appendix. It's a small organ, but it can cause big problems. Appendicitis is a very serious condition and can lead to death, but I believe you'll make a full recovery if you allow me to remove your appendix."

Thomas's eyes widened with fear. "You're going to cut me open?"

"If you agree." Burke would not perform surgery on a sentient person without his permission. "It's the only way to save your life."

Thomas groaned as another wave of pain washed over him. "Do it. Do it quick."

Burke looked at Louisa. "Will you get the chloroform ready while I tell the patient's family what's going to happen?" When she nodded, he went into the hallway. "Thomas has appendicitis and needs surgery," he told the quartet. "Louisa and I will do everything we can to save him." When Gertrude started to protest being left in the hallway, Burke gave her a stern look, then turned to Joanna. "If ever there was a time when my patient and I needed you to play, it's now."

For the next hour, the only sounds were Burke's orders to Louisa, their patient's even breathing once the chloroform took effect, and Joanna's playing. Instead of the slow, soothing music Burke had expected, she'd chosen pieces with fast tempos, almost as if she were urging Burke and Louisa to hurry, as if she sensed the urgency even more than they did. If that was her intention, she succeeded, for they worked quickly but efficiently, their movements seeming to keep pace with Joanna's music.

"That's it," Burke said as Louisa tied off the last suture. "I couldn't have done it better."

Though the strain of the past hour was visible in her furrowed brow, Louisa smiled. "Thank you for letting me assist. It's the first time I've been involved in a surgery like this."

"It's the first time I've performed it." Burke hadn't wanted to admit that until they'd completed the procedure. "Physicians used to drain appendixes, but the results weren't always positive. Just a few years ago when Robert Tait advocated removing the appendix, it was considered a revolutionary approach, but it's since been proven to be safe if performed properly."

Though Burke felt as if he were delivering a lecture, Louisa's expression said she was fascinated by the procedure's history.

"I'm thankful I read Tait's paper this summer. Otherwise, Gertrude might be a widow."

The music continued, but the tempo had slowed. Burke wondered whether that was because Joanna was tired or because she'd somehow sensed that the surgery was complete and that what was needed now was to relax and recuperate.

"Do you believe Thomas will make a full recovery?"

"That's up to God. You and I have done everything we can. The pain will be severe for a few days, but morphine will help." Burke would give Thomas the smallest dose possible to relieve his pain and would monitor him carefully. There would be no mistakes this time.

He continued his explanation to Louisa. "As long as the

incision is kept clean and dry, Thomas should recover. We'll keep him in the infirmary for a week to be certain healing is proceeding as it should." And to wean him off morphine as quickly as Burke could.

Louisa studied their patient. "He looks better already. There's more color in his face."

If he hadn't known otherwise, Burke would have said Thomas was enjoying a normal night's sleep. Lines of pain no longer etched his forehead, and his breathing was steady.

"We can let the family see him now." When Burke opened the door and stepped into the hallway, three anxious people rose from the bench.

"How is he?" Gertrude's face was tear-stained, but her voice was strong, reminding Burke that she'd once ruled over a schoolroom.

"Much better than he was two hours ago. He'll be asleep for a few hours until the chloroform wears off, and he'll have to stay here for a week, but I believe Thomas will be fine once the incision heals. Your husband is a strong man."

"I don't know how to thank you." The tears that filled Gertrude's eyes appeared to be tears of relief and gratitude.

Her father shook his head. "I do. Whatever your normal fee is, double it and we'll pay it."

"That's not necessary." Though the Albrights could afford a hefty bill, Burke would not charge them more than the fees he and Louisa had established.

"It is necessary," Mr. Albright insisted. "You've kept my daughter from being a young widow. That's priceless."

His wife clasped his hand and nodded. "My husband is right. There's no way we can ever repay you for what you've given us."

Blinking to keep her tears from falling, Gertrude attempted a smile. "Clive, you're the best thing that's ever happened to Sweetwater Crossing. Say you won't leave us."

Though Louisa blinked in surprise and Mrs. Albright murmured "Burke" to her daughter, Burke chose to ignore Gertrude's use of his uncle's name, although her repeated mistakes had begun to annoy him. "I won't leave until your husband has healed." That was all he could promise.

Once Gertrude and her parents had returned to the Albrights' home where Gertrude intended to spend the night and Burke and Louisa had gotten Thomas settled in the infirmary, Burke made his way to the storage room that housed the piano. Since Joanna was so intent on the song she was playing that she did not hear his approach, he waited until she paused before he spoke.

"Thank you, Joanna. They've gone home, so you can stop playing now. You must be exhausted." She'd played nonstop for well over an hour. Had this been a concert, there would have been a break.

"My hands are a bit tired," she admitted, "but I didn't want to stop until I was sure you didn't need me." Joanna extended her hands and began to flex each of the fingers. "I'm so glad that the surgery went well. Once again, you've accomplished your mother's definition for success. You've made a positive difference in more than one life. You saved Thomas and kept Gertrude from widowhood."

Mr. Albright had said the same thing, but while Burke had dismissed his praise, Joanna's filled his heart with joy.

"I didn't do it alone," he told her. "You and Louisa both assisted me. I don't know what you were playing, but it was so cheerful that it kept me encouraged." Burke paused as Joanna rose from the piano stool to stand next to him, her expression betraying her doubt. "It's true. I won't tell Gertrude or the Albrights, but the surgery was a difficult one. There were times when I was afraid I would fail, and then I'd listen for a second and know that everything would turn out well."

Burke was still in awe of how powerful her music had been.

"Thank you, Joanna. I don't know what I'd have done without you."

He was still thinking about her and the effect she and her music had on him when Louisa opened the office Monday morning. Burke had remained there since Thomas's surgery, not wanting to leave his patient unattended, but now that the pain had subsided enough that Burke could eliminate the morphine, Thomas no longer needed constant care. Burke was even considering moving him to the Albrights' house for the rest of the week.

"I would have been here sooner," Louisa said as she entered the office and laid her medical bag on the back counter, "but everyone I met wanted to talk about you. It seems Gertrude and the Albrights made certain everyone who was in church yesterday heard that you saved Thomas from certain death."

It wasn't the first time a grateful family had touted Burke's efforts, and he hoped it would not be the last. Saving lives was the reason he'd become a physician.

"I hope you told them that you assisted and that Joanna's music was as effective as the strongest medicine."

Louisa chuckled as she removed her hat. "No one wanted to hear that. They were all too busy trying to think of ways to persuade you to stay here permanently. I didn't have the heart to tell them you never planned to make Sweetwater Crossing your home. They wouldn't want to hear that when you've become the town's hero."

"I'm no hero." He was simply a man who'd done his job. "What I am is tired. These infirmary beds are almost as bad as sleeping on the floor. I should have listened to you and slept upstairs, but I didn't want to be that far from Thomas."

Though Thomas had come through the surgery successfully, there was always the possibility of infection. Fortunately, his recovery had reached the point where Burke could dismiss that worry.

"You should have let me spell you, but you're even more stubborn than my sisters, insisting on doing everything yourself." Louisa flashed a mocking smile. "It's time for me to assert my authority as the owner of this office and send you home. And as your reward for doing that, here's some mail."

She handed him two envelopes. A quick look told Burke that one was from Felix. The one that made his heart race was postmarked San Francisco. At last! Fielding had finally responded. Tamping back his eagerness, Burke nodded. "You're right. I'll go back to Finley House for a few hours. Maybe take a nap." But first he'd read the letter that might hold the key to his future.

Burke hurried home as quickly as he could without breaking into an actual run, somehow managing to control his curiosity until he'd passed the mansion's pillars. Then he ripped the envelope and withdrew the single sheet of paper, reading it twice before he sprinted up the steps and through the front door. If it hadn't been for the one stipulation, he would have called Fielding's response an answer to all his prayers.

"Joanna!"

⁂

Joanna closed the fallboard, straightened the sheet music, and rose. Now that she'd finished her morning practice session, it was time to go to Miss Heppel's house and begin sorting through her clothes. Later she planned to stop by the doctor's office to see how Burke—and Thomas, of course—were doing. It had been less than two days, but she'd missed Burke more than she had expected. Even though she understood why he'd stayed in the infirmary to watch over Thomas, the empty seat at meals served as a reminder that Burke would soon be leaving permanently. While she couldn't change that, she didn't want another day to pass without seeing him, even if it was only briefly.

246

"Joanna!"

As if she'd conjured him, Burke's voice echoed through the hallway. It was a single word, but she heard the excitement in it and knew there could only be one cause.

She hurried to greet him, smiling when she saw the huge grin on his face.

"It came," he said, holding out a letter.

"Your smile tells me it's good news. Come into the parlor and tell me all about it."

When they were seated in the wingback chairs facing each other, Burke began. "Dr. Fielding said he hadn't considered having an assistant, but my letter convinced him he needed one. He claims he's looking forward to working with me."

"Of course he is." Though she hated the idea that Burke would move so far away, Joanna was happy that his dream was becoming reality. Her dreams had changed, with some dying while others took their place. Perhaps that was what had happened to Burke. Research wasn't his first dream, but it was what he wanted now, and thanks to a man he'd yet to meet, it would come true.

"He wants me to start in January."

"That's wonderful news." For both of them. Burke would have what he wanted, and Joanna would have another two months before she had to bid him farewell. "I'm so happy for you."

As Burke's expression sobered, Joanna wondered what else the letter contained. "You look as if there might be a problem."

Burke shrugged. "I don't think so, but Dr. Fielding is a cautious man. He warned me that the work wouldn't be easy and that we might never accomplish what we set out to do. He said he wanted me to be certain that I'm prepared for disappointment, claiming that was inevitable, and said that I needed to consider the bad along with the good. That's why he doesn't want me to give him my answer until December."

That was probably good advice for most people, but Burke was different. "He doesn't realize that the thought of temporary failure won't discourage you. It would only make you more determined to help him succeed."

"You're right. I am determined." Burke's expression lightened. "But his point is a valid one. I'm used to seeing results immediately, or almost immediately. I knew within several hours that Thomas would live. Research is different."

"But when it succeeds, you'll be able to help many thousands of people."

"Exactly. That's what's so exciting about it—the possibilities."

If she hadn't been watching him so carefully, Joanna would have missed the momentary dimming of Burke's enthusiasm. "This sounds like everything you'd hoped for, but you look as if something about the letter bothers you."

Burke shook his head. "It's nothing that can't be resolved."

Joanna hoped that was true. Even though her heart ached at the thought of his leaving Sweetwater Crossing, she was genuinely happy for Burke.

"This is wonderful news." She infused her voice with enthusiasm. "We should celebrate."

"That's what I thought. I know what we should do." His grin was almost mischievous, making Joanna wonder what he had in mind.

"Have dinner at Ma's?"

"No." Burke elongated the pause, as if trying to build suspense. When he finally spoke, his answer surprised her. "I think we should remove the wainscoting and crown molding from your house."

It wasn't what anyone else would have considered a celebration, but Joanna and Burke spent the afternoon working on Miss Heppel's former bedroom. Burke pried molding and wainscoting off the wall while Joanna packed Miss Heppel's clothes, intending to offer them to Beulah's mother. The styles were too mature for Beulah, but Beulah's grandmother was skilled with a needle and would be able to remake the garments into ones suitable for a young girl.

As they worked, Joanna and Burke spoke of ordinary things—Thomas's recovery, Beulah's future pleasure in new clothes, what Emily might be serving for supper. There was nothing extraordinary about their conversation, and yet Joanna savored it for precisely that reason. Being with Burke made tasks that others might call boring enjoyable, leaving her with the conviction that this was an afternoon she'd cherish for many years.

The following days were filled with a thorough cleaning of the house and painting of the bedroom. The only room Joanna hadn't touched was the smaller bedchamber, the one she planned to use as a nursery. The bed linens there would need to be laundered, and once she found the key, she would open and empty the trunk. Other than that, the house was ready for her.

She'd decided that she wouldn't move until January, in part because Emily wanted one final Christmas with all three sisters living at Finley House. "The new year will bring many changes," she told Joanna and Louisa. "Let's not rush into them."

It had been easy for Joanna to agree, because staying at Finley House meant she had more time with Burke. Oh, how she'd miss him when he left!

The weeks had passed more quickly than she'd expected, and now it was the final day of November, and Joanna was feeling restless. Since Louisa and Burke were visiting patients, she had no reason to go to the doctor's office. Perhaps a walk would help. And perhaps today would be the day she received a letter from Marta. With each day that passed, Joanna's concerns increased.

Mr. Winslow grinned when Joanna entered the post office.

"I'm glad you came in today. You've got another of them letters from Europe."

Finally! "Thank you, Mr. Winslow." Though he appeared eager for a lengthy conversation, she added, "You'll excuse me if I rush away, but I've been waiting for this for a long time."

The house was empty when she returned. Emily had gone to the dressmaker with Della to help choose her wedding gown, and Mrs. Carmichael and Noah were playing in the backyard. Still, Joanna was taking no chances on being interrupted. She climbed the stairs to her room, fingering the thick envelope, trying to imagine what Marta had written.

Being careful not to rip it, she slit the envelope and withdrew the closely written sheets, her eyes scanning the first.

No! She closed her eyes, not wanting to believe what she'd read. It wasn't possible. It couldn't be true. But it was.

Twenty-Three

Burke walked quickly, eager to reach his destination. It was the final day of November, the day before he could send Fielding his decision. That should have been easy. A month ago, it would have been easy, even with Fielding's stipulation that Burke must remain single for as long as they worked together, but so many things had happened this month: Miss Heppel's death and the changes that brought to Joanna's life, Thomas's appendicitis and the feeling of satisfaction it had given Burke to have been able to perform a successful appendectomy, the way the townspeople urged him to remain. All of those had to be balanced against the excitement of searching for a way to prevent thousands of people from contracting pneumonia.

And then there were his feelings for Joanna. They'd grown with each day that had passed, filling him with contentment when they were together, making him wonder whether the undeniable allure of possibly creating a vaccine for pneumonia would compensate for the pain that leaving Joanna would bring. For the mere thought of being more than a thousand miles from her was painful. How much worse would the reality be? Joanna had become an important—an essential—part of his life. How could he walk away from her?

Burke had tried to weigh everything, but he'd remained indecisive. He'd prayed for guidance, but he'd received no answer. It was time to pray again, but this time he'd seek God's will in his own room rather than in the church.

He increased his pace when he reached the front pillars, then sprinted up the steps. Finley House was quiet when he entered it, making it the ideal time and place to pray. Closing his eyes for a second, he said a silent prayer that he'd receive an answer this time, then climbed the stairs.

When he reached the landing, the unmistakable sound of a woman's sobs filled the hallway. These weren't cries from physical pain; these were the sound of a broken heart. Someone was in almost unbearable anguish, and even though Burke knew it was not from a bodily ailment that he could cure as a physician, he could not—and would not—ignore such devastating pain.

He turned in the direction of the cries, trying to determine the source, then frowned. They appeared to be coming from the last room on the rear of the house, Joanna's room.

When Burke's knock was not answered, he debated his next step. Propriety said he should not enter her bedchamber, but he couldn't leave her, not like this. And so he opened the door and set foot inside.

Though his sisters would have been weeping face down on their bed, Joanna was seated next to a small dressing table, her head in her hands as sobs shook her body. Burke had seen people filled with despair when faced with a life-threatening illness. He'd seen others grieving the loss of a loved one, but he'd never seen someone exhibiting such heart-wrenching sorrow.

"Oh, sweetheart." The endearment slipped out seemingly of its own volition. "Tell me what's wrong. It can't be that bad."

Joanna stared at the man who'd entered her bedchamber. If anyone knew he was here, they'd be scandalized. She almost laughed at the irony. If anyone knew what Marta had written, they'd be even more scandalized.

Burke shouldn't be here, but she couldn't turn him away, not without an explanation. After witnessing her despair, he deserved to know what had caused it.

"You're wrong, Burke. It's more than bad. It's horrible." She gestured toward the pages she'd flung onto the table, wishing she could burn or at least crumple them but knowing she should not. Even now, though she'd read Marta's letter three times, trying to convince herself she'd imagined its contents, Joanna had difficulty believing the story she'd related was true. But it was. Joanna knew that just as she knew that her life had once again been irrevocably changed.

"Not all letters are like the one you received from Dr. Fielding and bring good news." Joanna wiped her eyes, grateful that Burke's presence had startled her enough that her sobs had subsided. "Ever since I opened that envelope, I've felt like I'm in the middle of a nightmare." She shuddered. "I wish it were only a nightmare, but this is no bad dream. I'm awake, and it's true."

Though he said nothing but waited for her to explain what had disturbed her so greatly, Joanna saw concern and something more, something that looked like sympathy in his eyes. If anyone would understand, it was Burke.

It was awkward to have him standing over her, and so she motioned to the other chair. Perhaps when he was seated, she would be able to muster the courage to tell him what Marta had written.

"Will you tell me what happened?" His voice was low yet filled with persuasion, urging her to confide in him. Was this how he dealt with difficult patients? "You know you can trust me."

She did. There was no one, not even her sisters, that Joanna trusted more. Still, the thought of telling anyone made her heart pound with fear. What would Burke think when he learned the truth? Words once spoken could not be retracted.

"Please, Joanna. I can't help you unless I know what's wrong."

That was Burke, a man dedicated to healing. He wanted to help her the way he helped his patients, the way he helped her turn Miss Heppel's house into one where she could be comfortable living and raising her baby.

Her baby! Joanna bit back the cry that threatened to escape. Taking a deep breath, she tried to control her emotions. Tears accomplished nothing. The past hour had proven that.

She looked directly at Burke. "I know you want to help, but no one can help me."

The concern she'd seen in his green eyes deepened. "I don't believe that."

"Believe it, Burke." Joanna took another deep breath, searching for the strength to tell him what she'd learned. "The truth is, I'm not married."

This time puzzlement crossed his face. "Of course you're not. You're widowed."

If only that were true. "That's what I believed, but it's not true. I was never married to Kurt. Not legally."

Puzzlement turned to shock. "How is that possible?"

Pointing to the letter she'd wanted to tear to shreds or toss into a fire, Joanna began her explanation. "Marta—she's my sister-in-law." Mirthless laughter spewed from her lips followed by a cough. "Marta, the woman I *thought* was my sister-in-law, sent me a letter explaining everything." Joanna trained her gaze on Burke, wanting to see his reaction at the same time that she dreaded it. "Do you remember that Kurt was a widower when I met him?"

Burke nodded. "Didn't his first wife die in a fire after they had an argument?"

"That's what he thought. It's what Irmgard wanted him to

believe." Irmgard, the woman who'd broken Kurt's heart and who was now breaking Joanna's.

"Kurt told me she was a moody person and that those moods could be extreme. They fought during one of the times when sadness overwhelmed her. According to what Marta wrote, Irmgard believed Kurt was the cause of her unhappiness and that the only way she'd feel better was to leave him. That's why she ran away, eventually staying with a cousin, but even when she was at her cousin's house, all she could think about was a life without him."

Burke's expression said he was as mystified by Irmgard's behavior as Joanna had been. She'd never known anyone who'd acted the way Kurt's wife had, and that made it difficult to believe what had happened.

"She soon became unhappy living with the cousin and took every opportunity to be outside. One night she wandered farther away than usual. When she returned, she discovered that the cousin's barn had burned."

Joanna coughed again, and this time it turned into a coughing spasm. She took a deep breath, trying to stop the coughs, but they only intensified. Not since she'd left Switzerland had she coughed like this.

Burke rose and poured water from the ewer into a glass. "Drink this. It'll help."

When the coughs subsided, she continued the story. "Irmgard told Marta it was a sign from God that a woman's charred body had been brought out of the barn and covered with a blanket. Realizing that no one could identify the body, Irmgard placed her own ring on the woman's finger, then fled, knowing everyone would believe the charred body was hers. She'd gotten her freedom from Kurt."

Burke was shaking his head, as if to clear cobwebs from his brain. Joanna understood the reaction. The first time she'd read Marta's letter, she'd been as incredulous as he appeared.

She took another deep breath, willing herself not to cough. "A month later when her anger at Kurt had faded, Irmgard returned to their home. By then, he'd gone to Switzerland to be with Marta, so Irmgard waited for them to come home, but only Marta did. Through no act of her own, Irmgard had gotten what she wanted—life without Kurt. His death had freed her from the marriage she'd grown to hate."

Burke was silent for a moment, digesting all that Joanna had told him. "It's an almost unbelievable story. Are you certain it's true?"

If only it weren't, but she knew otherwise. "Marta wouldn't lie. And as you said, the story is almost unbelievable. She would never have invented a tale like that."

Burke said nothing more, waiting for Joanna to continue.

"I wish it were only a story, but it isn't, and that means"—she placed her hand on her abdomen—"my baby will be illegitimate." Trying to hold back the tears that threatened to fall, she looked at the man who'd given her such good advice in the past. "Oh, Burke, what am I going to do?"

He pursed his lips as he pondered her dilemma. "You could say nothing and continue living as Joanna Richter. You and Kurt acted in good faith. You didn't try to deceive anyone. To the contrary, it was Kurt who was deceived."

She'd considered that idea. "That's true, but I'd still know that I wasn't really married."

"Are you certain you weren't? I don't know what the laws are in Switzerland, but even if it wasn't a legal marriage, I find it hard to believe that anyone would condemn you for marrying Kurt when he had every reason to believe Irmgard was dead. Besides, I'm not convinced you need to tell anyone about the letter. It's not their business."

"I'd still know, and eventually I would have to tell my child."

When another round of coughs wracked her body more violently than her earlier sobs had, Joanna reached for the glass of water.

"I don't think you should make any decisions today." Burke's voice was far calmer than her thoughts. "You've sustained a serious blow, and you need to recover from that."

Joanna looked at him, knowing her expression revealed her confusion.

"You may not have been hurt physically," Burke explained, "but Marta's letter wounded your emotions. Some doctors would say that you're suffering from hysteria. I'm not one of them, but the way you coughed after weeks without any attacks like that tells me how deeply this hurt you."

Joanna nodded her agreement. There was no denying how much pain the revelation of Irmgard's perfidy had caused.

"I may be wrong," Burke continued, "but I suspect your fears are for your child, not for yourself. I know you've been worried about how his father's death will affect him. This only worsens that."

Once again, Joanna nodded as Burke proved how well he understood her. She hated—oh, how she hated—the thought of anything that would make her baby's life more difficult.

"You're right. I am worried about that, but I don't see a way to give my baby the life I think he should have."

Burke shook his head. "You're wrong, Joanna. There is a way. You could marry me."

Twenty-Four

The instant the words were spoken, Burke was filled with peace. This was the answer to the prayer he'd been offering for days. It had come in a place he never would have expected—a woman's bedchamber—before he'd had a chance to kneel and once again ask for the Lord's guidance, but he knew that the words had come directly from God. Marrying Joanna was what God wanted Burke to do. The calm certainty that had settled over him, erasing his doubts and cloaking him with peace, told him that. Unfortunately, judging from her expression, Joanna was feeling no such peace. She appeared shocked, possibly horrified.

"Marry you?"

Her voice resonated with incredulity, as if he'd suggested she take an axe and murder her whole family. Burke felt a moment of annoyance that she was so reluctant to consider his proposal, but then he reflected on all that she'd endured today. Perhaps Joanna's reaction was similar to that of a patient who'd been told he had a serious illness. Perhaps she didn't want to accept her situation or the solution he'd proposed.

Though he wanted to gather her into his arms and comfort

her, Burke knew Joanna would not welcome his touch. Instead, using the tone that he reserved for distraught patients, he said, "If we marry, your child will have a father. I may not have sired him, but I can promise you that I'll love him as if he were my own flesh and blood."

If the window were open, he might have heard a bird calling or the breeze rustling a tree's leaves. As it was, all Burke heard was Joanna's ragged breathing. Though her tears had dried, her face still bore signs of her crying jag, and her breathing reminded him of the coughing spells that confirmed that her lungs were still not fully healed and should not be subjected to unnecessary stress, either physical or emotional. Learning that your marriage was invalid certainly qualified as stress. Burke didn't want to add to that, but surely she could see the wisdom of his plan.

Joanna stared at him for a moment before speaking. "You don't know what you're saying, Burke. Marrying me would be a mistake."

A mistake? How could it possibly be a mistake when God had put the words in his mouth? Struggling to maintain a conciliatory tone, Burke asked, "Am I that displeasing to you? I thought we were friends. Good friends, maybe even more than friends."

"We were." Joanna shook her head, then corrected herself. "We are. Yours was a generous offer, but I can't let you do this. I can't let you sacrifice your dreams to help me and my baby. Your future is in San Francisco with Dr. Fielding. He warned you that would take all your energy. Even if I were willing to go there, a wife and child would be a burden."

It was time to tell her of Fielding's stipulation. "Dr. Fielding agrees. Remember the day I received his letter and you sensed that something was bothering me? He said he'd only hire a bachelor."

Joanna nodded slowly. "That's your answer, Burke. The cost of marrying me would be too high. You'd lose your chance to follow your dream, and I'd feel guilty about being the reason for that. We'd both regret our marriage before a year is over."

"I wouldn't." And Burke hoped she wouldn't either. It was true that remaining in Sweetwater Crossing and marrying Joanna hadn't been his plan even a few days ago, but while it wasn't how he'd visualized his future, it would not be a sacrifice.

Joanna's expression left no doubt that she did not believe him. "Those are brave words, Burke, but they're the product of what my mother called the heat of the moment. When you've had a chance to reflect, you'll realize that your impulse—for that's what it was—was prompted by your desire to heal a wound. That's what makes you such a good doctor, but it's not a good foundation for marriage."

What an incredible woman she was! Even though she'd been dealt a devastating blow, her concern was for him, not herself. Burke could not imagine any other woman—not even Della, whom he considered both strong and selfless—doing that. It was up to him to convince Joanna of his sincerity.

"You're wrong, Joanna. It's true that I was shocked by your news. It's also true that I want to help you give your baby two parents, but it's not true that that was because of a sense of obligation."

He paused, wanting her to absorb everything he was saying before he continued. "I want to marry you because I care for you and because I believe we would be happy together." Though he wanted to tell Joanna he loved her, Burke knew she wasn't ready to hear that, and so he used the word *care* rather than *love*.

She stared at him, her eyes narrowed as if she were searching for the truth behind his words, but said nothing. Was she worried about herself or her unborn child?

"I don't have any experience with being a father, but watching Craig with Noah makes me confident that I can learn and that I would be a good parent to your child. Our child. If you marry me, he'll be my child as much as if I'd sired him."

260

There was a long silence, but just when Burke thought this would be a one-sided conversation, Joanna spoke. "You would be a good father. My instincts tell me that just as they tell me you'd be a good husband, but I still can't marry you."

"Don't you care for me at all?" That was the only reason Burke could imagine for her continued refusal. His mother had told him that some people loved only once. Perhaps Joanna had given all her love to Kurt. Oh, how he hoped that wasn't the case.

"I do, Burke. I care deeply."

Relief flowed through Burke as she dispelled his fears.

"That's the reason I can't let you abandon your dream of doing research with Dr. Fielding. That's what you want to do. It's what you should do."

It might have been true a month ago, but everything had changed. He had to make her understand.

"Marrying you is not simply what I want to do. It's what God wants me to do." Once again he paused, wanting to ensure that she heard everything he was telling her. "What would you say if I told you that what happened in this room was the answer to my prayer and that it showed me what God wants me to do with my life?"

Joanna's eyes widened with surprise, but then she shook her head. "I wouldn't believe you. How could my dilemma be the answer to anyone's prayer?"

He'd moved too quickly, making Joanna feel pressured when that was the last thing he'd intended. Backtracking, Burke said, "I wish Irmgard hadn't made everyone believe she was dead. If she hadn't, you wouldn't be in this predicament, but you are, and with every fiber of my being, I want to help you. I truly believe that marriage is the best answer for both of us, but I understand that you need more time to consider it. All I ask is that you pray about your decision. Will you do that?"

As tears welled in her eyes, Joanna blinked to keep them from falling, then nodded. "Yes."

Burke made his way to his own room, silently asking God to answer Joanna's prayers quickly.

⁓

"What should I do?" Joanna kept her gaze fixed on her sisters. As soon as Louisa returned from her office, Joanna had asked her and Emily to join her in her bedroom. There she'd repeated the story she'd told Burke, ending with his proposal. Their faces had reflected shock, anger, and sorrow, but now they were both calm.

"Marry him," Louisa said firmly. "He's a wonderful man, almost as wonderful as Josh."

Emily nodded. "I agree. He'll be a good husband and father, almost as good as Craig."

Joanna wasn't surprised by their response. Almost anyone would say that Burke had offered an ideal solution to her problem. "You don't have to convince me about that. I know what a fine man Burke is." Under other circumstances, she would have accepted his proposal with joy. As she'd told him, she had no doubts that he'd be a good husband and father, nor could she deny that she had strong feelings for him.

"I care for him," she told her sisters. "I may even be in love with him, but no matter how I feel about him, I can't let Burke give up his dream of finding a way to prevent pneumonia. Think of what that could mean to the world. That's much more important than helping me and my baby."

While Louisa seemed to understand, perhaps because she shared Burke's desire to eradicate the dreaded disease, it was clear Emily wasn't convinced. "There must be another way. I hate the idea of your leaving again, but couldn't Burke do both? You could marry him and go to San Francisco together."

Even if she were willing to leave Sweetwater Crossing, and

Joanna wasn't certain she was, it wasn't a viable solution. "That's not possible. Dr. Fielding was explicit in saying that he would hire only a single man. The work demands too many hours, and he doesn't want his assistant torn between work and family."

"Why would Burke agree to that?" A frown crossed Louisa's face. "I love delivering babies and helping heal illnesses, but I wouldn't want to do that if it meant I couldn't have my life with Josh. Doing nothing but work sounds like a horrible life."

Joanna didn't agree. "For the right man, I imagine the potential benefits would outweigh the hardship."

Emily's frown mirrored Louisa's. "Is Burke the right man for that kind of life? I know he's dedicated to his work, but he also seems to enjoy leisure time. Those walks you take almost every night aren't simply therapy, and I know you both enjoyed the day he took you fishing."

Joanna smiled at the memory of Burke's arms around her as he taught her to fish and the way they'd laughed when she caught the shoe. "That's true, but I can't let him forfeit this opportunity. There may never be another."

"There could be," Louisa said.

Though Emily looked as if she agreed with Louisa's optimistic suggestion, she ventured a different one. "It could be that being your husband and helping raise your child is more important to him than working with that other doctor. No one forced him to ask you to marry him."

Joanna glared at her sisters. "Stop it, both of you. Whose side are you on?"

"Yours, of course." Emily appeared surprised by Joanna's outburst. "We want you to be happy."

"And Burke is the man who'll bring you happiness." Once again, Louisa sounded confident.

"Louisa's right." Emily nodded her approval. "Marry him, Joanna. You won't regret it, and neither will he."

"I wish I were as certain as you two, but I'm not." And that was the problem. She couldn't—she wouldn't—risk Burke's future happiness, not even for her child.

∽

Burke quickened his pace as he walked down Center Street, trying to settle his thoughts. He believed that marrying Joanna was the right thing for both of them, but the way she'd avoided him, saying she was too tired to walk with him last night and leaving the breakfast table as soon as she'd finished eating, told him she hadn't changed her mind. There had to be a way to convince her, but Burke had yet to find it.

He was about to retrace his steps, not wanting to encounter anyone by walking on Main Street, when he saw Craig emerge from the schoolhouse.

"Working on Saturday?" he asked as he approached the schoolmaster.

"You could say that." The skin around Craig's eyes crinkled as he smiled. "I'm working on Emily's Christmas gift. This is the only place she won't see what I'm doing."

"And what is that?" Though his mother had prized hand-made gifts, Burke had always resorted to buying something at the mercantile. It appeared that Craig was more talented than he.

"Wood engraving." Craig's explanation confirmed Burke's supposition. "Emily writes so many letters and invitations that I wanted her to have personalized stationery. Josh knows a place that will do the printing if I make the design."

"Will you show me what you've done?" A detour into the schoolroom wouldn't solve Burke's problem, but it might clear his mind.

"Sure. Come in."

Craig unlocked the door and ushered Burke inside. As he'd expected, the building was similar to the one where he and his sisters had learned their three Rs. The sole difference Burke noted was the absence of a dunce stool in the front of the main room.

When Craig pulled a piece of wood from his desk and handed it to Burke, Burke let out a low whistle. "I didn't realize you were so artistic." The almost-completed design had Emily's initials in a fancy script surrounded by a wreath of flowers that Burke suspected were bluebonnets.

"I'm not artistic," Craig said, "but my predecessor is, so I enlisted her help. Do you remember the calligraphy on the invitations to Gertrude and Thomas's dinner party?" When Burke nodded, Craig continued. "According to Emily, Gertrude attempted to teach her pupils Chinese characters as well as calligraphy. That made me wonder whether she had a book with fancy fonts that I could borrow. She said she used to but had lost it, so she offered to design something for Emily, saying it wouldn't be a burden, because she enjoys writing in different scripts."

Craig took the engraving back from Burke and held it up to the light, scrutinizing it. "Do you think Emily will like this?"

"Definitely. It's a one-of-a-kind gift." And a reminder that he hadn't started selecting gifts for the Finley House residents. Maybe Craig had an idea. "I wish I knew what to give Joanna."

The schoolmaster shook his head. "I can't help you with that, but even though you didn't ask, I'm going to give you some advice about your courtship. And, yes, my wife told me about your offer to marry Joanna. Based on my own experience, you need to be patient and persistent. It took me months to convince Emily to marry me."

Months? Were the Vaughn sisters stubborn or simply slow to make up their minds?

"Really? I would never have guessed that."

"There were times when I was convinced my case was hopeless, but eventually she agreed."

"And judging from what I've seen, you're happy together."

"We are indeed. If you love Joanna, and I believe you do, don't give up."

It was good advice, advice Burke had every intention of following. "I won't."

Twenty-Five

Joanna reached for her gloves and bonnet, determined to find something to occupy her mind other than thoughts of Burke's proposal. Perhaps cleaning the second bedroom in Miss Heppel's house would do that.

Five minutes later, she stood in the doorway of what would become her baby's nursery. Though she'd planned to explore the contents of the dresser drawers, today the trunk caught her attention. Settling on the floor next to it, she pulled out the key ring she'd found in Miss Heppel's bedside table and began trying to fit keys into the lock.

The second one worked, and the lid opened easily, revealing a mostly empty interior. That was not what she'd expected. When she'd thought about it, Joanna had envisioned a trunk filled to the top with items that belonged to either Miss Heppel or her mother. Instead, it appeared only one thing had been stored here, a garment made of white silk. Carefully, Joanna withdrew the silk and examined it, sighing at the beauty. Intricate tucking and delicate lace trim turned what could have been an ordinary nightgown into one a bride might have chosen for her wedding night. This was a masterpiece.

Was the trunk Miss Heppel's hope chest? If so, where were the linens most women collected? And if the nightgown was part of her trousseau, where were the other garments? The only other item in the trunk was a small leather satchel. Unlike the distinctly feminine nightgown, this appeared to be something a man would carry. Was it meant to be a gift for her bridegroom?

Joanna pulled the satchel out and studied it. The stiffness of the leather told her it had never been used, and the style was old-fashioned, perhaps having been made twenty or so years ago. Joanna's father had had a similar satchel, one that had been a gift from Mama on their first wedding anniversary. His had been plain, whereas this one bore two initials: CF.

Joanna's breath caught in her throat. Given its age, the satchel couldn't have been intended for Emily's husband, Craig Ferguson. Could it have been for Clive Finley? The timing would have been right. Combine that with the items from Finley House that Miss Heppel had kept in her room and Joanna was almost certain this had been destined for Burke's uncle.

Why? Miss Heppel had claimed that she barely knew him. If that was true, there was no reason for her to have had a satchel with Clive's initials.

Joanna took a deep breath, trying to slow her heart rate. When she'd gotten it under control, she returned to study the satchel. Though her initial impression had been that it was empty, a small bulge told her there was something inside, the size and shape suggesting a book. With fingers that shook despite her best intentions, she unfastened the buckle and opened the satchel, withdrawing the book. She'd thought it might be another one purloined from Finley House, but it was not. This was a journal, a journal whose slightly worn cover told her it had been used.

Should she open it? Joanna bit her lip, trying to decide.

Journals were private, and yet they were designed to be read. Reluctantly, she opened the cover and saw Miss Heppel's name inscribed on the first page. Reading further would be a violation of privacy, and yet Joanna wanted—no, she needed—to learn more about the house's former owner. This book might hold the answers to the question of why Miss Heppel's room had had crown molding and wainscoting from Finley House, about why her trunk contained a satchel with Clive Finley's initials.

Putting aside her misgivings, Joanna rose, took a seat next to the window, and leafed through the book. There were no dates, simply dozens of pages filled with girlish handwriting.

She took a deep breath, hoping she wouldn't regret it, then began to read.

I never thought I'd have a diary. I never believed I would have anything I wanted to preserve in writing. All that changed today. The most handsome man I've ever seen came to town. He's tall, with auburn hair, green eyes, and the most wonderful smile. When he favored me with that smile, I knew Clive Finley was the man I was destined to marry.

Joanna cringed. Her questions were being answered, but the answers were far from reassuring. She turned another page.

Everyone in town is talking about Clive and how he plans to build a house for his sweetheart in Alabama. Fortunately, it will take months and months to complete it. That'll give me time to change his mind.

Poor Miss Heppel. Joanna's heart ached for the girl she'd been, one of many who'd been infatuated with the newcomer, just as Joanna had been infatuated with George, Emily's first husband. Though Miss Heppel had denied being infatuated, her words proved otherwise.

I did it. I told Malcolm I would never marry him, that he was not the man for me. How could he compare to Clive? He can't. He was angrier than I'd ever seen him. Strangely, he didn't blame me. He said it was Clive's fault and that someone needed to stop him from turning girls' heads. I think it was only bluster, but I'm afraid for Clive. Somehow, I have to find a way to warn him.

Joanna laid the book on the seat beside her and closed her eyes, trying to calm her thoughts. Mayor Alcott had made no secret of his disdain for Burke's uncle, but had there been more than scorn involved? They'd had a violent argument at Ma's Kitchen. Was that because Miss Heppel had refused the mayor's proposal? Had he been so angry that he was somehow responsible for Clive's sudden disappearance? That was something she and Burke would have to determine, but first she needed to see whether later entries in Miss Heppel's journal shed any light.

He stopped to talk to me after church today to tell me my playing was beautiful. There was no mention of the way Malcolm accosted him at Ma's, accusing him of trying to turn my head. Now I know what to do. He walks past here most days when he goes from the house he's building into town. When I see him coming, I'll open the front window and begin playing. Mama always said music was powerful. When Clive hears it, he'll know that I'm the woman he's supposed to marry.

The memory of Gertrude saying that Miss Heppel had tried to entice someone with her music flitted into Joanna's brain. Had others known of Miss Heppel's infatuation?

Music was powerful. Joanna knew that. But she also knew it had limitations. She'd learned that when George had been in Sweetwater Crossing, buying horses and choosing a bride. When he'd urged her to play for him each evening, choosing the songs and occasionally singing while she played, she had thought that was a sign that he loved her. She'd been as mistaken as Miss Heppel.

I thought he would ask me to dance at the church social. He didn't. My sole consolation is that he only danced with married ladies and old spinsters. Perhaps he didn't want anyone to see how he favors me. I understand his restraint, but there must be a way to make him admit that I'm the one he loves.

Sensing the increasing desperation in the way Miss Heppel's handwriting had changed, Joanna hesitated to turn the page. She rose to look outside. Had this been Miss Heppel's room before her parents died? Had she stood at this window and imagined herself walking down the aisle toward Clive Finley? With another sigh, Joanna returned to the diary.

Nothing's working. He treats me like he does everyone else. He's polite but never shows how much he cares for me. In another month, the house will be finished and he'll go back to Alabama to bring HER, that woman whose name I don't want to know, back here. I can't let him do that. I can't let him leave. I have to do something more.

Joanna's eyes widened when she turned the page and saw the unmistakable signs of tears blurring the handwriting.

Stealing is wrong. I know that, but I can't think of any other way to keep him from leaving. It was hard to carry

*those pieces of wainscoting from his house back here. I
wanted to put them in the attic, but I knew I couldn't get
them upstairs without Mama hearing, so I stored them
in the woodshed.*

The next entry was devoid of tearstains.

*I heard Clive was upset about the missing wainscoting.
I'm sorry to have caused him distress, but I had to do it.
If he doesn't acknowledge his love for me, I'll take some-
thing else—anything to delay completion of the house.*

Though Joanna had expected pages telling of the stolen
crown molding, books, and table, there were none. The diary
ended with one final entry.

*He's gone. Clive left last night without saying goodbye
to anyone—not even me. How could he have done that?
He loves me. I know he does.*

Joanna closed the book and laid it aside, her heart filled with
sympathy for the woman who'd penned those poignant entries.
This must have been what Miss Heppel had meant when she'd
said she'd done things she was ashamed of. She'd broken one
of the commandments by stealing, but if she was ashamed of
that, why had she filled her room with the stolen items? Was
it a form of penance, a constant reminder of her wrongdoing,
or was it something else?

Joanna wished she knew.

⟳

"We need to find out whether Mayor Alcott was involved in
my uncle's disappearance," Burke said when Joanna finished
the explanation of what she'd discovered in her new home.

He'd been relieved when she'd suggested they walk along the creek after supper, grateful that she was no longer avoiding him, and more pleased than he wanted to admit that she'd asked for his advice.

"People warn about a scorned woman's anger, but it's just as likely that a man who's been rejected would be equally angry . . . and equally dangerous." Joanna shuddered. "The mayor can be brusque and overbearing, but I hate to think that he might have harmed someone."

Burke agreed. While he didn't particularly like Alcott, he had difficulty picturing him as dangerous. He'd be more likely to threaten than to attack someone physically. Still, people were capable of almost anything if sufficiently provoked.

"If we ask him," Joanna continued, "he'll only deny everything. I suppose we could talk to the sheriff." She paused as a frog hopped into the creek, splashing water a surprising distance. "I'm not sure how helpful the sheriff would be either. That's why I think we should start with Mrs. Carmichael. She has an excellent memory and might recall if the mayor was in town when your uncle left."

Burke smiled at the realization that his own thoughts had reached the same conclusion. "That's a good idea. We don't have to tell her about the diary, only that we heard he was angry with Clive."

They walked in silence for a few seconds before Joanna spoke again. "Do you think I should tell Della that Miss Heppel stole those things in an attempt to keep Clive here longer? It would explain why there were delays in finishing the house."

"I'm not sure there's any benefit. What the journal tells us is that Miss Heppel did not send that letter of lies to Della, because she was as mystified as the rest of the town when Clive left. Unless she lied." Burke couldn't discount that.

"I don't think she did. What she wrote seemed genuine."

They'd been strolling, enjoying the unusually warm evening

with Joanna's hand wrapped around his arm in a way that Burke found reassuring. Even though she'd refused his proposal and tried to avoid him for a day, she did not shrink from his touch.

"I wonder whether I should burn the diary. The entry about the mayor doesn't prove anything, and the rest would only tarnish Miss Heppel's reputation. What do you think?"

If this was what life with Joanna would be like, consulting each other before making decisions, listening to the other's opinion, it would be even better than Burke had imagined. He could picture them fifty years from now, still acting like a team. But that was the future. Joanna was waiting for an answer.

"My mother used to tell me not to make any hasty decisions. She said I should wait a week before doing something irrevocable and see if I felt the same way then."

Joanna stopped and looked up at him, a smile teasing the corners of her mouth. "It's good advice, but you didn't follow it yesterday. You didn't wait even an hour before doing something hasty."

Is that how she viewed his proposal? It was true he'd acted quickly, but it hadn't been an impetuous act. "Asking you to marry me may have seemed impulsive, but it wasn't. I was listening to my heart."

Joanna's smile turned to skepticism. "Your heart told you to rescue a woman who was close to hysteria?"

"No." It was vital that she understand. His future happiness, hers, and that of her child were at stake. She had to believe him. And then Burke realized what he'd done wrong. He'd neglected to tell Joanna the most important thing, the one thing that might convince her.

"My heart told me to marry the woman I love."

Chapter

Twenty-Six

"You love me?" Could it be true? The past two days had been filled with unexpected revelations, first the almost unbelievable story of Irmgard's deceit, then the lengths to which Miss Heppel's long-ago fascination with Clive Finley had driven her. In between there'd been Burke's equally unexpected proposal of marriage. Though he'd said that it was what he wanted and what he believed God intended him to do, not once had he mentioned the all-important word: love.

"I do." Though the moon was only a tiny sliver, the starlight was bright enough to reveal the sincerity in Burke's expression.

Grateful that they'd reached the bridge, Joanna leaned against the railing as she tried to control the pounding of her heart. Was it possible that Burke's feelings were as deep as hers, and if that was true, did it change anything? There were still obstacles to surmount, problems to resolve.

"I think I began to fall in love with you the day Della and I arrived when you showed us the library before you took us to our rooms. You were so strong, so confident, and so caring."

Vaguely, Joanna recalled Burke calling her sweetheart when he'd found her sobbing after reading Marta's letter. She'd been so distraught that she'd barely heard it. He'd spoken of friendship, of caring, of wanting to help her. Now he claimed he loved her and had for a while. She started to shake her head, to deny that she was any of those things he'd described. The day she'd returned to Sweetwater Crossing, she'd been overwhelmed by the fact that Finley House, which she'd believed would be her refuge, no longer felt like home. She hadn't been strong. She hadn't been confident. But she had been caring. That much was true. And if Burke had seen her as more than she was, she'd accept the compliment, even though it was undeserved.

Burke shifted his weight, moving so that only inches separated them. "I'd never met a woman like you. Even though I knew I could never be worthy of you, you fascinated me and made me want to learn everything about you. That desire has never stopped. It's only increased."

Those were words every woman wanted to hear, balm to a battered spirit. Joanna wished she could tell Burke she'd fallen in love at the same time, but she hadn't, and she wouldn't lie. "I was intrigued by you from the beginning," she admitted, "but my bereavement was so recent that I didn't consider that I might be falling in love again."

He didn't seem bothered by her admission. "Then you do love me? What you feel is more than simply caring?"

There was no question about that. Joanna had told her sisters that she might be in love with Burke, but the truth was, there was no "might" about it. When she'd searched her heart that night, she'd admitted that what she felt was love, deep and abiding love. But even then, she'd known she could not marry him.

"I do love you, but—"

Burke laid his finger on her lips to keep her from completing the sentence. "There should be no buts. We love each other. That's what matters. That's why we should marry."

But it wasn't that simple. Joanna's heart wanted to say yes; her mind shouted no.

"Love isn't the only thing that matters. We need to be practical and think about the future."

"I have thought about the future—a future with you and our children. That's what I want."

Burke sounded certain, but Joanna's fears drowned out his assurance. "You can say that, but I'm afraid that if we marry and you lose the opportunity to follow your dream, your love will die."

As a frog croaked, then plopped into the water, Burke shook his head slowly. "Do you believe your love would die if something I did prevented you from ever again playing the piano?"

"No." How could he even think that? "I enjoy being a pianist. I like the idea that my music can touch someone's heart or help heal someone's spirit, but if it were a choice between being a musician or loving you, you'd win every time."

"Then why won't you believe that I feel the same way?"

"I don't know." Joanna was silent for a moment, pondering his question. He was right in sensing that there were other barriers keeping her from agreeing to be his wife. The problem was, she could not identify them. All she knew was that something held her back just as an anchor kept a boat from leaving port.

"Maybe it's because I don't believe I deserve someone as wonderful as you. You said you didn't feel worthy of me, but it's the other way around. I'm an ordinary girl."

"That's where you're wrong, Joanna. You're not ordinary to me. You're the most extraordinary woman I've ever met. I don't know what the future will bring us, but the one thing I'm certain about is that I want to spend every day of that future showing you how much I love you." Burke glanced in all directions, then smiled. "Right now there's something else I want to do."

Though she was almost speechless from the beauty of his declaration of love, Joanna managed to eke out the question that was foremost in her mind. "What is that?"

"This." Burke took a step closer, then lowered his head to press his lips to hers.

It wasn't Joanna's first kiss, but it was the first time a man's lips had sent shivers from her head to her toes, the first time her pulse had raced so much that she felt dizzy, the first time every one of her senses was heightened. Afterward, she couldn't have said how long it lasted, only that when the kiss ended, she felt both exhilarated and bereft.

"Oh, Burke. That was wonderful." She laid her fingers on her mouth, remembering the sweet sensation of having his lips on hers.

"There'll be more if you say you'll marry me."

Her doubts and her fears had begun to fade under the force of his nearness, but Joanna knew she couldn't agree. Not yet. "I want to marry you. I do, but I don't want to rush into it." Until she could identify and eradicate whatever was causing her to hesitate, it would be wrong to agree. As much as she wanted her baby to enter the world with two parents to raise him, she couldn't risk Burke's future happiness. "I want us both to be completely certain that it's the right thing to do."

"I'm already certain." Burke's fingers traced the outline of her lips, sending more waves of pleasure through her. "How long will it take you to feel the same way? Do you agree with my mother that a week is the right length of time to consider an important decision?"

If he kept touching her like that, Joanna would agree within seven seconds, not seven days. It was tempting, so tempting, but she knew she needed to wait longer.

AMANDA CABOT

"I need more time than that. Let's say a month. Ask me again on January first, and I'll give you my answer."

In the meantime, she would tell no one what she'd learned from Miss Heppel's diary. Those were secrets that had no reason to be revealed.

Her heart pounding with anticipation of what the new year might bring, Joanna smiled at Burke. "It's starting to get a bit cold, and we should probably talk to Mrs. Carmichael tonight."

He chuckled. "If that was supposed to dampen my ardor, it failed."

They found Mrs. Carmichael in the kitchen, sipping the warm milk she claimed helped her sleep.

"You two look like you have an announcement to make," the older woman said as she laid her cup back on the saucer. "Will there be another wedding before the end of the year?"

Joanna tried but failed to keep a blush from coloring her cheeks.

"I'm afraid not." Burke winked. "Craig warned me that the Vaughn girls are hard to convince, and Joanna's proving him right. We did want to talk to you, though. It's about the day my uncle left Sweetwater Crossing."

When Mrs. Carmichael's smile faded, Joanna wasn't certain which part of Burke's explanation was responsible.

"I told you everything I know, what little that was. The last time anyone could recall seeing Clive was that Saturday morning. When he didn't come to church the next day, the speculation began. It was all anyone could talk about."

"Did the sheriff or the mayor try to learn what had happened?" Joanna hoped that by including both men in her question she wouldn't reveal the reason for it.

Mrs. Carmichael shook her head. "The sheriff said Clive

was a grown man. If he chose to leave without making his farewells, that was his right. He refused to entertain the notion of foul play."

"And the mayor agreed." Though he phrased it as a statement, Burke asked the question that was on the tip of Joanna's tongue.

"If you mean Malcolm Alcott, he wasn't mayor yet, but he wasn't even here. He and Mary were on their wedding trip. As I recall, they came back a week or so later."

It was as Joanna and Burke had thought. Malcolm Alcott may have been angry with Burke's uncle, but he had nothing to do with his disappearance.

Burke stood by the front door, reflecting on what had—and hadn't—happened in the past week as he waited for Joanna to join him. He was more than ready to begin a formal courtship, giving Joanna gifts, taking her to supper at Ma's, letting everyone in town know that she was the woman with whom he wanted to share his life, but Craig had advised otherwise.

"Don't set the grapevine to speculating," he'd said the day after that memorable first kiss. "Joanna would hate that, and it'll detract from Della and Harold's wedding. Let them have their day."

Recognizing the wisdom of Craig's counsel, Burke hadn't deviated from his previous routine. He and Joanna strolled around town each night, doing nothing that would cause the gossips to suspect anything had changed. But it had. Burke sensed that Joanna's resistance was weakening, and that filled him with hope.

He'd already sent Dr. Fielding a letter, withdrawing his application to be his assistant. Even if Fielding would agree to hire a married man, Burke knew that was not the future he wanted. What he wanted was to stay in Sweetwater Crossing.

As Della had said the day she'd accepted Harold's proposal, it had become home.

Della's home was with Harold; Burke's was where Joanna was, and that was here. Even if she refused to marry him, he would remain here, helping Louisa treat the residents' injuries and illnesses and doing everything he could to make Joanna and her baby's lives happy ones.

"Did you have any special Christmas traditions when you were growing up?" the woman who occupied so many of his thoughts asked as they descended the steps.

With Christmas less than three weeks away, it was foremost on everyone's mind. Noah bubbled with excitement over the coming holiday, and Beulah bemoaned the fact that she wouldn't be able to spend it at Finley House. Though Emily had invited Beulah and her family to join them, her parents had insisted that they'd spend this Christmas the way they had all the previous ones, attending church, then returning to their own home.

Joanna's question revived happy memories. "It was the only time of the year that my mother made gingerbread cookies," Burke told her. "She didn't like the taste of molasses, but it was one of my father's favorites, so she made them in his honor. My sisters and I used to count down the days until Christmas Eve. That's when we were allowed to eat the first one."

Joanna smiled. "We had special cookies too. My stepmother's mother brought recipes from Germany, and my mother continued the tradition of spending the month of December baking German cookies. One that always made us laugh was called Pfeffernusse. That means 'pepper nuts.' Every year the three of us would announce that we wouldn't eat cookies with pepper in them."

The warmth in Joanna's voice told him the complaints had been in jest. "But you did."

"We did. They weren't our favorites, but it wouldn't have been Christmas without them. Have you ever eaten them?"

"I can't say that I have."

"I imagine Emily will bake some this year, so you'll be able to decide whether pepper should be an ingredient in a dessert."

"Am I allowed to be honest?"

Joanna let out a laugh. "Of course, as long as you eat at least three. They're small, so if you stop after one, Emily will claim you didn't give your taste buds a chance to savor them."

Even if the cookies verged on inedible, which he doubted, since Emily was an excellent cook, Burke was looking forward to the holiday. "I can see that I'm going to enjoy Christmas in Sweetwater Crossing."

And if Joanna agreed to be his wife, the next Christmas would be even better, for they'd be a family.

"I hope so. This will be a happier holiday than last year. It was only a few days before Christmas that I received Emily's letter with the news of our parents' deaths. And then on New Year's Day, I was diagnosed with scarlet fever."

"But this year we'll celebrate Della and Harold's wedding, and on New Year's, we'll become officially engaged."

"Maybe."

<hr/>

"Have you started to feel the baby move?"

Joanna tried not to let her surprise show. When Gertrude had invited her to have lunch with her, she'd expected the conversation to revolve around Christmas plans or Della and Harold's wedding, both of which were the major topics of discussion in Sweetwater Crossing. She had not thought Gertrude would want to talk about Joanna's pregnancy, particularly since her own had ended with the premature delivery of a stillborn baby.

Seeking to change the subject, Joanna gestured toward the plate of freshly baked biscuits. "These are delicious, so light and flaky."

But Gertrude was not to be diverted. "It's the most wonderful feeling. When my little Clive started fluttering inside me, I was the happiest person on Earth."

Once again Gertrude had managed to surprise Joanna. "You planned to call your baby Clive if it was a boy?" She would have expected Gertrude and Thomas to choose either Thomas or Wilbur, honoring the boy's father or grandfather.

"Oh yes. Thomas agreed that my father would have wanted him named after his friend. Besides, Clive Neville has a nice ring to it. Don't you agree?"

"I do." And naming a baby after the man who'd made an impact on the town wasn't much different from the Gleasons naming their son after Louisa. "Now tell me what spices you used in your peach jam. It's excellent."

This time Gertrude accepted the change of subject.

Burke patted his pocket, grinning when the envelope he'd stashed inside crinkled. He hadn't imagined it. Even though Christmas was a week away, he'd received one of the best gifts imaginable. The only thing better than this would be Joanna's agreement to marry him, but perhaps when she learned what Felix had written, the last of her doubts would vanish and Burke would have another early Christmas present.

If he were a whistling man, he would have whistled. If he were given to skipping, he would have skipped. As it was, he walked briskly back to Finley House, hoping Joanna was home from whatever errands she'd been running today.

"Joanna," he called as he entered the building that had been his home for three months. "Are you here?" The parlor was dark, the piano silent, but sounds of laughter came from the kitchen. Burke strode through the hallway and entered Emily's domain. As he'd hoped, Joanna was standing next to her sister, apparently helping to bake cookies.

Both women turned. "If you're looking for some freshly baked cookies, you're too early," Emily told him.

"I'm sure they'll be delicious, but I was hoping to talk to your sister. Can you spare her for a few minutes?"

Emily's smile turned into a grin. "You can have her for the rest of the afternoon. One helper is all I need, and Noah will be here soon."

Though she feigned outrage, Joanna's frown soon turned into a smile. "It's hardly a secret that I can't cook as well as you, but be honest, Emily. I'm better than Noah."

"Yes, you are, but I suspect that whatever Burke wants to discuss is more important than a batch of cookies."

It was. Burke didn't know how Emily had realized that, but he wasn't complaining.

The speed with which Joanna washed and dried her hands made Burke's already high spirits soar. Unless he was gravely mistaken, she was as eager to spend time with him as he was with her.

"The sun is still on the front porch," she told him. "Do you want to sit there?"

It was as good a place as any and had the advantage of being close. The sooner he could share his news with her the better.

"Something good happened, didn't it?" Joanna asked as they settled onto the pair of chairs they always chose.

"Something very good." Burke pulled the envelope from his pocket. "I received a letter from Felix today."

"Is everything all right in Samuels?"

Burke shrugged. "He didn't mention that. The letter was about what happened the night Mrs. Arnold died."

The furrows that formed between Joanna's eyes betrayed her concern. "How could that be good?"

"It seems I didn't give her a fatal dose of morphine." Somehow he managed to keep his voice as calm as if he were reciting yesterday's weather, even though Felix's letter had lifted the

284

burden Burke had carried for so long. He'd found a measure of peace in Joanna's belief that God had used Burke's mistake to end Mrs. Arnold's pain, but the sorrow that he'd made a fatal mistake had remained. Now it was gone.

"Then she died of natural causes?" Joanna shook her head. "That can't be, because you said four grains of morphine had been dispensed."

Trust Joanna to have remembered the details. "That's right. I gave her two. Edna gave her the other two." That was something Burke would never have suspected.

"I told you I was so tired that I left the infirmary to clear my head. Edna saw me and thought I was abandoning her mother, so she went to the infirmary. Since I'd neglected to record what I'd done, she assumed that either I'd forgotten or no longer cared that her mother was in pain. She knew it was past time for another injection, so she gave it to her but didn't tell anyone."

According to Felix, Edna had believed that Burke's delay in giving her mother morphine had caused her death, which was why she'd blamed him. But when she'd read the records and learned that four grains had been dispensed, she'd realized that she was the one who'd delivered the fatal dose.

"Edna's not a doctor. How did she know how to give her mother an injection?"

"That's probably the simplest part of this story. Felix had been training her to assist him. I'm certain he never thought she'd inject a patient unless he was supervising, but he didn't count on her wanting to do everything she could to ease her mother's pain."

Joanna was silent for a second, absorbing the story that still astonished Burke. Then she spoke. "Why didn't Edna admit what she'd done before this?"

"According to Felix, she didn't know that she'd made a mistake. Neither one of us told her how much morphine had been dispensed that night, because we didn't want to add to her distress. It was only a couple weeks ago that Edna saw the records and realized what had happened. Felix said she was devastated."

The letter had included a postscript from Edna, begging for Burke's forgiveness, and a second postscript from Felix, saying they both regretted the harsh words they'd exchanged before Burke left Samuels. Forgiveness was easy, in part because Burke's regret was tempered by the way Edna's mistake had strengthened his desire to forge a new life for himself and had opened his heart to the possibility of a future with Joanna here in Sweetwater Crossing.

"You must be relieved that you didn't make a mistake with the dosage."

That was an understatement. The letter had assuaged many of Burke's fears and filled him with hope. "I am. I made a mistake—there's no question about that—by not making a note of the injection on the chart, but at least I didn't give Mrs. Arnold an overdose."

Joanna must have sensed that he still harbored feelings of guilt, because she asked, "Is there a rule that says you must write what treatments you've done as soon as you complete them?"

"No, but it's always a good idea to do it soon after." He'd been so exhausted at the time that his handwriting might have been illegible. That was one of the reasons he'd left the infirmary to take a walk.

Shaking her head as if dismissing his explanation, Joanna said, "I know you felt an enormous guilt when Mrs. Arnold died, but don't you see, Burke? You weren't responsible. You had no way of knowing that Edna, or anyone, for that matter, would come into the infirmary while you were gone. You have no reason to feel guilty. You did the right thing. You eased Mrs. Arnold's pain." Joanna laid her hand on his and squeezed it. "I used to hate it when Emily said, 'I told you so,' but I'm going to say it now. I told you you were a fine doctor, and you are." She paused and gave him a smile. "Sweetwater Crossing is fortunate to have you here, and so am I." Her smile broadened. "I love you, Burke, but before you ask, I'm not yet ready to make a decision."

It wasn't everything he'd hoped for, but Joanna's unwavering belief in him was even more valuable than Felix's letter. That had exonerated him; Joanna's love exhilarated and encouraged him. New Year's Day couldn't come soon enough.

Chapter

Twenty-Seven

Joanna sat in front of her dressing table, smiling as she gave her hair the hundred brush strokes Mama claimed were so important. If only her parents were still alive, it would have been the best Christmas of her life. She had spent the day with her sisters and her extended family, a family that had become dear to her in only a few months. Like her own family, it had been formed by ties other than blood.

Joanna loved Emily's and Louisa's husbands as if they were brothers, not simply brothers by marriage. Noah was a pure delight, while Mrs. Carmichael acted more like a grandmother than Grandmother Kenner had. Della was the closest thing to an aunt Joanna had ever known, and Burke—ah, Burke. The mere thought of him made her almost giddy.

She loved him. That was unquestionable. He loved her, another unquestionable fact. Joanna had observed him carefully over the past month and had seen his satisfaction when he was able to help a patient. That and his repeated declaration that he could serve others by continuing as a practicing physician made her believe he would not regret not pursuing the opportunity to do research.

Even though Dr. Fielding had said he'd reconsider his stance on hiring a married man, Burke had insisted this was where he wanted to stay. Felix's letter had confirmed his skill, erasing the doubts that had weighed so heavily on him and helping to restore his confidence in himself. It would be an exaggeration to say that he was a new man, but he was definitely a happier one. And that made Joanna happy.

Her smile faded and her hand stilled. Brushing her hair wasn't important. Burke was. All the obstacles she'd thought kept them apart had tumbled, so why was she unable to give him the answer he sought? Why did she still hesitate to say the words that her heart knew were the right ones? Though there had to be a reason, Joanna could not find it. She wouldn't ask her sisters, because they'd tell her the same thing they always did: follow your heart. Marry Burke.

The problem was, though Joanna wanted to, she knew she wasn't ready. Something was holding her back. There were only six days left in the year, six days to erase the last of her doubts. If she asked him, Burke would give her more time to make her decision, but that wasn't fair to him. He needed to move forward, and so did she. There had to be a way to identify whatever was blocking her and eliminate it, but as Joanna laid her head on her pillow and fell asleep, the way escaped her.

The meadow was even more beautiful than the nurses' descriptions, the newly sprouted grass so green it made her eyes fill with tears of happiness. Oh, how wonderful it was to be outside again! She sighed with pleasure at the sight of the snow-capped mountains stretching into a faultless blue sky. What majesty!

At her feet, clusters of tiny flowers beckoned her to take a closer look. Joanna knelt in the grass, admiring the blossoms that were smaller than her little fingernail, additional proof of

*the perfection of God's creation. From the highest mountain
to the tiniest of flowers, not a single detail had been neglected.*

"They're so beautiful."

"Not as beautiful as you, my love."

Joanna turned, startled by the familiar voice. "Kurt!"

*He stood there, gazing at her for a moment, his smile radi-
ating the love she'd seen so often during their brief but happy
marriage. The smile widened as he raised his hand in a gesture
that could only mean farewell. And then he vanished.*

Joanna woke, feeling her limbs trembling as the last second
of the dream reverberated through her like the final chord of
a symphony, lingering in the air long after it had been played.
Closing her eyes, she tried to recapture the beauty of the Swiss
countryside and the poignancy of Kurt's farewell, but all that
remained was the bittersweet feeling she had each time she
turned the last page of a book.

The story had ended, and even if she reread it, there wouldn't
be the same sense of adventure, the same urgency to reach the
conclusion. But, at the same time that she regretted leaving
those characters' lives when she closed a book, she recognized
the possibility that another story was waiting to be read. All
she had to do was choose it.

As she brushed away the solitary tear making its way down
her cheek, Joanna began to smile. The dream was the answer
to a prayer she hadn't voiced. Seeing Kurt once more, even if
only in a dream, showed her that she hadn't closed the book on
her life with him. That was what had kept her from accepting
Burke's proposal. Della had said she felt freer once she said
goodbye to Clive, but Joanna hadn't done that with Kurt. The
dream of Kurt's farewell had accomplished what she needed,
letting her accept that that part of her life was over and that
she could begin to build a new life.

She hadn't been ready, but now she was.

Twenty-Eight

"I now pronounce you man and wife."

As Mayor Alcott's voice boomed through the church at the conclusion of the simple but beautiful service, Joanna bit back a gasp. The first time it had happened, she'd dismissed it as nerves, but when it continued, she knew that the gentle fluttering in her midsection was her baby's movements. And that made an already wonderful day even better.

Joanna's head told her that the timing of this momentous event was not connected to the decision she'd made last night, and yet she couldn't help but smile at the realization that her baby was making his presence known only hours after she'd taken the next step toward securing his future. What a glorious day!

Her smile broadened as she exchanged a glance with Burke. Even though it meant forgoing music, Della had asked Joanna to be her maid of honor with Burke serving as the groom's best man, and so they stood at the front of the sanctuary beside the newlyweds. Since Harold could not perform his own marriage ceremony, the mayor, whose attitude toward Burke had improved dramatically in the weeks since he'd agreed to remain as Sweetwater Crossing's doctor, had officiated.

The way Burke smiled told Joanna he was as touched by the couple's obvious happiness as she. Her heart, which had been brimming with emotion ever since last night's revelatory dream, overflowed with gratitude that Della and Harold had found true love. They'd both waited a long time for this day, and now that it had arrived, their joy was contagious, infecting the congregation with smiles almost as wide as their own. The town was united in wishing their minister and librarian a long, happy marriage.

Joanna rejoiced in that as well as the freedom she'd found by relinquishing the past's hold on her. Today was more than a new day; it was the first day of her new life.

"Shall we?" Burke bent his arm for Joanna to place her hand on it as they followed Della and Harold to the parsonage annex where the guests had been invited to enjoy cake while they congratulated the bride and groom.

"I can't recall ever seeing a happier couple," Burke said as he and Joanna entered the now-crowded building.

"I agree. They're both glowing." At Emily's suggestion, Della had chosen a light blue poplin for her wedding dress, the color highlighting her eyes. No artifice had been needed to make the bride's cheeks rosy. Sheer happiness had done that, just as it had made Harold's eyes brighter than Joanna had ever seen them. Though he was responding to his parishioners' well-wishes with his usual courtesy, his gaze kept returning to his bride as if he were counting the minutes until they could be alone together.

Though Joanna was also counting minutes, she tried to keep her expression from revealing her impatience.

"It was considerate of Gertrude and Thomas to give Della and Harold their house for a honeymoon." The honeymoon would be a short one, because Harold had promised to be back in the pulpit on Sunday, but at least he and Della would have some time to themselves.

Burke nodded. "From what I heard, it was Thomas's idea. I agree that it's a good one, because they're less likely to be interrupted there."

"I wonder whether Gertrude's parents told him how several parishioners called on my father for guidance the day he and Mama were married. Thomas may have wanted to spare Harold and Della that."

Joanna looked around, smiling when she saw Thomas bring his wife a piece of cake. Louisa had claimed that he was besotted with Gertrude, and that appeared to be true, particularly today. Perhaps Della and Harold's happiness reminded him of his own wedding day.

Turning back to Burke, Joanna said, "My parents used to laugh about those interruptions each year on their anniversary."

Burke wrinkled his nose. "I doubt they laughed then."

"Probably not." Joanna and Kurt had spent their wedding night at a *Gasthaus* near the sanatorium but had returned the next day to stay in one of the sanatorium rooms reserved for visiting family members. "My father claimed that a minister was always on call—a lot like a doctor, I imagine."

"I've had my share of middle-of-the-night summons to a patient's side." A chuckle punctuated Burke's words. "I probably shouldn't have admitted that while I'm trying to convince you to be my wife. Can you pretend you didn't hear that?"

Someone jostled Joanna's arm, reminding her that she and Burke were supposed to be circulating instead of standing here near the door, absorbed in a private conversation.

"I can't pretend that, but it doesn't matter. I've made my decision." As she'd dressed this morning, Joanna had realized there was no reason to delay telling Burke what she'd learned from her dream.

"You have?" Hope and apprehension vied for dominance in his expression.

"Yes," she said softly, "but this isn't the time or place to discuss it. We can't leave until Della and Harold do."

The next hour seemed to last a day. As anxious as Joanna was to be alone with Burke, she wouldn't do anything to detract from Della and Harold's celebration. This was their wedding day, a once-in-a-lifetime moment to cherish.

Afterward, Joanna could not recall a single conversation she'd had, and only fragments of the hour remained in her memory. She recalled Gertrude looking almost coquettish as she talked to Burke, Beulah eating cake with Noah in one corner, Louisa engaged in a discussion with the woman who ran the tearoom, Emily cutting and serving cake. And all the while, the newlyweds made their way around the room, accepting congratulations.

When they reached her, Della bent forward to whisper in Joanna's ear. "I hope you'll be Sweetwater Crossing's next bride. You and Burke belong together."

Unable to respond without admitting that she had the same hope, Joanna merely smiled, then wished the bride and groom much happiness.

At last, Della and Harold took their leave, and within minutes, the guests dispersed. The party was over, all except for the cleanup. As Joanna approached Emily to offer her assistance, her sister shook her head. "You don't need to stay. Craig will help me clean up, won't you?"

"As long as Mrs. Carmichael takes Noah home so he doesn't try to help us. I don't want to consider what our son's idea of cleanup might involve."

Emily shared a laugh with her husband, then turned to Joanna. "See, you're not needed. You and Burke can leave."

Did everyone realize how anxious they were to be alone? Joanna had hoped she and Burke had hidden that, but it appeared they hadn't.

"Thanks, big sister." She nodded to Burke. It was time.

❦

Had there ever been a longer afternoon? Burke's heart had nearly burst through his chest wall when Joanna said she'd made her decision. The softness of her smile filled him with hope that she was ready to accept his proposal, but until he heard the words, he couldn't dismiss the niggling fear that she would refuse him.

He'd wanted to leave the reception that instant, but reason—Joanna's reason—had prevailed, and they'd waited until almost everyone had left. In the meantime, Burke had been cornered by the mayor, who appeared to be taking credit for his decision to stay here permanently, by Gertrude, who spent far too long telling him what a gifted physician he was and how grateful she was that he wasn't leaving Sweetwater Crossing, and by half a dozen others whose conversations had made no impression on him. All he could think about was being alone with Joanna. And now—finally!—they were able to leave.

"Where shall we go?" Though the days were at their shortest, it was still light outside, which meant that they might be observed. The place affording the most privacy would be the section of the creek behind Finley House, but there was always the possibility that Mrs. Carmichael had let Noah and Beulah run off some of their energy there.

"The bridge."

Joanna's suggestion was an excellent one. Far enough from the center of town that they would have some privacy, it was also a romantic spot, or at least so Harold claimed.

"The bridge it is."

Though Burke wanted to run, that would be unseemly, and so they walked slowly, barely speaking. Was it his imagination, or was Joanna as nervous as he?

When they finally reached the center of the bridge, he turned to face her, extending both hands in an invitation for her to place hers in his. When she did, his heart skipped a beat. Harold was right: this was a romantic spot, for Burke was here with the woman he loved, the woman he hoped returned that love.

"Are you ready to give me your answer," he asked, the break in his voice betraying his fear that she would refuse, "even though it's not yet 1884?"

"I am, but . . ." Joanna hesitated for what seemed like forever before saying, "It may be silly of me, but I'd like you to ask the question again."

"It's not silly at all." Burke's sisters had told him about their husbands' proposals, making them seem romantic. Women want to be asked, they'd told him. They want to know that they're loved. And, how he loved Joanna!

"This past month has taught me so much." He tightened his grip on her hands as he spoke. "I've learned patience while I waited for you to make your decision. I've learned that serving as Sweetwater Crossing's doctor and continuing to train Louisa is more than just what your sister wants. It's what God intends for me. Most of all, I've learned that my love for you continues to grow. It's become deeper and stronger each day, and I know that will continue for as long as I live."

When her eyes shone with happiness, Burke continued. "I love you, Joanna. I love you with all my heart. I love you and the baby you're carrying. Will you do me the very great honor of becoming my wife and letting me be a father to your child?"

Joanna's smile signaled her answer, but just as she'd wanted the formality of an official proposal, he craved a verbal acceptance. A second later he received it.

"Yes, Burke. A thousand times yes." Her face radiant with happiness, Joanna leaned forward and pressed her lips to his. It was the briefest and yet the sweetest of kisses, confirming that his hopes and dreams had come true.

He would have returned the kiss, but Joanna shifted her weight, breaking the contact as she said, "You aren't the only one who's learned a lot this month. I learned that loving you doesn't diminish what I felt for Kurt. There's room in my heart for both of you. Kurt was part of my past. You're my present and my future."

She gazed into his eyes, her expression so filled with love that Burke's heart overflowed with happiness as she said, "I love you now and I always will."

Those were the words Burke had longed to hear, words that mirrored his own thoughts.

"I can picture us saying the same thing when we've been married for half a century," he told her. "Our hair may be gray and our eyesight might not be as sharp, but our love will still fill our hearts and make each day we have together one to cherish."

Joanna's eyes sparkled as she nodded. "It took me until last night to accept that Kurt was my past and that I needed to put that past behind me so that I could enjoy the present and look forward to the future. We can't predict what the future will bring, but I know that our time together will be glorious." Her lips curved into another brilliant smile. "Oh, Burke, I love you so much. There's nothing I want more than to be your wife."

Drawing her into his arms, Burke lowered his lips to hers, sealing their commitment with a kiss filled with all the love he had for her. Waiting had been difficult, but it was over. Nothing would keep them apart now.

Twenty-Nine

The satchel was heavier than she'd realized. Joanna shifted it from one shoulder to the other as she approached the house that would soon be her home, then paused when she saw Gertrude approaching from the other direction. The way the older woman waved left no doubt that she wanted to talk.

"Are you ready to move in? I heard you were waiting until after Della's wedding, but I hadn't realized you'd move the very next day."

Joanna laid the satchel on the ground next to her. It might not be polite, but she didn't want to invite Gertrude to come inside today. The house was not quite ready, and when it was, she'd decided that the first visitors would be her family and Della and Harold.

She probably should have brought her sisters here weeks ago, but she'd needed more time to recover from the discoveries she made and—surprisingly—neither Emily nor Louisa had pressed to visit.

Today Joanna wanted to walk through the house, envisioning it not only as her home but as Burke's. While it was nowhere near as large as either Finley House or the one Louisa and Josh were building, she and Burke had agreed that this was where they'd begin their married life.

Managing a small smile for Gertrude, Joanna said, "It'll be another three weeks before I move." Three weeks and two days until the January 19th wedding she and Burke had decided on. Since Gertrude seemed to expect an explanation, Joanna gestured toward the satchel. "This is most of my sheet music. I've started practicing here each day."

"That's probably a good idea. It'll give you a chance to become accustomed to living alone." Gertrude frowned. "I'm not sure you'll like it. You probably don't remember, but I tried living in town when I first started teaching. It was convenient, but I was lonelier than I expected, so I moved back to the ranch."

Her frown turned into a smile. "I love that place. When my parents started talking about selling the ranch to Thomas, I didn't want to leave all the memories. Fortunately, Thomas still wanted to marry me."

Joanna hoped her confusion wasn't apparent. She'd thought that the Albrights had moved after Gertrude announced her engagement so that she and Thomas could build a life as a couple without others interfering, but it appeared that the actual sequence of events had been different.

"You can always move back to Finley House if you don't like being alone."

"I won't be alone." The words came out before Joanna had a chance to consider them, perhaps because Gertrude seemed to have reverted to her schoolmarm days and was giving unsolicited advice.

Her former teacher narrowed her eyes in a gesture Joanna knew meant that a lecture was forthcoming. "Of course you won't be alone once the baby comes, but that's months from now." Before Joanna could reply, Gertrude continued. "I wanted his baby so much, but he wouldn't agree. Foolish, stubborn man."

Once again, Joanna was confused. Louisa had told her how Gertrude and Thomas's baby had been stillborn and how Gertrude had grieved. Now she was acting as if there'd been no baby.

Sensing that Gertrude needed reassurance, Joanna said, "I won't be alone at all." She hadn't told anyone other than her family and Mrs. Carmichael, because she and Burke had agreed that the official announcement would come in church on Sunday, but there was no reason not to confide in Gertrude, particularly if it might comfort her.

Joanna had never seen her former teacher in a mood like this. Perhaps she was having regrets over giving her home to Della and Harold, even though it was only for a few days. Perhaps hearing some good news would jolt her out of her melancholy. "Burke and I are going to be married."

For a second Gertrude stared, her expression incredulous. Then she shook her head vehemently. "You're mistaken. He would never marry you. He's promised to someone else."

Though she wondered how Gertrude had learned of Edna, Joanna did not ask. There was no reason to add to Gertrude's distress. Instead she said, "Burke's first sweetheart married someone else, and Kurt died. There's nothing keeping us apart."

"Are you certain?" Gertrude's question surprised Joanna with its ferocity. She had expected congratulations, not an almost hostile interrogation.

"Absolutely." When she was met with silence rather than felicitations, Joanna decided to say nothing more. If she was fortunate, Gertrude would leave and she could enter her house, put this awkward conversation behind her, and do what she could to make the house into a home for her and Burke.

"When's the wedding?" Gertrude's question sounded almost grudging, as if she still did not believe Joanna.

"January 19th. You'll come, won't you?"

"Of course." Gertrude stared into the distance for a moment, then shook her head. "You'll have to excuse me now. My mother's waiting for me."

⤫

"Horse!"

Burke smiled at the boy who was pointing out the front window. Noah's enthusiasm for horses was well known, and yet Burke couldn't dismiss his sense of apprehension. Why was a horse outside before breakfast on a Monday morning? He rarely saw any on this part of Creek until later in the day. The Albrights did not venture out until midmorning, and the men working on Josh and Louisa's house approached from the opposite direction. The only explanation Burke could find was that someone had come to summon either him or Louisa.

He joined Noah at the front window. Though he expected to see someone mounted on a horse, it was riderless. The second surprise came when he recognized the horse. "It's Enoch."

"Enoch?"

Burke hadn't realized he was speaking so loudly, but his words must have carried to the hallway, alerting Joanna as she descended the stairs.

"Why is Thomas in town so early?"

He wished he could answer the question, but the sight of Enoch filled him with apprehension. As much as he wished there were an innocent explanation, he feared there was not.

"Thomas isn't riding Enoch. The horse is saddled but running loose."

"Horse loose."

"Yes, Noah. He's running loose." Burke laid his hand on the boy's shoulder and urged him to return to Emily in the kitchen. The child didn't need to overhear Burke's concerns.

"I can't imagine why." Joanna stood next to Burke and peered

301

out the window. "Thomas is so careful with Enoch. He'd never leave him like that."

"That's exactly what I thought." Thomas had mentioned that Enoch considered the Albrights' other horses his herd and that he headed to the stable whenever they came into town, but he wasn't doing that this morning. Instead, if Enoch were a human, Burke would have said that he was pacing.

Joanna spun around and grabbed her cloak from the coat-tree. "I'm going to ask the Albrights what happened."

His sense of dread increasing, Burke nodded. "I'll go with you." It was possible Thomas would need his medical skills again, but even if Burke's concerns were unfounded, he did not want Joanna to be alone.

Without bothering to don his coat, he hurried across the street with her and waited impatiently while she knocked on the Albrights' front door.

"Joanna. Burke." Mrs. Albright's face mirrored confusion and concern when she opened the door. "Is something wrong?" The apron she wore and the flour on her hands told Burke she was in the midst of preparing breakfast, oblivious to anything that might have happened outside.

"That's what we came to ask you." Joanna gestured toward Enoch. The horse was pawing the ground and whinnying. "Is Thomas here?"

"No. He and Gertrude went back to the ranch after church yesterday. I don't expect them in town again until Saturday." Mrs. Albright gave Enoch another look, then shook her head. "I can't understand why Thomas's horse is here."

Unwilling to distress the older woman with the possible reasons, Burke said, "Thank you, Mrs. Albright. Joanna and I'll let you know what we discover. You might want to ask your husband to take Enoch back to the other horses. That might calm him."

As they walked toward Finley House, Joanna laid her hand

on Burke's arm and looked up at him. "You believe Thomas was riding and Enoch threw him."

"That's possible. Horses will normally return home after throwing a rider, but from what Gertrude said, Enoch considered his home to be with her parents' other horses. That could explain why he's here." But it did not explain why Enoch hadn't gone to the stable behind the Albrights' house.

"I thought Enoch was a gentle horse. He must have been spooked by a snake or a javelina. Or maybe he caught his foot in a hole the way Josh's horse did. It might have been an accident."

Burke hoped that was the case. "We'll know more when we find Thomas. Let's take your buggy."

While Burke harnessed the horse, Joanna went inside to retrieve Burke's medical bag and to tell Emily they wouldn't be back for breakfast.

"Which way to the ranch?" Burke asked as he guided the horse past the front pillars. The sun had begun to rise, dispelling the darkness but not his fears.

"West." Joanna's face reflected her concern. "You're afraid Thomas is badly injured, aren't you?"

"My instincts say yes. It's the only thing that seems to make sense." Burke took a deep breath, trying to calm his thoughts. "I wonder if Thomas was on his way here because Gertrude is ill."

Joanna's eyes closed as if she were offering a silent prayer. When she opened them, she said, "I hope not, but I can't imagine any other reason he'd have come into town so early."

They rode in silence for a few minutes, each lost in thoughts of what might have happened.

"The entrance to the ranch is on the right," Joanna said as they crested a small hill. "You can't miss it."

What Burke couldn't miss was the form on the side of the road near the open gates. He reined in the horse and jumped out of the buggy, racing toward the man who lay so still. When he reached him, Burke knew there was no need to search for

303

a pulse. The man lay on his back, his eyes staring sightlessly into the sky.

"It's Thomas." Joanna's voice reflected the horror Burke felt. When she gripped his hand, Burke did not know whether she sought to give or receive comfort. All he knew was that they were bound together by a new tragedy.

"This was no accident. Thomas was murdered." Burke pointed toward the blood-soaked coat and shirt.

Joanna shuddered. "I don't understand. Everyone liked Thomas."

"Someone didn't. He was shot at close range."

Chapter
Thirty

Joanna stared at Thomas's body, horror making her whole body tremble. "Oh, Burke, what will Gertrude do?" She raised her gaze to meet his and saw sorrow reflected in his eyes. "It was awful when Kurt died, but at least I knew it was from natural causes. The doctors did everything they could to save him and Grandmother."

Almost involuntarily, her eyes moved downward, propelled by the hope that she'd simply imagined the still body and the lifeless eyes. But she hadn't. Joanna shuddered again. "This is so much worse than what happened to Kurt. I just don't understand it. Thomas was such a mild-mannered man. Why would anyone want to kill him?"

Burke wrapped an arm around her waist and drew her close to him, giving Joanna the comfort she needed so desperately. "It'll be the sheriff's responsibility to discover that. I'll go for him once we take Thomas's body to the ranch and tell Gertrude what happened."

Her heart aching over the thought of the coming conversation with her former teacher, Joanna helped Burke lift Thomas into the back of the buggy, then climbed onto the front seat next to Burke.

"How can anyone kill?" she demanded, her voice fierce with anger as they turned into the drive leading to the ranch house.

"Murder's been part of human history ever since Cain and Abel," Burke reminded her.

Though his words were matter of fact, the harshness of his tone told Joanna his anger matched hers. As a physician, Burke was no stranger to death, but violent death, because it was so unnatural, was more difficult to accept.

Joanna sighed. "My father used to preach about 'thou shalt not kill' at least once a year, but that didn't stop someone from killing him. And now someone's killed Thomas." She took a deep breath, trying to calm her emotions. "I can't dwell on that right now. Gertrude will need me to be strong for her."

Burke reached for her hand and squeezed it before he reined in the horse in front of the ranch house. "You can do it. I know you can. You're a brave and strong woman, Joanna."

Her confidence boosted by his faith in her, Joanna prepared to descend from the buggy. "I think it'll be better if I break the news to Gertrude alone, so give me a minute or two before you come in."

She knocked on the front door. When there was no immediate response, she entered and closed the door behind her, not wanting Gertrude to see Burke and the buggy with Thomas's body.

"Gertrude!" she called out.

The off-key singing that stopped abruptly left no doubt that Thomas's widow was inside the house. She emerged from the kitchen, her eyes widening with surprise when she recognized Joanna. "What are you doing here so early?" Gertrude's greeting was less than welcoming, perhaps because she hadn't expected visitors before breakfast.

Though Joanna wanted to hug her, Gertrude was not one for hugs, and so she said simply, "I think you should sit down." She led the way into the parlor and waited until the older woman was seated before she continued. "Something horrible has happened. I wish it weren't true, but Thomas is dead."

Gertrude shook her head so violently that one of her hairpins tumbled to the floor. "That's not possible. He's out feeding the chickens."

"No, Gertrude, he's not. Burke is with him."

Gertrude's blue eyes lit with what appeared to be pleasure. "Burke is here?"

"We saw Thomas's horse by your parents' house and knew something was wrong, so we started looking for him. We found him at the entrance to the ranch."

Once again, Gertrude shook her head. "I told you, he's feeding the chickens."

Gertrude and Thomas had no chickens. Joanna started to correct the older woman but stopped, recalling how Father had said that people in shock might say or do odd things. That must be what was happening.

At the sound of footsteps in the hallway, both women looked toward the door. As Burke entered, Gertrude jumped to her feet, raced to him, and threw her arms around him. "Tell me it isn't true," she demanded.

Gently, Burke disentangled himself from her grip. "I'm afraid it is true." He pressed his hand on the small of Gertrude's back and propelled her back to the chair. "We need to bring Thomas inside. Where would you like me to put him?"

The widow looked around the room, her eyes moving wildly, not resting on any one spot. "It doesn't matter. Nothing matters." Finally, she pointed to the floor in front of the pot-bellied stove. "Put him there. He always liked that stove."

Gertrude remained silent while Burke carried Thomas's blanket-covered body into the parlor, her face as expressionless as a stone statue. When Joanna tried to comfort her by touching her hand, she knocked it away.

"I need to fetch the sheriff," Burke said. "I'll ask your parents to come too."

"No!" Once again, Gertrude gave her head a violent shake. "I don't want anyone, Clive. Just Joanna. She's the only one who knows how I feel." Though she'd rejected Joanna's gesture of comfort only seconds before, Gertrude reached out to grasp her hand. "You'll stay with me. You have to."

"Of course I'll stay with you, but Burke needs to tell the sheriff what happened."

As she mentioned the sheriff, Joanna realized that Gertrude hadn't asked how Thomas died. The blanket covered everything but his face, hiding the blood-stained clothing and the evidence that his had not been a peaceful death. Gertrude's lack of curiosity must be another sign of the shock she'd suffered.

"Do it. Do whatever you have to." Gertrude, the woman who'd taught her pupils that discipline could be maintained without raising one's voice, practically shouted at Burke. "Just leave Joanna and me alone."

"I'll be back as soon as I can," Burke told Joanna as he left.

Once the front door closed, Gertrude rose, keeping Joanna's hand gripped in hers. "I don't want to stay here any longer. There's nothing I can do for Thomas. Let's go for a walk. I need to visit my garden." She spoke almost mechanically, her eyes flashing with an emotion Joanna could not identify.

"Perhaps later when it's warmer," Joanna said, trying to calm the obviously distraught woman. "There's nothing blooming now, is there?"

"Of course not. It's winter. But we need to go there. Come on, Joanna." She tugged Joanna's hand, releasing it only when they were outside. "Don't dally. There's no time for that."

Practically running, Gertrude reached the flower bed in half the time it had taken the last time she'd brought Joanna here. When they reached it, she looked down at the rectangular plot that had been covered with blossoms during the summer, then turned her gaze on Joanna.

"I had to do it, you know. It was the only way."

She was making no sense. "What did you have to do?"

"Kill Thomas." Gertrude's tone was matter of fact, as if she were discussing the price she'd paid for flour rather than her husband's murder.

Joanna stared, wondering if this was further evidence of Gertrude's being in shock but realizing it wasn't. What had seemed odd before now made sense. Gertrude had had no reason to ask how Thomas had died, because she'd been there. She'd been the one who'd pulled the trigger. No wonder the shot had been fired at close range. Thomas would have had no reason to fear his wife.

"Why?" Why had this woman whose eyes bore a madness Joanna had never before seen killed the man she'd married?

Gertrude looked at Joanna as if she were a pupil having difficulty learning a simple lesson. "I couldn't have any barriers separating Clive and me. I always knew he loved me and would come back for me, and he did. He's just as handsome as he was then. He hasn't aged a bit."

Burke. She was speaking of Burke.

Joanna had thought it odd that Gertrude had called Burke by his uncle's name so many times but had dismissed it as a slip of the tongue triggered by the strong resemblance between Burke and Clive. It appeared that she'd been wrong and that there was a deeper, darker reason why Gertrude confused the two men.

"Clive Finley is dead." Joanna needed to bring the older woman back to the present.

"Of course he is." Pointing toward the now dormant flower bed, Gertrude smiled. "Why do you think my flowers grow so well? Clive is buried beneath them."

Was this another delusion? Though Joanna wished that were the case, the bed was the right size and shape for a grave, and Gertrude would have been strong enough to dig it. An hour ago, Joanna would have dismissed the idea of her former teacher killing someone, but after her confession that she'd murdered Thomas, the story of Clive being buried here seemed plausible.

"I thought he died in the war." That was the story everyone in Sweetwater Crossing—everyone but Gertrude—had believed.

"He might have, if he'd gone back to Alabama, but he didn't." Gertrude's expression grew somber as she looked at the place she claimed to have buried a man. "I begged him to marry me, but he wouldn't. He said he was promised to Della and that she was the only woman he would ever love. He wouldn't listen when I told him I'd give him more love than she could."

Gertrude turned beseeching eyes on Joanna, begging for understanding. What Joanna understood was that at some point Gertrude's mind had taken a terrible turn, her reasoning becoming twisted.

"I couldn't let him go to her, so I shot him just like I shot Thomas. Thomas thought we were going for a romantic ride before breakfast. Foolish man. He didn't know that would be the last ride he'd ever take. I didn't want to do it, but I had to. How could I marry the man I love if I already had a husband?"

Joanna had heard of madness, how it warped a person's mind, how it blurred the lines between right and wrong. Though she had never suspected it of Gertrude, her former teacher had slipped from sanity into madness.

"What happened to Clive?" Joanna wondered how Gertrude had lured him to the ranch. Like Thomas, he probably did not anticipate any harm from this normally calm woman.

Gertrude's lips twisted into a macabre smile. "I told Clive my father needed to speak with him out here before the four of them met that night, but Papa and Mama weren't here. They were already in town with your parents. No one knew that Clive had come out here. They all thought he'd left for Alabama early. No one knew he was buried here."

The pieces to the puzzle were starting to fit together, and the picture they formed was a frightening one.

"Did you write the letter to Della and sign my father's name?"

Gertrude nodded. "I had to. I didn't want her to send someone here to look for him. I would have copied your father's handwriting, but I didn't know what it looked like, so I used a font I'd seen in an old book. You know how good I am at calligraphy. It was easy enough to copy another font and pretend I was your father. It fooled Della for all these years." There was a note of triumph in Gertrude's voice.

"I still don't understand why you killed Thomas." She'd claimed she was paving the way to marry the man she loved, but Clive had been dead for decades.

Once again, Gertrude regarded Joanna as if she were slow to learn. "He can't marry me if I'm married to someone else. Thomas was an impediment. I had to get rid of him just like I have to get rid of you. I can't let you marry him." Slowly and deliberately, Gertrude pulled a gun from her pocket. "Don't think I like doing this, Joanna. I don't, but it's the only way."

⁓

Thank you, Lord. Burke knew it was no coincidence that he was here. He was preparing to drive back to town when he saw Gertrude leading Joanna out of the house. Though he wanted to get the sheriff's investigation started, Burke's instincts told him something was wrong, that there was no good reason for the women to be walking outside in the cold.

The pace Gertrude was setting and the way she gripped Joanna's hand made Burke suspect that grief had overcome Gertrude's common sense and that she might need a sedative to calm her, and so he grabbed his medical bag, climbed down from the buggy, and followed them, staying out of sight by darting from one tree to another. The ground was still soft, muffling his footsteps, but nothing muffled Gertrude's voice.

The story she related was worse than anything Burke could have imagined. The woman Sweetwater Crossing had admired for decades had killed twice, not in the heat of passion but coldly, deliberately. There was no doubt that Gertrude wasn't in her right mind, but that didn't excuse what she'd done or what she planned to do. The gun she had pointed at Joanna had already killed once this morning. Burke couldn't let her press the trigger again.

Show me how to stop her. He closed his eyes for a second, seeking a way to save the woman he loved. Gertrude's tale made it clear that she'd suffered from unrequited love decades ago when his uncle had lived here and that she was having trouble distinguishing him from Clive. Perhaps careful use of that delusion was the answer. After another brief prayer for wisdom and strength, Burke placed his bag on the ground and stepped away from the tree.

"Gertrude, darling, why are you all the way out here?" He deepened his accent, hoping that made him sound more like his uncle. Della had once told him that while the physical resemblance was great, his uncle was a bass rather than a tenor.

As Burke had hoped, Gertrude's head swiveled toward him, though she kept the gun pointed at Joanna, her finger on the trigger. "Oh, Clive, I knew you'd come to me." Her voice was soft and higher than usual, giving the illusion of someone much younger.

So far, Burke's plan was working. Gertrude had returned to the past. Now he needed to get Joanna away from her. He could only hope Joanna recognized his ploy and would do nothing to disrupt it. Although another woman might have been trembling with fear, she stood almost motionless, only the briefest flash of her eyes and pursing of her lips telling him she'd received his silent message.

Feigning surprise at seeing Joanna, Burke continued. "Why did you invite that woman?" He wouldn't use her name, lest that shift Gertrude's mind back to the present. "Is that any way to treat the man you're going to marry? This was supposed to be just us two."

Gertrude glanced at Joanna, as if only now registering her presence, then turned back to Burke. "You love me, don't you?" Once again, her voice was that of a simpering young woman.

He wouldn't lie, but he needed to sustain her delusion long enough for Joanna to escape. Burke extended his arms in a welcoming gesture, hoping Gertrude would accept the invitation. "Come here and let me show you how much."

She started to move toward him, then stopped abruptly, staring at Joanna as if she were a stranger. "What are you doing here? Go away. Leave Clive and me alone."

As Burke had hoped, Joanna picked up her skirts and ran behind the tree where he'd left his bag.

He manufactured a smile for the woman who'd lost her grip on reality. "We're alone now, honey, but why are you holding that gun? You wouldn't hurt me, would you?" Though he believed she was deep in her delusion, Burke wouldn't risk becoming another victim of Gertrude's madness.

"Never, Clive. I love you."

"I know you do. Now put that gun down and come here. I want to hold you."

Dropping the gun, she giggled. "I've waited so long to hear you say that." Like the young girl she once was, she giggled again, then ran into his embrace.

It was exactly what he wanted her to do. When Gertrude raised her face, inviting his kiss, Burke wrapped his arms around her, pinning her arms to her sides. There was nothing loverlike about the way he held her or about his voice when he called out to Joanna.

"I need my bag."

Wrenched back to the present, Gertrude began to struggle, trying to escape from the arms that imprisoned her. "What are you doing?" she demanded, stomping her foot like an angry child. "You're not Clive. He wouldn't hurt me."

Nor would Burke. "I won't hurt you, Gertrude, but I can't let you hurt anyone else." Two murders were two too many. God willing, there would be no more.

When Joanna reached them, he directed her to open the bag. "You'll find a green bottle of chloroform and a gauze pad. Soak the pad and bring it here."

"No! I don't want you to hurt me!" Gertrude's struggles increased, and she began to kick Burke's shins. "Let me go! I haven't done anything wrong."

Burke waited until she lifted her foot again, then pushed her backward, softening her landing on the ground as much as he could. While he attempted to keep Gertrude immobile, he nodded at Joanna, then turned back to Gertrude.

"Don't fight us," he cautioned her. "This is for your own good. It's what Clive would have wanted."

When Joanna had soaked the pad with chloroform, Burke held Gertrude still while she pressed it over the woman's nose. The struggles subsided, and Gertrude's eyes closed. Once he was certain she was unconscious, Burke picked her up.

"We'll need to restrain her before she wakens," he told Joanna. "Do you know where she might keep rope?"

"Probably in the barn. I'll go ahead and see what I can find while you bring Gertrude back to the house."

But before they could reach the house, they heard the sound of an approaching buggy. Seconds later, both of Gertrude's parents stood next to Burke and Joanna, their faces dark with fury.

"What have you done to my daughter?" Mr. Albright demanded. "Why are you carrying her, and why is she asleep?"

"We need to get her inside," Burke said as calmly as he could. The Albrights would undoubtedly protest when he tied Gertrude's wrists and ankles, but he didn't want to give her too much chloroform and couldn't take the risk that she'd try to escape before the sheriff arrived.

Perhaps not wanting the Albrights to see Thomas's body in the parlor, Joanna led the way to the back door and through the short hallway to Gertrude's bedroom.

When Burke laid her on the bed, Joanna straightened Gertrude's skirt, then handed him the rope.

As recognition dawned, Mrs. Albright screeched. "You can't do that!"

"It's for her own good."

Something in Burke's tone must have convinced them, because neither Albright said anything more until he'd finished restraining Gertrude.

"All right, young man. This travesty has gone on long enough." Mr. Albright's voice was harsh with anger and fear. "Tell me why you feel the need to treat our daughter like a common criminal."

Burke saw the sympathy on Joanna's face. Even after being held at gunpoint by Gertrude, she still wanted to protect the woman's parents.

"I wish it weren't true, but your daughter killed two men and threatened to kill Joanna."

"That's not possible. Gertrude wouldn't do that." Mrs. Albright practically screeched the denial.

"I'm afraid it is true," Burke told her. "There's more to the story, and the sheriff needs to hear it as well as you." He turned to Joanna. "Will you go for him? We'll wait in the kitchen."

It was one of the longest half hours of Burke's life. The Albrights spoke softly to each other, shooting occasional glances at Burke as if he were the criminal, but at last Joanna returned, accompanied by Sheriff Granger.

They sat around the kitchen table, silently listening as Joanna recounted what Gertrude had revealed.

When she finished, the sheriff ran his hand through his hair in what appeared to be a nervous gesture. "Two murders. I can hardly believe it."

"She wasn't in her right mind." A lawyer might call that an extenuating circumstance, but Burke suspected a jury wouldn't take it into account. The only way Gertrude would escape hanging was if she was confined to an asylum rather than being held accountable for her crimes.

Mrs. Albright shook her head. "I don't believe it. Gertrude has always been a good girl. She never showed any sign of . . ."

"Madness?" The sheriff completed the sentence.

"No, never."

Mr. Albright laid his hand on his wife's in an attempt to comfort her. "It appears we didn't know her as well as we thought." He turned to the sheriff. "What are you going to do?"

When Sheriff Granger hesitated, Burke suspected he was imagining the pain that seeing their daughter hanged would bring to the Albrights and perhaps to the whole town. For years, Gertrude had been its well-respected schoolmarm.

Though he wasn't a lawman, Burke couldn't let the sheriff be swayed by his friendship with the Albrights. "We can't take the risk that Gertrude might harm someone else." He doubted he'd ever forget the fear he'd felt when he'd seen that gun pointed at Joanna.

Sheriff Granger was silent for a moment before he said, "You're right. She needs to be put in an asylum."

Blood drained from Mrs. Albright's face when she heard the sheriff's decision. "That would kill her. Gertrude is a sensitive girl."

"I have no choice, Mrs. Albright. It's either that or a trial."

Her face crumpling with shock and sorrow, Gertrude's mother rose, shoving her chair aside. "I can't listen to any more of this. That's my baby you're talking about." As sobs wrenched her, she stormed from the kitchen.

Mr. Albright was silent for a moment. "My wife is right. Being confined to an institution would kill Gertrude. Is it possible there's another answer? What if we turned this into an asylum? We could put bars on Gertrude's windows and keep her locked up unless one of us was with her."

"How would you do that when you live in town?" Though the sheriff had not dismissed the idea, he was clearly dubious.

"We would move back here," Gertrude's father said. "I don't think anyone would be surprised if we told them she was devastated by Thomas's death and that we needed to be with her. We'd make it clear that she isn't able to have visitors."

He paused for a second, as if trying to consider every aspect of his hastily constructed plan. "We'd be very, very careful."

Burke heard Joanna's gasp and realized she was as disturbed as he was that the sheriff would even entertain such a scheme. While Burke understood the Albrights' desire to protect their daughter, there was no ignoring the fact that she was a dangerous woman.

"The risk is too high," he said firmly. "Gertrude needs to be in an asylum."

When the sheriff nodded, Mr. Albright rose, his face contorted with grief. "I want to tell Lorena what you've decided." He left the room, searching for his wife. Only seconds later, Burke heard him cry, "Oh, Lorena, what have you done?"

Moving in unison, Burke, Joanna, and the sheriff headed in the direction of Mr. Albright's voice. They found him in Gertrude's bedroom staring at the form lying on the bed, a pillow clasped to her face.

Burke hurried to the bedside, although the body's unnatural stillness told him there was no reason to rush. Pulling the pillow aside, he saw proof that Gertrude had suffocated.

"How did she get her hands loose?" he demanded.

Mrs. Albright's blue eyes filled with tears. "I couldn't leave her like that. She said she wanted to hold Thomas's pillow, so I untied her. Before I knew it, she wasn't breathing."

The woman was lying. Burke knew that as surely as he knew she'd believed she was saving her daughter from an unthinkable future when she held the pillow over her nose and mouth.

He doubted Gertrude had spoken. She was probably still under the effects of the chloroform when her mother tried to spare her being sent to an asylum. And death had not occurred as quickly as Mrs. Albright had implied. Asphyxiation didn't happen immediately. It took minutes.

Lorena Albright had killed her daughter just as surely as Gertrude had murdered her husband and Burke's uncle. The question was, would anything be served by accusing her of the crime? The almost imperceptible shake of the sheriff's head said he was unwilling to do that.

Burke turned toward Joanna, whose face was contorted with sorrow as she looked at the woman who'd been first her teacher, then her friend. When she met his gaze, she too shook her head. Perhaps they were right. Perhaps justice had already been served, although not in a conventional way. Gertrude was no longer a threat, and her parents would have to live with the memory—and the guilt—of what had happened today. Perhaps that was punishment enough.

"This might be for the best," Sheriff Granger said. "You can have a double funeral and bury her with Thomas. We can tell people that Thomas was killed in a fall from his horse and that Gertrude died of grief over her husband's death. Folks will speculate, but there's no need to say more, no need to sully the Albright name."

"Thank you." Mr. Albright nodded slowly, then wrapped his arm around his wife's shoulders. "Thomas needs to be laid to rest in the cemetery with his parents, but I think we should bury Gertrude out here, don't you? We can extend the flower bed."

The tears she'd been trying to hold back trickled down Mrs. Albright's cheeks. "She would have liked that."

Joanna, who'd been silent since they'd entered the bedroom, nodded. "She said she wanted to be near Clive."

And though it was only her body, not her spirit, that would be with him, Gertrude's wish would be answered.

Mrs. Albright let out a deep sigh, fixing her gaze on Joanna. "I know it's asking a great deal, but do you think that someday you'll be able to forgive my daughter for wanting to kill you?"

When Joanna took a deep breath, Burke wondered whether she was remembering how many loved ones she'd lost this year and how close she'd come to death herself. Could she forgive? He wasn't certain he could.

Slowly, Joanna reached forward to touch Mrs. Albright's hand. "I already have. I remember how dedicated she was when she taught all of us. That was a gift she bestowed on so many pupils." Joanna paused for a second. "I only wish she'd been happier."

Gertrude had been more than unhappy. Like Kurt's first wife, she'd suffered from what some called a disease of the spirit. Perhaps someday physicians would find a way to cure it or at least mitigate its effects.

Her face reflecting relief, Mrs. Albright turned her hand to squeeze Joanna's. "Gertrude wasn't as fortunate in love as you."

"I've been blessed."

Burke moved to his future wife's side. Her pallor and the way her hands had begun to shake told him it was past time to take her away from the scene of so much sorrow. For her sake and that of the child she carried, she needed a chance to remember that life was filled with promise, but first there were things they had to do.

"Joanna and I have both been blessed," Burke said as calmly as he could. He touched Joanna's shoulder. "We need to tell Della what we've learned." Perhaps then they could put the past behind them.

❦

Joanna was thankful that Burke had taken the lead in explaining what had happened. As they'd ridden back to town, she'd suggested that her sisters and their husbands needed to hear the story too, and so they'd asked everyone to gather in the parlor of Finley House. It was fitting, she realized, that everyone learn about Clive's final days while seated in the house he'd built.

As she'd expected, there were gasps of shock as Burke revealed the extent of Gertrude's madness and the lengths to which she'd been willing to go to ensure that Burke, whom she'd continued to confuse with his uncle, would marry her, and Della's eyes had filled with tears.

"It's over now," Burke said. "The last of the questions that brought Della and me to Sweetwater Crossing have been answered."

Grateful that her hands no longer trembled and that she'd had no coughing fits, Joanna nodded. "We can only pray that Gertrude is at peace."

There was a moment of silence when everyone appeared to be praying. Then Harold turned to his wife. "We could bring Clive's body into town, have a proper funeral, and bury him in the cemetery. Not the same day that we bury Thomas, but soon after."

Della met his gaze, her eyes shining with emotion. "Thank you, my dear, but that will accomplish nothing good. Let his body rest where it is." She faced Burke as she said, "I came here to see Clive's grave, but I never thought it would be under a bed of flowers." A small smile crossed her face. "That's more fitting than Gertrude probably realized. Clive loved flowers as much as I love books."

Neither Louisa nor Emily made any effort to hide their shock. "Gertrude showed me that flower bed," Emily said, "but I never thought it was covering the biggest secret this town has ever had."

Louisa nodded. "When I saw it, I thought the secret was that Gertrude had planted it without her mother's knowledge. I didn't dream there was anything hidden underneath."

"I wonder what she thought each time she tended those flowers. Did she regret what she'd done, or did she believe she was justified?" Joanna would never know, just as she'd never know whether the regrets Miss Heppel had mentioned were over the efforts she'd taken to keep Clive from leaving Sweetwater Crossing. Some secrets would remain secret.

⁓

That evening as they walked toward the bridge, Burke wrapped his arm around Joanna's waist and drew her closer to him. "Today was a day neither of us will ever forget, but as horrible as it was, I think we have reasons to give thanks."

"I'm thankful that you realized something was wrong and followed Gertrude and me." Joanna didn't want to think about what might have happened if Burke hadn't felt compelled to learn why they were headed away from the ranch house.

"That was God's prompting," he said firmly, "but there are other reasons to be thankful. First, there are the answers we received. We were both determined to learn what had happened to Clive, and we succeeded. As tragic as the story is, I know Della is more at peace now."

Peace. Was that the feeling that was stealing over Joanna, the sense of completion that she found when she turned the last page of a book and the characters' dilemmas had been resolved? Perhaps it was. The lingering mystery of Clive's final days had caused her more anxiety than she'd wanted to admit. Now it felt as if the light breeze that rustled the leaves on the live oaks was dissipating her worries about how not knowing what had happened to her fiancé had affected Della.

Joanna nodded, silently telling Burke she understood.

"Just as importantly, we no longer have clouds hanging over us." He smiled as he pointed upward. Though there was no moon, stars twinkled across the dark sky. "No clouds, literal or figurative. I'm not saying that there won't be problems along the way—undoubtedly there will be—but our love is strong enough to overcome them."

Burke was right. Though they couldn't—and shouldn't—forget the past, for it had formed them and brought them to this point, it was time to focus on the future. "When I returned to Sweetwater Crossing, I dreamt of creating a new future living at Finley House. That dream disappeared the first day when I realized how much had changed—including me. After that, I didn't want to think about my future, because it was uncertain. I felt as if my dreams had died, but then you arrived and I started to have better dreams than I'd ever had before."

Burke paused, waiting until Joanna looked up at him before he said, "You weren't the only one whose dreams changed for the better. I thought I knew what I wanted my future to be, but I was wrong, so wrong."

"Do you know what the best part is, Burke?" Without waiting for him to answer, Joanna told him what she'd realized as the months had passed. "I may never need to dream again, because my fondest dreams are coming true. Thanks to Miss Heppel, I have a home of my own, but the greatest thanks go to you. Thanks to you, I have a way to use the talents God has given me to help others. Thanks to you, my baby will have a loving father and I'll have the most wonderful husband any woman could want. I can't predict what the future will bring us, but I know it will be a glorious one, because we're sharing it."

Joanna pressed a kiss on his cheek. "I love you, Burke Finley."

"And I love you. I can't wait to see what the new year brings us. What I know is that 1884 will be a year we'll never forget."

Epilogue

"Are you ready for Burke?" Louisa asked as she straightened the coverlet.

"*We* are." Joanna smiled, her gaze fixed on the infant sleeping in her arms, the love she felt for this tiny bundle of humanity overwhelming her with its intensity.

"All right. I'll leave you alone." Louisa opened the door. "Come on in, Papa."

Without waiting for Louisa to leave, Burke burst into the room. "Are you all right?" he demanded.

Joanna nodded, watching as the worried lines that marked his handsome face vanished when he saw her propped up in bed and holding a baby. Louisa had claimed that he was the worst expectant father she'd encountered, that he wouldn't believe her when she told him everything was going well, but Joanna had thought her sister had exaggerated. It appeared she had not.

"These have been the longest six hours of my life," Burke declared as he studied Joanna's face.

It was love that made him so frantic, the same love that made

325

Burke insist on fetching Louisa the minute Joanna's pains began, even though they both knew it would be hours before the baby arrived.

Joanna gave her husband an indulgent smile. "You're a doctor, Burke. You know that childbirth is not a painless event. I'm fine—a little sore, of course—but so happy." She lifted the baby and pressed a kiss to the tiny nose. "Look at him, Burke. Our son is perfect."

The last of Burke's worries faded, and a grin split his face. "A boy? Louisa wouldn't tell me even when I threatened to stop teaching her."

That was an idle threat if Joanna had ever heard one. Almost daily Burke told her how much he enjoyed having Louisa as his partner. Sweetwater Crossing's women and children relied on her for all but the most serious of ailments, while the men—still convinced that women weren't suited to be physicians—gave thanks that Burke was there to treat them.

Joanna feigned indignation. "How could you have had any doubts? Didn't I tell you we were having a son?"

A shrug was Burke's first response. "Yes," he admitted, "but you've been wrong before. Don't forget that you were certain Emily's baby would be a boy."

"Must you remind me of my mistakes?" Joanna's heart overflowed with happiness every time she thought of her niece, the first of a new generation, who'd been named after their mother. "Prudence is a beautiful little girl."

"She is indeed," Burke agreed before transferring his gaze from Joanna to the infant in her arms. "And Curtis is the most handsome little boy in all of Texas."

The boy whose wrinkled red face was far from handsome began to squirm. Joanna shifted him slightly, hoping he'd remain asleep for another minute or two. "Are you sure you don't mind naming him that?"

Burke shook his head. "For the hundredth time, no, I don't

326

mind. 'Curtis' pays tribute to the man who sired him. It's a good name for our son."

Joanna looked from the baby to the man she loved so dearly. "Our son. Do you know how much I love hearing you say that?"

"Probably almost as much as I love saying it." Hesitation etched Burke's face. "Do I dare hold him?"

"Of course you do." She slid Curtis into his father's arms, smiling when Burke's smile turned as doting as hers.

"We're going to have so much fun," Burke told the still sleeping baby. "You and me, your mother, and any brothers and sisters the good Lord sees fit to give you."

That was Burke, planning for the future. Joanna chuckled at the realization that he'd already forgotten how much he'd fretted while she was in labor.

"Siblings will have to wait a while, but Curtis will have another cousin."

Burke turned his attention from his son to her, his eyebrows raised in a question. "Emily or Louisa?"

"Louisa. When I told her she was a cruel taskmaster to make me keep walking when the contractions hit, she said I could do the same thing to her in seven months." The news that all three Vaughn sisters would have children close to the same age had been almost enough to make Joanna forget her pain. Almost.

Burke's smile turned into a full-fledged laugh. "Three babies in one year. Didn't I tell you this was going to be a great year?"

"You did." The memory of the tragic way 1883 had ended had faded, replaced by days, weeks, then months filled with joy and anticipation.

"Just think, Burke. This is only the beginning."

Author's Letter

Dear Reader,

Were you surprised by what happened to Clive Finley? I knew "who done it" from the day I proposed the series in the summer of 2020, but a few things surprised me as I was writing *Into the Starlight*. Miss Heppel decided she needed a far bigger role than I'd originally envisioned, and the mayor insisted that he too was an important part of Clive's past. As an author, I love it when my characters take on lives of their own.

It was such fun creating Joanna and Burke's story, but oh how I hated typing the final sentence. Though Joanna tells Burke it's only the beginning—and it is indeed the beginning of their future—this is the end of the series. That's always a sad time for me. My fictional towns and the people who live there become real to me, which makes it difficult to say goodbye to them, but I have to . . . at least for a while.

This may be the last of the Sweetwater Crossing trilogy, but it's not the last of my stories. If you haven't already subscribed to my newsletter, I encourage you to do so. That way you'll be the first to know what's coming next. You'll find the link to it along with information about all my books, advice for aspiring writers, and more on my website: www.AmandaCabot .com. And if you haven't already read the first two Sweetwater books, I encourage you to spend some time learning how Emily discovered the truth about her father's death and what secrets Louisa uncovered. Emily's story is *After the Shadows*. Louisa's is *Against the Wind*.

Thank you for joining me in Sweetwater Crossing and my other fictional towns. Your support means the world to me!

Blessings,
Amanda

Turn the page to start
reading another intriguing
historical romance from

AMANDA CABOT

Chapter

One

Someone was watching. Though a shiver of dread made its way down her spine, Evelyn Radcliffe kept a smile fixed on her face. No matter how her skin prickled and how every instinct told her to flick the reins and urge the horse to race forward, she wouldn't do anything to worry the child who sat beside her.

She took a deep breath, then exhaled gradually, trying to slow her pulse, reminding herself that this was not the first time she'd sensed the Watcher. The feeling would diminish when she reached the outskirts of Gilmorton, and by the time she was an hour away, it would have disappeared. It always did. The only thing that made today different was that she was not alone. Today she had a child to protect.

Evelyn took another breath, forcing herself to think about something—anything—other than the danger she'd sensed. It was a beautiful day and an unusually warm one for so close to Christmas. The sun was shining, bringing a genuine smile to her face as she gazed at the now dormant cotton fields that brought so much wealth to this part of Texas. White gold, she'd heard some call it.

"What's wrong?"

Evelyn turned toward the girl who looked enough like her to be her sister. Polly's hair was silver blond rather than Evelyn's golden and her eyes were a lighter shade of blue, but she had the same oval face and a nose whose tip flared ever so slightly, just as Evelyn's did. Besides the difference in their ages, Evelyn's skin was unmarred, while a prominent strawberry red birthmark on her left cheek destroyed Polly's hopes of beauty.

"Nothing's wrong." Evelyn wished the child weren't so sensitive. "I'm just anxious to get home." Logansville was three hours away, far enough that the Watcher had never followed her. But Polly didn't need to know about the Watcher. Evelyn tickled the girl's nose. "You know Hilda can't be trusted to heat stew without scorching it."

The distraction appeared to have worked, for Polly giggled. "She's a bad cook. Buster spit out the oatmeal she gave him 'cuz it had lumps. Big lumps."

Lumpy oatmeal was a better topic than the fear that engulfed Evelyn almost every time she came to Gilmorton. Mrs. Folger had told her she needed to confront her fears. That was one of the reasons she insisted Evelyn be the one to make these trips. But Mrs. Folger didn't know that even ten years later, Evelyn could not bear to look at the building she'd once called home and that she detoured to avoid that block of Main Street. Mrs. Folger scoffed at the idea that someone was watching, calling it nonsense, but Evelyn knew better. Someone *was* watching, and it terrified her.

The tension that had coiled inside Evelyn began to release as the town disappeared from view. She wouldn't have come to Gilmorton if she had had a choice, but unless she was willing to be gone for more than a day each time she made a delivery, there were no other outlets for the lace the children made. The owner of the mercantile gave her a fair price for their handi-crafts. Today there'd even been enough money left over after she'd bought provisions that Evelyn had been able to purchase a piece of candy for each child. That would make Christmas morning special.

"When you're a little older, I'll teach you how to make oat-meal."

Evelyn laid a hand on Polly's shoulder, wanting contact with the child who'd become so dear to her in the month since she'd arrived at the orphanage. Arrived? She'd been deposited on the front step as if she were no more important than the piles of clothing some parishioners left when their children had out-grown them. Like worn dresses and overalls, Polly had been discarded.

Unaware of the turns Evelyn's thoughts had taken, Polly grinned. "I know how. I watched you. You gotta stir, stir, stir."

"That's right. You're a smart girl."

"My daddy said that too. He said I was the smartest girl in the whole county and that I was worth more than a thousand bales of cotton."

Polly's smile turned upside down, reminding Evelyn of the story she'd told about her father being put in a box in the ground. Evelyn was all too familiar with those boxes, but she'd been fortunate enough to have her parents with her for thirteen years before the night when everything changed. Polly was only six, or so she said.

Think about Polly, Evelyn told herself, not the night when it had rained hard enough to muffle her screams from passersby. The sheriff had told her he'd arrested and hanged the man re-sponsible. He'd assured her she had no reason to fear, and yet she did. Ten years wasn't long enough to erase the memories, particularly when she could feel someone watching her.

"I miss my daddy." Tears welled in Polly's eyes. "I want him to come back."

"I know you do."

Despite her nod, tears began to trickle down Polly's cheeks. "Buster said some girls get new daddies. He said people come looking for good little girls." She looked up at Evelyn, pleading in her eyes. "I've been good, haven't I?"

"You've been very good," Evelyn reassured her. But that wouldn't be enough. Three couples had come to the orphanage since Polly's arrival, and all three had been unwilling to adopt a child with such a prominent birthmark.

"It's Satan's mark," one woman had announced. When she'd heard that, Evelyn had been tempted to gouge the woman's cheek and give her her own mark.

"I want a new daddy." Polly was nothing if not persistent. Persistent and stubborn. No matter how many times Evelyn and Mrs. Folger asked, she refused to tell them her last name. "I can't," she insisted. "I can't."

Evelyn made a show of looking in every direction. "I don't see any daddies here. Maybe if we sing, someone will hear us."

As Polly's eyes brightened, Evelyn smiled. Singing would be a good distraction for both of them. And so they sang song after song. Neither of them could carry a tune, but that didn't bother them or Reginald. Evelyn imagined the gelding twitching his ears in time to their singing, and her spirits rose with each mile they traveled. Polly was once again cheerful, there was no rain in sight, and it would be another month before she had to return to Gilmorton—three reasons to give thanks.

Her smile was as bright as Polly's until she saw it. It was only the slightest of limps, and yet Evelyn knew something was wrong. Unwilling to take any chances, she stopped the wagon and climbed out. A quick look at Reginald's front right leg confirmed her fears.

"What's wrong?" Polly asked for the second time since they'd left Gilmorton.

"Reginald's lost a shoe."

Peering over the side of the wagon, Polly grinned. "I'll find it."

Evelyn shook her head. "You need to stay in the wagon." Though the sun was past its zenith, the day was still warm enough that snakes could be out, and ever-curious Polly might reach for one. Evelyn glanced at Reginald's hoof one last time. There was no choice. She wouldn't risk permanent injury by having him pull the wagon all the way to Logansville.

"We're going back to Gilmorton." As much as she wished otherwise, it was closer.

"Okay." Polly watched wide-eyed as Evelyn unhooked the wagon. "What are you doing?"

"We need to leave the wagon here." Even though it meant that anyone coming by could steal the contents, she had to take the chance. "Reginald can't pull it until he gets a new shoe."

Evelyn lifted Polly out of the wagon and placed her on the horse's back. "Hold on to the harness."

Normally agreeable Polly turned petulant. "I wanna walk with you."

Evelyn wouldn't argue. "All right, but when you get tired, Reginald will be glad to carry you." The horse was exceptionally good with children, which was fortunate, given the number who called the orphanage home.

"This is fun!" Polly exclaimed as she began to skip down the road. It was no longer fun by the time they reached Gilmorton. Polly was tired and fussy. To make matters worse, the blacksmith was in the middle of shoeing another horse and told Evelyn it would be at least half an hour before he could see to Reginald.

"Whoever shoed this horse the last time deserves to be shot," the blacksmith said when he was finally able to inspect the gelding's hoof. "He didn't know what he was doin'."

Evelyn tried not to sigh. Mrs. Folger had wanted to give Buster a chance, claiming he had an aptitude for caring for horses, but it appeared that the matron had been mistaken. "Did he do any permanent damage?"

"Nah." The blacksmith scraped a rough edge off the hoof. "Just be sure to bring Reginald here next time he needs a shoe. He may be gettin' on in years, but he's a fine piece of horse-flesh."

Evelyn and Polly rode the fine piece of horseflesh back to the wagon. Fortunately, the contents were all there. Unfortunately, the delays meant that they'd be very late arriving home. In all likelihood, everyone would be asleep, even Mrs. Folger. The matron wouldn't be pleased, but at least Evelyn hadn't lost the supplies she'd purchased today.

Darkness had fallen long before they reached Logansville, and Polly—worn out by the walking as well as the excitement of the day—slept on the bench next to Evelyn. Though she stirred occasionally, each time she did, she drifted back to sleep. This time, however, she sat up, rubbed her eyes, and pinched her nose.

"What's that smell?"

Evelyn sniffed. "It's smoke." She squinted, looking for the source of the odor, but saw nothing.

"Phew! I don't like that."

"I don't either, but we're almost home." Though it was late, someone must be burning trash. "It won't smell as bad once we're indoors."

Evelyn had already decided to let Polly sleep with her tonight rather than risk waking the other girls. That prospect, along with the promise that she could help stir the oatmeal tomorrow morning, had buoyed Polly's spirits when the only supper Evelyn could offer her had been the cheese and bread she'd purchased while waiting for the blacksmith. Though Gilmorton had a restaurant, that was one place Evelyn would not enter no matter how hungry she might be. When they reached the orphanage, she would warm some milk for Polly.

They were almost there. Within half an hour, Evelyn would have Reginald in his stall and Polly in her bed. The horse tossed his head, perhaps disturbed by the smoke that had intensified.

As they rounded the final bend in the road, the cause of the smoke was all too clear. The light from the almost full moon revealed the ashes and rubble that were all that was left of the building that had been Evelyn's home for the past ten years. She stared at the blackened foundation, trying to make sense of something that made no sense. Well aware of the danger fire posed to a frame structure, Mrs. Folger was vigilant about safety. Yet, despite her caution, something had happened. The orphanage was gone.

So were its inhabitants. There should be close to two dozen children swarming around, yet Evelyn saw nothing more than a few men. Though her heart was pounding so violently that she feared it would break through her chest at the realization that she'd lost her home, she clung to the hope that Mrs. Folger and the children had escaped and had been taken in by some of the town's residents. If not . . .

The possibility was too horrible to consider. Her mother had told her not to borrow trouble, and Evelyn wouldn't. Instead, she'd ask the men what had happened. Surely everyone had been saved. But though she tried to convince herself that she would be reunited with the matron and the other orphans, in her heart she knew that was one prayer that would not be answered.

Evelyn bit the inside of her cheek, determined not to let Polly see her fears. But she failed, for the child began to tremble.

"What happened to the 'nage?" Though Polly's diction was far better than one would have expected from the shabby clothing she'd worn when she was abandoned, whoever had taught her hadn't included "orphanage" in her vocabulary.

Evelyn wrapped her arms around Polly and willed her voice to remain steady as she said, "It's gone." And, if what she feared was true, so were Mrs. Folger and the children who had been her family.

As she descended the small hill and approached the front

drive, Evelyn saw that the men were wandering around the yard, their casual attitude belying the gravity of the situation.

"Ain't no one left," one called to the others, his voice carrying clearly through the still night air. "Smoke musta got 'em."

No. Oh, dear God, no. It couldn't be true, and yet it was. Once again, she had lost everyone she loved, everyone except the girl who clung to her, her own fear palpable. Once again, it was night. Once again, she was powerless to change anything, but at least this time it had been an accident.

Evelyn shuddered and said a silent prayer that Polly wouldn't realize the extent of the tragedy. Somehow, she would protect her. Somehow, she would help her recover from all that they had lost in this terrible accident.

"Can't figger it out," another man chimed in. "Who woulda wanted to do 'em in? No mistakin' them kerosene cans, though. Somebody set the fire."

Evelyn gasped, feeling as though she'd been bludgeoned, and for a second everything turned black. The fire wasn't an accident. Someone had deliberately destroyed the orphanage, planning to kill everyone inside. Including her.

"Where is she?" The memory of the voice that still haunted Evelyn's dreams echoed through her brain, shattering the fragile peace Mrs. Folger's assurances had created. Tonight proved that she wasn't safe, not even here. Someone wanted to kill the last of the Radcliffes.

Why? That was the question no one had been able to answer ten years ago, the question that had kept Evelyn from leaving the sanctuary the orphanage had promised. Now that promise was shattered.

She closed her eyes as fear and sorrow threatened to overwhelm her. The life she had built was gone, destroyed along with the building that had been her refuge and the people who had become her family. *Oh, God, what should I do?*

The response was immediate. *Leave.*

It was the only answer. She could do nothing for Mrs. Folger and the others, but she could—and she would—do everything in her power to give Polly a safe future. The question was where they should go. Evelyn stared at the stars for a second, then nodded. Gilmorton, the one place she would not consider, was east. Resolutely, she headed west.

"What happened?" Polly asked again, her voice far calmer than Evelyn would have expected. Either the child was too young to understand the magnitude of what had happened, or she'd experienced so much tragedy in her life that she was numb.

"We need a new home." For the first time, Evelyn gave thanks that Polly had formed no strong attachments to anyone other than her. That would make her transition to a new life easier. While grief had wrapped its tendrils around Evelyn's heart, squeezing so tightly that she had trouble breathing, Polly seemed to be recovering from her initial shock.

"Okay." Though the child tightened her grip on Evelyn's arm, her trembling had stopped. "Where are we going?"

"It'll be a surprise." At this point, Evelyn had no idea where she and Polly would find their next home. All she knew was that it had to be far from here, far from whoever had set the fire, far from the Watcher.

Polly was silent for a moment before she said, "It's okay, Evelyn. You'll be my mama, and you'll find me a new daddy."

Amanda Cabot's dream of selling a book before her thirtieth birthday came true, and she's now the author of more than forty novels as well as eight novellas, four nonfiction books, and what she describes as enough technical articles to cure insomnia in a medium-sized city. Her stories have appeared on the CBA and ECPA bestseller lists, have garnered starred reviews from *Publishers Weekly* and *Library Journal*, were a *Woman's World* Book Club selection, and have been finalists for the ACFW Carol, the HOLT Medallion, and the Booksellers Best awards.

Amanda married her high school sweetheart, who shares her love of travel and who's driven thousands of miles to help her research her books. After years as Easterners, they fulfilled a longtime dream when Amanda retired from her job as director of information technology for a major corporation and now live in the American West.

HEAD TO THE 1880S TEXAS HILL COUNTRY FOR ROMANCE AND MYSTERY

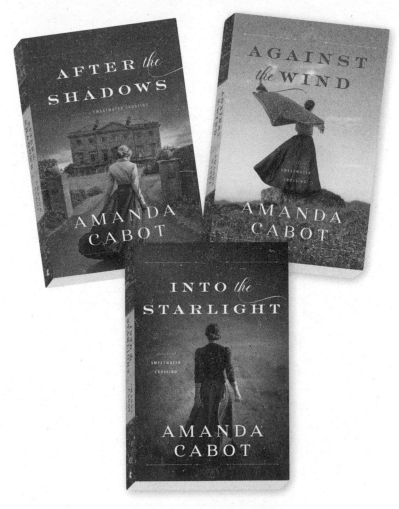

"Cabot's realistic portrayal of characters often on the margins of history really shines in this new historical series."
—*Library Journal* starred review

Don't Miss the Books in the
MESQUITE SPRINGS SERIES!

"Cabot expertly combines suspense with
a pleasant romance. A moving and uplifting tale."
—**Booklist** on *Out of the Embers*

a division of Baker Publishing Group
RevellBooks.com

Available wherever books and ebooks are sold.